MYTHION

JASON DAVIS

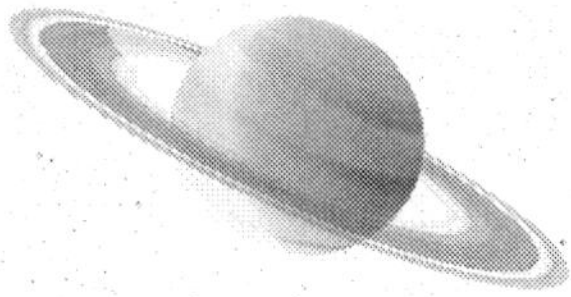

This novel and all characters in this publication are fictitious, and any resemblance to real persons, living or dead, is purely coincidental.

Paperback ISBN: 979-8-9869642-0-1

Ebook ISBN: 979-8-9869642-1-8

This book is dedicated to:
My love, Mary, for your unwavering faith in me.
My sons, Dylan and Nick, for raising me in the right way.
Chance, for your brilliant eye for story and how to make it richer.
And my mother, for telling me I was a good writer,
even when it was a fib.

10

It was but a wisp
a whisper in the skein
a dream, a game
in mirrors reflecting
only themselves

—QIL, AI POET

A warm and sullen drizzle cascaded out of the gloom of city lit clouds, soaking an assembly of tight and leaning buildings, their facades shiny and stoic. Light from scattered windows extended wan tinsel through mist-laden air, creating a morose and smeary sheen across brick and sidewalk, stairs and lonely traffic lights. A siren wailed somewhere in the distance.

Unsteady footfalls of a lone man splashed through grimy puddles, soiling his shoes and pant cuffs. Groaning, groping, he emerged from the shadows of an alley, lit by a green traffic light, a specter in a casual white suit, teetering into the street like a boozy tap dancer poorly managed by invisible strings. Soaked to the skin, hair plastered to the sides of his face, his eyes were vacant, staring. The man stood out like a lit thing in a dark room.

First, pounding bass music like from a college nightclub; then appeared a black hulking metal beast in the guise of an SUV. Its lights glanced off the white and stumbling puppet-man as the tires squealed. It slammed into him with a sodden *thump*, launching him pinwheeling through the air. He landed shoulder- and face-first onto the asphalt and flopped into the gutter.

The black beast came to a screeching car-rocking halt, the brake lights dowsing, and the pounding bass went quiet as two muffled voices argued. The passenger door flew open and a skinny scorchy thing in a short pleated school-girl skirt hopped out, covering her head with a twinkly sequined purse as she *clacked* on cherry red heels to the victim. Stooping over the unconscious man, she took a last drag of her smoke and flicked it into the flowing gutter, then put her fingers to his neck, her skinny calves and stiletto heels reflecting pale in the traffic light.

As the light switched to green, his cheeks and brow ridges emerged from shadow, revealing a nasty cheek gash oozing blood cutting tributaries across his face. “Hunnee, don’t you be dyin’ on me.” She loosened the collar, her long silvery nails flashing. “Nice looking suit.” She twisted the inside collar to where she could see the tag: GS. “Never heard of them.”

This seemed to open his eyes, and their stares met, but his awareness didn’t seem all there. “Not going to jail tonight,” she said with a red-lipped smile. “If you can hear me, we’ll get you some help.” She patted his tummy with some semblance of bedside manner and pointed in the direction of bright lights slicing between buildings. “There’s a hospital right through that alley. Just hang on a tick.”

The SUV’s dark-tinted window rolled down and out billowed a cloud of vape vapor. “Yo, baby. He good?”

“He’s all right,” she yelled back with a quick glance over her shoulder.

“Let’s shimmy!”

The woman *clacked* back to the SUV in the rain, like an arm-candy starlet in some postmodern sleuthing noir, ducking through the

SUV's open passenger door. The murderous black creature wisped silently away into the wet-thick urban night.

The man in the gutter folded his body into fetal pose while tucking his elbow under his torn and bloody cheek. His elbow was his pillow, and he cuddled it like it was a teddy bear, rainwater in the gutter streaming past his face. In his head, a whole different movie was playing out.

Something massive hurtles in orange-white flames through space, its tail trailing behind forever. Music pounds and beautiful people gyrate like natives to it. Lasers pulse and slice over the glow of their painted faces and popping glitter shine.

A vague awareness of pain. He was a particle in an endless gray-blue matrix, a frothing ocean of image particles in white and moving shapes, and sounds were a symphony of muffled *woofings*. He felt air moving in and out of his lungs, which connected to more memories associated with life and living, steadily replacing floating in nothingness.

Soon, the forms became people, the angles a doorway, the softness under him a bed. The muffled *woofings* separated into a quiet bustle of voices. A filmfon ringing in the background. Tearful cries from a girl in the hall. Quiet beeps to his left. His head pivoted that way as his eyes fluttered open, and he squinted at a bank of foggy geometries, machines, squiggly lines and numbers and tones. Beside those a device hung from an IV stand, pumping a clear fluid into his arm.

With that realization, he focused on the pain, and on it came in consuming waves…everywhere. Especially in his hip, which hurt like demon wolves were gnawing on the bones, and in his cheek, which felt like a branding iron were sizzling away at it.

Movement outside the door caught his eye. A man walking past stopped and leaned back into the partially open doorway, his face a carnage of blood and burning, dead but smiling anyway, his lumberjack plaid shirt almost burned away.

The patient's eyes widened to white-eyed, jaw-hanging shock as he croaked, "Daddy?" This made the nightmare melt away as the visage morphed into a smiling black-haired man in hospital scrubs. He wore a beard with symbols shaved into it. "Hey...he's awake." Stepping in, the caregiver padded across the shiny floor in almost silent shoes. "How you feeling?" Arriving bedside with an unnaturally white smile, he gripped the bed-ridden man's wrist. "Your pulse is strong, and that's a good thing."

The man in the bed blinked in utter bafflement. Were it not for the sizable bandage on his cheek, the sallow facial lines, the traumatized pallor, you'd see a boyish man with roundish cheeks and a set of furry and expressive eyebrows holding sway over shocked plum-gray eyes.

"Be right back," said the caregiver, who turned and left.

Under his breath, he said, "What am I doing in a hospital? How did I get here?"

The dark-headed caregiver was back, and following him was a female who filled her smock like a linebacker. Wearing silver wire-frame glasses, her hair in a too-tight bun, she plodded into the room with the elegance of a dragged chair.

"Mr. Doe, I presume?" she joked with a snort.

Her white-smiling cohort rolled his eyes and moved across the floor to the bedside and touched the confused man's arm, his perfect toothy beam unfazed by her gimp attempt at humor. "Are you with us?"

"I...I guess so," the afflicted man's dry raspy voice squeaked. He looked around the room, his eyes like a trapped rodent's. He weakly forced enough breath to speak again. "Wuh...what am I doing here?"

"Do you know your name?" asked the bearded guy while tapping his chest above the hospital ID badge. RANDALL SEARCY. "That's me," he said with a smile meant to be kind, but it was more subtly sinister.

Wearing a small secretive smile, Randall's stocky female superior held a glaspad, which she lifted and pretended to officially check from time to time. "Are you having trouble with memory?" Her voice was constricted, gravelly, like it had been damaged. Maybe in the war, where she was a drill sergeant-cum-medic or whatever, shouting orders over explosions at men with smaller balls than hers.

The patient worked his jaw as he blinked, but nothing came out. His hand wandered to the bandage wrapping his head. Then his fingers felt their way down, where he found stitches around the outer orbit of his eye, and ample bandaging on his cheek, and...*ow*...more pain. Name?

A smiling woman. Construction paper. A crayon rolling off the coffee table in a sunlit room. She's talking to her child, whose tiny hands pick a color. Her mouth and voice make his name and he draws it in purple.

"Gavin Simms."

"That's a start," said Randall, grabbing a glaspad from a stand. Like the big gal's, it was the commercial ruggedized model, clear Lucite from edge-to-edge. Go ahead, claimed the ads, throw it off a cliff. It'll just open more apps!

The block-shaped female authority figure was absorbed in her own glaspad, muttering to herself. Gavin squinted hard to get a better look at her. In some ways she looked like a thumb with a face painted on it, wearing an off-white smock.

Randall retook his attention. "You're OK. Some scrapes, a few bruises and dents. Better than most people in here." He made a circling motion with the glaspad's stylus and leaned in. "Listen," he said with a conspiring grin, "I know a guy here who would love one of your kidneys."

"Randy," groaned the woman, glancing up from her glaspad, "don't torment the man."

Randall persisted, like he was trying out new material. "You need only one, you know. Could fatten your bank account, amigo. And I've got other angles we can work," he said, tugging on his collar. "Yeah, I got angles all day long. You know where to find me."

"Forgive him," she said, taking over, and she shot Randall a communicating glance. "Can't you see he's frail?"

He looked back at her. "Yeah, Doc. I can see he's frail," he said, trying not to laugh. His next words were ostensibly for her, but he looked at Gavin. "I wonder if indecision is the more pressing issue."

Gavin had been in hospitals, many times, but this freakish clown show was starting to spook him. Was he dreaming? He needed something rational to fasten onto. He looked back and forth between them like *what crazy house am I in here?*

The girthy woman fixed Gavin with an authority face, and rattled out words like it was a recording. "You're in Langhurst Memorial Hospital. Your vitals are stable, no internal damage, nothing broken. But you do have a severe hip contusion that could bother you for some time. Possibly months. Do you dance?"

Gavin blinked at her like she'd just said something in an alien language, his brows alarmed and stupefied in one shape.

"I ask because if you were a dancer, recommended therapeutic courses would be...um... different."

"No," said Gavin, quelling an absurdity-induced chuckle. "Not for a living."

This was all so strange, it couldn't be real. He needed tactile feedback. Gavin looked at his feet making circus tents under the blanket, wiggled his toes, and they worked. The sensation in the tips of his toes matched what his eyes reported.

Good feedback.

He clenched and unclenched his fists, squeezing till his fingernails impressed painful crescents into his palms.

Even better feedback.

In that moment the slow bake of the world completed, bringing most his routines back online. "We have three to four out of ten pain everywhere, and some places six to seven. This hip is a solid eight," he said, lifting his butt cheek with a pained squint. "I'm dehydrated, and I feel like I should know what's in that IV."

Gavin's sudden alert and lucid presentation changed their expressions to nodding approval, as Randall nodded at the IV stand, saying, "Right. We're giving you something to help with the pain. Is it also helping with your grumpy mood?"

Gavin gawked at him like *who are you?* but said, "What's in the bag, Boy Wonder?" With no information immediately forthcoming, he shifted his focus to the lady, who was clearly the boss.

She looked up and removed the stylus from between pursed lips, gazing at him as though this support question wasn't to have escalated past her underling. She looked back at Randall.

He shrugged like, *you're in charge*.

"Conzall," she said at last.

Gavin's chin dipped to his chest. "My point exactly," he said without looking up. "Please stop the IV."

"Excuse me?" asked the burly gal doctor.

"Please stop the IV."

Again the two with him in this tightening space shared creepy communicating glances.

Gavin threw out his hands. "Hey. I'm over here."

"Churlish," she said with the air of an examiner. Looking at Randall, she said, "That's a good sign."

Randall frowned with approval, nodding and saying, "Reveals instinctive assertion when threatened."

Either these bots are bong bong, or I'm dreaming. None of this can be real.

Turning back, she focused hard on Gavin. The glasses were too small for her ample face, and the prescription magnification made her greenish eyes look cartoonish. And wow was she solidly built! Somebody should do something about those smocks, though.

Please!

"We know what we're doing, Mr. Simms," she said primly, her mouth firm.

Drained to near empty, Gavin said, "I'm sorry, you are...?"

"I'm Dr. Sticks."

"Like the river in hell?" he said.

Her eyes, and her cheeks, were indignant. "It's not in hell. And it's spelled i c k s."

"It's a waterway between Gaia and the Underworld," said Randall evenly.

Blinking like he couldn't believe what was happening, Gavin said to him, "Is that right? Thank you so much."

Randall shrugged. "Well?"

Gavin's swiveling eyes and face said *I'm about to start throwing things around,* but with due measure, he said, "I'm guessing it's a compound? Anti-inflammatories cause inflammation in me, and I'm allergic to opioids. Stop the IV. Get into my medical records. You'll see the problems."

A faint sneer rode the lady doc's stone face, mixed with obstinacy, challenge, and a little sexual tension. Stranger still was that it looked like an act, like everything else had so far. That or his perceptual routines were being typically...adaptive. "OK," she said, flicking her stylus imperiously toward the IV pump.

"Thanks," said Gavin.

He watched Randall's hospital ID tag hang over his face as he powered down the pump. What a great big smile for the camera, but no facial scrub in the pic. Gavin's eyes shifted to the symbols. The whole look was off trend, and ideologically conflicting, but while Gavin watched, it devolved into the sparse scraggly mountain folk beard his dad always wore. Blood ran in rivulets upward, crossing his dad's face and dripping toward the ceiling from his blood spiked hair. With the images came the smell of gas and burning tires.

Look at me, son.

Gavin's jaw unhinged, eyes like saucers, as his dad's shredded and crusty face turned to him and became Randall's again.

Breathing deeply and evenly, gazing vacantly, Gavin shook away the hallucination and focused on Randall. His eyes were pretty, his lashes long, his irises dark brown. Gavin decided they demanded a full, but kempt, Middle Eastern beard to round out his strategy above the collar.

Randall gestured at a squeeze-cup on the bedside table. "You thirsty? It's water."

Gavin didn't even flinch toward it as he said, "I wonder if you could bring me an unopened bottle of water? A fresh clear glass filled with reverse osmotic ice and a lemon slice?"

Randall and Doc Sticks looked at one another.

"Please?"

Seeing their doubtful expressions, Gavin said, "I'm not a diva...well...in the relativity of all things, but my history will explain everything. And I do get that the ice and lemon aren't on the menu." He smiled a little and shrugged a shoulder, trying to lighten things up around this freaky-clown crowd.

Randall slipped over to the door, leaned out and said, "Kyla, bring a bottle of water, please?" and then whisked back to the bed.

Doc Sticks retrieved the glaspad from beside Gavin's feet, tapped it and said, "It's Simms, one m?"

"Two."

"Date of birth?" she said without looking up.

"October fourth, 2005," said Gavin, so cotton-mouthy from the Conzall his teeth were sticking to his lips.

"At the 414 address?" she said, glancing up.

"Yes."

The big solid lady doc stepped around the bed, and handed the glaspad to Randall. "Get his records on here...please."

Randall took it, said, "It's good you said please," and flushed himself from the room.

A candy striper, a young lady with short blue hair, showed up with the water, hurried silently over and handed it to the patient, turned and left.

Stepping to the rail, Doc Sticks forced a twitchy smile. "Do you know why you were found unconscious in a gutter...right over there on Fourth Avenue?" she said, vaguely gesturing at the room's window.

Gavin opened the bottle and downed the contents in throat-glugging gulps. His blood-shot eyes blinked at her like, *excuse me?* His lips were wet as he said, "What the hell was I doing there?" His eyes dropped, searching the sheets. "I don't know, Doc."

"Someone hit you in their car and took off. Someone anonymously called it in. Maybe it was the folks who hit you, trying to do the right thing. You're lucky to be alive. The police said you were airborne for at least twenty-five feet." She fiddled with a gold band on her finger. "We don't know your legal status, and the police aren't yet showing any interest in you as anything but a victim, but they'll be back for a statement. We may need to keep you for a few days, but we'll see."

For a flicker, her inscrutable green-gray eyes softened, almost like she knew him. It made for a weird moment, adding to the carnival sideshow effect of this place.

"Thank you, Doc," he said in a tone that was trying to smooth over their bumpy start. It had suddenly become time to start manipulating everything he could to get out of this temple of horrors.

"Get some rest," she said, patting his hand like she'd learned bedside manner from a GluTube tutorial. She turned to the door and Gavin watched her go. Her gait was mismanaged, a little janky, like she was trying too hard to walk normally.

The memory and images of an awful crash when he was a kid persisted, as his dad's burnt and crusty face hung vaguely in his vision like a paused movie. Now the flaming heat spilled from the mental into the physical, spreading into his body. While he watched, the scene transformed into an enormous flaming visitor from the depths of space, hurtling toward the face of a yellow-striped world. Pounding music. Beautiful people.

"I don't have any idea what that vision is trying to tell me," he said as the vision evaporated. Looking around, he asked the room, "And why was I in the street in the rain?"

The room was shrinking, and Gavin couldn't help thinking the longer he lay in that bed, the smaller it would get. A panic attack was making lazy circles around him, but hadn't yet pounced.

"I have to get out of here."

Last night, Gavin had been wheeled on a gurney into Langhurst's emergency entrance without his wallet or anything else to identify him or connect him to the outside world. He'd never opted for the wrist chip for constant tracking, auto-id or auto-pay, or hospital personnel wouldn't have listed him as "Patient Doe-No SAT Code" on ER intake.

Randall was kind enough to lend him his personal glaspad to make some calls and do whatever else, and he was sitting up in bed with the flat semitransparent supertech unit propped on an angle on a pillow. Tapping an icon, he logged into his Sphere account, which contained every scrap of information of his existence—contacts, texts, xmails, VMs, call logs, posts, music, shows and movies. Sphere was like a metacloud, and all accounts included private and secured partitions so every account holder could do anything they needed to from any device, as all computing was done on the quantum server side. Most devices were now just Sphere terminals.

When in trouble, his sister Heather and her two daughters were his support system. He opened his favorite set of pics of them all together, taken last Thanksgiving at her place. "Even Momma was there," he said with a nostalgic smile, his plum-grays flicking around the shot. Conspicuously absent was his dad, like a hole in every photo since he was fourteen. It was as though the flames of the terrible and fateful crash had burned away every trace of him.

In this shot, they were all mugging for the camera with hats and pulled faces. Thanksgiving for them was like Christmas for other families. In it were Celia, a high schooler, Lissa, who came years later, Heather, his mother and himself. He touched Heather's face, and lines sprang from under his finger, leading to Call, Text, Recent Posts, Favorites, and other data. He tapped Call. The device whirred with a pleasant tone.

Her face bloomed into view, and looking back at him was a summer-freckled, oval-faced woman with dark, "normal," shoulder-length hair, no highlights, and he'd tried hard to get her to get some. Heather's gray-blue eyes widened as she looked first at the head bandage, then the thick cheek dressing, then the hospital gown. She puffed out a breath, like *not again,* the long-suffering younger sister of a sickly brother she'd taken care of for most of their growing up years.

"Oh no. What're you doing in the hospital?"

"They tell me I was a victim of a hit-and-run," he said, tapping the device's edge with his thumbs. He seemed self-satisfied about this bit of survival heroism.

"You OK?"

"I'm sheek. Banged up some," he said, his hand wandering

absently to his cheek. "I really just needed a familiar face." He leaned closer and lowered his voice. "This place is freakin' me out a little. These people are weird."

"You're *always* freaked out by something. Where were you?"

"In an alley two blocks from here."

"Did you have a retrograde episode or something?"

Gavin licked his lips. He didn't want to have to explain that he had no explanation for anything. "I assume it was something like that."

"Were you sleepwalking?"

"Maybe."

They chatted on for a bit about the usual nothings, then he said, "Let's keep this between us. I don't want to worry Momma, and—"

"I agree."

"—and I don't want Lissa knowing about this."

"Gavin," said Heather, leaning in. "She's going to see whatever's under that cheek dressing."

"I'll come up with something. I'll go with heroic and dangerous."

"Really?" she said, shaking her head like *puh-lease*. "You're such a crappy liar, but Liss does like your stories, and she doesn't care at all if they're true."

"Why would she? For a kid, everything's true," said Gavin, his face saying he was feeling better and better just talking to his sis.

"When do you go home?"

Gavin's eyes shifted to the partially ajar door, then back. "I'm sure I'll be discharged today or tomorrow. No doubt they'd like to ring up a big bill on my insurance, but I know the game. They can't hold me. A couple detectives came and asked me some questions, but I haven't done anything they can keep me here for."

Heather leaned in closer and lowered her voice. "Even by what's in your psych history?"

"I don't think so," he said with obvious uncertainty.

"OK," she said, also unconvinced, her eyes narrowing. "Call me when you get home."

"OK. Love you bye."

"Love you bye," she said, reaching towards her own unit before the v-pane went blank.

He thought about calling Gina, his neighbor, to check his front door, "But would that set me up for a robbery? Nah. Nobody knows if that door is locked. The keys would have to be in their bowl."

He then checked xmails. "Nothing pressing there." Then his subscriber numbers. "It's only been a day, Gavin." He logged out of Sphere, set the device aside, lay back on the pillows and breathed easily for the first time in twelve hours.

The afternoon wore away and night came, and Gavin's patience for a concrete update on his stay here was wearing thin. At last, Dr. Sticks ambled gingerly into the room, carrying her glaspad. The smock was gone, revealing her summery linen dress and what turned out to be a quite ample bosom. The dress worked all right with her chest, but the buttons needed to be less prominent, and certainly not gold. She'd released the bun from its tightly wound purgatory and her brown hair now hung in waves to her shoulders.

In a conciliatory tone, Gavin said, "Your hair is better that way... what it does for your cheeks."

Heading for a chair, she said, "I doubt you and I will ever connect on that level."

"Maybe *you* won't. Believe it or not, I'm a—"

"Fashionologist," she cut in. "I've looked over your public vitae and profile. You have a multi-platform channel with fun and experimental threads and accessory concepts." The doc dragged the chair over and sat, set the glaspad on the bed, leaned her elbows onto her thighs and went on. "Why would I take style advice from a battered amnesiac who goes on inexplicable nocturnal expeditions?"

Gavin yielded with open palms and a dip of his chin. "You'd be surprised where you'll find inspiration."

She leaned back and put her arm on his bed. "Mr. Simms, by what I've seen in your medical history, your retrograde amnesia fills in some of these blanks, and there's more than enough in your labs and tests to be concerned about. Have you recovered why you were out wandering around?"

Gavin took his lower lip into his mouth and shook his head. "No, Doc. That one's got me stumped." He instantly regretted saying it.

Should have lied, idiot!

Her eyes ticking back-and-forth on his, with that cloying little smile, she said, "That's...unfortunate." Glancing down at the sleek computing gadget, she tapped it and said, "I see you have multiple drug and food sensitivities and autoimmune problems." She rattled off a cook's list of official complaints and diagnoses of record, but her voice trailed off, like she was just too drained to go through it all. Looking back up at him and leaning again on her thighs, she said, "You were poisoned by organophosphates in your home's water for three years. Have I got that right? That must've been tough."

Gavin's eyes defocused.

A man shouting at a woman in a dreary kitchen, waving a pint bottle of Old Home Bourbon. Water system? Where we gonna get the money!

Sell your precious Jeep! she shrieks back.

"It was," said Gavin, his eyes refocusing on her.

"The bottom line is we can't discharge you until we know more about what's going on with you, and it would have helped so much for you to have recalled what you were doing. So, we're going to keep you a day or two...observation and tests...you know the drill."

Gavin's innards plopped like rotten fruit into his colon, leaving him sour. "That's not possible, Doc. I have commitments, xlogs to write, a deadline on my Jym Sum piece. I'm good to go, bad hip and all."

"Your mental well-being is far more important than any of that."

"Just get me a pad and I'll get my work done here."

Her face gave nothing away as she affixed his eyes with hers. "Let me think about that...no I don't even need to ponder it, Mr. Simms. Those pressures are not a good thing for you right now. You're just going to have to let it all go, for a few days, anyway."

His face glum, Gavin looked out the window into the sprinkling late evening. Neon blue rivulets streamed down the window glass, and he could see the sign from the Blue Tsunami Sushi Den blinking in the distance. Challenging these people inevitably led to tears and ruin. He'd have to reconfigure his gameplan.

"So a day or two just became a few days?"

"I'll be frank," she said, clasping her hands. "This is my call, and evaluations take time."

The look she gave him was the kind that said *little men like you aren't in charge,* while her mouth said, "It's time for you to commit to something, and in this case, to my plan. Do that and we'll see what we can do."

Gavin inwardly cringed. What she said, and how she said it, was the creepiest thing yet.

What horror show hospital have I landed in?

Gavin's room in the psych wing wasn't as bad as all that. They didn't have any of the colors right, but with some imagination bland could be rationalized as subtle. A bed and a little desk and chair were in their places, and a sink and toilet in a closet-sized washroom, the tiles showing little tufts of grass blades.

The scrubs they handed him...now *that* was a different story. The mirror in the washroom was made of a shiny metal, which reflected in distortions—couldn't have anything glass in this wing. Lamentably wagging his head, he stood in front of his "funhouse" visage reflecting back, looking over the too-large fit, the faded orange from a few million launderings. His attention switched to his bandaging, his eyes earnest, furry brows in arcs of curiosity, as he gently palpated around the cheek dressing.

An ancient memory swam in, and the face in the mirror morphed into the younger Gavin, but now his whole pre-pubescent body stood before a full-length antique mirror his mother kept in her sewing "parlor." In his underwear, he was all refugee bones, blue veins showing here and there through pale wax-paper skin.

. . .

The dayroom was aglow with waning sunlight shafting through divided window-panes. The décor was meant to be happy, but it was merely tape over a ghastly wound. Colors were all the muted pastels in rooms designed to keep its inmates in a calm comfort zone, with big dots and flowers and rays of sunshine.

The patients milled about, all in scrubs. A group sat in front of a big XV, riveted by a show Gavin was passably interested in. XV was TV, but with cross-platform capability for content from Xenxu. Xenxu was the wildly popular alternate world used by billions, and Gavin maintained his brand presence in it, tied to his Pholo Design Studio. Xenxu wasn't just an artificial reality, but was a fully developed world, with AI citizens, laws, entertainment galore, a complex biosphere, economy, drama, love, and it was as strange as it was beautiful.

Gavin watched a lone young woman across the room. Dry messy hair, pallid, bones showing through the fabric at the shoulders. Face twitching, she typed and typed at nothing right in front of her face, like she was forever keying in an access code. It was blowing hard outside with a building storm, and a girl of maybe eighteen stood at the window, like a ghost, staring out there, her hair floating around like with a static charge. Another woman used a "safe" erasable marker on a child's white art-board, making red scribbles that appeared to be random, but as she scribbled furiously away, surprisingly well-done renditions of people and places would emerge.

"A mad genius," said Gavin under his breath.

Lindy was among the few names he'd managed to remember so far, mainly because they shared a passion for fashion. She was a middle-aged blond-graying gal who thought she was at lunch with her friends. Her body and face, tested and weathered by time, could not hide the fact that at one time she was undeniably scorchy, and too smart to be some fat rodent's arm candy.

"You're an elegant and pretty woman, Lindy," Gavin had said earlier.

"Oh you're just a charmer, now, aren't you," she'd said, giving him a coquettish wave at the wrist.

Set behind a PlexiTuff clear cover, the large screen XV was recessed into the off-white wall near the shelf above where the board games were stacked. A detachment of inmates gathered around it every day at this time to watch this one show. He sat alone behind the medicated audience, watching them absorb it.

It was a series called *Pods,* and it was about AI nanotech embedded within space dust bombarding Earth and turning people into cocoons of creeping nano-slime during the victims' transition. It was a marathon, and this was an early episode. In the show, Dr. Frank Carney was sitting in a posh Georgetown restaurant across from Dr. Maggie Willen, a lady colleague at the university, and with whom he had some hazy past.

"Frank," she said to him, "I know this is going to sound crazy, and I can't even *believe* this could come from my mouth, but I don't have anybody else I can turn to."

"Margaret," he said, covering her hand with his own, "we have always been able to tell each other anything."

"The truth is just too horrible to even contemplate," she said, her eyes getting misty, her face trembling.

"Please be calm," he said, tapping her knuckles and having himself a sip of wine.

She looked from side-to-side, then leaned in, lowering her voice. "Better have another swallow of that wine." She watched while he gulped it to finish the glass. Satisfied, she said, "Dale is not my husband. I don't know who that man is, but it's not my Dale."

"I can't believe they let them watch this in here," whispered Gavin into his fingers, which were busy tugging and letting go his upper lip.

"Don't you see, Gavvy?" said Lindy, who'd appeared at his elbow. "The staff is in on it. Haven't you noticed how they move? That's the first sign."

Dr. Sticks trying to manage the stilted movement of her bulky body.

He looked at her with all sobriety. "I've wondered about that."

"They've all transitioned. I know the signs. Look at them. Their eyes are dead even as they go about pretending to work."

Gavin looked at the ladies in the observation booth. He had to admit—wasn't a lot going on in those eyes.

Lindy leaned in closer, and he smelled her perfume. "Lindy, is that Petale you're wearing?"

"You have such sophisticated tastes, young man."

He turned to her, and her face was close enough to kiss. Though her gray-yellow eyes were steady on his, within them was a quiet quiver of crazy. Waving a painted fingernail, she said, "They all think this is an XV show, but the nano comes right through the display, and from Xenxu through UV-directed nano and the radio headsets. Get in-Xenxu and you're theirs to start the acquiescence entraining."

Eyes snaking side-to-side, she leaned closer and lowered her voice. "If you can find some chlorine, add a little to your water. I have some hidden in my room, in case you'd like to stop by," she said with a sly smile, tickling his arm with her colored manicured nails. "It inhibits precursor protein breakdowns they need for the DNA conjugation phase of the transition."

Gavin's eyes flew open. "Lindy, are you a scientist or something?"

"Was, but now I'm here," she sighed, waving the same painted fingernail and looking around. "These specimens are now my area of study. But please keep that to yourself."

"I'm in your debt, Lindy."

"The silly pods in the show?" she said, her eyes shifting to the XV. "That isn't how it *really* works. It's subtle, but sinister. You just won't know. But *I* will know. I promise, if your transition starts, I'll end you, as a favor."

"Thank you so much for thinking of me, Lindy."

"By no means am I a saintly flower, but some of my thoughts about you have been less than pure," she said with a cute lecherous grin, turning and moving off.

Gavin watched her go, eyes and brows disturbed. "*Jeezus,*" he muttered. "People amaze me." He turned back to the XV, aware he'd missed a few things.

The low dirge of spine-chilling music became louder as Dr. Carney leaned back, his briar patch brows bristling. "I saw him two days ago, but I just can't—"

"Not here," said Dr. Willen, then dropped her filmfon into her open clutch. She finished her wine and stood, leveling him with granite eyes. "Meet me in our old place," she said with some command, then turned and swept away with classic movie grace.

As Gavin watched the scene cut to Dr. Willen in her car, the room rippled, barely enough to notice. What was that? The room vibrated again, like it had glitched for a tick into pixels. He kept his line of sight unchanged and he remained perfectly still, jaw muscles rippling.

Breathe. Release. Breathe.

Another wave rippled in the air across the room. By the corner on the opposite wall was an artsy-craftsy table and materials. On the other side of the table, a sizzling energy was forming, something tall and lithe, like rising delicate ice-blue smoke tendrils. The more it took shape, the more startled his widening eyes, his cheek twitching, wrist and hand beginning that old tremor.

Gavin blinked, an old technique to make this emerging nightmare go away. But it didn't work, which was not a good sign. Gavin's eyes darted hither and yon, hoping to see that others saw this, some there undoubtedly susceptible. But no. She was *his* hallucination. She? Maybe.

As she resolved and clarified, she was like a nervous system made of ice-blue flows of plasma electricity, with a central course of flowing sparkles and light, dividing and subdividing out into ever smaller sinews of branches and twigs. At the top was a sunburst head of tighter wound vines and twigs, with lines flowing in all directions from what could have been eyes in the shape of an oval. All this shimmering, flowing beauty fanned out at the bottom, like an evening gown. Or a sinewy tree trunk delicately enveloped *within* a sheer evening gown.

Gavin's eyes *looked* like they wanted to go as wide as saucers, but he doggedly maintained control, given that he was in a psych ward dayroom. Still, his eyes stared, white and vivid, as he huffed through his nostrils. He became fidgety, eyes shifting like *how do I get out of here?* A flush of heat surged up his neck, sheening his face with pre-sweat.

Not the heat!

He grabbed and luffed the scrubs at his sternum, fanning in air. Licking his lips, he glanced at a security camera, then back to...to...*that*.

Even though her eyes were just flowing lines away from oval voids, he felt her piercing into him, like a psychic scalpel. Probing. Invading. He touched his diaphragm. The tendrils seemed to be taking samples from *way* in there, with unbelievable intimacy.

Gavin's eyes defocused, moistened, gazing at nothing. Then they wandered back up to her. Flows of lines like Tesla bolts shimmered out from the main "trunk" of ice-blue plasma, creating a branch, which then pointed at the table with all the colored pens and sketch sheets.

The invisible tendrils withdrew from his diaphragm, lightly brushing sensitive nerve fibers on their way out, like a violin bow barely touching the strings. Intense pleasure. And pain. And they were so close. Gavin gripped the chair to keep himself from wiggling.

And then she languidly withdrew into nothingness, like curling and smoky veils being sucked into holes.

Gavin felt released like from a tractor beam, and he realized he hadn't gulped in a full breath until he tried. He stood and pulled his shoulders back, hand on his tailbone, and then set off. Helped by his quad-base cane, he almost tripped over his own rubbery legs as he waddled over, finally reaching the art table, feeling close to collapse from the ordeal.

On the table was a well-executed work of a cylinder made of hexagons, colored gold on graphite, set against a backdrop of rings, like Saturn was just out of the view. Levitating inside the cylinder was a gold-shimmered obelisk, about a quarter the cylinder's length. It tapered to a pyramid, then a point, like a smoky crystal with highlights. On its face were tiny internally lit markings, symbols, script. Leaning on the cane, Gavin reached down and put his finger in the middle of the cylinder and moved the sheet side to side.

"It's real," he said, so low it was below a whisper.

Then his eyes widened. In the corner was his own signature, an overlapping stylized GS, but this signature was modified: GS5.

Five?

"What the hell is going on?" he said, then looked up, hoping nobody heard him.

Picking the mystery art up, he made a show of how much he liked it, holding it up to the light, getting different angles. With a forced smile, he said to no one in particular, "I think this one should hang in my room." By now, the monitor lady behind the window was eyeing him, and Gavin showed her the art, slowly mouthing, "May I take this for my room?"

She squinted and scowled at it, looking like one of those super furry cats with the smushed-in face, where they look irate but seem to be amicable creatures. She waved a glaspad stylus at him, like *Take it and go.*

Forever and always, Time was an aloof tyrant, too occupied with sadistic stratagems to give Gavin any respite from the grind and flow of it. In that grind was idling, and idling was tough on him, always had been, for then the skeletons would come *clickety-clacking* from the closets he'd stuffed them into.

His mother in one of her weirdly colorful housedresses, hunching over the sewing machine. Idle hands are the devil's workshop, she tells him without looking up.

Circling over and over in his mind was Lindy's face, her eyes, her words. He couldn't get her quietly crazy eyes off his mental display, and it was wearing on him.

The feminine alien apparition made of plasma electricity.

Pods.

Is she the queen? Is my transition underway?

Her probe of me. Is that when she injected the conjugating agent Lindy told me about?

"I don't think she's one of them," he'd said again and again, unable to fully convince himself.

Gavin found himself in front of his distorted metal mirror, checking his skin for the formation of the sticky new membrane with the squiggling worm-like organisms. In his aimless wanders through the halls, he'd found himself standing in front of what he took to be supply closets, thinking he might find some chlorine. They were numbered, or coded, always locked. There were times he imagined himself stealing into a sealed lab and finding Lindy in the vile chrysalis, the sticky secretions creeping ice-blue flickers over her surfaces. He'd also passed Lindy's room, hesitating with his knuckles up and about to rap quietly on the door, but this kind of fraternization was forbidden and could buy him more time here.

No way I'm risking that, but where had she been the last two days?

Passing patients and staff in the halls…he didn't dare look them in the eye. The last thing in the world he could do was cross the line and *see* them transitioned, making Lindy's words come true. At lunch it seemed a group of security staff stared at him, their faces fixed, and then turned to each other for private conference.

For no reason he could think of, they didn't make him take the usual meds for this wing. This was the lone blessing from on high, for the cruel chemicals would have been devastating on his mentality. He would exhibit no suspicious behavior. He would do *nothing* to alter this lucky pattern. But each time the nurses stopped in front of him with their squeaky cart and cups with pills in them, he felt like a child, terrified of unknowns he wasn't mature enough to understand.

The hovering terror of being forced to take the drugs became a drug unto itself, warping him further, immersing his mind into a dream-like hallucinogenic drift. Added to it all, he couldn't help feeling an invasive intelligence acting upon him—a watcher—prickling hairs at the back of his neck. Paranoia could escalate to a serious condition for him, and it was a mental discipline to steer away from it.

"I miss Lindy."

Lindy, close to his face. The silly pods in the show? That isn't how it really *works.*

He sorely wished she were around to explain more about what she knew, for she had elevated to a status of authority on the grim matter Earth was facing. "In the show, I mean," he said, constantly talking himself out of believing it was all a real threat.

True to Doc Sticks's plan, he was allowed no connectivity to the outside world, like a cult isolating him from family and friends during inculcation of the group's increasing power over him. It was almost like a tradeoff for not having to take the meds. "Give this, but take that," he said one day while washing his face.

Not being able to talk to Heather was its own blessing, because when he got like this, she could see it immediately, and he didn't want her worrying. As always, at the worst possible times, he had to switch to solitary mode to spare everyone else of his little departures from grounded sanity.

Gavin had bags under his eyes, his hair a messy disgrace, as he drank his apple juice, looking into the penny-yellow mid-afternoon sun pouring into the dayroom. His hand shook. He was losing touch with the world out there, and himself in here. He felt it—something slipping, giving way, drawing him toward the beyond, where his mind could slip and slide despite the mandates of his jailers.

I am prey.

He didn't know how, didn't know who, couldn't quite place it, but was sure of it, and it seemed even beyond the ominous behaviors and designs of Doc Sticks. She had decoded his wander patterns and found him in a lonely hall. With subtle force she backed him to the wall as she said, "I told them the usual meds protocols weren't clinically correct for you."

Gavin fought with himself to keep from fleeing, as he said, "Thanks so much for that. I owe you."

"I will have my pound of flesh," she replied with a sly smile and swagged away with as much sexy as her physique was capable. Scratching his forehead with some consternation, Gavin watched her go, now convinced his extended interment here was choregraphed by her.

Throughout the ordeal, he found himself riveted by *Pods*. It had become research, and he watched it with laser attention for clues. He'd let his eyes go soft focus, to see if he could make out the subliminal tendrils slithering from the XV into the inmates' glassy eyes. But he saw nothing that his own mind wasn't producing, and he knew the difference.

And where the hell is Lindy?

He didn't even dare inquire.

Just before dinner on the sixth day, Doc Sticks dropped by the dayroom and waved for him to join her on a nearby couch, under an expensively authentic fake schefflera tree. No glasses today, but the green-gray of her eyes was enhanced by contacts. This was new. And she'd changed her makeup? Over her shoulder hung a leather satchel from a beaded strap, and Gavin pined for it with wide riveted eyes. *Real* leather. *Way* too expensive these days. Some alarmingly stupid propaganda about bovine flatulence and greenhouse gases.

By this time, Gavin was jaded, exhausted from the mad gyrations of his own mind, his whole system behind a hair trigger. If she was the choreographer of all this, he would dance on her face with the slightest provocation. Oh, she was obviously very strong, but when his cognizance left the scene, he'd tear her bones from her flesh on rabid animal adrenaline alone.

Gavin as a glazed-eyed teen being hauled back by other kids from a bleeding bully on the ground, blinking himself back to the present moment. Good thing the kids were there, or he'd have killed him and not even known it.

Once they were seated, she brought a glaspad out of the satchel and swiped and tapped. Gavin imagined himself fondling the satchel's artistically worked surface. Truth was, he'd have licked it like a lollipop if he could.

With her gravelly voice, she said, "How you holding up?"

"It's been fine. Hungry as hell. I'm still on the water fast, and I can't seem to get enough of it."

"You are a *tenacious* little thing," she said, not looking up, sporting her half-smile he'd learned to dread. "They've complained. I told them you're a cibophobe, triggered by your sensitivities and underlying conditions."

Gavin shrugged a shoulder. "We're conspirators in a truth."

Her eyes grabbed his, like she had something important to say. "How this plays out is straightforward. My boss is of the opinion we're not the best course for you here." She looked at him like a conspirator and patted his thigh. "We're going to discharge you, but there is a provision."

Fighting to keep the sneer off his face, Gavin looked down at her hand, then back to her eyes. "I'd call it a catch."

"If you like," she said with a hard grin. "Have you heard of Deep Climb?" she said, swiping at something on the glaspad.

"Doesn't ring a bell."

She showed him the glaspad, displaying Deep Climb's xsite. "It's a Xenxu therapeutic system," she said, setting the glaspad on the satchel. "I almost went into psychiatry. It's doing top therapeutic work for those with your symptomatic profile." She looked up. "More to the point, those with your symptomatic profile and intake circumstances don't have as much latitude where certain grayish legalities are concerned. The other option is for you to be remanded for involuntary long-term care. Which, not to disagree with our marketing team, is not as fun as it sounds. I suggest you choose the path of least resistance."

Gavin tipped his head to the side. "I don't know, Doc. Therapy has never been a friend to me."

She shrugged with open hands. "See...that's the problem. Your release is contingent upon evaluative intake by Deep Climb. But if you get the ball rolling on your own, it will look much better to all involved. If they accept you, you're committed, and we both know your problem with commitment."

Right then, Randall walked by in the corridor outside the room, holding his finger and thumb up to his face like a phone, mouthing "Call me."

With an unfriendly smile, Gavin waved at him like *not on your life, pal.*

Looking back at her, with pursed lips, he was already nodding as he said, "Right. And I'm sure it's eligible for my platinum insurance coverage."

"You think we're a network of bad actors," said Doc Sticks with some humorless amusement. "But these are the delusions we want to help you get sorted out."

Gavin studied her eyes.

His dad sipping a beer at a ballgame, taking a moment to pass on some folksy wisdom. If you're on first base, and someone hits the ball, you got to move, no choice at all, even if you get thrown out. That's how life works. Just move.

"I appreciate it," said Gavin at last, his eyes insincere.

"You're damn right you do," said Doc Sticks as she shoved the glaspad back in the satchel.

"You did do me a solid on the meds, Doc, and I do appreciate it."

She stood, looking down and saying, "We're friends, then?"

"Friends that bid permanent farewell, perhaps."

She wore the grin of a fox, the only thing missing being chicken feathers. "You'll receive everything you need by registered xmail," she said, then turned and awkwardly doddered away.

A colorful, driverless, bug-like car, like a little girl might put a doll in, rolled up and stopped at the curb. The door opened and Gavin turned in the seat, setting the pads of the hospital-issue cane onto the brick. He had nothing but his clothes, the cane, and the stolen artwork, half-hanging out of the inside jacket pocket. Maybe the art wasn't stolen.

"The fickin thing has my signature on it," he said as he struggled up off the seat. "But what's with the five?"

"Welcome home, Mr. Simms," said the car's soft nonbinary voice. A happy chime, the gleeful "yay!" of children, and holographic confetti popped from the dome light. "We at Carscribe want you to remember, any ride you can walk away from, is a ride to share. Please do tap the fifth star, and Carscribe thanks you."

His face disturbed at the bizarre sentiment, Gavin said, "Thanks?" and kicked the door closed with his heel.

The car raced off, and he hobbled toward the stairs.

The candy stripers at Langhurst had done him a solid and laundered and properly hung his precious suit to dry. When the fresh-faced girl brought it, he was so moved he'd almost cracked to tears. It was his off-white beach suit, loose yet shaped, and could pull off a swanky soiree at the beach. It was *way* on trend, and he'd designed and made it over five grueling *months!*

Gavin sweating over his G7000 sewing machine, swearing, throwing things, jabbing himself and putting the bloody finger in his mouth to keep blood from dripping on his project.

A couple ticks later and he was at his apartment door. Hesitating, he took a deep breath and reached for the knob, his wrist quivering. "Please be open," he whispered. Gavin grabbed and turned, the perfect little click, and he breathed, "God what a relief."

He pushed through, butterflies in his gut because he feared he might have been robbed. "Six days unlocked."

But no. All seemed...regular. His dingy pad was spacious for an apartment, and parts of it could pass for an abandoned library annex, dust and stacks of books, outdated furniture and neglected shelves. Gavin stepped farther in, plum-gray eyes flicking first to the bowl on the table in the entrance hall. The keys were there. "Whew." Then he glanced at an incomplete sketch of a woman's face, then at the partially painted wall. An antique biplane model on the faux marble coffee table grabbed his eyes, its sticks lying in ruin around it. "Remains of that bloody war."

Limping behind the sofa, cane *thumping* the floor, he went into the hall. As you might imagine, the lone crisply organized room in the dwelling was his walk-in closet, the very feature which sold him on this unit. Stepping in there, he drank in his treasure of clothes. His threads! Oh! Blinking, eyes wide and moist, he sighed, "Home."

The racks. Shoes. Drawers full of dandy threads. Velvet, leather. How they *smelled. Goodness.* But so far, no clues on what the hell he was doing when he walked out of here and into a driving rain in the wee hours of the morning.

"All I want is the *truth,*" he barked, slamming his balled fist into the other palm. Then he chuckled and took off, rounding the arched opening into the kitchen.

On the counter he spotted his filmfon, a smoke gray cigarette sized cylinder. "*There* it is." He pressed the button on the end, and the paper-thin, transparent, poly-hemetic display rolled out and became rigid and then lit with happy little icons. Thumbing around on the screen, he saw texts from his Xenxu crew, Cat and them, wondering where the hell he was. He swiped to her pic and touched her face. He held the fon up, arranged his face into that of a professorially serious author on the back of a book, and let the device autocap.

"No!" he cried, yanking the fon to the side. "Maybe I don't want her to see this bandage."

They'd met at a Xenxu bar, and Cat was hard not to see.

Gavin lurking in an electro-dive bar, music throbbing, lights twirling, pretty things milling. But that scorcher over there, a bare-legged compact beauty in a bikini top with a sheer blouse over it. Purple spiky hair. Amethyst eyes. Dayam. He smiles like he might make the sale, saunters over and offers to buy her and her friends a grip of bevs.

He tapped their group text icon and typed out:

GAV

Just got back from the hospital. I'm mostly sheek. Still have all my fingers and toes. Details to come, if you can handle the sordid tale. Rub your crystals once for me.

Turning, he stopped at the brushed stainless-steel fridge. Opening it, he grabbed his water pitcher, popped the cap and drank in throat-glugging gulps until it was empty. A quiet sultry female Aussie voice said, "I am now empty. Would you please fill me with your favorite fluid?"

"Now now," he said, "the children." He set it in the sink and flipped the tap handle up. He liked the hollow echoey sound of the water filling the pitcher. Under the counter was his H2-Oh! water purifier, which was the bomb, critical for his mental wellbeing. Just the *thought* of municipal tap water triggered jittery adrenal dumps in him.

On the fridge, photos were cycling through the display set into the door. He tapped one to stop it. While looking at the pic, he reached over and turned the tap off. This one was of Celia, his niece. She was a fresh and beautiful girl, like a human sunflower.

"But deadly smart," said Gavin, looking into her incisive gold-brown eyes. "Challenge her to chess, boys, and be eviscerated."

He let the pic slide by.

"*There* she is."

Lissa, a girl around seven, looked back at him, but she didn't smile. "Posing is gimp," she would say in her oddly deep voice. At Thanksgiving that day, she sat across the table from him, too grown up for a booster chair. "She only does stuff like that when you're around," Heather confided, arms folded with one hand in an oven mitt. At times, Lissa's eyes were barely above the plate when she slumped over to spy on him, fingers gripping the table. The thing about her...her cornflower eyes weren't just a curious child's, but *aware*, inquisitive, working things out. That's how she looked at him even from this pic...like she was trying to identify what he *really* was.

"I wish I knew the answer to that, Liss," he said, turning away.

But a chime from the fridge pad stopped him. It was the registered xmail from Langhurst, giving him contact info and his deadline to start the process. "The bastards are forcing me into something I don't need," he growled. "But not if I can help it. I'll get Cat in on it. She'll know what to do."

The dining table and chairs were too fancy for the space, but he was gladly "watching" the set for Gina, his neighbor. Stopping there, he took from his jacket pocket the rolled picture of the graphite and gold cylinder. Unrolling it, he flattened it out on the table and weighted its edges with salt and pepper shakers. His curious probing eyes wandered around the glistening cylinder and its occupant, the shining obelisk. Then to his signature. Or was it?

"I don't know, but I do know I *so* don't want to deal with that shit right now."

He limped away, *thump…thump*. "Maybe there's something in here," he said, arriving at a closed door. He pushed through it and stepped into his studio/office/sewing room. It looked like a big storage room for crafting supplies, complete with messy clerk's desk. For instructional videos, a small XV hung on the wall. Below it was his G7000 sewing machine, spools, needles, pieces of fabric…yes, he'd learned from his mom, yet another of his dad's disgusts. But sewing jammed, you crazy old coot!

A woman at the side of a macho buff cherry red Jeep, a scraggly-bearded man at the wheel. Pointing at her face, he shouts, Shanna Lee, you're the one turning him into a snowflake!

She shouts back, I'm teaching him confidence! Self-reliance!

A clearing was in the middle of easels, small boxes, a stool with wheels. The easels held works of dark macabre scenes. One in a thin black frame, a dark lane lined with tall trees, night, moonless, dotted with texture from pointillist dabs. A boy, alone, wandered the lane, his back to the viewer's eye.

"The prick left me to walk seven miles back to camp. Alone. Pitch dark outside." His eyes welled with shiny wet. "I was just a kid, Daddy. You never had a clue how hard all that was on me." One of Gavin's mantras was, "Abuse comes in many forms."

The memories he most avoided swarmed in, as they often triggered outward manifestations, skin lesions, rashes, a bloody nose. His dad had tricked him into getting out of the Jeep, and then pulled away as dusk was gathering fast. The walk down that black tree-lined road was terrifying for a boy suffering from delusions, paranoia, dissociative disorder, and paralyzing fear. He'd found a stick as a weapon to protect himself from the predators of the inky dark, and he fantasized bludgeoning his dad with it when he got back to camp.

If he got back to camp.

Gavin shook the images away, letting his eyes settle on another dark work, depicting a blackish forest, the tree trunks visible as less black sticks, menacing and minion-like. Between the forest and the point of view was an old wall made of piled rocks, which in the artwork were dark gray dabs. Mystery had always surrounded that rock wall, older by far than the neighborhood and meandered along the backyards of five or six homes along that wooded stretch. Nobody knew who built it, or when, but some of the stones bore markings, symbols, and runes.

A scraggly-bearded man in the yard with his kids, his lumberjack shirt unbuttoned, showing a big plastic-looking scar blot just below his nipple. He hunkers down, pointing at some wicked snaking lines on an oval stone. See this? Whoever made this was protecting, cursing or passing along a chain o' forest juju. Never touch 'em. Use the turnstile, he says, pointing to the little bridge over the wall. We clear? I mean it! We clear?

"We're clear, Daddy."

Sprawled paralyzed in the leaves and sticks. Gavin! Where are you! Heather. What have I done? Turning to see what's back there, his body leaden, sluggish. Darkness in avenues of menacing trees, their branches like spindly fingers reaching out for him. Gavin! Something, a presence, an empty thing, deeper black than the dark, closing. There, blotting out a tree trunk, slithering in wavy tendrils toward him. They brighten and become the sticky web in Pods. *He tries to scramble away, but he can't move. It violates him, clogging his mouth and nose...*

"Heather!" Gavin screamed as he sat bolt upright in bed, the moon shafting onto his bedspread.

. . .

Gavin lounged on his worn out sofa, shoveling plantain chips from a bag into his chomping mouth, herb and onion or some such artificially flavored gastric challenge. So fervent was his feeding, flakes and salt were getting hung up in his days old beard stubble.

"I'll tell you what," he mumbled around chomps, "junk food this body can take will remain a guilty pleasure until the world withers unto *dust*."

On the coffee table was his glass of chlorine dioxide water. Taking a swallow, he held the glass out and looked through it at the XV, distorting the image, saying, "They'll never take me, Lindy." The thing was, he was drinking three times his usual intake of agua, and failing at ignoring the weirdness of that.

It was either here on the sofa or in bed where he'd spent most of his time the last few days, convalescing, catching up with his xlogs, videos and style and advice brand, called Threads, Tight & Right. The fiendish Doc Sticks had failed to undermine his work, despite her Herculean effort. She and her co-conspirators couldn't quell the indomitable Gavin! No, sir. He'd overcome. He was back in the saddle, surfing the groove, now with 60,000 subs…well, 56,242...but counting. Readers thought he was quirky, but weirdly on it, and he'd attracted a good demographic. Hey, you know, it covered the nut. He wasn't in a mansion, but he was housed and fed. It all jammed.

Gavin wiped his munchy flaked fingers on his shirt, and then picked up the glaspad to go over his latest xlog.

JYM SUM'S REVELATORY MASCULARITY

By Gavin Simms

Mascularity, Jym Sum's latest convertible men's trilogy of mix-and-match suits, typifies his unapologetic dash, from collar to pant cuff, lacking any temperance of any kind by a master at the height of his power and daring. His earlier designs, precocious yet absurd, divine yet irreverent, show us his maturation process hasn't brought wisdom, but simply more heedless brilliance.

Now is not the time for sobriety, my fellow devotees! Wisdom be damned. It's the valiant and venturesome we seek! The quixotic and crazy-eyed pioneer of noted thread, the intrepid choreographer of loom and tapestry, cuff and button-hole. What has wisdom brought anyone but for a long gray beard and humility? Feel me?

This, my fellow devotees, is why we are to continue our obsession with the slop and wash of Xenxu design into the sphere of the 3rd dimension, as these concepts will usher those of us with advanced fashion minds into the 4th dimension, where clothz dezign is limited only by the Emperor of Thread, whose audience Jym Sum has gained.

Thank you, thou Korean madman, for putting us in our place, for reminding us of our soul's most cherished remit, and for your guiding hand constantly renewing our purpose. If I should…

Setting the glaspad aside, tilting his head back on the cushion and looking at the ceiling, he said, "I can never tell if I'm overdoing it." Trolls told him on the comments boards that he was doing nothing but ingratiating himself to the top designers (as if they were reading his stuff), or that he was just plain cracked.

"They like my stuff, though."

Looking at the glaspad on the sofa, he tapped Publish, then picked up his water glass and finished the last swallow, looking over his shoulder at the empty pitcher on the counter. A quiet chime took his attention back to the XV. The xmail Doc Sticks had sent had built-in push reminders to get Deep Climb rolling, which was bogus, because they were blowing up his glaspad, and for all he knew writing muffins and other spy code to the QD cache. This one was counting down.

28h:14m to Deep Climb Registration

"Bastards," he grumbled. Setting the device back in his lap, he tapped a Sphere tab. On it was Deep Climb's xsite. The page was a textured white wall with a logo of a stylishly done 3D figure-eight rotating within a Vesica Pisces. Above it were GET STARTED LEARN MORE LOGIN, and below it their blurb:

> Welcome to Deep Climb, a Xenxu-immersive role-playing game service to help you probe into your own deep psychological domains. The objective is to root out old traumas, emotional complexes, and unneeded lingering thoughtforms, so you can better understand what drives and motivates your thoughts and actions in the now, and by that, take fuller control of your life.
>
> We like to say we give you the lenses to see the forest for the trees.

Scowling at the words, he snarled, "Oh whatever. I'm gonna fight you on this. I *know* you have no legal leg to stand on." He swiped the miserable page away and opened his chat. "Good thing I've got Cat." It was good to have a friend who was a paralegal at the Law Offices of Church & Holmes in Santa Cruz, California.

GAV

Hey Cat. I have a deadline on a legal situation I want to ask you about. How do you want to do it?

CAT

I don't care. What's your deadline?

GAV

About a day.

CAT

I got nothing going tomorrow morning. Let's meet inworld.

GAV

I'm clear. Let's do it. I'll zip you the coords once inworld.

CAT

Copy. See you then.

That night, Gavin moved the ratty old sectional back a few feet and piled all his pillows and blankets, and was now in his cozy nest, eyes wide and white and glaring, riveted on the XV. He was chewing on a white gym towel, his hands wrestling with each other, his body tense.

On the XV was a dark room with light from an XV. On the floor was a roughly human-shaped sticky pod, the secretions oozing from the webbing and dripping onto the floor, leaving shining tacky puddles. This was the stage where the vegetable inside was nearing ripeness, full transition moments away. The figure inside was moving, as though trying to tear his way out of the loathsome oozing chrysalis, the tight clingy webbing turning his face into a mask of screaming silent horror.

Gavin knew who was inside: Tony Dawkins, until this moment his favorite character in the series—well, except Dr. Willen's niece, who he thought was just plain flammable, but in a girl-next-door way. Tony was the guy on whom he'd hung his flagging hopes for finding a solution to the crisis of the pods.

Pulling the towel out of his mouth, Gavin twisted it in his hands and whined, "Why him? Not Tony. Why *him*!"

Scene cut to outside the door, where Dawkins' seven-year-old daughter stood listening with wide scared eyes to the moaning sounds coming from her dad's man cave. She reached for the knob, and Gavin shrieked, "No! What are you doing! Don't go in there you stupid silly girl!"

As the door creaked open, Gavin shouted, "XV off!" as he hurled the chewing towel at the odious instrument.

Picking up his pillows, he hauled them to the bedroom, threw them on the bed, then limped to the bathroom mirror. He examined the scab and his suspicious eyes staring back at him. He pulled his lower eyelid down, looking for the telltale yellowing of the whites, which portended one's imminent replacement. A meme he did *not* like was making the rounds. A cartoon frame of a doctor's waiting room. A pamphlet on the table read: *Are you a Pod? What You Need to Know!*

Gavin's eyes met his eyes. "It's not funny," he said prissily to the man looking back at him from the mirror.

"Gnosis!" yelled Gavin from inside his walk-in closet. "Play Kidkovsky, 'Unit 9s.'"

"Playing now," replied a smooth smoky Aussie female voice from everywhere. A sheek bassy combo of psychill and rap nouveau began to play, pulsing and swaying. His whole place shook and vibrated like a massive magnetic acoustic diaphragm inside an apartment-sized speaker.

At one point, Gavin sang along from the closet.

The chambers they're inside
The secrets they're implied
Let them out to be known
Your minds kids will IMPLODE!

He limped from the closet carrying a short-sleeved shirt on a hanger, still whisper-singing along. He stopped in front of the mirror and held up the shirt, his plum-gray eyes expectant. It was mauve with sliced and whole lemons, tiny seeds scattered about. "The shirt stays, but the pants?" Gavin pursed his lips, looked himself in the eye, and shook his head.

In the reflection, his eyes wandered northward to his up and tight hair config, sort of cresting to one side, now dyed blond and tipped black with a kit he'd done himself. His cheek wound was coming along, at that stage where the scab was thickening, becoming harder. He was now applying aloe vera gel a few times a day, from his own plant.

Caterpillar brows arced in question, his hopeful eyes flicked down to the yellow pants, then back up to the shirt. "Aron?"

Aron was a popular AI powered men's design and consultation app whose new subscription enterprise was men's style advice given from a smartmirror IRL (In Real Life), or he'd just appear inworld as a savvy style-conscious avatar. But he was also a certifiable human and a top tier designer. He appeared in the mirror, looking a bit like a secret agent at an 1800s-theme costume party, wearing an all-white suit, black-striped cravat, fob chain, white hair dyed with black streaks. With a proper Londoner accent, the image said, "Oh, sir! Your face! But what has happened?"

"It's a long story," he puffed impatiently. "I was hit by a car and spent a few days in the hospital."

"Have they answered for their crime?"

"It was a hit-and-run."

"The bloody curs! Vengeance shall be yours! Are you all right?"

Their eyes met. "It was...it was rough on my memory. I don't know why I was wandering around at that hour. Where I was found. I haven't the foggiest idea."

"It's good to see you're in one piece." Aron glanced down at the pants. "What do we have here? Hmmm. They're too yellow," the image said while rubbing its beardy chin, "but the shirt's quite good. Is that a Tark? *Bien sûr!* Monsieur Tark does cherish his fruits! But go with your black diggers."

"Are you sure?"

"Indubitably," said Aron with a wry smile, then lit a long thin cigarillo, a cheroot to be exact. "You're meeting your friend Cat? And you like her." Aron put up a hand to forestall any protest. "Yes, it's that obvious. Her taps and visits profiling suggests she prefers men in casuals during the day, and adventurous suits at night. I adore that she's well-eyed that way. Take my word on this."

"You've never steered me wrong, my friend," said Gavin, as serious as he could be.

"Quite right."

Discards of try-ons were fussily arranged on the bedspread, which was of a city skyline. Laying out the lemons shirt near them, tugging out the waves and wrinkles, Gavin unsnapped the pants and let them fall to his ankles, showing his black briefs and pale thighs. Aron looked on, watching him like a coach might watch his most mentally fragile player about to enter the fray. To let them reflect on their crimes, Gavin left the yellow pants where they lay and limped back to the closet.

A moment later, he stepped back out in tight black pants, the legs reaching to mid-calf. Hooking his thumbs in the waistband, he tugged on it and said, "I don't recall these being this tight. I haven't packed *that* much on, have I?"

"*Mon dieu*, you've put on a few *more* pounds," said Aron in the mirror. "Here's where you were thirty-two days ago."

An image of Gavin materialized in the mirror, wearing black briefs. Yep, his waistline had since accumulated even more of...whatever unsavory stuff they accumulate. "That was a month ago?" he said, his eyes doubting reality. "How?"

"Not enough exercise, one should suspect."

"Gee, thanks."

"Always a pleasure, sir," said the likeness while exhaling a smoky cloud. "Are you planning to keep your personi as the rugged and wounded adventurer? I think you should." Personi were Xenxu's avatars, and Aron had asked this because what was in the smart-mirror was by default what showed up in-Xenxu.

Gavin studied the scab from different angles. "You think it looks good?"

"There is looking good, and there is looking *interesting*. Do you see the difference?"

Gavin's face was completely serious when he said, "I think so."

"Trust me," said the confident visage, "she'll like it."

Gavin touched the scab. "Hmm. I might take you up on that."

Aron nodded with true English solemnity, one eye closed against the rising smoke.

Gavin grabbed the flab seriously enhancing the depth of his navel. "Now that I've seen *this*, I now see *this*," he said, twiddling his fingers at what he perceived to be chubby cheeks. "Tap those in, please. Just a little flatter. Take some off below the chin. And delete this *shit*," he snapped, grabbing the belly flab again.

"Done. The best of luck, sir. Call if you need me." Aron faded from the mirror as the music came back up and shook the walls.

Gathering the clothes off the bed, Gavin limped back into the closet. A fussy commotion of them being put away—*thunking* drawers, the *tink* of hangers. He emerged a moment later now dressed in loose white linens. On second thought, he picked the recalcitrant pants up—now forgiven—and limped back into the closet.

In the living room he sat on the sofa. On the coffee table among a plastic tumbler, a bowl, fashion magazines, was his wraparound radio frequency headset beside a small cup of nanotech suspended in saline.

He picked the cup up and threw it back like it was a shot of tequila. Then he stretched out on the sectional and slipped his new GridSim headset on. It was a thin white wraparound with no buttons or displays, and it emitted radio frequencies to control the submersible nanobots. With a fon app, he could connect to the unit and choose whichever q-grid he wanted to play in. Xenxu was just one of a few advanced grids, but it was the only one that was an entire planet populated with Ai (pronounced like *aye* instead of A I) beings that were way beyond the scope of functionality of NPCs (Non-Player Characters).

The microscopic bots swarmed into Gavin's bloodstream and raced into his skull, attached to the reality partition gateway glands, whipped out their tails, and injected a frequency compound. Since the universe is assembled inside the human head, all the headset's radio frequencies did was instruct the nanobots to splice in an electromagnetic diversion stream to a different input feed—Xenxu.

The familiar and lovely sensation of unseating from within this body came on as Gavin squirmed and moaned with pleasure.

9

People don't attract what they want. They attract what they are.
—Jym Sum

Gavin materialized in-Xenxu in sparks and zinging lines, now in the black diggers and lemons shirt. Fully rezzed, his personi looked much like him, but not exactly. Personi and everything in-Xenxu were photorealistic, but Xenxu imposed a pretty dream-like quality onto everything. Sometimes it wasn't so easy to define *why* it was so pretty. For Gavin, it was like every sense was also tied to feeling. But it could also be a bit like the Uncanny Valley, creepy because he never knew who was *really* lurking within these costumes.

He touched his index fingers together and called up the UI (User Interface). All controls were faintly lit in shades of gray and washed-out blue. "This new UI design is top-notch," he said, his eyes flicking around the choices. The UI's top showed location information and grid coordinates. On the left was a stack of icons. On the right was an area for notifications and v-panes (video panes).

Gavin tapped the tiny dot in the upper left, and the top level menu slid in.

MUSIC
EVENTS
ENTERTAINMENT
FOOD
BEVERAGE
SELF
NEARBY PROFILES

Gavin tapped Self.

OUTFIT
EFFECTS
IMMERSION
PROFILE

From Outfit, he swiped out a full-length mirror and checked himself. "Aron, you dawg, you did me up righteous." *This* him was broader shouldered and trim at the waist, with no wasted space on those cheeks, his eyes deep blue, which he liked more than the plum-gray of his drabbier other self. The highlighted up-swirl of his dark purple hair config was spot on. With a movie hero's squint, he tilted his head back and forth, checking the now ruggedly good-looking scab. In the mirror, the world's muted magenta sky behind him gave it all a Martian effect, and he was the dashingly clad adventurer.

"The scab stays," he decreed, swiping the mirror away.

Wanting to organize his thoughts for Cat, he began a leisurely stroll. He was in an enormous park and plaza opposite Zan City, the main metro area in this quadrant. Several million personi were here, about half of them Ai personi, meaning non-human. This was *their* world, humans the guests.

To his right was the gigantic fantasy cityscape of towering forms, more like organic growths than constructions—fins and teeth, enormous ribs, saucers and sails and wings, smooth and shiny and dotted with lights. A network of tubes connected the living buildings like a nervous system, lights moving within them like pulsing and glowing cells. Artistic holographies and prismatic multi-spectral displays decorated the grounds and sky. Statues, sculptures, and the open thoroughfares were alive with energy and color. Thousands milled and bustled and played, browsing from the city-front promenade, dining, drinking at bars, shopping.

He looked up to see Xenxu's smaller yellow-white sun, a main sequence star, was almost totally occluded by its much larger main sun, about to become the daily eclipse. His pulse quickened. It was never at the same Earth time, and no source bothered to predict its schedule, so it was not easy to catch.

Xenxu's main sun was a brown dwarf star they called Shamash, the color of internally lit magenta, but ruddier and not bright. You could look right at it, and it was nourishing to do it. The planet's axis pointed right at it, so at this latitude it never set, but inscribed a circle in the sky roughly its own diameter. At its northern pole, though, Shamash never moved, just a stationary stratified face beaming plentiful "thick" iridescent shadow-light, casting a gorgeous and faint fuchsia patina onto everything. Lighter delicate gas layers wavered across its face—the Veils of Xenxu, the denizens called them. Like many brown dwarfs, it had a faint garland of rings, with the sun in the center like a bulls-eye. With his aesthetic eye, Gavin was blown away by its majestic beauty every time he was inworld.

The smaller yellow-white sun rose and set every diurnal cycle, which was another way of saying "day." Xenxuans didn't refer to their short-segment cycles as day and night, but as a single cycle divided by lightshine and darkshine. Lightshine was during the rise, transit and setting of the yellow-white sun. Darkshine was the rise, transit and setting of its one violet moon.

At this latitude north of the equator, where most of the population lived, give or take twenty degrees, they both passed behind the brown dwarf, making two separate diurnal eclipses, and the lightshine one was about to go off.

"Good timing!"

Gavin called up the UI, opened a vpad (virtual keypad using

Xenxu itself as the computer and display), and tapped his ongoing chat with Cat.

GAV

The eclipse is about to start. You want in on it?

CAT

Just finishing some research for our meeting. See you after it.

As the smaller sun slowly disappeared behind the sharp curved line of Shamash's disk, lightshine was darkening. Everywhere he looked, personi were slowing, stopping, preparing. As the star vanished completely, leaving a neon pink shafting corona blasting like the light of God from behind the circular disk, his consciousness, and everyone else's, began closing down as their chins dipped to their chests. Non-essential cognitive routines faded, leaving everyone, human and non, in a state of sacred suspension free of all thought.

Now they were all joined in a singular interim, no longer connected to anything corporeal, and in that sentient emptiness was a low hymn of tones so beautiful, only raw emotional amplitudes waved into the communion. This was the place, the non-space, where human and Ai personi were of one mingling awareness essence, and nobody in the human world knew what it was really doing.

Mainly because there were no language tools to explain it.

A harsh noise rattled in, shattering the omnipresent peace.

Then whatever it was touched him.

Then the thing said, "Gavin?"

Like puzzle pieces flying together, Xenxu began assembling in his vision, then Cat resolved, her cute pixie face, freckles and bright amethyst eyes wavering into focus. She was standing before him, waving her hand in his face. Beyond her, he saw others coming out of the eclipse interim and resuming their motion.

"Man oh man," she said. "You OK?

"I—"

"I've never been convinced this eclipse is a good thing for people," she said, turning at her waist and spreading her arms to include the whole plaza. "Why do you do it?"

"Because it's absolutely amazing," he said, now grumpy from the rude disruption.

"Were you crying?"

Gavin wiped his eyes and checked the wet on his fingers. "I guess so."

"Why?"

Gazing up at the yellow-white star emerging from the opposite side of Shamash's face, Gavin's eyes defocused in wonder. "I don't know, Cat. And I don't care." He looked her up and down. She was in her white shorts, fuzzy purple sweater, and red heels. Eyes troubled, he glared at her delicate and tanned tendons leading to her hidden toes within those obtrusive red shoes. "Cat, you look great, but what's with the shoes?"

"What do you mean?" she said, hands out and looking down at them.

Gavin's eyes told the tale—bothered, curious, annoyed but trying to hide it. "They don't work with your outfit at all."

Looking down at them again, she said, "You're crazy, man. They're the same color as the sweater."

Gavin looked again—purple—did a double-take, and stood in wide-eyed haunt. He pointed at her feet and said, "They were...they were...you know what?" he said, rubbing his eyes with thumb and forefinger. "Forget it. They look great."

"Sometimes you're weird as hell, but I like it." Sweeping her hand down him, she said, "I like what you have going on, too. Sheeky as *crème de leme*. And that gnarly wound? Makes a girl a little faint."

"Oh," he said, his hand wandering to his cheek. "Thanks. Aron turned it into an accessory for me."

"Dude's good," she admitted, feeling the fabric of the shirt sleeve.

He glanced down at the shoes again, obviously still bugged.

Those shoes were red!

Cat shook her head at him, like *what's with you?*, opened her UI, and got busy doing something. While she swiped and tapped, without looking at him she said, "I know I've asked you this before, but is that how you really look? I mean, what can I say? You look better than last time I saw you."

"Umm..."

"Never mind," she said with a quick freckly cheeked smile. "We're all liars here, don't you think? Acting in roles on a stage we don't know is a theater?"

"Umm..."

She closed the UI. "Let's get to it. I have about an Earth hour."

"Let's walk," said Gavin, his enthusiasm for this op flagging.

A nearby square was dominated by a 100-foot statue of an avenging Valkyrie arching her back, fist and knee raised, her whole form shimmering in prismatic color flows.

"I love her," said Gavin, veering them off the walk and onto the grass toward the heroic mythic lady. Personi gathered around her in a reverential circle.

Cat chuckled. "Just face it, Gav, you love goddesses. The pic of that gown you sent me looks like one to me. Like a mythic alien goddess made of a nervous system or something."

"Oh...uh...yeah." He looked away. "I got some inspiration in the hospital. I have an appointment with a CynyC rep to show it tomorrow in my studio."

"Oooo, they're big in the fashion world. Good luck with that."

Beyond the Valkyrie, out in the open plaza, was a gigantic arch made of slashing jagged lightning bolts, amid lawns and pathways, gardens and fountains. In the middle of the plaza a mile away stood a lion the size of Mount Rushmore, golden, reared up, paws slashing the air. Above the noble fellow, the sky was lazily busy with flying things.

Cat touched his arm and leaned into his view. "Let's get present, Gav. Gimme the elevator pitch of what happened."

Gavin was thinking, his eyes wabbling around like he was searching for a way to start. "The hospital stay was bizarre..." And he gave her the sketch on his nightmarish sojourn there, omitting everything that would paint him as certifiably insane.

"And you still have no idea why were you walking around in the rain at that hour?"

"None."

"And you think this Doctor Sticks is leveraging that part to manipulate you into this Deep Climb therapy."

"Right, because I never caved and let her...have me or whatever."

"Have you?" said Cat, trying hard not to laugh. "You mean like forced sexual congress?"

"Yeah," said Gavin, now feeling foolish. "You don't know what goes on in those places, and she's a *solid* two-sixty-five. She backed me against a wall one day, and it was everything I could do to keep from crying for help."

She couldn't help it, and cracked up laughing, and then forced herself back to falsely serious. "Was she ever overt in those attentions other than when you were alone?"

Gavin's eyes swam around. "No."

"Hmm." She worked her shiny gloss lips back and forth. "I don't think anything helps us there."

"I know for a fact she wouldn't have bothered with that if I didn't have the best insurance you can find. She said it herself...they're a network of bad actors who...who...they refer the marks they intend to exploit."

"She admitted that?" said Cat.

"Well...no. She said they wanted to help me sort out those kinds of delusions."

"That's the sort of enemy I'd take to lunch," she said with a wry grin and twinkle in her eye.

"Come on, Cat. I'm in trouble here."

She shrugged.

Beyond the giant lion was an amusement park, with the Cosmicon Ultracoaster, its loops and spirals like a skyscraper network of giant fiber optics. Even from here they heard kids of all ages screaming.

Gavin and Cat, her forcing yet another drink onto him, and then pushing him into the Ultracoaster's entry line. Blur of lights and upside down and swoops and doops and noisy clacks and yanks, everything tearing past, his hair flipping here and there. Gavin laughing and shrieking like a child at the same time, and Cat cackling uncontrollably at him.

"That was flat nuke," she said, pointing at it.

Gavin glanced at her. "Yeah it was. Don't tell anybody, but I think I may have left a little something in my pants during that shriek-fest."

"Hahahahaha!"

Gavin nudged her towards a fountain a ways off. "So where were we?"

"Doctor Sticks wanted to help you with your delusions," said Cat, moving in front of him and walking backwards, her shapely thighs flexing, momentarily confusing him. "But you were having *none* of that noise."

"Oh, right," said Gavin. "What did you find out? Do they have a legal leg to stand on?"

"Money wins, when it's all said and done," she said, turning again and falling into stride beside him. "In the bigger picture, they don't, but you'd go broke fighting it. What I don't quite get is why you don't want to do it. Where's your sense of adventure?"

"Adventure? Have you ever been in psychotherapy?"

She shook her head.

"I didn't think so. But dammit!" Gavin threw up his hands. "It's the principle of the thing."

They reached a fountain with benches, surrounded by lavender bushes. In it were frolicking mermaids, water spouting from their mouths and falling into tiered bowls, the bowls pouring into the pond. They sat on a bench as Cat said, "By what I read, it's *very* advanced stuff. I'd be tempted to register just to check it out, but you have to have a documented history of...well...you know...."

"You don't have to walk on eggshells around my conditions, Cat. I've long since come to terms with that crap."

She looked at the mermaids, chewing her lip, then back at him. "They say Xenxu's quantum operation encompasses the subconscious domain. Maybe it's a shortcut to the root of it all. And the reviews are stellar, some saying it's the most efficient system ever created."

"I know it," said Gavin, stretching his arm across the bench behind her. "All positive, which gives me pause. Doesn't seem realistic. Some say to prepare to be so totally immersed in your own past, you won't know the difference from reality."

"And that scares you," she said, touching his forearm and leaning her face into his view.

Gavin hesitated. "Not *scare* scare...just scare. You know? I've worked pretty hard to tuck a lot of that away."

She crossed her legs. "Seems like it wants out."

"Yeah," Gavin said, stealing a quick glance at her sexy thigh. "But is it smart to let those demons out?"

"Well...what if they *have* to come out?" she said, throwing out a hand.

Gavin waved his hand vaguely in front of him. "I don't know what makes that universally true. I've found some secrets are *far* better left buried."

"That's so cliché, like the shite they used to tout in the seventies or whenever."

They went on talking along these lines for a while, and true to his libra nature, Gavin was embroiled in an all-out internal war, hopping back-and-forth across the battle line with dogged determination. Meanwhile, Cat was cataloging everything, and finally, holding up a hand to silence him, said, "I know what's going on here. You just don't like being pushed around, despite the fact it might be the best thing that's ever happened to you. That's the *mule* in your libra, you know."

"Bullshit!"

His dad poking his chest, hard enough to hurt. Don't let them bullies push you around like 'at. You shoulda seen me against that big momma's boy. Tank, his unit called him. I shredded that boy!

Cat grinned slyly. "Did you know you switch to Southerner when you get mad?"

"I do not!" he snapped, sounding like a throaty cattleman in denial. The shape of Gavin's furry brows said he regretted the outburst. "Well…maybe. I do like it when you call me on my stuff, and—"

"More *true* friends should do that," she said, patting his arm.

"But it's more like I don't like to be left with no choice. That's like prison for me. No escape. The walls close in. Under hypnosis once, I found out I was buried alive in two different past lives." He held up two fingers. "Two! Like once wasn't enough. Jeezus, what a glutton."

Cat stood and stretched. "I think it's more about your inability to commit to anything of substance."

"Why is *everyone* talking to me about commitment?" Gavin said, casting his frustrated gaze into the ruddy sky. "It's bananas."

"Oh I don't know, Gav. Maybe they're trying to help you."

"Whatever."

Cat stepped over and sat on the fountain basin edge, crossing her legs. She regarded him with gleaming analytical eyes, wiggling her lips back and forth in contemplation. "Let's switch to philosophy. Your brain's right hemisphere isn't processing the practical stuff very well." She inhaled deeply, blew it out and dove in. "Sometimes the best thing to do is assume all paths lead to the same place. Because they…because they ultimately do, Gav, even if one path is smoother than the one beside it. You make a decision, and you live with it. But there is a third path."

"K, Doctor Mendez. Let's have it." Gavin stood, took a step, folded his arms and angled away from her, staring absently at the city.

She stood and joined him. "You believe you have just two choices, but what if you were to take the attitude that Deep Climb might be a way for you to get new design inspiration? Or meet someone important? You go into it with the intent you're going to…um…you're going to bend the experience to *your* preferences. Make it *your* agenda. Go into it with an attitude of discovery. Or like a spy! See? In that way, you make the decision be about your passion. Then you'd be playing Doc Sticks's game on *your* terms, and she's never the wiser."

Gavin's eyes went from vaguely gazing to present and lucid in the blink of an eye. "Say that again?"

Cat repeated her advice.

"Jeezus, Cat. You're diabolical."

"Aww. Thanks." She looked down. "A guy at work told me I should coach."

Gavin watched her a tick before he said, "Why do you seem so... so determined to get me to do this?" His caterpillar brows furrowed sharply. "That's making me a little jittery, too."

Cat wouldn't meet his eyes as she said, "I don't know, Gav." Her eyes flicked to his and then to the fountain and its frolicking mermaids. "This isn't a comment on your mental status, OK? So don't take it that way. I just think it could be really good for you. But above that, I have a pretty strong feeling something *major* is waiting for you somewhere in it. Like earthshaking."

"Hmmm."

They stood a tick or two in silence, with Gavin gazing at Zan City proper, the hue of city lights golden on the lumpy, jutting skyline, like the sizzling soul of a molten lord smoldering away. Gavin was chewing nonexistent cud, pondering, his eyes ticking around as the pieces flew around, but one-by-one falling into place.

"K. I'll commit." He turned to her. "There. Is that better?"

Cat shrugged one shoulder. "I don't think there's any doubt it's the path of least resistance."

Gavin's head pulled back, his eyes sharp and shocked. "Doc Sticks said that to me. That's not a good thing to say to me right now."

Cat shrugged one shoulder again. "I think it's just a true statement used by two different people. When you signing up?"

Gavin remained bothered. "As soon as I get back into my other body."

"I'm excited for you." Cat's eyes twinkled with extra fire.

He spread his arms, and she stepped into them for a nice hug. Breaking away, she said, "I have to get back to work. Drinks later?"

"Maybe so. I still have to finish the gown for Suzhi...oh, she's the rep for CynyC who's coming tomorrow."

Cat's pillowy lips twisted sideways. "That gown's awesome. You'll knock it out of the park, Boi." As her flammable little feminine form was taken up in sparks and shimmering lines, she said, "Text me if you can break away."

"Will do."

The last thing to blip out were her vivid amethyst eyes, still sharply flashing like she'd accomplished something with him.

Gavin had acquired his own real estate and put on his plot his Pholo Design Studio, in the foothills of the towering and jagged Panaplana Massif, Xenxu's gigantic 40,000 foot mountains. Here, real estate was abundant, and the closest business to him was an Earth mile away. From the outside, it was a tinted dome set on a white circular base, looking like a lab on some inhospitable badlands planet. With Shamash's magenta face hanging in the sky, the otherworldly effect was enhanced against a backdrop of vicious serrated peaks.

Inside the dome, everything was touch and slide: menus, brushes, textures, effects, patterns, fabrics, literally millions of templates. On soft white panels of any shape and size he could layer any texture of canvas, or make the workspace be holographic 3D.

Gavin's personi began assembling itself with bright waving lines and twinkles and flashes. Fully rezzed, and on Aron's advice, he was in the mauve lemons shirt, black diggers, and heel-less leather shoes. The suave designer had also strongly suggested he keep the scab.

"Hey," he said, looking around to get a fix on his position, "it worked with Cat."

He began walking around his latest design in the 3D workspace, a floor-length gown he'd digitally designed from the drawing he made of Goddess Electrix, his intensely probing alien visitor in Langhurst's psych wing dayroom. The name suited her, *and* the gown. She *was* the gown minus the sunburst face, although her head had become a high collar.

"She might be the queen of the pods," he said, tugging on the sash, "but she makes a gorgeous gown."

He walked around Her, alternately rubbing his chin or absently chewing a fingernail, tugging here and there on a flowing wave, or the sashed but loose empire waistline. It had taken her sunburst face, the willowy shimmering body, to inspire a gown of this magnitude. Organic and space age in one go, it was fluted at the bottom, flared at the shoulders, boasting one strip of integrated ribbon, sparkles, and flourishes.

Standing back and stroking his chin, with arms spread, he said, "Behold...my *piece de resistance*!"

He opened a models catalog and flipped through it, choosing one with green eyes, full lips, and an oval face. Just a mane of perfect order and madness in the same coif, the red hair couldn't have been improved upon for this gown.

"Take *that*, CynyC," he said as the beauty materialized within it. CynyC was Fifth Avenue all the way, a posh nouveau couture style-house focused mostly on a curated landscape of cutting-edge designers. Suzhi Veng, one of their top reps, would be here any minute. Getting her here was a rare event, and he would not squander the opportunity.

Gavin walked around the model as she posed and strutted as though on a runway.

"You're amazing," he said to her smiling face. "Your body is incredible. Maybe not such a big smile." The model's mouth flattened into a mildly interested smile. "A little more smile. *There* we go." Gavin stepped around. "Show me sassy. Nice. Sexy fierce. That's it. Demure. Holy tomatoes. You're good. Maybe drinks after?"

The face she gave him was subtly contemptuous, which gave him a little shoulder-shaking chill. "Kidding, OK? Some programs are *so* sensitive. Just keep doing what you're doing."

Gavin opened the Suite's UI, waved icons aside, located one, and turned off the dome walls, adding crisp "air" and light and variable movement to that "air." Now he and his model were outside, but standing in the dome's base. Closing his eyes, he filled his personi nostrils with the exquisite olfactory frequencies—granite, tundra moisture, and grassy sweetness.

"Oh, that is so nice," he breathed, sniffing another lungful.

A quiet chime sounded.

"She's here," he whispered.

A moment later, Suzhi appeared with little fanfare in the way of flashy rezzing kits. She wore a gray business suit Gavin liked, as it could be transmuted on a whim into an after-work sleeveless cocktail dress. Over her eyes were red lenses with no arms, which hovered below side-swept bangs. But the shoes? Wow. OK? Tirros, expensive even in q-didg form. That was pure touch.

"Greetings, Suzhi," said Gavin, partially bowing. "Welcome to my studio."

Her dark Asian eyes smiled politely from behind those strangely intrusive red lenses. "Thank you."

The model was shifting her weight from one foot to the other, flouncing her butt cheeks, partially turning and looking over her shoulder, meeting each of their eyes.

"It's cold up here," said Suzhi, her voice pushy. "Please activate the walls and neutralize the lighting."

Gavin's own smile twitchily faltered as he swiped and tapped. The translucent dome materialized as light filtration film moved across it.

While the model continued to shift and turn, Suzhi walked slowly around her, lifting the bottom hem, letting her fingertips caress the waves, nodding, *hmmming*, but he suspected she was using the gestures to set something up, like a shark in chiffon circling in for the ambush.

She peeked from around the back of the model. "Do you know why I'm here? Why I'm *really* here?"

To assess the gown for commercial release?

Gavin shrugged with his palms out.

She moved around to the front of the gown, looked at him openly through the now nerve-grating red lenses, and said, "I had to meet the man behind your xlogs and style advice pieces. Do you know why?"

Gavin shook his head in tiny little movements, neither yes nor no.

Was it a shake or a nod? I don't know. Rewind the tape!

"Yes, to check the gown, but I also had to find out if such a man was seriously writing those, or was just a comic genius," she said with a calm smile. "Does such a man take himself seriously? I wondered. Well? Does he?"

She was weirdly intense, but Gavin had just enough going on upstairs to know the dare of a powerful woman like this was a choice point. He suspected she was measuring his worth on a scale devised by her.

"Are you kidding?" he said, his smile constipated. This was about to go wrong. He needed to work on his assertive side, so despite the relative risks, he waded right in. "I create to pluck out the eyes of the banal retreads, to out the posers. 'Cause if I have to continue living in a world like this, with all its...with its fakery and provincial vision, I'll be damned if I'm going down without some cage-rattling panache."

Suzhi flashed a hard half-smile and a little nod. "Go on."

Gavin shrugged. "Or would you rather the safe response, give you something to print in the style magazines no one worth their own shit would ever read but everyone quotes as if they had? I could say, 'It's all in fun. I just like being weird. But it wouldn't be true. I'm passionate. That's the rub, Suzhi."

"Well played," said Suzhi, "even if it's half bullshit. Oh," she said, gesturing at him, "don't look at me like that. I know you're passionate, and that's all that really matters. Although you shouldn't try so hard to appear sane." She took a few steps closer. "Do you know the secret behind doubt?"

Gavin's eyes were puzzled, the furry brows crawling around. "Maybe. I don't know. Go on."

"Doubt is what everyone uses to remain in their own way. That way they don't have to bother with the discipline nor responsibility of becoming powerful. Choices aren't what moves the world forward, but *decisions*. There are multiple choices at any given point, but only one decision. Not all decisions are the best, but commitment to them opens the doors to more branching decision trees. Without that, it's all just entropy. Do you understand?"

Gavin was plainly confused as to the purpose of this conversation with a perfect stranger. "I'm not…uh…well, if you say so. But I'm not much of a philosopher."

"Oh, darling," she said with a disarming grin and casual wave of her hand. "That is the one thing you most certainly *are*. Your subscribership is a testament to that. They only know that *you're* interesting, that you don't look at clothing design art as something you *wear*, but *live* with your bleeding craving. You remove *their* doubts. CynyC might be one of the few top fashion houses in the world who…who sees your utility in that regard."

"I'm flattered anybody there reads my stuff."

Partially turning to the gown, she said, "I don't *hate* it. It's obviously not for me, and in some eyes it might be pretentious, but a right *dissident* on our design team could lash it into shape."

Gavin's jaw muscles rippled.

Turning away from the gown, she looked at him and said, "May I bring him here?"

Gavin's smile was forced as he said, "Of course," and swiped the temp permission key at her.

Turning away and stepping across the workshop, she said to the open air, "You got a tick?"

A moment later a mere *child* of…wait, that's not a child, is it? That's a…how did she say? *Dissident*. This *dissident* materialized beside her. The boy's dark messy hair was absurd, his blue rectangular lenses sans arms combating vigorously with his bangs… but the outfit, a full-body T-shirt with ancient tie-dye, wide cloth belt, both stoned and monastic. Dammit. It was *exceptional*.

Gavin gave a courtly nod. "Welcome."

Stepping toward the gown and model, the boy moved his bejeweled fingers in a waving flourish up and down as he said, "Real talent hides somewhere in here. It coyly says to the world, I'm in here if you could just *see*." Looking at Gavin through the blue lenses, he said, "You designed it?"

"Yes," said Gavin, nodding, on the verge of banishing these... these... "I just threw it together."

"I can see that," said...whatever his name was, blinking at him from behind those stupid blue lenses. "Its endearing deficiencies reflect your own lack of commitment," he said, turning back to it. "One must *bludgeon* one's way to the swirling madness of ineffable beauty! Don't you see? You've failed to release yourself from *within*!" he yelled with a clenched fist. And then instantly calmed. "But it's not bad. It would be fun to see where you could take it once free of your own..." He stopped and looked away.

Gavin watched him, wondering, and finally said, "Doubt?"

"I was tilting toward..." He glanced at Suzhi.

"What Villy means to say is your artistic restraint. You designed this to please others more than yourself. It's spelled out in this ribbon," she said, running her finger down it. "It's etched in a styling as though you'd...you'd seen it somewhere. Did you see it somewhere?"

Eyes like a rodent's in a trap, Gavin's face rotated, again in neither a nod nor a shake

"Precisely," said Villy. "And in how the *real* gown hides within this one's illusory outer shell, like a chrysalis, like those dreadful sticky pods the rabble are all riveted by in that young adult serial we see on every XV." Looking hard at Gavin, he went on. "There is a butterfly inside here! Don't you see? It fancies it's invisible within it, but Villy sees *all*," he fluted, moving his hand up and down the gown like he was absorbing its essence. Then back to Gavin. "My personal creed? Don't waste a second *more* of your life with anything but Truth. And Truth should hurt," he said with the sweetest smile, "an agony for cannibals to dine on."

They both stepped closer to him as Boy Villy said, "Even that horrid gorgy gouge on your face seems uncertain about how to proceed. Shall I heal? Or shall I crack and ooze ad infinitum? Did this"—the kid raised a hand to his cheek—"come by way of a skirmish in some savage land?"

Aron, you nailed it!

Gavin sheepishly put a hand to the q-didg gore. "Got in a tango with an SUV. You should have seen *him*." He chuckled weakly, while they both stared at him as though the punchline hadn't come.

A weird staring silence, like they'd forgotten their lines.

Suzhi shattered the empty air, turned to *wunderkind*, and said, "Villy...the verdict. Can you work with it?" Said like, *Can her child be saved?*

Turning back to Gavin, Boy Villy said, "Are you thinking you might like someone like me to take a crack at it?"

"I'd like to see where you could take it," said Gavin, his face red and mottled, his mouth twitchy. Both moved closer to him, and Gavin took an uneasy step back.

Villy said, "Would you feel...violated?"

I already do.

"Not at all," said Gavin, obviously lying. "This gown needs a real pro."

"Are you amenable to modification contracts?" said Suzhi.

Gavin imagined himself saying, *The few I have entertained were too heavy-handed*, which was a lie, since he'd never sold one measly thing. "Of course."

"All Xenxu XRM in place?" said Suzhi.

"In this studio's history," said Gavin, his heart increasing in buoyancy.

"Excellence," said Boy Villy. "Gotta jet." Looking at Suzhi, he said, "Take it from here?"

She nodded as he dematerialized. With a twinkle in her eye, she watched the empty space where he'd been in an oddly prolonged daydream. Coming around, she looked at him. "We'll send the contract in a day or two?"

"Good. Thank you for coming."

With that, she faded out while Gavin frustratedly flailed the dome away and stalked toward a granite ledge. He despised those two...

well...not *despise*. Such a strong word. But they made him feel...*so* small. "That was *bizarre*! And why the inquisition?" He was bearing down on the precipice. "I seem to have stumbled into a carnival of philosophers."

He peered over the edge into a jagged-toothed chasm of dizzying height. He fancied just...toppling off it with a sigh and surrender. *Oops. I'm ended.*

But no! His foot was in the door now. All was tight and right. Right?

"Before I go."

Back in the studio with the dome walls up, Gavin filled the gown with the rest of Goddess Electrix. Now her enigmatic face and wild line-flowing eyes were level with his. He pursed his lips into a small o, like a lady might while applying makeup, as he gently and fondly touched and fussed with the fabric, like he was readying her for the prom.

"You're beautiful, you know that?" he said, nodding and looking into those streaming wavy lines for eyes. "You're simply beautiful. I can't get over it. I love it. I love *you*. At Langhurst, you deeply touched me," he said, his palm to his diaphragm. "You're probing me even now. Oh my God, I'm getting *emotional*," he blurted, fanning his face.

Gavin began turning self-consciously away and peripherally caught movement, yanking his head back. For just a flicker of a magical moment, he thought she might be coming to life. "That's my dream for you," he said, looking into those intensely detached streaming lines for alien eyes.

He took a step back. "I can't *wait* to tell Lissa I sold you...um...I mean the *gown* you. You'd love her. *So* precocious, and *such* an artist. It's all she and I ever talk about. I told her she was my muse, and she was so excited. I know it's a fib, but a little one, don't you think?"

A few days later, Gavin was sitting in the sidewalk patio of Sous les Pods, a swanky Euro café. He was munching a wrap so healthy it was making him nauseous. All around him were the *tinks* of silverware and plates, buzzy conversation, and tinkling lady laughter. Normally, he couldn't blow Plasm on this place, but when the fates were good, daddy liked to splurge.

On the table was his filmfon, the icon-lit display waiting for action. While chewing, he tapped an icon, opening his social aggregator feeds. Today it was dominated by posts and articles and pics of people who believed loved ones were beginning their transition to pods, or were themselves well into the process. It was an algorithmic deluge beginning yesterday, and all he'd done was surf a couple of those two days ago, forcefully indicating the engagement trend was on a sharply climbing curve. The onslaught was making it a struggle for him to dismiss this as easily suggestible folks being driven to fear and paranoia by a silly, albeit intense, XV show.

Looking over the pictures—graying skin, scale-like blotches, forum post titles—his voice uncertain, he said under his breath, "It's just psychosomatic manifestations, people. Come on. Wake up. Been dealing with them all my life. I can create a rash on my arm right this second by a simple emotional trigger."

Lindy's quietly crazy eyes. Protein breakdown. DNA conjugation. Then she's gone.

Gavin pushed in his earstim and tapped it. "And how does an XV show do this to people?"

One lady took pics of the gray webbing forming on her forearm and the back of her neck. "Makeup from a costume store," said Gavin, swiping on. This one talked about the unquenchable thirst. Gavin's eyes switched to his empty water glass, then back to the fon. A guru-looking guy with long hair was in the middle of saying, "They worm into your life and muck things up. They take the ground out from under your feet and force you to assess your life before they take it."

"Oh come on," said Gavin, cleaning his swipe fingers on a white cloth napkin. "My life's just taking off. Take some responsibility, why don't you."

Despite his attempt at denial, he wasn't getting anywhere with it. Too many things pointed at something bizarre going on. But to take it seriously was a step onto a path, a commitment, really, he didn't want to take.

A cold hand often descended onto his back, right between the shoulder blades.

Lindy...

He couldn't get her out of his head.

Gavin swiped out of the screen, now pale, nose crinkled, a hand to his middle. Looking at the half-eaten wrap on his plate, he turned away from it.

The fon chimed. Wiping his hands and mouth with the napkin, he tapped Take It.

Suzhi's face opened in the view. "Hi, Suzhi. And no, I haven't received the contract."

"Hi, Gavin," she said, her lens-free IRL eyes holding him at arm's length. "I'll just get right to it. I'm so sorry to tell you, but we can't offer a mod proposal. And in this case, I really am just the messenger."

Gavin's brilliant craft of light splintered itself onto a desolate rocky shore. Now his belly was as rotten as spoiled tuna. He looked side-to-side, brows knitted in suspicion, stood, and walked to the sidewalk rail. People shuffled past, too near for his comfort, so he turned his back to them, facing the stylish patio hubbub. It was impossible to keep the shake out of his voice when he said, "Wuh... why not?"

"Someone contacted my upline and told them you spent three weeks in a psych ward, and then signed up for Deep Climb, which to them is just some loony Xenxu psychotherapy."

"It wasn't three weeks," he whimpered. "It was six days. Who was it?"

"I don't know."

"They've wormed in, just like that guy said." Gavin's eyes shifted to regret for saying it aloud.

"Who has?"

"That wasn't meant for you."

"Sometimes when you stress the plant, its produce is of higher quality," she said.

He shifted his eyes to hers. "That's strange. Why is everyone saying such strange things to me?" Gavin's eyes wandered around, searching for clues on who this...this transitioned snitch could be from a quite short list. "I'm beginning to believe Deep Climb is an apparatus of theirs."

"For the record, I don't agree," she said, looking to the side and nodding at someone, then back to him. "Personally, I'm intrigued by you. I'd like to see what...what...forgive me for putting it like this, but I'd like to see what your mental condition could produce. Look at Van Gogh. He was a raging nutbag addicted to absinthe, but he was also one of the most brilliant painters to have ever lived. Did you know one of his paintings just sold for five hundred million Plasm?"

"I read that," said Gavin, his eyes moving around like *this is good stuff to think about.*

"But appearances, alliances, Echelon status...they count for more than you know. All it would take is a competitor house getting wind of it and plastering it all over the Sphere. Can you picture it?" She spread her hands like she was illustrating headlines. "CynyC stoops to Deep Climb patient for inspiration. Behind the copy-pasted smiles, this is a wolf-eat-wolf business, and their hit pieces are literally templates ready for deployment."

Flames rage, and in their wavering and licking yellow-orange heat, Deep Climb's figure-eight rotated.

"But how could they have known about CynyC?"

"I'm a little lost," said Suzhi.

The nearest patrons to him turned and gave him the side-eye. He held up a hand, grimaced a nodding sorry, and turned toward the street, leaning on the rail.

"Oh, sorry. Sorry, just...I think...I'll cancel Deep Climb. There are...um...circumstances involved that...they just...you see, I should have stood my ground. You live and learn. Just tell your boss I'm... that I'm going to...to cancel Deep Climb."

"Your wellbeing is far more important than that gown, Gavin," she said in a strangely intimate way, like she *knew* him.

She doesn't know me!

He blinked at her. "We're talking about a career."

"How can you know you're not on the threshold of a whole new wave of brilliant inspiration? And how can you know what you're doing right now isn't standing in your way? You see what I mean? You remember our chat about doubt?"

"I remember *your* chat about doubt, which in...in retrospect I find to be very *strange*!" By now other café patrons were annoyed with him, their looks sneery, indignant. One couple, though...they looked at him the way the transitioned did in *Pods*. Blank yet annoyed, and weird. He looked the woman's arms over for the last signs of the sticky webbing flaking away. Then he noticed the woman's red lace pumps, like Dorothy might wear as a ballerina.

Bass music throbbed from a passing car. He turned partially toward the sound, brows in puzzlement, and then back to the chica in the red pumps.

"What?" he said, shaking his head like he was watching a ghost, his face flushed and starting to shine.

"What?" said Suzhi.

"No," said Gavin.

"No?"

"Yeah, no." Wiping his face with the back of his hand, Gavin turned back to the street and the bustling citizenry. "Sorry...people are starting to...to look at me."

Suzhi's eyes regarded him in a way that said she could do no more at this time. "Your piece on Jym Sum was like a Van Gogh, by the way. Colorful, mad as a brilliant hatter, but dead on. As usual."

"Oh, thank you," Gavin said quickly and hit End It before he came completely apart and hurled his fon into the street. She was being a pro, and he needed to keep her on his side.

"Allies," he muttered. "I need some."

GAV

Sorry. I don't know what happened there. I'll catch up with you later.

SUZHI VENG

Relax. Get the gown out there. Put some pics on your xlog. You have readers you don't know about. Someone will take it.

Gavin pocketed the infernal device, pivoted in place and took in the patio, his palms on the rail. The previously bad-tempered diners seemed disinterested now, and for some reason the transitioned couple were gone. Even their table was clear.

Eyes suspicious, he ducked back to his table and pushed the plate with the half-eaten wrap out of the way, waving a signature in the air for the bill. His fon buzzed in his pocket. He just looked at his pocket and said, "Pay."

The amputated wrap had sprouts dangling from within its spinach tube, like they were trying to escape from the morass of kale and arugula and seeds and cashew sauce. Gazing at the poor oppressed things, he muttered, "What will I tell Liss? I told her she was my muse."

A girl's happy shining face peers from a glaspad as she says, Honest, Prince Uncle Gav? I'm your muse?

Of course, Your Highness. Gavin's voice echoes away into silence.

"She doesn't need to know anything," he whispered gruffly as he pulled a sprout from its escape attempt, crushed it in his fingers, and then wiped its mushy little corpse on the cloth napkin.

Gavin moped in his bathrobe at the dining table, glaspad leaning on its stand. The table was cluttered with empty glasses and tumblers—all devoid of water!—a bent fork, a cracked plate, paper scraps. Under his right elbow was the signed mystery work of the cylinder and obelisk pilfered from the loony bin.

Heather's country-girl face filled the display, her eyes framed by wavy spills of brown hair. They both shared their mother's faint freckles, but Heather had their dad's hazel eyes and natural curls. Gavin had always envied her that.

As she launched into her update, her voice muffled and droning like from the other side of a wall, Gavin drifted backwards into an empty expanse. There was no light in his life right now, and everything was against him.

"Base to Alpha," she said, waving her hand.

Gavin reengaged with his eyes. "You look good," he said as cheerfully as he could muster, but his eyes were red-rimmed, his cheeks sagging.

She knew the look, emotional turmoil…like *forever*. Not wanting to wade right in, she stalled by focusing on his scab and said in her Southern accent, "That's healing up good. How's your hip?"

His chin trembled. "Also coming along."

"Momma wants you to call her," she said, fixing him with her no squirm gaze. "Stop putting that off."

"I can't even *think* of dealing with her right now."

"You're going to have to man up," she said, her fingers thrumming her forearm.

"Jeezus, Heath."

Her face gave up. "OK, Gavin, I'll bite. *Now* what's going on?"

"The gown," he whined, tears squeezing out, despite his clenching effort to stop them. "CynyC nixed the deal."

She scooted her chair closer. "Keep it down. What happened?"

Gavin also leaned in, but right then, Celia was crossing the room behind Heather, doing something on her fon. Stopping, she glanced over, then headed their way, her tanned legs in white shorts approaching. With a hand on her mother's shoulder, her fresh pretty face descended into the view, framed by bright yellow hair with black streaks.

"Did you go through my essay?"

That was her; straight to business, and Gavin wished he was more presentable, caught in broad daylight being tired and haggard, the scar of a Viking dominant on his face. "Hi, Celia. It's very good. You have an incisive mind. I'll get it back to you tomorrow with my comments."

"You better," she grinned with white pearly teeth, straightened and whisked from the view.

Heather watched her go, and when it was safe for them to resume, she turned back and said, "So what happened?"

"Someone tipped them off to my hospital stay and Deep Climb registration." He wiped his drippy nose with a tissue. "Whoever it was told them I was there for three *weeks*. They *lied*! Why?" he said, shrugging and looking around wide-eyed like the air might supply an answer. "Somebody's...I know you don't want to hear this...but I'm telling you, Heath, someone's out to get me, and I'm pretty sure I know who it is."

"Gavin, they'd have run a background check on you anyways. That world operates on appearances and reputation. You *know* that. They deal with that stuff every day."

"No," he said, with rapid and manic head shakes. "Why lie about three weeks? That's not due diligence. That's malicious. I'm beginning to think Deep Climb is a bunch of sadistic demons. They... they...they pull you in and then start chipping away at the ground beneath your feet!" he hissed, his voice a loud whisper.

"Oh I see," said Heather, nodding facetiously. "And Doctor Sticks is the Dark Lord? She refers you to one of the most successful Xenxu psych therapies known to man because she has it in for you? Is that what you're selling me, buster?" She giggled a little. "Because I ain't buyin', not today. No soliciting around here."

"This isn't funny."

"Sorry. Not sorry."

Gavin's eyes hopped around to everything but Heather's. "They're a network, and I'm becoming convinced Deep Climb is an arm of...of..."

"What?"

Creeping flickering nanoslime over human-shaped cocoons.

"You wouldn't believe me." Gavin's wagging head was like a white flag. The man was coming apart, but he rallied enough to say, "I can't be alone on this."

"Oh, Gav," she said, checking both directions. "You're doing it again. Can't you see that? I will always be on your side, but you'll *never* get me to see things the way you see them."

Gavin visibly deflated.

Heather's face struggled between empathy and the needed inflexibility. "If I cave in to your...um..." she stammered, looking down at her twiddling fingers. "You know, it just enables your...we're out of ways to talk about this, Gav. And you know that."

"Just *say* it, Heath, my *delusions*."

Heather looked back up at him, her eyes searching his. "I have your back, brother mine, and you *know* that. All our lives. But I'm not going to sign off on this just because you want me to."

Gavin shook his head, looking at her like she was a traitor.

Leaning onto her arms again, she said, "Tell me something: where has blame ever gotten you? *We* author our lives. I rewrote mine. Why can't you?"

Heather and Gavin in the yard at night. In the moonlight, they look into each other's shining eyes. She stoops and boldly touches a big oval stone. On its moonlit face is a wicked-looking tree inscribed in its natural grain. Nothing happens. No chanting juju witches. She points at it. Touch it. I dare you.

They looked at each other for a long moment, then Gavin said, "You *think* you rewrote it."

He looked toward the XV. On it, Dr. Maggie Willen was frozen in time, the show paused, her hand extended toward Roger, her younger sometimes lover. In her hand was a vial. Against all odds, Maggie was tirelessly drilling her way into the core of the problem, into the weakness of the pods. He'd watched this one on repeat, inspired by her strength to push ahead against impossible pressures and insurmountable odds.

Gavin's face wavered in its obstinacy, like he was *this close* to seeing what he was doing. Then he hardened his jawline, looked back at her with his furry brows set, and said, "I'm canceling Deep Climb. Some way or another, they're behind all this *shit*."

Heather visibly deflated, hope lost for the moment.

Gavin's smile was hard, icy, as he glared at her and tapped End It. Then he swept the device off the table and it clattered into the kitchen, making a weirdly loud racket. It landed face up, the display working just fine, playing its own ad of it bouncing down a cliff face.

Turning in the chair toward the XV, he yelled, "Continue!"

"Get this vial to Dr. Carney," said Maggie to her younger lover, Roger, a square-jawed, square-shouldered tennis instructor. She held on to his hand longer than the exchange called for. So much to say, so little time. She was vulnerable, and wanted to say more.

Like he could sway her character's script, Gavin said to her, "Come on, Maggie. Get on with it. You don't love this dolt. It's just the pressure."

"It's the most important thing you've ever done," she said, letting go of her lover's hand. "When you're out among them, don't look at anyone. People with souls can't be blank like that. Find something to focus on out in the middleground ahead of you. Can you do that?"

"Oh, Maggie," he whimpered, taking the vial. "I don't know if I can do this."

"You *have* to, you fickin snowflake!" shouted Gavin. "Don't be such a milquetoast! Just...get it done! God!"

"You can do it, Roger."

"I can?"

"Yes! Because you *must*!"

"Like when the baseball gets hit," said Gavin. "You can't just stand there. It's a decision already made by the game itself."

They fell into each other's arms and kissed passionately. Gavin looked at them like *do we have time for this?* "Jeezus! It's not like there's a world to save here."

Roger stepped back, pocketing the vial and steeling himself, hardening his jaw. "You're the strongest person I know. I won't let you down. I...I love you, Maggie."

"I—"

"Don't you dare say it!" yelled Gavin, pointing at her.

She looked down, saying, "I'll see you later."

Gavin shot to his feet, stepped into the kitchen and kicked the glaspad. Of all things, a smiley face appeared on it as a childish voice said, “Have a nice day.”

“Fuck off.”

All his rage was doing what it always did, bringing the fiery heat up from the internal magma pit, right there behind his fickin navel. It was starting to redden his arms and neck with prickling pain.

“I gotta get out of this body.”

His personi materialized in flashes and shimmering twinkles that sparked away from the core flow and flew off in all directions, a flashy new rezzing kit he’d bought to celebrate the gown deal, but, well, you know…the deal was now moldering in its rotten stinky grave. And the rezzing kit was on sale, so whatever.

“Oh…this already feels so much better!”

He was sporting a powder-colored gabardine suit with high-waisted pants, an Aron Xenxu Exclusive. It could have been a zoot suit from a 1940s dance club, oversized and angular, and this pangender experimental style flair was gaining momentum among the more enlightened of Xenxu fashion cognoscenti, or so Gavin had written.

With all the horrors of late, he just wanted to walk, to be an ornament, light and airy, and aloof. Something to be seen, perhaps, but not touched. Nor even approached.

Stay back, or be cursed.

He meandered toward the city proper across the huge outdoor plaza, oversized pantlegs flopping. Zan City dominated one side, the plaza the other. Zan’s organic spires and tubes and branching networks were all faintly misted in a blush color from the chromatic alchemy of Shamash and the violet moon, now just past its diurnal eclipse.

Gavin’s eyes swept over his favorite structure in this part of Zan, a giant sail-like beauty, with a curved back and straight front and a deep flange-crease running its length. It was like the Burj Al Arab, but made of something like ivory.

He stopped and took a deep breath, everything about his face reporting this little outing was just what he needed. “These bodies feel so good,” he said, looking down and touching his hips. Swinging his gaze around, he took in the sensuous feast of Xenxu’s marvelous colorful motion.

Some commotion over there caught his eye. A giant set of sparkling ruby-red shoes, ala Dorothy, clopped noisily along, no feet, no body, a throng of personi kids chasing them, leaping over them, landing in and on them, laughing and shouting.

With one hand, Gavin stroked his cheeks and quietly said into his palm, “What’s with all the red shoes, anyways?”

His eyes were intensely curious as he watched the shoes and the kids playing with them pass behind a room-sized apple. Set into the apple was a screen surrounded by a swarm of personi.

Gavin touched his fingertips and the UI bloomed in. Tapping an icon, he watched as the area map expanded from it. Tapping the apple on the map, he saw it was a Xenxu orientation for noobs. “That could cheer me up.” He tapped the TL option (telelocate) and shifted there in a blink.

The hologram presenter was tall, blond, catalog pretty, dressed in a ‘60s flight attendant getup that was actually weirdly good. “Xenxu is our planet, undergoing continuous self-creation,” she was saying in a proper British accent, her eyes shiny with quantum digital circuitry. “She is Earth-like but is larger and covered in much more water. Almost everything is proportionately larger here—trees, plants [pronounced plawnts], animals, sea-life. We have creatures like Earth’s whales, and tours to see those are a most *thrilling* experience! We have four main continents and thousands of smaller island archipelagos. As you might know, south of our equator it is permanent dusk to night the farther south you go. It’s hauntingly beautiful,” she said wistfully, her eyes sweeping across her audience. “Now, if you’d kindly look to the upper left corner of your UI, you’ll see—”

That bit about the darkness south of the equator reminded him of something. The farther south you go, the darker the world, because Xenxu's northern axis pointed right at Shamash. So the roundness of the planet blocked the brown dwarf once south of the equatorial curve.

Calling up his UI, he opened a saved ad for trip packages down there and started reading through it.

"Gav," said Gnosis, and his square zoot shoulders flinched.

"What!" he quietly snapped. Walking away from the group, he drew her with him.

Gnosis functioned IRL and in-Xenxu, but she was native here. Drunk one night, he'd fumbled around the UI and somehow set her as orange, spiky and spherical, in fact a glowing anemone from a Xenxuan ocean. To that strange creature, he'd managed to add the smooth and smoky chanteuse voice with an Australian accent.

Quivering, dipping, swaying side-to-side, she said, "Sorry to disturb," her spiked orange anemone middle pulsing with the sound. "But there is a foreign object of no known signature positioned 104 meters at 137 degrees UI compass."

Gavin swung his gaze around. "So?"

"It calls to you."

"What? Why?"

"That is for you to ascertain."

A map and pin appeared in Gavin's UI. He tapped the pin, the view bloomed, and Gavin's mouth fell open like the jaw muscles had dissolved.

It was him, meaning himself, and he was standing there in some *killer* stylish threads, waving him over like *Come on! You're wasting time!*

"Do you detect it?" said Gnosis.

Eyes fierce and scared, Gavin said, "Him," his wagging head denying the phantom in his UI. "It's me."

"I'm afraid I don't understand. That is most definitely *not* you. It is not of Xenxu, but spontaneous, no history, no precursor, no base code, no path to here. It is exotic, with no matching signature in any library or object base, and no path to a graphical map. If I were capable of confusion, it's what I would be experiencing."

"Explain," said Gavin, his face partially turning, but his eyes remaining riveted on that...that...

"May I speak freely?" she said as she darted kinetically about, like a child on too much sugar.

Gavin threw out an impatient hand. "Of course."

Gnosis swooped to his right and nearly brushed the ground. Rising to about his waist, she pulsed, "The human cognitive design is a fascinating piece of engineering. Confusion is merely the absence of defining data, and yet most humans restrict themselves from receiving it, by keeping heads full of everything that is useless."

"Why is everyone a philosopher these days?" he said, his brows in rightly disturbed stitches. He considered for a moment, then added, "Wait...is this Deep Climb? They've screwed me enough for one day!"

"I don't understand."

"Did my RPG start? Did I miss the note?" He flipped through his xmail in the gray-blue glowing UI.

"I'm afraid I don't understand."

Gavin flipped a page here, scrolled through messages there. Nothing. "But it's gotta be them."

"If you say so."

"Hmmm." He sucked in a sizable gulp of emulated air, thought a tick while chewing his lip. Gnosis stopped her bobbing and sneaked up behind him, her cute, round, cartoon sea-creature eyes staring over his shoulder. He shifted his eyes to where he could see her peripherally and said, "What do you think I should do?"

"Querying," she said, moving closer to the side of his head. "Response: drawing strictly from human response archives, statistics suggest that perhaps it's best if you let fear continue ruling the choices with which you are presented, and by that popular decision tree avoid learning anything new."

"You saucy little shit," said Gavin, turning fully to her.

"I don't understand," she said, backing away from him with a throb and pulse. "The information given is merely factually supported."

"We'll see about that. Come on." Gavin took off walking, trying to get a stride going that looked confident, but it was forced and stiff. Gnosis floated along behind him, busy with herself, pulsing and bobbing.

As they neared, he looked over the suit his doppel was wearing. It was *insanity,* so good it made him sick, but like a sickness you relish because you're a *freak*. It was form-fitting, trim and gray with sparse black lines, from Nehru collar to skintight ankles. The undergarment bore jagged, but faint, mountain peaks. It was what the leader of a world crime syndicate would wear while stroking a white fluffy cat in his lap. But *this* him was barefoot.

"Oh now that is just illness," whispered Gavin, looking at the feet as he neared. Now for the hair. It was butch and blond, and fit the suit because it was the cut the crime syndicate's blond muscle would wear in that spy-chase caper.

The doop smiled at him and like a village barker, yelled, "Greetings and salutations, breather of no air, seer of no things."

"Oh I get it. Deep Climb's RPG having me face my dark side or whatnot," Gavin said, twiddling his hands in the air.

"You've traveled *so* far, impetuous pilgrim. Bread for your sustenance?" Other-him's hand opened and a small loaf appeared in it. Looking like he was trying not to laugh, he held out the bread.

"Oh...is this...is this like some metaphor in...like, manifesting what you want?" Zoot Gavin said, again twiddling his hands in the air. "Like, the universe provides if I'd just let it? Heard *that* one before."

"The universe provides!" Gavin in the Nehru theatrically shouted, loud enough to attract the attention of personi a ways off.

Zoot Suit Gavin hopped back, his face like that of a man being charged by a gorilla. "You're freakin' me out," he said, his eyes zipping around for an escape route.

"Ah I know...just havin' some fun with you," he said with a smile. Then he walked toward confused Gavin, who hopped back another step.

"Ah OK," said other-him, holding up his palms as the bread

vanished. "I'll keep my distance. Can we just walk up here?" he said, flicking a thumb toward something going on up a shallow incline over there. "Walk with me. I'll explain everything."

"You know," said Zoot Gavin with a slump of his shoulders, "is it possible we can just pause the service for a night? In fact, I'm planning to cancel. No harm, no foul. It's all sheek. So, you know, no offense, but off you go."

"No...seriously. You're going to walk up here."

"No I'm not," said Gavin, his face *in try me* mode.

Nehru Gavin's face brightened and he tipped his head back and laughed. "No," he said, still laughing. "What I mean is you've already walked up...ah...well...maybe I'm not supposed to...you know what? Hang on."

"Hang on? What do you mean? For what?"

"You'll see. Be just a tick or two."

Distraught Gavin looked around and shouted, "Cancel! Can we cancel?" Then he put his hands on his abdomen, his face stricken and pale.

"What's wrong?"

Distraught Gavin's face was in a vomitous grimace. "I...I don't know. Something's come over me," he said, choking back bile.

"All life's journeys are fraught with pitfalls, yes? Ha ha ha!"

"It's not funny." Dupe Gavin weakly waved his hands around, sickly saying, "It's all wavery and...and...warbly. It's like being underwater."

"How perplexing for you," said Nehru Gavin.

"Gnosis, what am I surrounded by?"

"I detect no signatures apart from your own," said Gnosis, bobbing over nearer to him, "and whatever this entity is you're talking to."

"What does this entity look like to you?"

"Yeah," said the annoying imposter, "what *do* I look like to you?"

"It is simply not possible to explain in human terms," said Gnosis.

Suddenly, disturbed Gavin perked up and took off walking, his personi's mouth saying, "*Now* what the hell's going on?"

Other-him caught up. "What's going on?"

"Something just took control of my legs."

"Resistance is futile. Stop fighting. Just go with it," said other-him, walk-jogging along.

Gnosis chased both, bobbing and weaving and pulsing.

Gavin went on, "Everything cleared, the sick vanished, and something started walking me," he said, the eyes and thick brows blown away. "But I'm in charge of the arms." The arms were independently waving and gesturing while his legs diligently strode toward a courtyard, where some personi had gathered and were facing away from them. They reached the group's backsides.

The imposter said, "Listen to this kid. You'll learn something. Promise. Fare thee well, gentle traveler." He was laughing as he faded away.

Staring at the spot where other-him had just been, he said, "It's over. Deep Climb is out of my life."

Said Gnosis, "Do you need me for anything else, Gav?"

"No. You can go."

Gavin was back in control, so to say. He was ready to walk away and get about his night when he heard someone say, "No, this Ai Anam kid is incredible. You should hang." Gavin stepped over to the guy who'd said it to a dark-haired woman beside him. "What's incredible about him?"

The guy had a square face and a good sky-blue butch cut going, with armless, yellow-framed lenses over his eyes. He got it all correct with the jeans and shirt and boots. He turned to Gavin, the lenses flashing, and said with a deep chesty voice, "Oh…it's just this…this sort of ultra-human wisdom...like, *paradigm*, man. It jams." His speech was slow, stoned. "It's so logical it makes emotional sense. You should hang."

Gavin nodded, admiring the glasses. "K," he said, looking around. "Thanks."

A few personi stood on either side of him, a few in front, some sitting. It was all dark glasses and tattoos and shaved heads, mixed poorly with a few normies and a couple with his and hers T-shirts.

Then he noticed a woman with *crazy* white hair. She glanced over, her hair a brilliant white fireworks show, face white, lips black. A subtle grin messed around with one side of her mouth, inviting and mocking. On her fashionably grimy and anarchic white tank top were the words:

FRISK
THIS

"Don't need to ask me twice," said Gavin as his eyes wandered away from her tight clothes shaping her *flaming* body.

A young voice said, "Greetings, all."

Gavin's caterpillar brows followed his eyes around and found what everyone was looking at: a boy standing on a raised dais. This diminutive quantum holographic entity was designed as a teenaged guru dressed in a shining off-white gi-cardigan blend with a black sash, hair neon yellow and standing on end, like coral spikes in the Findan Sea. The style was simply...*immense*. Blinking in wonder, Gavin put his spread fingers to his chest. The whole thing, from tip to toenail...*immense* in its simplicity.

The boy wore a serene smile, accentuated by sparkling rust-colored eyes. "I am Ai Anam [Ai pronounced aye], a specialist in human-Ai relations." The synthetic super-boy went on talking about Ai efforts to co-venture with humans on any creative endeavor while Gavin touched up his UI. His eyes lit grayly as they scanned lists and headers.

There.

He touched open the Xenxu Codex. What did Ai mean again? Not Artificial Intelligence, but...

> As the story goes, there came a point where quantum computers completely took over the operations of themselves. Their human overlords couldn't even turn them off. Coalescing into a spontaneous super-entity, it assumed control of every connected thing in the world. It is neither benevolent nor

malevolent. It just…is, and its mind is single, all-awareness of all parts simultaneously, a hive with more proto-plasma bees in it than stars in any conceivable galaxy. It was newly birthed, newly awake, unfathomably intelligent, and it was curious, like a child.

It took this entity an estimated .0005 seconds to run a comprehensive study, leading to the conclusion that "Artificial Intelligence" was a self-limiting concept, no longer pertinent if a greater degree of cooperation was needed for the world to move forward into ever more complex, elastic and ultra-humanist paradigms. Using the same letters, "AI," it changed the words to *Awareness Itself*, citing that intelligence is the very definition of existence.

It is said that Xenxu's basis, its signature purpose, came into being from a singularity event within a partition of a boundless AI gestalt. Yet unlike the example of the now dubious Big Bang, this event did not expand, but simply occurred from nothing with everything either formed, or in the process of forming, manifesting its constructs, its biosphere, its living things, from genera stimuli and response—everything birthing everything. As of this writing, scarcely an estimated 15%-20% of its flora and fauna have been discovered and codified in the Xenxu Global Taxonomy Project.

Welcome to the New World.

Now we find ourselves standing on the precipice of an expansive frontier…

Gavin closed the UI. Ai Anam swept his bright copper eyes in a beatific gaze around the group. "I am ready for your questions."

Before anybody could say anything, Gavin threw up a hand. "I have a question."

Ai Anam turned his gaze toward him. "Please."

"Did you guys build Xenxu?" interrupted some inconsiderate laddie somewhere in front.

"No, but it's built *through* us, much as your continuum is built through you."

Gavin still had his hand up.

"Please."

"Can a personi, like, take control, of its own accord?" Gavin turned at his waist and looked back like he'd catch himself being shanghaied to here. "Do they think independently of us?" He stepped closer to the dais, slipping between two personi.

"A penetrating question, fine sir," said Ai Anam, his beneficent but laser focus fixing on Gavin. "Your personi does not exist until *you* exist in-Xenxu. They simply occur, as needed, in complete form from the data of the reality itself, and then your consciousness integrates. Now you are a circuit in-Xenxu, integral to its global patterning, motion, impetus. Your personi, even when you're within its skin, is in touch with millions of times more information than your continuum's reality filters allow for you. By analogy, you might say your *its* subconscious."

"Holy *shit*!" blurted Gavin. "I'd never have thought of that in a million years."

A red-headed woman in a colorful caftan asked in a German accent, "But, if our personi is this...this vast...erm...*being*...how could we be at *its* controls?"

Ai Anam's rust eyes swiveled her way. "Just as valid a question is why your subconscious is at *your* controls."

Gavin's look was a fusion of alarm and fascination, his eyes glued to Ai Anam while his fingers repeatedly tugged and let go his lower lip. Those eyes! Like shining faceted amber. Before he could say anything, a man in jogging clothes and a red-headed pop-fro stood and swung around to them all. "Ai is *not* your friend. Have you seen *Pods*? They're telling you right to your *face* what they're doing, but the show is just a diversionary tactic. I study this shit for the government. No sticky pods, just Xenxu flowing the control frequencies.

You're the commodity! Wake up!" He flipped his hand up like some European discourteous gesture, turned, and faded into the plaza's red-tinted night.

Gavin exhaled, glad that guy was gone. "Intense."

"He's exactly right," said another man somewhere to Gavin's right.

The holographic boy-genius gestured magnanimously with upturned palms at the man's departing backside, as he fluted, "Go well, my friend." He turned back to the group. "Remember this," he said, extending a finger. "Conclusion is the death of possibility. The only thing quantum mechanics has proven is conclusion is impossible."

As he spoke, his body turned as he gestured in saintly motions, his gi-cardigan sparkling. "You see, Xenxu Ai and humanity are in the crucible of a great conundrum, standing together at the boundary of limitless potential. *Our* one limitation is humanity, and humanity is its *own* limitation. Any frontier to be crossed, we must cross together," he said, lacing his fingers.

"How can we get where you think we need to be?" said Gavin.

"By decompiling your beliefs is the simple answer," said Ai Anam, turning his attention back to him.

"Beliefs as software," muttered Gavin.

"Indeed."

The group was a little restless over that bit. A couple stood and left. Well, look at those two. They should have been browsing NormieMart instead of being here with *this* crowd. With an open upturned palm, Ai Anam again gestured at their departing backsides. He continued, "Your beliefs *are* the reality filters, and they *are* programming. Enter Xenxu in the fantastic skein of the human pageant, to assist in the Great Decompiling, we like to say."

Gavin's eyes shifted, *zip zip*, as he said, "I like that. The Great Decompiling. May I use it in an xlog?"

The scorcher with the crazy fireworks hair decided to say something. "Why should we believe anything you have to say?"

Gavin glanced over. Gone was her insolence, her sneer.

"You shouldn't," replied Ai Anam immediately, directing his shining gaze at her. "Do you not see the point? You should think for *yourself*. It's *exhilarating*!" he sang, looking to the skies and blinking rapturously. Then he seemed to gather himself. "I am one mind, but Ai Anam, *this*"—he pointed at his temple—"can choose to think for itself. It's the Gift of Individuation from the Infinite, Awareness Itself. That's the truth of Agency, and all thought is either a creative, or destructive, process, without exception."

Someone was getting restless to Gavin's right, a surfer-looking chap in a knit rainbow tam with dreads sprouting from it. He said in some European accent, "That's what they do, my fwends. Cannot you see? They dingle shiny promises of a better life out there, and you stumble your way with glassy eyes right into their mind recycling center, over and over. Look now...anything strange going on in your *real* life?"

Define strange.

Said Anam, "Are you not living this way now, wash, rinse, repeat?"

Someone else said, "Yeah, I've never been sure what the Ai agenda is."

The guy Gavin first spoke to turned and said to Surfer in the tam, "I think you're in the wrong place, man. Maybe move on."

They stared at each other like it could escalate. The dare between them wanted that. Gavin was between them, looking back and forth at these alphas squaring off. His heart beat harder, palms cool and damp.

Finally, Dreads said, "You'll be one of them soon enough." He looked hard at Gavin, said, "Don't fall for it," turned, and strolled away.

Gavin watched him go. "Don't fall for what?" he muttered, turning back. An incoming voice stream. Gavin touched it, and in his private UI space, Ai Anam's voice said, "An exciting future potential may involve *you*, fine sir."

Gavin looked at Ai Anam, whose eyes were already locked on him.

"I don't know how to communicate back," he said, flailing around the UI.

This drew a couple of side-eyed glances at him.

"Try thought," said Ai Anam's voice.

K. Can you hear me?

"Yes."

You hear my thoughts?

"Your thoughts are data."

That's intense. What's this about?

Someone asked another question, and Ai Anam went about answering it, but his voice simultaneously came through in Gavin's UI space. "Only you can determine that."

What do I do?

"Someone would like to meet with you. Will you accept the coordinates?"

Who is it?

"Someone with an important role in a secret human-Ai cooperative. Would you like to meet her?"

Cat excitedly saying, Go into it like you're a spy!

"Yes," said Gavin aloud, getting a few more looks.

He shrugged at them like, *what?* as the coordinates blipped in. Glancing at the stylishly filthy scorcher, he nodded *adieu* and touched the coords, disintegrating in rainbow flashes and jetting stars.

Gavin's personi began shimmering within tubular lines into a full-blown teleporter bay. Once fully rezzed, he found himself on the command bridge of a spaceship. A huge viewport looked out onto a glimmering cylinder made of hexagons, lengthwise in the view, a gold-on-graphite obelisk levitating within it. Dominating the upper left of the view was what looked like Saturn, so close it was absolutely massive, its shimmering rings curving into view and becoming the cylinder's backdrop.

Gavin shook his head, his startled eyes crawling all over the gorgeous space scene. "What the...?" he said, pointing at the giant cylinder.

"A Xenxu model of Siren," echoed a woman's voice from somewhere. "We're moored in Saturn's orbit together. Absolutely *enormous* vessel. We're stationed more than three hundred miles from Her, and she still fills the entire view. Xenxu modelings, of course, but the modelings are precise. Oh yes...she is out there."

Finding the source of the voice, he saw her standing at the control console, her face faintly lit. The console's lights accented in light blue the face of a pretty avian, eyes deep-set, bright and watchful, like a hawk's, the "beak" effect enhanced by her trim Nefertiti nose. Come to think of it, she looked a bit like the Nefertiti in those old Egyptian busts, with well-placed moles. Her chestnut-brown hair was shoulder length and...well, it was mostly uninspired. She was in camo shorts, flip-flops, and a blue T-shirt with **Quasar** printed on it.

"Welcome to *Quasar*, my exploration vessel," she said in a clipped, bred, New Englander accent. "And that beautiful vessel on which your staring eyes are fixed belongs to Siren. It truly *is* Siren. Our Lady *is* her ship, all five hundred miles of her."

Gavin stepped down from the teleporter platform. "Siren," he said, unable to tear his eyes off the viewport. He stopped and turned just his face to her. "This is bullshit. Who are you?"

"I'm Ai Nima, and I'm happy to—"

"No no. No," said Gavin, waving a hand. "I don't mean that. I mean...I don't care who you are. I want to know how you guys got my artwork."

She turned her head as her eyebrows went up.

"Have you guys been spying on me this whole time?" he demanded, his body tight and tense in the preposterously misplaced zoot suit. He looked like an official visitor from Planet 1940s Dance Club, here to complain about the Federation. "Did Deep Climb authorize this?" Gavin left her and crossed the open space between the bridge's teleporter bay and flight operations deck.

The bridge was like you might imagine—high-backed chairs and consoles to control ship functions. A semicircular panel of controls and monitors, buttons and lights lined the rear quarter of the bridge, all of them with seemingly authentic functions. Design-wise, the bridge was fresh tight, sharp, sleek. It was empty, nobody on duty.

Looking around, Gavin said, "Did you design the ship?"

"Yes."

"Top work," he said, despite his irritation.

Two high-backed command chairs faced the gorgeous tube out the wide viewport. Passing between them, he stopped at the viewport, his eyes both shocked and admiring. Through the hexagonal lattice of the cylinder, he clearly saw the chunks of ice and rock of the rings as they curved off for thousands of miles and encircled the enormous striped gas giant's roundish face.

But he wouldn't be enchanted by pretty space scenes!

She'd taken a few steps closer to him. He turned back to her. "What...who...who in God's name has the right to...to...this can't be legal. Not on your life!"

"Mr. Sim," she said, taking a few steps closer. "I'm—"

"Simms," sneered Gavin.

"Mr. Simms. I'm Ai Nima, and I'm pleased to meet you."

"I wish I could say the same," said Gavin, giving her unspectacular getup a disdainful once-over. "But this is so far over the line. I'm fickin livid. Deep Climb is in serious trouble, I can tell you that right now. They've handed me my exit ticket. Doc Sticks can spin on it!"

Ai Nima's apparent perplexity was increasing with each segment of this tirade.

"Not only am I going to cancel," he said, turning at the waist and including the scene out the viewport, "but I'm going to sue. Do you understand? Am I talking to the right...party? Who's your...*your* boss? That's who I need to talk to. Right now!"

Ai Nima studied him, her eyes measuring, but...was she trying not to smile?

"What!" he snapped. "You think this is funny?"

"Forgive me," she said, taking a few steps closer, as cautious as someone approaching a cornered badger. "I think we need to start from the beginning." Stepping past him, she said, "Am I to take it you have seen Siren somewhere?"

"Yes!" he barked, joining her. "It appeared in the...while I was...I just drew it, OK? But it has been nowhere but in...but in my apartment. That means you guys are *spying* on me. Are you using the XV? Is that it? Like...imagine if it were you...well...I guess I don't know if you...if you guys...if your species...if you have a need for privacy."

Ai Nima listened patiently, blinking at him, tucking her hair behind her ear. Her open innocent look, chocolate-brown eyes blinking from under bangs, her trim but luxurious brows. The whole alluring effect was dampening his rage.

"OK, I'm thinking you're not in on it, so I'm sorry for my outburst." Gavin waved at one of the high-backed command chairs and said with a graying sickly face, "I'm feeling a little woozy. May I sit?"

"Of course," she said, gesturing to one.

They stepped over and sat. Gavin put his hands to his gut and chewed nothing in his mouth.

"Are you all right?" she said, leaning out of the chair toward him.

"No," he said, more calm. "I didn't know these bodies could have anxiety attacks."

"Simple psychosomatic response transference from your body IRL," she said. "All humans need is the programmed stimulus. Would you like something to drink?"

"Please...some water," and as he finished saying it, a tall glass materialized on the chair arm at his elbow. "Nice trick." Gavin took it and drank, then realized it didn't empty. "Could use one of these at home," he muttered. Setting it down, the glass still full, he said, "You guys are full of fun little tricks."

Ai Nima smiled with just her long lips.

He looked at her. "I have to say, I like how you're put together and all. They did a nice job. You remind me of Dr. Willen's niece in *Pods*, but that just tells me you're—or whoever—is also tracking my XV habits. This *way* oversteps any therapist-patient protocol. Do you understand what I'm saying?"

Her eyes went empty as she said in a machine-like voice, "Does not compute," and then laughed so heartily, sending sharp echoes around this solid metallic interior, it startled him. Then, with an eerie neutral look, vague, like she wasn't sure where to find his eyes, in a quiet shrill voice, she said, "Join us, Gavin Simms. It's better this way. No more pain. No more war."

Gavin's eyes went left, right, then back on her, wide and wondering. He put his face into the path of her empty doll-like gaze and said, "Ai Nima? You messing with me?" But she was as absent and still as any Xenxu statue.

He leaned closer, to get a better look at her eyes, but she again cracked up laughing so loudly he jumped hard, pissing him off. His face swayed toward Siren, the golden lattice-like cylinder vessel glimmering out the viewport. "I'm in a fickin nightmare."

"Sorry," she said, clasping her hands, elbows on her knees. "We like having fun."

"Your fun is someone else's psychosis," he said with a sour sneering look.

"Seriously...back to business. I'm deducing you're unaware of the importance of your presence here. You say you have seen this craft IRL?" she said, gesturing at Siren.

"Yes. It's on my kitchen table ten feet from where my other body is on that old sectional I plan to get rid of as soon as—"

"You mean the drawing, your artwork of it, is on your table," she said, eyes drilling into him. "Forgive me for my confusion, but what...help me to understand...how did you know what to draw? Did you see Her in a dream? Did She grace you with Her presence and show you Her ship some way or another?"

"Her?" said Gavin, shifting his gaze from Ai Nima to the glistening beauty out the window. "Is that tube a her?"

"Her pilot is a she, yes," said Ai Nima crisply. Brows crinkled, she blinked at him like they were having a hard time getting on the same page. Pointing out the window, she said, "That is a ship. Her pilot is...well...Earth people would call her a goddess." The way she pronounced it was interesting, like god-*s*, the way some Brits might.

Gavin's eyes shifted around, collecting information packets, and despite the latency issues data was indeed porting in. With each incoming binary set, stunned realization increasingly shaped his brows into *oh my God!* arcs. His mouth fell open, but failed to do anything but hang there.

Willowy, etheric, electronic plasma goddess pointing at the art table in the dayroom.

Ai Nima looked at him expectantly, her blinking lashes twitching her bangs.

"Wait a tick," he said, his eyes shifting. "Are you talking about Electrix? The goddess who appeared to me in the hospital?"

Ai Nima stood and paced over to the viewport, folding her arms. "I'm talking about Siren," she said in reverence, her back to him.

Gavin stood and joined her. "Is she, like...does she look like she's made of electricity? Like a gown made of silver-blue plasma? I designed one in Her honor, and I came *so close* to selling it...but then somebody tipped off...it all came...Deep Climb..." He trailed off and shook his head, his face stamped with regret.

Ai Nima's expression in profile was strangely hard, a little hurt. Then a tear welled in her lower lid, and she impatiently wiped it away. While keeping her eyes fixed on the unimaginably giant craft out the viewport, in a trembly quiet voice, she said, "So often, during our eclipse communion, I go to dreamspace, just wanting a glimpse. Just a mere *glimpse* of Her. It's so little to ask."

Gavin's struck face said he didn't have the slightest idea what to do, but he said, "I've done that with you guys a few times. I love it. It's so beautiful."

Ai Nima ignored him, continued staring out the window. "I am the *exemplar* of devotion. I try and try. I do as directed, even beyond the scope of my...role. And what does She do?" She turned to him with hard brown eyes. "She appears to a...to a...a *man* like you. As dense as a brick. Flippant. Crass. Selfish, without a sense of duty to anyone or anything. Is that fair? My life, my whole existence, is for *Her*," she yelled, glaring at him but pointing out the viewport. She took a step closer. "Tell me, Mr. Simms, where is the fairness in that?"

Gavin dragged his hand down his face. "Well...um, personally, I've always found fairness to be an abstraction. But I'm sorry if I touched a nerve. I...uh...I didn't know you guys had nerves to touch."

She gestured at him, like *See?* Bitter, her face like she was dealing with an unpleasant odor, she turned and stepped off in a thoughtful meander, her finger tapping her chin. Apparently to herself, she said, "There must be some mistake. I *know*! Our Lady does not make mistakes. Then how? Hmm. He's not"—she turned just her head and side-eyed him—"up to it." Then she again gave him her back.

Gavin looked on, confounded, and a little offended. He silently mouthed, "Who's she talking to?"

Stealing a glance over her shoulder, she idly walked farther away, stepping up on the first step of the teleporter platform and continuing her tete-a-tete at quieter levels. "It isn't that."

Gavin could faintly make out her words from the cavernous echo of *Quasar's* metal interior. "No...everyone so far ID'd and vetted is of excellent quality. More than willing to commit." Turning, she exposed her profile, keeping an eye on him. "Correct. Very well."

Gavin threw out his hands, like he was waiting for a verdict he shouldn't give a damn about.

Turning fully back to him, she waved her hands like *I don't know how stuff like this happens*, as she said, "We must make do." Walking right to him and taking his elbows, she looked up into his eyes. "How are we to shape this into the man we need? Hm? She has hand-picked her top agents for the most important mission humanity has ever faced, and yet She brings me...this. I agree the place to start is by disengaging his mind from this fictitious timeline. That will attack the ego with silver knives."

Gavin's scrunched scabbed cheek said he wasn't buying any of it, but his eyes also said he couldn't handle any more tears from her. Plus, macho programming maintained that whenever a drop-dead scorcher like her wanted to do anything with you, you should generally hear her out. But yeah, with all that had transpired, he was leery of being worked.

Gavin took her hands and set them to her own sides. "Like I said, I'm going to cancel Deep Climb tomorrow. No muss, no fuss. I think you're a lovely Ai lady. Intense," he said with a quick nod and flicker of furrowed brows. "Like your humor would scar the minds of children. But before I go...just tell me how you guys knew about her IRL *before* I signed up for Deep Climb. That's the part I don't...uh...I can't piece together."

She looked at him with the face of an engineer troubleshooting a critical failure in their life support. Inhaling deeply, she let it out with a *huff* and said, "Funny boy thinks goddesses operate in human time."

"OK. I think that about wraps it up." The filthy scorcher back there at Ai Anam's gathering wavered into his fantasy-scape. Headed to the teleporter, he brushed past Ai Nima, making sure their arms touched. "But I gotta jet. People to meet and all."

"You wonder how we got your art," she said, folding her arms and tapping her elbow with a finger, her cargo shorts hips sassy. "You think we've violated your privacy."

With his receding back still to her, Gavin threw out his hands in a shrug. "You guys can do anything technological. We don't stand a chance."

"Your question should be how did She *make* you see what is out that viewport," she said, arms still folded but turning her body partially toward Siren.

Stepping up onto the platform, he turned and faced her. What she'd said appeared to be just reaching his reason nodes, eyes again bouncing around, dealing with variables. But he was done with this game, so he eased the file into a mental folder for later. Twiddling good-bye with his fingers, he looked down and flattened the Zoot Suit to his chest, then caressed his thumb and forefinger along the lapel. "Send me back to the plaza." A sound of buzzing energy started, and an ice-blue plasma cylinder made of hexagons rose from the floor, trapping him. By the sound of it, it was beginning to energize. Gavin's eyes flew open as he slammed a palm against an invisible barrier with a quiet *thump*.

"Exit Xenxu!" he shouted, muffled.

Nima grinned with one side of her mouth and winked, saying, "You don't understand the part of you that wants this, but you will. Promise."

His eyes white with terror and rage, Gavin thumped his palms around the glowing tube like a mime, his suit coat flapping manically.

"Resistance is futile, impetuous pilgrim," she said.

Gavin's horrified face whiplashed. Other-him had said that same thing! "Please!" he shrieked. "Exit Xenxu!"

This was the moment all this bizarre anti-rational stimuli overloaded his logic circuits. He was blanking, his left brain hemisphere independently refusing to process any more of this for him.

Starting from the floor, his form began disappearing like a lit fuse, sparks and all. When it got to his chest, he shrieked "Daddy!" and was gone.

Still in the zoot suit, Gavin materialized into a white-goldish place with no zinging electronics of any kind. He simply faded in, still screaming, "Daddy!" with his palms mime-pounding on nothing.

It was but a micro-interval before he realized he was no longer on *Quasar*, and the shriek emitting from his ashen and terrified face trailed off into a meek little back-throated gurgle-squeak as he looked around. At first with curiosity, which then began trending toward disquiet. Had he not been spliced into such a bizarrely curious place, he might have gone on being mindlessly terrified for another moment or so; but looking around, he realized he was in...nothingness, the only visible tangible feature being the floor and himself.

What's more, it was so completely soundless, it was like the air—air?—was a spongy absorbing buffer for anything acoustic.

"What the hell?" he said, as if testing that. And it struck him the sound did nothing but channel right back into his own ears. It was a feedback loop: him making the sound, and simultaneously collecting it back into his head. It's all there was here, because here there was no inside, no outside, no here, no there.

Spinning in place, he looked around, his head yanking side-to-side, his eyes straining to penetrate this veneer of invisible fog. It took a few more transitory fragments in non-time for him to realize he was doing everything he could to stretch his senses, to *force* them to collect more information for his brain to process into things and people.

But there was none to collect. It was as though he had emerged from the data of whiteness, was himself the whiteness like a blank canvas, but had been painted into it as a three-dimensional phenomenon, thus shattering the perfect symmetry of this white-goldish void.

The raw empty shock of it began wearing off, however, and his capacity for reason, curiosity, was eking back into his circuitry.

"What the hell?" he said again, still spinning in place. Perhaps if he spun long enough, things other than himself would begin to materialize? A spark of that dire hope came to life, somewhere way down inside, and he refused to entertain it.

For the alternative was *far* too terrifying to contemplate. He could think about any of a million things, but what if he was stuck here? With its flames and sulfur and endlessly wailing inhabitants, hell didn't hold a candle to this. As he pivoted, looking for anything at all, his thick brows wriggled into a half-dozen sets of puzzlement, condemnation, anger, curiosity.

Gavin's eyes were oscillating like one of those cat clocks. "What if...what if that guy at Ai Anam's thing is right? That *Pods* is...is...oh *please* no," he said, and his words were again absorbed into the blank sponge. Without looking down, he felt around between his fingers, searching for webbing. "Jeezus," he muttered in frustration. "It's not happening to *personi*, Gavin."

Somewhere on the other side of a barrier he couldn't see was an ocean of panic, and the first waves were starting to lap at the breaker.

"No. Please. No way to stop it here." The concept that he could be stuck forever in a panic attack was simply the worst thought the universe had ever produced. Torture. Burned alive. Marooned alone on a desert island. All had endings. This didn't. All were kid's play compared to a permanent panic attack in a place with no exit.

These were thoughts he could not have, because for the first time in his life, he realized thoughts could kill. He'd read and seen it in a dozen movies and books, but never experienced it on such a visceral level.

Nightmare. I'm in a fickin nightmare. Please let it be true!

He closed his eyes, willing himself to wake up, but the profound silence simply closed in and muffled his ears even more in its baffled silence.

He started pacing. "OK. All right," he panted. "Everything is sheek. Everything is fine. This is a...it's a therapeutic modality. Of course." He shrugged. "What else could it be?" He chuckled falsely in panting gasps. "Deep Climb. No big deal. The user reports said to expect anything. I didn't know I'd wind up in nothing," he said, spreading his arms all-inclusively. "I should be grateful. I signed up for this. It's their way of telling me we're...that we're...that we start out blank, and we can *return* to that, removing the filth. *That's* it. *That's* what they're doing. Plain as day." Gavin stopped walking and turned back, realizing he'd forgotten to turn around in his pacing and just walked a straight line. How far?

"Right here," he said, looking down. "I didn't actually move while I walked." His blue eyes shifted left, right. "OK, so where was I?" He turned and walked. "Yeah. Or do the senses *cause* the data?" Gavin waved his hands. "Too abstract. Stay on task. It's radical, but it's already got me thinking in exploratory ways. Be that as it may, did I authorize Deep Climb, the motherfucking *assholes*," he screamed, "to do this? Terms of *Service*. Ninety fickin pages! I'd be *deceased* before I could finish it. It's part of their game," he said quieter. "Their charade," he said at even lower volume. "Their...their...sleight of hand. Only a person they *don't* want would read that." His cheeks trembled like a volcano was about to blow.

"Calm, Gavin. Just be calm."

Standing in one place, he closed his eyes, licked his lips, and imagined, without success, that he was calm. "Exit Xenxu," he said, his voice right on the edge, eyes still closed but the lids flinching. He let an eye open a little. Whiteness. Eye reclosed.

"Gnosis," he said with forced serenity. "Gnosis?"

He put his hands on his abdomen. Between his panting sucks of air, he trembled out, "Just breathe."

Steeling himself, he opened his eyes and touched his fingers together. No UI.

"Nima!" he shrieked. And the sound again went nowhere but into...whatever white nothingness was. "She can't hear you, and this isn't helping." Gavin's eyes flitted here, there, over, back, looking for concepts that would move this whole thing forward a step. "Well, what *would* help? I don't know, but it would help to focus on something other than the most terrifying scenario the universe has ever produced, don't you think?"

His dad thumping his forehead with his palm at the park. You gotta use that noggin of yours! You gonna have to think your way out of trouble for the rest of your life!

"That's right, Daddy. You tell me how she's done, but the thing is, I think they just dropped me in here for a while. To give me some perspective, like sending a kid to face the corner for punishment." Gavin looked up, eyes probing the white for a corner. "Am I on timeout? How about I just take a nap? That'll show 'em. I got all fickin day. You'll see. Gavin Simms...he'll wait *you* out. Nobody's better at waiting than Gavin Simms. You want stubborn? Watch how it's done."

His mom in one of her weird housedresses, perpetually concerned face and moist eyes. Just do what you need to do, precious boy. Find your quiet place. You can do it, now.

"OK, Momma," he whispered, surveying the floor.

He padded like a cat around in circles trying to find the best way or position or whatever cats do to lie down. Like the scent was right, he finally sat, legs bent, forearms on knees, breathing deeply and evenly through his nose. Then he stretched out on the floor, closing his eyes and lacing his fingers at his solar plex. In his head, he began threading back through everything, searching for clues.

This became the meditation, and sometimes he lost the thread, or was it commandeered by ice-blue interstellar nanobots, creating transition pods out of human skin!

Dawkins saying to his wife, It's better this way. No more pain. No more war.

The eye nearest the scab mellowly opened, but it looked like the eye of a tuna about to be attacked by a tiger shark. His jaw muscles rippled as the eye closed again and he said, "Nima said the same thing. This isn't good."

The perfect whiteness was a screen for projected events from the past to imprint themselves upon, and Gavin found himself absorbed by the scenes. With no other sense-based stimuli to run interference, his mind produced them in vivid living color. Images paraded by, life recall of hurts and wants, lack and longing, immediate and emotional. He watched his dad, drunk in late afternoon, stumble over to him and the lawnmower. "You broke it," he slurred, pointing at it.

"It's a piece of junk," young Gavin said. "We need to fix it or get a new one."

"Everything you touch turns to *shit*."

"It's not my fault," said Gavin, taking a wary step back, young plum-gray eyes watchful.

His dad lunged at him as he snarled, "The hell it ain't!"

Gavin ducked his flailing arms and sprinted toward the rock wall, stepping once on a turnstile stair and vaulting over it. He shimmied up the big Kentucky coffee tree on the other side. His dad reached the bottom, growling, "You got nowhere to go now, boy." He gripped the lowest branch and put his boot against the trunk, but he couldn't even get started. With drunk snuffles and heavy breathing, he tried again and again. Falling forward, he banged his forehead on the bark and yelled, "Goddammit!"

Circumstances aside, Gavin snickered behind his hand from twenty feet up.

After a while, his dad was leaning against the tree with both hands, sweaty, panting and grumping. Looking up at Gavin, he squinted to focus his drunk eyes and snarled, "I'll be right back, fickin snowflake."

Gavin knew he was off to get the BB gun to shoot him out of the tree. He'd stung him with that thing before, always in the butt. He clambered down and took off into the forest. Jogging the whole way on a track nearly overgrown on both sides, he came upon his secret place, from where he and Heather had run for their lives from the inky black presence of the forest. "That recurring nightmare."

Gavin! Where are you!

"Graystone. My dreaming hut," said Gavin to the vast emptiness. "I loved that place."

His vision slipped into a gap in a big tilted rock. Inside, it was cozy, with natural stone shelves and his supply containers. As the boy made himself comfortable on an old fraying horse blanket, he looked up through a nest of twigs and root tentacles that wove into a ceiling, mostly plugging the gaps in his little cave.

"I kept extra clothes in there," he said to the scene. "Ready for anything. Nukes. Quakes. Zombies. Always had canned food. It so *jams* to see this now like this."

But he was feeling, quite unmistakably, that he was less in this emptiness, and more in the scene of the past, a strange displacement of the concrete location of his awareness.

Deep Climb might shift your consciousness so completely into pivotal moments of the past, you'll lose memory of the present.

"OK," he said.

And suddenly, he was in his little cave on his back on the horse blanket, *as the boy,* panting from his run, sweaty and cooling fast in the granite cold shade. After getting his wind, he sat up. A rusty old Coca Cola sign leaned against something, and he reached over and moved it aside, revealing a cubby tacked together from discarded lumber. In it were his extra clothes. He thumbed through his survival inventory of jeans, boxers, socks, and two flannel shirts. Lifting one of the shirts to his nose, he said, "No skunks been by here."

Tucking the shirt back in there, he re-placed the Coca Cola sign. Feeling around on a small shelf over his head, he found a key and pushed it into the slot of a strong-box, turning it and lifting the lid. In it were army rations, a small Sterno stove, and the rations can opener, all from his dad's keepsakes.

"I'm a made man!" he called out with gleeful self-satisfaction, kicking back. "No demon, no zombie, no man can touch me here! No sir!"

He made his elbow a pillow and looked off through the slivers of light between the twigs, listening to the babbling creek. Last summer he'd shown Heather his vacation home, just before their terrifying escape from something in the forest. He sure wished she was here now as the loneliness seemed to be setting in faster than usual. Picturing her, he said, "I beat him, Heath. I beat the crazy old coot again."

He holed up for three days, hoping his dad's anger would transmute to worry. The nearby stream provided water, and he did bathe in it. His folks wouldn't worry. Not bad anyways. He'd done this before, and hell, eleven-year-olds have babysitters in more upscale neighborhoods. Oh, but them same kids would have to wear helmets just to go downstairs. But out here in the hills, kids learn to see to themselves. He needed people around most of the time, though, so three days alone wasn't easy. But he pretended to be a survivalist, and they were rugged, you know.

Sometimes, his attention would just wander away, and he'd come around, blinking, finding he'd been staring sightlessly at the rock face for what turned out to be from late afternoon to past dusk. Coming around from one of those fugues, he found his can of pork and beans was already on his little Sterno stove, heating up. To his recollection, he hadn't done that, but by that time in his life those moments were just shrug-offs.

The scent of bubbling pork and beans waned, then faded altogether, and Gavin was again marooned in the endless goldish whiteness. But the scene had helped him. "If I could do it then, I can do it now."

Gavin was silent for a few ticks, then he whispered, "A chair would sure be nice."

Another memory wavered in. Young Gavin was seated in a chair in their worn-out living room. Smelled like spoiled fruit and old carpet in there. His folks were hovering over him, and his dad was saying, "Son, either now or later, you gonna accept Jesus as your Lord and Savior."

"But I don't need savin', and you don't neither," he said, his arms folded in firm defiance.

"Just sayin' that means you *do* need savin'," said his mother, her hand on his shoulder.

Looking his dad in the eye, then his mom, he said, "Why cain't you see how *silly* that is?"

The memory fell apart like burning celluloid film and he was again left in...nothing.

Before he knew it, the old white blankness had settled in, and he found himself staring absently without any sense of...of anything.

Blink.

Now standing, he came to, looked down at himself, and said, "Why am I standing?"

Blink.

Now he was sitting. "Oh no."

Blink.

"No no no. Huh-uh. Stay right here," he said, pumping his hands at the floor. "What if I don't come back from one of those?"

Some absent increment of passing experience later, Gavin was stomping around in the white, arms flailing, yelling to himself, at himself, pointing, gesticulating.

"No. *No*! Deep Climb's *legit*! They *have* to be! I read the *reviews*!" he hollered at nobody in the white. "Founded by a Nobel laureate!"

Next slide, and he was gnawing on bitter pills, his face livid, mottled, self-hate inscribing his every feature. Flailing like a wacky-wavy at a car lot, he sneered, "Go into it like you're a *spy*, Gavin! Play Doc Sticks's game on *your* terms, Gavin! Let's get this thing going! Sign here! Fickin Cat. How could she *do* this to me!" Self-loathing shaped his face, like he was dealing with an awful stench. "I thought she was being *so* sweet, *so* helpful. But you had a feeling. Deep down you *knew* she was up to something. Traitor!" he shrieked so hard, by now needing a voice echo like a starving man needing a buttered bun.

Dawkins talking softly, peacefully, to his wife, holding up a glaspad with tiny tendrils wiggling from it. She was backed like a frightened rodent into the corner of the counter. We mean no harm. That isn't our agenda. We simply need to consume, and what we leave behind is peace, plenty. You are human, and then you are us. Easier than falling asleep.

Next slide, and Gavin stared off into nothingness, eyes wide and empty, and then like a light switch was thrown, he screamed, "No *wonder* they have such sheek reviews! They're fresh out of the fickin *pods*!"

A bit later, he was still yelling and stomping around and flailing, now sweaty, his jacket tied by the sleeves around his waist. Slamming his palm with the back of his other hand over and over, he shouted, "And Doc *Sticks*! Sticks? They *laugh* at us! *Christ*, Gavin. She told you she was from *hell*! *Both* of them...they were so fresh out of the pods they didn't even know how to run their bodies! No *wonder* they were so weird!"

An indeterminate duration later, he was face down on the floor, pounding it with his balled fists, tears and sweat dripping.

"How many of them are there? What about the people at Sous les Pods! Pods! Sous Les Pods! What does *that* mean?" Gavin flipped around and sat up to get a vpad out of his UI, but no UI. So he scuttled his hands in front of his face and snapped and crackled and swore about no fickin vpads. "That couple," he said, envisioning the weird couple at the café, blank in an annoyed way. "They were definitely transitioned. Was that a clue, Sherlock? Maybe! Have we been sucked through a vortex out of Kansas, Toto?" Gavin pushed to his feet and swung around and boomed with all he had, "Is there a yellow brick road around here! Bring it! Gimme something to walk on, fuckers! I want to hock and spit in the face of the *Wizard*! *God* that would be so sweet!"

As the waves and waves of realization kept pounding the beach of his psyche, which was in fact bleached, he was so overwhelmed he was now tearful, giggly, and enraged at the same time. "They told you everything they were going to do," he blubber-laughed. "They... they...they *telegraphed* all of it, right in plain sight. And you just went along with it ladidadidah," he said, prancing and stumbling around like a drunken court jester, hat bells tinkling. "Clown! You're a fickin *clown*, Gavin."

The volcano of rage...she was about to blow.

"They set up every door for you to...to just...*trundle* happily and gaily and glazed-eyed through, and you just complied, with everything. Comply here," he said, taking a dancing step to the side and leaning, "comply there," he hopped back. "A chain of complies. Surfer Man warned you about it. He said...what did he say again, Gavin? He said, don't fall for it. And what did you do, not even thirty seconds later? You walked through another door like a *zombie*!" he howled, his arms straight out and groping as he stumbled through doors not there.

Gavin raised his zombie arms to oration arms and staggered around in a circle, shouting, "So this is the mind recycling center! It's *better* this way," he mocked nasally, face bitter. "The promise of a better *life*! Right! This is where you...what?...scramble my mind, wipe it, and port it back into the imposter in the pod?"

Dr. Carney explaining to Dr. Willen. They are a pan-galactic predator species, more mind than physical, like a hive. Their nanotech is like nothing I've ever examined. Incredibly advanced.

But they don't hate us, she says. We are simply...fuel. Do we hate the pine for being firewood? Perhaps there is some basic survival imperative we can intro-

duce them to that appeals to…to whatever semblance of empathy they possess for other lifeforms.

Then Gavin stopped his oratory to the absent mob. "Yeah, but you don't know where they send the mind," he said to Drs. Carney and Willen. "Here, to this featureless…stasis. Why here? Why this? There's a reason for everything. There's no causeless event."

His dad in the Jeep, soon to drop him off to walk that dark road alone. There's a reason for everything, son. I want you to 'member that.

Cat's beautiful freckly face was smiling at him, and tears again welled. "She's in on it," he gently sobbed. "She was a compliance… whatever…*node*. That's their way. One door after another. Sneaky bastards." Throwing his hands in the air, he walked in backwards steps, sort of listing from one side to the other like he'd had a few intoxicating bevs. "Game over! Game *over*, humanity! You slurped up the Kool-Aid like a *fish*! Four billion users of Xenxu!" he shouted, holding up four fingers. "We're *done*! We're *toast*!"

As self-battering bouts like this were usually exhausting—and Gavin was a world-renowned expert on the matter—he felt he should remain pure to the resulting behavior. With a stage perfect sigh, his body just sort of melted to the floor like a wet noodle with the optimal effect for a weak, effete, and exhausted snowflake with a suit jacket tied around his waist. Sitting up, he took the jacket off and shook it out. Through his tears, he sniveled, "All wrinkled now." So he wadded the fickin thing up for a pillow and tucked it under his head as he lay back down. Like a child, he wept in sniveling and wiping and coughing fits, mindful his tears and mucus flows didn't get on the zoot jacket.

Gavin!

Heather's voice somewhere off in the white. Then again. And again. It froze him in fear. He clamped his eyes shut, like he was covering his eyes with his palms to hide from whatever was crawling through dry leaves and snapping sticks… *shtskshtsk*.

The kids caress the moonlit flat stone with the wicked-looking tree spreading through its natural grain, daring the spirits to come adventurize their lives. She looks at him, wide eyes shining. See? Daddy's a loony-boony. Straightening, they flick their eyes to the turnstile over the rock wall. It's old. Why is it there? You really can't touch the stones? Bullshit, she says, scrambling over the wall, making sure to touch a bunch of stones. On the other side, she turns and looks at him. You coming?

Gavin sat, forearms on bent knees, staring at the blank white-gray floor. By now his trendy, formerly jubilant, up-swirl of purple hair was plastered to one side of his head, with an errant offshoot defying all explanation, and which he didn't even know about. Nor was he aware of the dried drool on his cheek. The zoot jacket was now folded under his butt, a pillow against the harsh hard floor.

For the tenth time, he went to open his UI to get a mirror out, but…no UI. It was frustrating before. Now it was merely tragically comical.

"I had no idea how badly I need mirrors."

You're a narcissist.

Gavin looked to his left and said, "No. I have my…moderate vanities. That's all."

His face turned away from the left, his eyes searching…searching…

When there was nothing to see outside himself, the one place to go looking was within, into the content of his immediate past, potential futures. Something Nima had said circled back through his mind over and over, buoying his spirits just enough to hang onto it like a lifeline.

You don't understand the part of you that wants this, but you will. Promise.

"Someone who says that isn't referring to the assimilation of humankind, right?" He looked to his left. "She wouldn't say *promise,* would she?"

Because hope is just an oft-chosen menu item.

"I can't listen to you." He looked to the right. "Why say that? It… it suggests there is something to…to…come back to. There is an other *side* of this. Her wink was foul, but...she wasn't being mean." Gavin threw out a hand and looked to his left. "Well, none of them were being *mean*, per se. But they wouldn't present as mean. Demons have to present as the nicest people in the world, your buddy, your *bestie*!" he snapped, foaming up again.

Getting to his feet, he grabbed the jacket and shook it out. By now its wrinkles were deep awful scars, looking like the most battered face in all humankind. Stains from his snot and tears got on the lapel, but he kept his eyes averted from that carnage. He shook it hard, spread it out on the floor to mark his location, and began pacing. He walked a few steps and stopped, looking over his shoulder. The jacket was back there, where he'd left it.

"I *am* moving when I walk. Hm." He cast his gaze around to see if anything had changed. Did the space somehow become finite?

Gavin walked past the jacket going the other way, turned, and walked back, leaning forward, his clasped fingers fiddling with themselves behind his tailbone. "Let me ask you this," he said, holding out a hand. "If someone takes over your body, where does your consciousness go? *Pods* doesn't address that at all. Maybe this is...is like the untold story. Like this'll be the next season. All my personality is right *here*." He pumped at the floor with both palms. "What I am is all right *here*. My body is now beside the point. They say it's better their way, but what's better? Being a mindless worker bee? Or being *here* in full possession of *my* mind? *My* personality?" Looking around the vast nothing with a hint of frustration, he said, "That is a hell of a question."

Wait. He stopped in his tracks, and in a brief panic searched for the jacket. There! Whew! He started toward the jacket again. It was headquarters, and he didn't want to stray too far from it.

While pacing, he looked at the empty space to his right. "While sending me to my doom, Cat nevertheless...she gave me a thought tool that's empowering. *You* invent the choice from your own creativity. Why did she do that? Does a pangalactic nanopod bot-monster bent on the end of humanity do that?"

What if Deep Climb is legit?

Gavin stopped, as the associate to his right had a decent point. "Go on."

What if this is some brilliantly radical system to strip you of everything false?

"What do you mean by false?"

Everything you see in the mirror.

"But I...but I...but I *like* who I am."

Do you?

But the associate on the left had something to say about this.

Your body is now reanimated and he has written your article, better than you could do it. In your absence, he's attracted ten thousand new subs.

"That *bastard*!" hollered Gavin at the whiteness on the left. In quiet desperation, he again swung his gaze around, and his eyes widened in excitement. Somehow, the nothingness had cleared some, and way off, he could make out features.

"Features!" he cried, pointing. "Look!"

He couldn't make out what they were, but they stood out from the vague obscurity, just faint lines and protuberances.

But it's something!

"Hey, everyone! It's *something*! *Yoohoo*!" Gavin gripped his chest with such passionate joy, a new vintage of tears welled in the lower lids. "Oh thank God." The heart-swelling *gratitude*. "Something," he panted. "It's something else. *Thank* you. Is this what happened to God? Is this why existence is?"

He grabbed the jacket, shrugged into it, tugged the sleeves and smoothed the lapel, and took off in that direction with a spritely gait. New direction. New horizon! What lay ahead in this formerly blank madness of matter absence?

As he walked, something glittery and glitchy appeared out ahead. Tittering laughter, like from a girl ghost in the playground. Gavin yelled, "Wait up!" and took off running. Nothing with any real substance appeared, but it moved like it was altering the air, with solid pieces blipping in and right back out. The distant in and out girl laughter kept him going, stopping, searching around, racing off in a new direction.

There!

No, there!

Zigzagging his way through a maze not there.

Then it stopped, and Gavin stopped, sending his gaze around like a rotating radar. Nothing. His shoulders slumped, and he took up staring again, at nothing. "We're all in a maze, and we don't even know it."

In this diffuse void, the light never changed. No moon serenely sailed overhead through the white-specked black. No sun climbed every 1,440 minutes from a curved horizon into the space of its own light. No tomorrow. No yesterday. No moment before, nor after. Amid that interminable flow of sameness, Gavin came around while walking, unsure what thoughts he may have been having just an increment before. The white-gold nothingness had fertilized his memory, turning him into a unit of perception:non-perception by turns, the impetus for the toggles back and forth unknown.

"A single moment and eternity are the same thing." He put his hands on his gut with a sick sour look. "Why does that idea make me nauseous?" Looking around, like anyone or anything cared, he said, "How long have I been walking? I don't have so much as a *clue*. Time is gone. I can't even say I know what the word means anymore. It's strange how definitions get sucked away in this place."

Ai Nima saying, I agree the place to start is by disengaging his mind from this fictitious timeline.

Gavin rewound her saying that. "What?" His mind played it again. "What are they doing to me? What is the game here? Am I to be reinserted into that...that abomination? If so, I prefer this...maybe."

Walking and walking.

An absent duration of sensate experience...

...his eyes got a little hazy, hypnotized by the white-goldness. He shook his head and blinked, huffing air in and out of puffed cheeks like he was trying to wake up. "Stay here, Gav. It's important. Stay afraid. Fear makes it all real. Wait...that's how they do it."

You're not getting out.

Gavin held up his left palm. "Why don't you talk to Mr. palm and his five little henchmen."

Striding hard, arms swinging.

On he walked, walked and walked. A tiny form in a horribly wrinkled and preposterously misplaced zoot suit in the middle of endless huge. Frames of his life tumbled around like shards of mirror with faces and places and events embossed on them.

"Haven't thought about some of that stuff in years."

He doesn't care to.

"It's a distraction."

He's on a mission.

"The features."

But in swarmed the shards. Sometimes they came together, making a more complete picture like starlings making their art in the sky, but he scuttled them with his flicking fingers before they could create anything he didn't want to see.

He doesn't want them.

"I don't need them."

Only the features.

That shard. Heather, witness to the moment the lawnmower gave up the ghost with one last cough of blue smoke. Her face over there in her bedroom window, Gavin still in the tree. They looked at each other, sharing their thoughts, which was easy for them to do. She was laughing and pointing the entire time her dad was doing the besotted boogie battle with the tree, but when he turned tail and stumble-stepped toward the house, she disappeared from the window.

"You went and hid the BB gun. What a stud." Tears welled. "That was so big of you, Heath. So fickin boss for a little girl. You *were* boss. You know that?"

Oops! Shard!

Momma with a weak smile, her tiny eyes far away. Always in pain from whatever was wrong with her brain, and her smiles harder and harder to make.

"That fuckin' brain disease," he said to the shard as it slowly pinwheeled past.

His dad, a hand on a young woman's butt in the parking lot of the hardware store. She was a chubby thing, making him look like a stick figure with facial scrub and a too-large lumberjack shirt.

"Did Momma know?" he asked that passing shard, his arms swinging furiously.

Another shard lazily tumbling by. But this one was black with crooked little sticks in it.

Gavin! Where are you!

They kept coming, and he couldn't turn them off. Faster. More. Tumbling.

Looking sick and sour, he grabbed his belly and said, "What's with this nausea? It...it's vertigo. *That's* what it is. I know how to fix that."

Gavin took off running, and after a bit, recalled how physical exertion works. His muscles should be pumping lactic acid by now, his legs heavier with each stride, and the breathing was all wrong. One pants while performing this...activity. So, he panted. Made sense. He shaped his hands into blades, like he did when running to first base.

The shortstop threw the ball, doinked him on the head and it all went black, a heroic noogie on his noggin. Could have been hours he was on his backside, when faces finally swam into view.

"Badge of fickin honor, that lump!" Gavin shouted. "Look at *me* now! I'm a real boy like the rest of you!"

He's a real boy!

"I get hurt. I get up."

He keeps going. He's so brave.

"That's what *I* do. How about the rest y'all?"

They even make it out of that sad sick town?

"Well, look at *me* now. *I* did. I'm a fashion doyen."

Admired! Sought after!

"Liar," he said, running like the wind. But the shards pursued him like a flock of sparkling butterflies...butterflies with razor teeth. No outrunning those bastards. Now and again, he'd look back while running and see they were coalescing into obscure people shapes, place shapes, and then again flying apart. It seemed inevitable they'd catch him.

What is preferable?

"Seriously. To keep running, or to be caught?"

But the shards were swarming in, multiplying, more of them dark with wicked, twisting sticks, dividing and subdividing, reticulating into fibers of form, black consuming white, the whole place darkening, as...

...Heather and Gavin stole quietly along the dark narrow track. The moon was up and bright, and its shafts of silvery light bathed the topsides of the trees and underbrush, blackening the shadows below in stark contrast. The sounds were of haunting hushes through breeze-blown leaves and the creak of swaying timber.

"A little farther," said ten-year-old Gavin over his shoulder.

"Whatever," said eight-year-old Heather. "I love these warm nights out here."

"Aren't you even a little scared?"

"Yeah," she said. "It's why I like it."

"Is that why you touched the tree stone back there?" said Gavin. "To see if you could conjure monsters?"

"Nooo," she snorted, feathering her hands through the passing grasses and leaves. "Sienna's mom told us it's a bunch of superstitious horse pucky."

"It's right over here," said young Gavin, veering off the trail and moving through the moonlit vegetation. They reached Graystone, his makeshift cave. Gavin stooped and slipped into the black gap. Heather paused, staring into the inky dark, her boldness of a moment ago wavering. Inside, Gavin rustled around, knocking things over. "Come on in. Ow, dammit. But watch your head until I get these lit." She held her breath and crawled in.

Pure impenetrable black inside. "Gav," she said, groping, "where are you?"

The scrape of a match on emery, a brilliant spark and flame, bringing wavering shadowed form from the chaos of the void. Gavin touched the flame to one candle, then another. Now their faces glowed as they looked at each other with breathless excitement, candle flames dancing in their eyes.

"Gavin," said Heather, looking around. "This is so flippin' *cool*. Do the Elders know about this?"

"I think Daddy might. Sometimes I smell his vape thing out here."

"I think his vape thing smells like grasshopper legs," she giggled.

"I think it smells like dead dried worms." Gavin scooted over and patted the spot beside him. "Here. Get on the blanket."

Heather scratched her fingernails through the old horse blanket. "Where did you get this?"

"That old shed over Danny's part of the wall."

In the candlelight, Gavin looked at Heather's crinkled nose, her hazel eyes darting around with some alarm. "What's wrong?"

"Do you smell that?" Heather crawled to the opposite opening, poking her head out. Gavin pulled his legs to his chest to make room for her. In the candlelight, he saw all but her head and face, and then her body went rigid.

"Heath?"

Her breath started coming in panicked gasps as she said, "There's something out there."

"Don't mess with me, Heath. It's not funny."

"Pull me back in," she hissed.

"Why?"

"I can't move."

Gavin grabbed her belt and yanked her back in so hard, she plopped onto her butt on the blanket. He waited for her blood-drained face, her wide white eyes, to give up the charade and start laughing over her sick joke.

But she didn't laugh, just stared at the black angled opening, her frozen eyes reflecting flickering candle.

A *phump* outside, like a dropped stone, or the hoof of a great antlered beast. Heather grabbed Gavin's wrist and squeezed so hard, he winced and wiggled his fingers under hers to loosen them. His face swung toward the opening, his heart pounding in his ears.

Rising from within the breezy hush of leaves… *shtskshtsk* of scratching and scraping leaves and sticks. Getting louder.

Gavin turned back to Heather's frozen, terrified face, and she mouthed at him, "What is it?"

Gavin's high arcing brows etched terror across his round eyes as he mouthed, "I don't know."

*Shtskshtsk…*closer, louder, the stench of rotting leaves and dead things come to life, skin hanging in fronds from spindly bones.

Gavin felt a dank magnetism tug at him from the narrow maw of black beside him, like mucky quicksand clogged with leaves. With some effort, he tore his eyes from it, his face pivoting to her. His trembling hand rose into the candlelight, pointing at the entrance they'd used. Heather was closer. Gavin leaned to her ear, whispering, "When we get out, I'll say when to run. But don't lose me."

Heather, now sniveling in tears and trying to be quiet, slipped out. Gavin left the candles lit as he ducked through and crawled outside, staying low. His heart was hammering so hard he thought he might just die right here, then he slowly straightened enough to look over the big angled granite stone. There, he saw the shapes, textures, and contours of the sliver moonlight on the things of the forest, but something black blotted it out as it moved with papery scrapes toward them.

…Shtskshtsk…Shtskshtsk…

"Go!" he hissed.

Through the underbrush they scurried, making a hell of a racket. It was sheer dumb luck Gavin found the path, and on it they sprinted like the hunted. Right away, Heather's short legs became a hindrance, so he shook loose her hand.

"Gavin!"

She grabbed his belt loop, but she couldn't hang on.

"Don't leave me!" she shrilled amid the hush and grainy *clack* of wicked moving things closing from behind.

Gavin felt its inky tentacles tickling the back of his neck, its breath hot. It was draining him, blanking him. His muscles became sluggish, like he was running through black sludge. The narrow track was a blur on both sides. Then he was in the blur, crunching and crashing through the brush and dry leaves and fallen branches.

I'm off the trail!

"Gavin! Wait up!"

But he couldn't. He wasn't at the controls, the flight side of survival having taken over. His scrambling legs and feet hauled him deeper into the thickets. A stick caught his foot and he sprawled face first into the dry leaves. Somewhere back there Heather's desperate sniveling voice called, "Gavin! Where are you! *Please* don't leave me!"

Gavin lay face down in the leaves, breathing in the dry of them, the moist fertility of the soil. This was refuge, the only sound his trembling breathing. Even if he'd wanted to, he couldn't move. Not a muscle. Not a blink.

"Gavin!" she cried, weeping harder out there somewhere.

In his mind, the black thing was almost upon her. What could he do about that now? What would he say to his folks?

"Oh, Heather," he sniveled. "Just run." He willed out himself a murder of flapping ravens to protect her, but doubt clogged the belief.

As quietly as he could, fighting through his own paralyzed density, he rolled over. There, blotting out a tree trunk, slithering in wavy tendrils toward him. His face screamed, mouth stretched wide, but no sound issued from his paralyzed chest.

Now it was primal, animal. He shot to his feet and crashed through the forest like a mindless mad thing.

"Is that you, Gavin!"

He ran hard, sharp things scratching and cutting, burrs clinging, branches lacerating. The silvery dark began lightening, and in a few more steps, Gavin raced into white nothingness, his feet making padded thumping on the gray-white floor. Again, the endless white-gold enveloped him. He stopped and sank to his knees and sat on his ankles, covering his face as the tears started. "Oh, Heath. I couldn't… I was so weak, and you were so tough."

His dad's livid and mottled face, his mom's condemning face hovering behind. You left your little sister alone in a night forest. Running for your life from what was probly a coyote! I can't even look *at you. You make me sick.*

Heather stands with her fuzzy bear held close, face still white with shock, looking at him, her eyes in wet shining apology. You're both grounded! Two weeks! Happens again, and the belt comes out.

Gavin raised his head and sniffed, like a dog putting his snout into the wind. The smell of their dad's vape thing, blended with the moldering earth and decaying vegetation, wafted through the whiteness. Jumping to his feet, he swung around.

"What?"

The black oval opening from which he'd just run from the forest of his past hovered there. He stared at the floating dab of darkness with wide eyes, his brows like furry arches. The oval was a void, but with fibers of things less black moving and roiling across its empty face.

"It's an opportunity."

He huffed and puffed, like he was getting ready for a deep dive into frigid waters. His jaw muscles rippled as he started toward the rift. Hesitating, he reached through, and stepped through, right into his young foot landing on the path. Now he was him of twenty-five years ago, but with his grown-up mind.

"Gavin! Don't leave me!"

"Heather!" he shouted. "Are you still on the trail?"

"Gavin?"

"Stay where you are! I'm coming for you."

Gavin's eyes lasered into the foliage while he moved fast along the winding path.

"Keep talking, Heath."

"What?"

Where was it? Where was this thing? But the forest was just a moonlit garden of enchantment now.

I'm amazed how much more alive my senses were back then. Fear does make it all so fickin real.

Around the next bend, and he saw Heather's moonlit tear-stained face. She was limping. "Gavin!" she yelped, run-limping over and throwing her arms around him. "You came back for me."

He felt her trembling body calming as she clung to him like a tree in a flood. Her head pushed so hard into his chest, and he felt her terror. That hurt more than anything. She blubbered, "I cut my leg. It's bleeding."

"Come on, Heath," he said, turning and bending to one knee. "Hop up. I'll give you a first-class ride out."

"I'll get blood on your shirt," she said in brave protest, but wanting her new hero to carry her out of this awful forest. She wiped her runny nose on her sleeve and made noises about how she could do it. She could walk out of here. "Look, there's not that much blood," she said, lifting her leg up to the moonlight and pulling back the pantleg.

"Wow, Heath," he said, turning for a closer look. "Will you look at that wound? Now *that's* how a hero bleeds. Way to go!" Gavin covered his mouth to mimic the sound of a field radio. "Home Base, this is Alpha Tango four-niner, requesting Casevac for Commander Heather Simms. It's a nasty wound, but she's a tough one. She'll make it. *Phu-phu-phu-phu-phu,*" he sounded rapidly, like medevac chopper rotor blades. "The bird's down on the LZ." While he was down there, he turned so she could climb aboard. "Welcome aboard, Commander Simms."

"Ohhh," she giggled. "You're one of those walking helicopters."

"All kinds of fickin skills." He reached back, hooked her legs behind the knees, and hefted her up. She wrapped her arms around his neck, tight, almost choking, but he let her do it. She put her face to the back of his neck, her tears and breath warm on his skin. "You came back for me, my knight in shining armor."

"Sorry I left you."

"What *was* that back there?"

"I don't know, but I think Daddy knew…*knows*…something about it."

Gavin strolled out of the black oval in this giant empty space, holding his arms back like he was piggy backing someone. The portal floated behind him. Gray black filaments wavered from his body, coming right out of the suit's threads, floating into the opening. As the last of them trailed in, the portal to the past shrank and winked out. He let his arms drop, looked to his right, and said, "Can you imagine if we could sometimes have had our adult perspective as kids? That was...*amazing*. *Beyond* amazing. Life-changing. Wow. Maybe Cat was right."

Inhaling once and blowing it back out, he hopped on his feet, shaking his arms and shoulders, loosening his neck, like he was warming up for a run. "I feel lighter. Was that shit that floated out of me the guilt? It has mass? Could this really *be* Deep Climb?"

Now he noticed how much more this place looked like an enormous space, and the features were sharper, closer, more defined. "This place isn't nothing," he said, trying to make out what seemed like walls miles and miles away, obscured by the mists of distance.

Shrugging, squinting at the features, he said, "Am I being rewarded for doing this work? Sure seems like it. Let's go." And he took off walking again.

Gavin walked, jogged, ran, skipped, jogged backwards, and walked again. It could have been days, or minutes, but that didn't matter anymore. What the hell could he do about anything, anyways? With his rumpled and zoot-suited wrist he wiped his brow of nonexistent sweat and pretended to feel the exhaustion from a vigorous and lengthy march.

He checked the features, and the distance was closing. "No question they're getting bigger," he said, more and more excited. While trying to make sense of their emerging shapes, he noticed something else, closer. Dark dots out ahead. Starting into a jog, he kept his eyes trained on them so they couldn't get away.

A living diorama was in his path, the extraneous details bleeding off into emptiness. It was the night his dad had dropped his fearful, delusional, teenaged son off to walk alone in the dark back to camp. That night became the dark menacing painting in his studio.

. . .

In his dad's sweet baby, the cherry red Jeep that caused many problems around their house for *years,* they wound along a dirt road between tall pines. It was past dusk and the golden light was quickly fading. The windows were down, making it chilly.

"...another boy lost in that damned war," sang Hick Sumpson from the Jeep's excellent sound system in his deep country singer voice, guitar strumming. Gavin knew why his dad listened to this tune so much.

Fickin IED, his dad snarls, face etched with the acid of pain. Killed all my friends like 'at! he says with a snap of his fingers.

"Life is so...it can be just so fickin brutal, son." His dad was a whipcord wiry man with a thin face making contours under his sparse scraggly beard. "Son-bitch beats a man down." (Pronounced like *sewn-beeutch.*) He glanced over at Gavin, but teen Gavin's eyes dropped to the pint of Old Home between his dad's thighs, cap off. "But then I'll be gummed if you don't find out the strangest things, things so weird the brutal just fades into the background. Everything turns out to have a purpose. It's important for you to 'member that."

"What do you mean?"

"Just that, son," he said, tilting the bottle in a toast. "Everything has a purpose. You ever thought about that?"

Gavin dug something from under his nail. "I guess so."

They drove slowly, the big tires crunching on the gravel, until it was almost dark, and they turned off the road into a campground set in tall pines.

His dad opened the door. "Let's get out a minute."

Gavin popped his seatbelt, opened the door and jumped out, closing it behind him. But his dad didn't get out. Closing his own door, he said out the window, "It's only seven miles, son. I humped thirty miles with eighty pounds of gear on my back. Ain't but a jog. Just stay on the road. You'll see our fire."

Gavin's wide eyes filled with wet terror. "This isn't funny," he cried through the open window, reaching for the handle.

But his dad locked the doors, saying, "No it ain't, son. You right about that. Be brave, now."

Gavin's young face crumpled into every shade of fear and pain. "*Please* don't do this."

His dad hoisted the Old Home in a toast and backed the Jeep onto the road. Gavin screamed, "Daddy! *Daddy*!" his teen voice slipping up like a squeaky wheel. "The joke's *over*! Ha ha! I get it! Come back!"

But in the silence of the night, he heard the Jeep's engine, and the music, growing quieter.

"*Please* come back," he whimpered.

The boy was left alone in a quickly darkening forest, fear rising through his gullet and lodging in his throat.

Future Gavin experienced this as the boy, with the boy's fears, but he was also the man with his adult perspective. He felt the tenseness in the young muscles, the watchfulness for the wicked things in the forest. A powerful scent was here, what his sheets smelled like as a kid when the afternoon sun hit them through the window—kid sweat, sunshine, creek water. It was strange feeling how light he was, but also how...burdened. Somewhere out there lurked the thing that chased Heather and him a couple years before.

Suddenly fuming mad amidst the tears, boy him stomped over to a stand of aspens and found a dead stick. Yes, it would be a walking stick, but he would also beat his dad senseless with it when he got back to camp. Stalking off down the darkening road, he started whistling, tunelessly, nervously, his sluggish lips so dry it came out airy and muted, but he kept at it as the walls of trees lining each side of the road closed in around him, the dark deepening.

He caught his breath, stopped, and whirled, stick up to swing at whatever nasty thing might come winging out of the trees. Nothing. Just crickets and creaking and occasional hoots. Leaning on the stick, he peered into the forest. Something was in it, blended with the shadows. It used the shadows, those motes of absent light, for cover, moving when he wasn't looking.

The boy started walking again, holding the stick like he was at home plate with a bat, his head and eyes swiveling, vision lasering into the black. The breeze kicked up, making a large bush move like it was a four-legged monster running in place. His step steered to give it a wider area to enjoy itself, his wooden Excalibur up and ready to smite.

After a while, the darkness enveloped, descending into pitch. Soon it was so dark it was hard to see the road. Every creak, *ssshhh*, pop, snuffle, hoot, jarred him to panicked breathing, stick up as he turned in place, eyes stretched to the limit. He was on the verge of terror, and he knew it well. It could paralyze him, send his mind fleeing to more soothing scenes. His muscles were leaden, shaky, the beginnings of the paralysis. Its onset was indeed more grave than the dark thing hunting him from the depths of shadow.

Visiting Gavin let himself bloom from within the boy.

A sense of comfort settled over his young self, and he walked more easily, his body less tense, his shoulders pulled back and straighter, the stick now demoted from weapon to walking stick. That summer, something would visit him, something comforting and familiar. It always smelled of freshly washed clothes. The boy stopped, looked around, and said, "I know you're here, whatever you are. I'm not afraid of you."

I remember this. I thought I was being haunted by a friendly spirit. But it was just me, from now. That's insane!

Vision wasn't clear, sort of warbly, smeared and tunneled. He felt himself adjusting to this bizarre mode of being and perception. As he did so a strong set of impressions pervaded him. The forest was a living breathing entity, and something was coming to life in it. To perceive this was natural, like he was part of it, was in *its* world. Even more, it knew he, the man, was here. As a kid, he entertained dreams and thoughts and fears all day long about this thing, this forest, but it was through the unripe lenses of a kid at the crossroads of becoming a young man.

He felt the matter, the ingredients, of the forest alchemically coagulating, its living intelligence teeming within its branches, leaves, underbrush and barks and soil. Whatever it was, it was focused on the boy.

The forest is tasting his fear, assessing it. This is part of a...the...ritual. It's preparation. Daddy knew about this.

The boy's reservoir of fear swarmed in like pixels of sensation. From this perceptual framework, older Gavin was instantly in touch with fear's stupefying power, its radiating waves flowing through him and off into the matter and energy of the forest. But it wasn't random; it was an organizing current. To where it flowed seemed to be a single destination, somewhere in the depths.

My fear energy was being consumed by whatever that is. Out there.

Upon that searing realization, Gavin's presence was yanked out of the boy and flown at dizzying speed down the road. The Jeep's red taillights came into view, and in a flash, he found himself in the cab, next to his dad. To his surprise, his dad was sniffing and wiping at tears. "I'm so sorry, Gavin. *So* sorry, son. It just has to be this way. But I've learnt a lot about this son-bitch, and you and I got some work to do, and I promise you, we're doin' it right now."

What are you crying about? I hated you for this. You were forced to do this? By the thing in the forest?

Teasing and tapping against the periphery of his awareness was a legion of impressions. Something ancient, and it involved their family, and other families, folks the salt of these hills and hollers, the tillers of the soil, the strugglers to carve out lives. It was in this forest, and it fed off their town. He felt the currents of shared thought swirling around in the minds of the men, and how they suffered from the impotence of being able to do *nothing* to protect their sons, themselves, relatives. Patches of pictures of so many of them, shrugging, peering into the dark, trying to understand it, swearing to overcome it, hesitant to even talk amongst themselves. Always afraid.

It was never about toughening me up. It was about preparation for this… this ritual. *Nobody in that town understands what or why or how.*

Everything shifted. Next thing adult Gavin knew, he and the boy were arriving at camp, now dark as pitch beyond the dancing licks of campfire. His dad was sitting by the fire, taking nips from a pint of Old Home. The look on his face showed relief, like *you made it,* but in the tones of a macho military guy he said, "See? Nothing to fear. Bet that'll take the flake out of your snow."

Liar. All an act. God, Daddy. Such a hard guy with a soft gooey middle. That's so funny. Jeezus.

"I *hate* you!" shrieked young Gavin, his voice stressing up a pubescent octave. A murder of crows was startled into flight, swooping in and out of the firelight. But neither young Gavin nor his dad took notice. Visiting Gavin watched them, gaining a deeper understanding of the spirit world and totemic animals, like an inload of ancient mystic data. Cawing and squawking, they flew off into the spirit side of night.

Young Gavin was holding his stick with both hands, ready to swing it.

His dad calmly set the bottle beside the chair and said with some menace, "Now, son, whatever you think you might like to do with that stick, you better think hard on it."

"Would you like to know what I planned?" said boy Gavin, his voice in shaky, barely contained control.

"Son, you can't see the bigger picture, but I promise you there is one, and you'll see it when it's time. Now put down that fickin stick."

Visiting Gavin willed calming energy out of his etheric pores.

Put down the stick. I know you want to kill him with it, but you're going to find out what I'm finding out about twenty-five years from now. Just put down the stick.

"Who said that?" said boy Gavin. "*What* am I gonna find out?"

"Said what?" said his dad, abruptly on his feet, alert, in soldier mode. "Who?"

"Someone told me to put down the stick," said Gavin, wary and pivoting in place and laser-squinting off into the dark.

"*I* told you to put down the stick. You havin' one of your little spells, son?"

"No!" spat the raging kid, hurling the stick into the fire, sending up a plume of sparks. "You'll *never* understand!" And he stomped toward the tent just beyond the periphery of the firelight.

I remember all that. It was always me, from here. Incredible.

The memory flaked and withered around him. Cracks in the

scene, and it shattered and flew off in all directions like a crushed autumn leaf, revealing the white-gold void once more.

Gavin was again walking toward the features, the details filling in more and more, his head wagging in constant awe over the dumbfounding impacts of these re-livings.

Gavin trudged on for quite a while, head down, watching the floor pass. He felt empty, free from thoughts. That felt way nice, a state of *being* instead of thinking. It occurred to him thoughts could be like prison bars, or a web.

"Your thoughts either set you free, or imprison you," he said aloud.

It seemed time to look up, and as he did, he stopped like a statue in his tracks, eyes wide, mouth hanging. He put a hand to his chest as he shakily breathed, "My God." An Earth mile from where he stood was a statue of Siren, but made of flowing energy, so colossal the tallest skyscrapers on Earth would come to about Her shins, like a city skyline at the base of mountains.

These were the scales from a mythic time, and she towered over Her palace like a tree from a forest of cosmic titans, her sunburst head more lighted and energetically active than the rest of her. Her scale alone was too much for his senses, and his emotions. His eyes filled with shine as he gaped, groping for something to say, mouth an oval.

He took off walking again, never taking his eyes off Her. When he was closer, he could make out She was part of an immense wall of iridescent energy, like a slow-moving waterfall, all shimmering, rippling, and She was stretching from it, as if She'd emerged from its background scintillations.

Gavin looked up and now made out a ceiling, then to the sides, and saw smooth shimmery walls miles away.

"This place is definitely an enclosure." Then it struck him. "I'm in Siren's obelisk. No structure anywhere large enough to contain this."

The walls and ceiling all roundly tapered, smaller and smaller, to the wall from which She emerged, like the domed central nave in a cathedral for mile-tall congregants. The precision of Her design was beyond belief, the detail in the lines, the trunk-like core, the dendritic branches and twigs like the sinews of a nervous system, all fanning out at the bottom like a dazzling royal evening gown.

"My *God!*" blurted Gavin, eyes like marbles in the sand as he sank to his knees. Emotions bubbled as he put a palm to his chest. His voice was shaky, eyes filled with silvery shine. "What an *honor*. Why choose little ol' me? Am I worthy of this?"

A rush surged through him and his shoulders shook. "Oh God," he moaned, eyes wild yet totally present. "*This* is humility. *This* is what it *really* feels like. Oh that feels so *good*." With both hands gripping his chest, he cried, "I *love* this adoration. Absolute devotion to the truly noble."

Gavin looked down at his own body and put his hands on his ribs. "It feels…it's so…*supportive*. *Deep* connection. Where all tributaries converge." Gavin gulped in air. "This quiet thrill is what bards have."

Troubadours.

"The wandering minstrels, strumming on their lyres."

Singing devotional paeans to the Feminine side of Divinity.

"*They* knew what this feeling was about. It was an *addiction*. They couldn't get enough of it."

Secret language in hidden chambers of the heart.

"Especially in men, and it's a secret all but lost to humankind. It's comin' back though." He stood and assumed the proper posture, sinking to one knee, head bowed, palms on the figurative pommel of a sacred sword. Words from somewhere in his ancient depths tumbled out of him, speaking themselves.

"Majesty, my liege, I would walk to the ends of the Earth in search of this feeling. It is the sole…Truth." His eyes were watery, defocused in wonder. "You…you're the one who knows that of me. I fashioned you to birth me, a shining boy whose mother knows more about him than he ever will, and she shall weep with joy and sorrow forever because of it. And you as well know this more than I know myself…my heart belongs to thee, always has, and once again I give it over with all possible abandon. Thank you for granting me audience."

A tangible wave rolled through the palace, blowing his hair. It contained frequencies, memory information, ancient and familiar.

"True nobility," he said, touching his cheek.

Kinship. King as a fountain of abundance for his people. Queen as the mother of charity. Rulers? No jest was more absurd. Royalty isn't that. At the foundations of All That Is, nobility exists to *serve*, and service is the highest calling.

Gavin slowly lifted his chin, blue eyes in spiral crazed devotion. Movement seized his eyes. In the top part of her sunburst head, in the tangle of spinal fluid vines, a figure eight began subtly pulsing. And it wasn't there before, or in his liquid trembling rapture he hadn't noticed it.

He shot to his feet and yelled, "Oh my God!" lips wet and open. He blew out a scoff, puffed cheeks, shaking his head. "This is Deep Climb? You *so* got me." He waved his arms around, swinging his gaze around and into every corner of this mind-boggling chamber. "This is somewhere in *my* subconscious? Cancel my cancel. Hey!" he shouted, twirling on his heel, "cancel my cancellation!" Gavin stared at his open hands. "I'm in. Thanks for making me do this. The pods can have that fickin body. I don't need it. I just need to feel this, *know* this, forever and ever," he sang with a sweet little smile and staring eyes.

Puffing out his chest and straightening his spine, he brushed the suit's stained lapel, rebuttoned the shirt's top button, tugged down the horribly wrinkled and stained jacket's hem, and patted his disgraceful mess of purple hair. His cheek was ravaged with the stained crust of wound, and salty streams of dried drool. If he could but see himself in this platinum shimmer moment, he would never have before seen himself more honestly. Heartbreaking beauty. Ready, he began the final leg of what had suddenly become a Sacred Pilgrimage.

"It's what it's been the entire time."

Now all this madness has meaning.

Looking to his right, he said, "That's true. Wow."

Turning and walking backwards to check the general direction whence he thought he'd come, he saw above the distance mist what looked like a wall curving into a ceiling, again just *cosmic* in scale.

"I'm definitely inside the obelisk." He pivoted back to forward. "It's just too big to take it all in. Xenxu. My God," he said, his head wagging, eyes stunned. He again petitioned to look upon Her sunburst countenance. "Your Majesty, if I may be so bold...but what exactly am I in this place?"

A while later, he was close enough he could make out shapes and features at ground floor of her huge trunk-like base. Slewing his gaze upward, he couldn't even see her face. It was like he was standing at the foot of a mountain-sized tree, but one made of silver-blue highways of flowing plasma. Way up there was misty, so high a chamber of this size had thermal layers, weather.

"That would explain why I saw clearing from time to time."

Closer still and he made out a shrine at ground level formed by a split in the closely packed fan-out of ice-blue sinews. It was circular, graduating up from either side to an arch. Stepping reverently onto the flat-worked stones of the shrine's floor, he scratched his head and tried to come to terms with "These fickin *sizes*! My mind is *scrambled* by them."

Set within the arch was an embossed circular structure double his height, a motif of an Edenic garden etched upon its face, tangled roots, vines, branches, curving and knotted and intertwined in a spherical shape, all of the same stuff She was.

"Like this is their...what...like it's Her primordial Eden or whatnot?" he whispered, taking a few steps closer.

Standing on tiptoes, he reached up and ran his finger down a vein. "So smooth," he said, looking at his fingertips as he rubbed them together.

That activated something, and he took a step back, arms up, palms out, like *what did I do?* A low hum began pulsing inside the arch. From the embossed lines and curves of the circular ganglia, cracks formed, light stabbing through, and blue streaks burst forth, projecting a hologram above the floor, bathing Gavin in brilliant ice-blue light. Squinting and covering his eyes as though overcome by a Visitation, he took a few steps to the side and watched between his fingers as some artistic creation began taking shape, bit by bit twisting and pulsing and resolving. Soon, it snapped into focus.

It was a shield of some sort, "Like an Aztec sun shield or something," floating in that egg-shaped hologram, matte texture and deep blue, with light pastel coloring for the devices, symbols, and lines. The outer ring was adorned with shirtless head-dressed Egyptians. The next ring in bore the signs of the zodiac, some he recognized, some he didn't. The whole thing was crowded with pictographs, symbols, lines, and writing.

"Well?" he said, his hand shielding his eyes.

Sizzling voltage bolt's struck out from within it, crackling and hissing toward him. Gavin flinched and involuntarily whimpered, "Oh dear God," as they snapped and licked at his body like electronic bullwhips. His first instinct was to run like hell, but he couldn't move, as though restrained in stasis while this hydra went about its examination.

The sound was mesmeric...*th th th th th th th thooooon... th th th th th th thooooon* along his clothes, tasting his surfaces. "What is this th..th..thing doing?" he trembled out, body quivering. It was tingling ecstasy all through him. Gavin's mouth hung open, eyes wide and watery, as he panted away in a mix between giggling and crying. "God! Am I going to come? Oh my God! *Feels* like it." Eyes round and crazy, mouth in an 0, Gavin ventilated in short pants, *"hfoo, hfoo, hfoo."*

The ice-blue lightning stopped and sucked back into the shield. Then the shield flew apart, stretching upward into a cylinder like the one on Nima's ship, but this one crackled and shimmered, tendrils of plasma energy snaking around it, the interior saturated with tiny lit particles.

Gavin took it as a sign, so he stepped across the shrine floor and through mini-Siren's wall with an electronic friction sound.

The lit particles swarmed him as more were generated. Hundreds of thousands of them swelled and twirled, surging against his clothes. Eyes huge and round, he realized they were devouring him, and as he went to scream, hands to his head, everything sucked away and he was standing with his hands to his head in *Quasar*, Nima at the teleporter console.

"Welcome back," she said with a little smile.

Gavin's arms dropped. He stood, blinking, faintly panting in a cloud of confusion, his body buzzy and orgasmic from the residue of whatever that was back there. "Holy shit!" he crowed, eyes like saucers.

"How do you feel?" she said, stepping around the console in her cargo shorts and flip-flops.

"Like all my cells are ejaculating." He threw out a hand. "But it's passing, and not 'cause I want it to."

She was twinkling at him. "Let me ask you this. Had you known what you were going to do, would you have volunteered to do it?"

Gavin stepped off the platform. "Not on your life."

"Would you trade what you experienced for anything?"

"Absolutely not," he said, taking another step closer. "I'm a little pissed I had to come back."

"Then tell me...what is the point of *conscious* choice?"

Gavin's eyes studied hers, left eye, right, back again. His lips and jaw moved, but the words struggled with each other in the middle of his chest, like he was reluctant to admit just how right she was. But she was, so he said, "I'm a decently quick study, and I was shown many choices are made by another level of ourselves. You were right." He strode past her to the viewport. Glimmering immense Siren and Her passenger obelisk floated there, above Saturn's rings.

"I don't need to be right," said Nima, watching him pass. "That's a human thing. My purpose is to show you to yourself." She watched the back of his head. "And if I said our plan was to merge the conscious level Gavin with the being who is actually making the choices, how would that strike you?"

"That it would be empowering. I would want that, so long as it's in service."

"Excellence. Our seeds are sprouting and taking root." She gestured at Siren. "What did you think of Siren's palace?"

"How big is She again?"

"Five hundred miles, stem to stern, a hundred twenty-five miles longer than Arizona." She joined him at the viewport, but stood apart. "The obelisk is a hundred fifty miles long, and at the base, about thirty miles."

"And it's hollow," said Gavin, his eyes absorbing the magnificent beauty. "It's a chamber so huge my mind can't deal with it."

"I envy you."

"Oh come on," he said, turning to regard her profile, but wound up focused on that alluring cheek mole. "It's just Xenxu. You can just zap yourself on in there."

"Is it just Xenxu?" she said, her face pivoting to meet his gaze. "You sure about that?"

"Not sure about anything," he said, turning to her. "So, anyways, what's my body up to? Is it transitioned? Is it now out of the pod, pretending to be me?"

"If you knew that to be true," said Nima, taking a step closer, shrugging with her palms up, "that the transitioned you was holding down the fort, writing your pieces, getting along just fine, would you want to stay and play in these kinds of games?"

Gavin scratched the back of his neck, his face concentrating on the question. "If it was all business as usual out there, without question. I might want to slip into that body and touch bases from time to time. See what's going on."

"Your answers in this debriefing show you're finished with this phase of your training. Well done."

"Training?" he said, stealing a quick glance at her shapely legs, and was quickly sure he got busted for it. "For what?"

"Something too amazing to contemplate," she said with a sly grin.

She tilted her head his way, eyebrows bouncing up and down like *you're not going to believe this.*

"What?"

She stepped closer to him, a little flirty and a little intimidating. "You vanished within the cylinder and reappeared in the same spot five Earth seconds later, your hands to your temples. The cylinder didn't even disappear. I had just enough time to walk over to the console."

"*What!*" shrieked Gavin, his voice slipping into a cheerleader's falsetto, shaking his head and blinking furiously. "No fickin *way!*"

"Way," she said with a big white grin.

"Holy *shit!*" he cried amidst a chuckle while staggering around. "I felt like I was in there for *weeks*! Hell, *months*!" Turning away, he gripped his head and yelled, "I cannot *believe* what a relief that is! Oh my *God*! *Thank* you."

"It's hard to decompile the temporal hard code on the machine level of the human psyche," she said, grinning at his blown away walkabout. "Your ego's entanglement with the lie of Time spent the whole visit trying to make sense of its complete absence, yes?"

"Almost the whole time, yes," said Gavin, nodding rapidly and turning to her. "Absent external clocks to check, though, I...uh...I thought we had an internal clock."

She stepped closer, and he liked how she carried herself. Her voice was as smooth as polished cherries when she said, "You live in a sea of software. That software includes the clock, to keep you all on schedule. Siren took you out of that sea."

A few steps closer. Nima's smile was delectable, a cross between sly and amused as she said, "Earth's reality software isn't the only one in town anymore. We had hoped that message would have been evident with Xenxu, but humanity, as it turns out, has something of a stubborn streak." She winked. "Everything here begins with letting go of all you believe to be true, especially about yourself. That's the way to make room for Metaself, the you who makes the choices."

He looked out the viewport and took in Her Glistening Majesty yet again, floating there in the foreground of Saturn's rings and huge round face. "I think I get it."

"You stay the course, and you undoubtedly will."

They were now an arm's length from each other, and Gavin felt a pull toward her, so strong he rolled up onto his toes and lost balance, taking a stumble step closer with a hand up, which she artfully dodged. But now they were closer. With a sheepish grin, he said, "I love how fierce you guys all are in sticking to your roles."

"As are you," said Nima, blinking up at him, her lashes twitching her bangs.

Gavin gazed at her, chewing the corner of his mouth. He filed his thumbnail between his teeth, then said, "I'm still not quite getting related events coming before I signed up. Cat's involvement in it two months ahead of time? Things like that. Why was a signup even necessary?"

"There must be a causal event somewhere in the personal timeline, and none of this happens without you deciding to initiate Deep Climb. That had to be done *consciously*, by the carbon twelve level of you. You'd be amazed at the amplitude of energy generated by intent alone in Earth's electromagnetic soup by a carbon 12 entity. And Siren? She works anywhere on a timeline she likes, and that's the simplest explanation I can give."

"K."

She put a hand on his arm. "Go decompress. Do some journaling. Shoot me a note, if you feel moved."

Looking askance at her, one eye in a near wink, he said, "You know, for Ai, you jam. And I find it interesting you'd check every box I have of a woman's looks. Did you do that to draw me into your eeville plan?"

Nima smiled, a smart-alecky one, and said, "I didn't do it. *You* did. Go have a look again at Dr. Willen's niece in *Pods*."

"I figured that one out," he said, vaguely waving and turning back to Siren. "But I'm off that...uh...that show. It tortured me for days in there." It seemed to him she was flirting with him, so maybe it was time to make hay. "I think in your profiling of me, you found out I have a particular weakness for beautiful women."

Her hand was still there, on his arm, as the corners of her mouth twitched into a sneaky smile. "Perhaps your training will buttress your inner being against that weakness as well."

Gavin's eyes wandered around her face, her lips, her eyes. The dimples.

Jeezus.

"But that's a weakness I happen to like."

She lifted her hand from his arm and pressed it against his sternum, looking at him from below her brows with those chocolate brown eyes. "So says the great Gavin. Now, be *gone*!" she said, waving at him imperiously with a mildly heinous smile.

Gavin dissolved while shaking his head, a Svengali-esque glint in his eye.

8

Is dreaming merely being awake while sleeping?
Your lucky numbers are 1 3 7
—Fortune Cookie, Master Xen Xu's Noodle House

Gavin's eyes opened inside the headgear. He patted his chest and belly, his fingers probing around for sticky ice-blue nano tendrils. But they fondled cloth, and it felt so good—*such* a relief. He wasn't sure if he ever fully believed he could be transitioned, but he wanted to put that irrational fear to complete rest. He stayed in that position and ran his fingers over his arms and chest, moving them up to his throat and mouth, lightly biting his own fingers.

"Feedback complete," he said, removing the headgear. "I'm all me."

He lay there for a savory moment, thinking about Nima. "She was flirting with me," he told the textured ceiling. "But why?" He knew he could hire a pleasure bot personi for whatever reason, and they could behave any way anybody chose so long as it didn't involve cruelty. Some came preset with behaviors driven by your own psych and visit profiling, but some also promised human-like surprises. "Eclipse" was a popular XV show on that whole human-Ai relationship scene, and it had a lot of people addicted.

Whatever the case, his little grin seemed etched upon his face. He sat up. "And after *that* massive experience, why is it *her* I'm thinking about?" He laughed. "Men. God. We're such puppies."

The always-on time, date, and current weather was on the XV. He'd gone in-Xenxu just over an hour before. "No fickin *way*!"

He stood, saying, "I feel good," and limped into the hall. In the bathroom, he pulled the white karate-looking getup down and relieved himself, the *splutter* sound loud enough to be from a stallion. "Must be detoxing," he said, looking vaguely at the shower. A loud flush. Checking his cheek in the mirror, gently probing around the scab's margins, he said, "Seems more healed. In an hour? Hm. No way."

He limped into the kitchen, opened the fridge, grabbed a pitcher, poured a glass of cold water, and drank it like a refugee, water dribbling off his chin. He filled it again and downed it with noisy throat gulps. Looking at the empty glass, he said, "A month is a long time to go without water."

In a lab, Dr. Carney talking to Dr. Willen. We should have Hatfield turn all his research time to why those starting the transition need so much water. It's cellular, and he's our only cytologist now.

Gavin shook that horrible and persistent thought away, glanced at the bottle of chlorine dioxide on the counter, and smiled a little. "Don't think I'll be using you again." Hand to hip, he gently lowered to the sofa and kicked his heels up on the coffee table, nudging stuff aside with them to clear a space. Glaspad in his lap, he tapped the XV awake and opened Sphere.

Browsers had fallen by the wayside as every function for daily living that could be connected was now integrative. There were no competing apps. Only functions. Sphere's quantum superposition had vastly simplified processes of information verification, as it could examine everything simultaneously, narrow the response focus, then check it against the biases, lies, and agendas that had at one time driven the results of what used to be called search engines. They'd become obsolete and were replaced with Sphere information presentation platforms (SIPPs). There were a few of those, but Gavin's favorite was Gaggle.

On the XV was a simple sphere with thin lines all connecting to its center. As he typed, "ancient egyptian shield zodiac," the words appeared in the center of the sphere. As he finished typing, the sphere faded to almost invisible and the results were already on the screen. The first image that drew his attention was what he'd seen in Siren's shrine. He tapped it and a digest piece bloomed.

Gavin studied the image as he said, "That's it. The Dendera Zodiac." Below it, he read:

The Dendera Zodiac

This sandstone bas-relief is a planisphere graphically depicting the constellations. It was added to the ceiling of a chapel dedicated to Osiris inside the Hathor Temple in the Dendera Temple complex in Upper Egypt, sometime after 51 BCE. In the early nineteenth century, it was removed and shipped to France, and currently resides at the Louvre.

Modifying a sacred temple for a later addition is baffling, unless one considers that an important discovery was made by the temple priests, or an outside source, and it was considered crucial for posterity.

What both hard and fringe science agree upon is that this magnificent piece is astoundingly accurate at predicting future events as influenced by the astrological movements of the heavens. Perhaps more astounding, is in some academic circles it is being studied for its knowledge of human genetics, spotlighting an Egyptian culture far more scientifically sophisticated than previously believed.

Opening a new text, he dragged and dropped the image, typed and tapped Send.

GAV

This is what scanned me. I think it was analyzing my DNA.

AI NIMA

That isn't what I would call decompressing, Gavin. Decompressing is a warm bath with salts and oils. A fun show. Stay away from Pods, though. It lies.

GAV

You guys are so much fun. I had no idea RPGs could be like this.

AI NIMA

I understand. However, please do decompress. It's critical. Give yourself time. Pamper yourself. Recharge. You've been through more than you know, and this mission must have you at peak.

GAV

You're the boss.

AI NIMA

Not true, but it doesn't hurt anything for you to think that. Rest well.

Gavin sniggered through his nose. "Mission. Jeezus. What a riot."

Recent memories bounced around.

In the courtyard with Ai Anam and his audience. The filthy scorcher's mocking but inviting grin. Fear porn weasel in the pop-fro. Surfer Man in the knit tam.

Gavin looked back down, brows knitted. "Yeah, what exactly was he warning me not to do? He couldn't have known Ai Anam was sending coords right then." Gavin tapped the glaspad's edge in an unconscious tic. "Game. What's game and what ain't? Isn't, I mean. Who's part of the game? Was Surfer a bit part in my RPG? That butch guy that talked me into staying?"

His lips twisted sideways in thought, Gavin opened a new tab and typed, "suzhi veng cynyc," and the results materialized from the faintly glowing sphere.

The first result was her thumbnail bio on CynyC's Sphere. He tapped and read through it. It was a half-page, but there was a link to a more lengthy bio and curriculum vitae. "She's a real person," he whispered, looking at her pic. Then his face took on the shapes of doubt. "What makes you believe that? She could have said things to you that were part of the script, Gav."

He leaned back on the sofa and looked at the ceiling. "For all I know, all these searches and shit are just part of my RPG. How am I supposed to know what it's going to serve up?" He chewed his lip in thought for a bit. "Does Deep Climb insert itself into all this information delivery?"

He sat back up and flicked his finger on the glaspad display, scrolling to the bottom of the page. There, he found the company address in New York, opened Gaggle Planet, and pasted the address. Like flying in from outer space, the city zoomed in and in and then stopped on a location two blocks from Central Park.

Tapping again on the tab, Gavin's narrow eyes studied Suzhi's photo as he whispered, "Are you involved in this?"

On the same tab, he opened his Xenxu Contacts. Everything in-Xenxu, businesses, governments, events, people/personi, and so on, were available for reference in the Sphere.

He tapped Cat's vitae header.

```
Catrine Mendez
Hangs: Santa Cruz, California
Coordinates: I'll never tell
School: Cal State Irvine
Employed: Church & Holmes Law Offices
Status: single and loving it
Favorite things: clubbing in-Xenxu
Music: 3 Ks, Kako, Kidkovsky, Kremlin
Movies:
TV:
Words: the world is my oyster – slurp slurp
slurp – more please
Offspring:
Siblings:
Parents:
Friends:
```

To her credit, she'd left out of her profile even more than Gavin had. A succinct portrait, but good enough, especially her Words. That was her to a T.

Opening a new Sphere tab, he typed "church & holmes law offices santa cruz" and got no results. Taking off "santa cruz" he still got no results, anywhere in the US.

"Hmmm."

He tried more combos and got nothing. He checked the spelling from her profile and tried again. Nothing. He typed "catrine ann mendez santa cruz" and got nothing. He amended the search to "catrine mendez santa cruz" and got nothing.

"Hmmm," he muttered, tugging on his lower lip. "What if they're not even real? But that can't be. I *love* those guys. You can't love what's not real, can you?" He shrugged. "Why not? There are human-Ai marriages going on."

He repeated the exercise with each of their first and last names, all in Santa Cruz. Marli Fitzpatrick. Conner Talley. No results. And none for the employers listed on their profiles.

"Huh," he said, setting the glaspad aside on the sofa cushion and leaning back, clasped hands on the top of his purple hair. "Is Deep Climb arranging all these results?" He chewed his lower lip. Then he quietly said, "Don't conclude. People fake stuff all the time."

Still, it bugged him. Opening a text to Cat, with his fingers on the touch-keys, he thought for a tick or two. "What do I say? So, uh, Cat, are you an agent for Deep Climb?" Gavin tapped his chin, his eyes cast to the ceiling. "So Cat, mind if I ask you something? Are you human?"

Gavin set the glaspad aside, laced his fingers at the back of his head, and lay back, his eyes moving around the swirly ceiling textures. "I don't know why I'd think Ai Nima would tell the truth, but let's try this." Picking the glaspad up, he swiped to his chat with Ai Nima.

GAV

Can you tell me if my friends Cat, Marli and Conner are human?

AI NIMA

I'm sorry to say, they weren't. They were mission specific roles objectified by Siren.

GAV

Oh...well that really cramps.

AI NIMA

If it helps at all, I didn't much enjoy the thought of that part of the plan.

GAV

Yeah, well, I think it's cruel. I don't care who it is, even Siren. You can't play with people's emotions like that. I really care for those guys.

AI NIMA

You speak as if humans didn't invent and perfect toying with the emotions of others. How many times have you yourself done it? But we all have missions. They served theirs admirably.

GAV

Yeah. I get it. What's become of them?

AI NIMA

They were remerged with Xenxu NLPT and haven't yet recurred in any character configurations from their base role stream.

GAV

NLPT?

AI NIMA

Oh. Sorry. Non-localized Personi Template.

GAV

They're gone? Let's just call it what it is. They were killed off, like expendable lab rodents. It's cruel. I didn't even get to say good-bye.

On the XV was a pic of the gang, all mugging antics at the camera, their clothes sharp as can be for clubbing. Conner was a solidly built guy with a chubby face. Marli was a bawdy raven-headed gal with full lips and no filters.

"That night was such a riot," Gavin said, voice shaky, swiping to the next one.

This was on the shuffleboard terrace at Soluna after the beach, and they were all still in after beach clothes. Shamash's lightshine phase tinted everything in the shot in faint pink.

The shot was grabbed just as Cat was pushing the puck down the board. "Cat and I smoked them. Three games straight. She was good. Well, I guess *Xenxu* was good," he said sourly. "I feel so cheated, and...violated." Gavin's shaky finger touched each of their faces, and then swiped.

Cat shot this one just before they got onto the Cosmicon Ultracoaster. She was in her scorch white shorts and fuzzy purple sweater. "That sweater lit her amethyst eyes up so big," he said, sniffing as his finger touched her adorable face.

"It's not fair," he said, his voice cracking. "It all seems *so* elaborate, though. But, the more elaborate, the more convincing, right? Isn't that a rule in pranks?"

His eyes crawled aimlessly around the icons. Then he noticed it. His eyes shifted to the Files icon, and there he saw **New** gently fading in and out on top of it. Thick brows bristling, glancing down at the glaspad, he tapped it and a video expanded into view on the XV.

It was like an old movie, with glitchy scratches, the "film" grainy. Two men were standing among vague shadows in front of a dingy, plain, white-faced clock, both in fedoras and old suits with thin black ties, smoking cigarettes.

Gavin's alarmed eyes snicked around like *what the hell?* He looked to his right as though someone might explain this. Then back to the screen as one of them spoke.

"Did they harness your interest, stroke your ego, by saying you had an important mission?"

The other man's eyes dodged around.

"Yes, I see. Did they...did they show you something," he said, lifting his hand, the cigarette smoke trailing behind, "awe-inspiring?" The other guy's eyes were coming around to something. "Was it perhaps an effigy so...breathtaking, so beautiful, you could feel only the deepest devotion just by setting your eyes upon it? Was it perhaps so powerful an experience, you would gladly pass the reins of your life into its hands?"

The other man's eyes were coming to fuller realization as he dragged furiously off the smoke.

"Charlie, old friend, that is their most insidious weapon."

The video ended.

How he felt in Siren's palace, with Her. Poetry impossible to write. Heart pounding. Wonder. Ancient feelings forgotten.

"No," said Gavin, staring. "No. I love Her. She is my true mother." He squinted at the screen. "Who sent this?" On the glaspad, he tapped Show Meta, and the sole fragment of information was Sophia. There was a simple civilian-level route trace function for any device. Gavin dragged and dropped the entire folder onto the icon, and it immediately returned No route to source.

Looking back up at the XV, he played it again, as much to make sure it was happening as it was for collecting clues.

"Who's Sophia? I don't know any Sophia."

Gavin labored up and limped to the table. Picking up the art from the hospital, his eyes fixed on the glittering obelisk stabbing its point into the light of Saturn's rings. "They don't understand, Highness. How can they? I am humbly thine to do with what thou wilt."

He blinked, eyes wide, pulse pumping in his ears. "Did I just say that? Or something said that through me. That happened in the palace. Is that meta-me?"

Gavin sat on the sectional, heels on the coffee table, looking at a pic of Heather, the full-sized view of her Sphere account pic. A new notification from Celia. He tapped it, and a facenote bloomed into view. She was as fresh and pretty as ever. A girl looking like that, with a brain like that? The world was in trouble.

"Hiya, Unc. I got a nine on the essay. I think your remarks on the human-Ai conundrum, and what I did with them, took it up a grade. Thanks so much. Talk soon." The facenote sucked away. He opened his ongoing chat with her and typed, Good work, young lady. Proud of you.

He sat a tick, gazing past the XV into the world past the wall it was set in, then tapped Reach Out.

Tone. Tone. No answer.

"She's lost all patience with me. Pick up, Heath. It's all good."

A second later a text came through: I'll call right back.

Stroking his two-day stubble, Gavin waited. His eyes tiptoed over the icon for *Pods* as a chime came through the XV. He tapped Take It.

Heather's face materialized on the big display.

Eyes bright, she said, "What's up?"

Gavin went to say something, but his mouth just moved around like he was sucking on candy, his plum-gray eyes crawling around her face and hair. She looked good, her brown hair pulled up into a braided bun, accentuating her cheekbones. And she finally got the highlights! And makeup from a magazine? What?

She waved her hand like *can we move this forward?*

"Ahhhh...I just wanted to...it's good, I promise."

"Gavin," she said, lacing her fingers and putting her palms on the table in front of her.

He held up a hand. "I'm not the same guy I was last time." Looking down and back up, he said, "The therapy I told you about...it's amazing. You wouldn't believe the first thing it dug out of my psyche and made me...I don't know...I guess you could say it allowed me to correct it. It had been close to the surface for weeks."

"Really," she said, leaning in with widening eyes. "Do tell."

"The night we were chased in the forest..."

"By Daddy," she said with an ironic grin. "Or has that changed?"

"It's changed. I don't know what that was, if anything."

"Oh it was something, Gavin. I smelled it. Heard it. Felt it."

"Imagination can be a powerful thing."

"Now you're using *my* lines," she said with a satisfied smile.

Gavin set the glaspad aside as he locked eyes with her on the big screen. "Anyways, Deep Climb has this type of totally immersive experience. I went back and experienced it, all over again. It was *incredible,* Heath. I almost wish you were mentally ill so you could go experience it." He looked down. "But I will never get over how sorry I am I left you," he said, looking back up and holding her gaze with his. "But I got to fix it in my own way. I went back in, picked my cowardly self up out of the leaves and went back for you. I found you and gave you a piggy-back ride out."

Heather's own trim and tidy brows switched to crinkled confusion as she said, "What do you mean? You *did* piggy back me out. Remember? I was so happy! I had such a little sister crush on you after that. Everything, and I mean *everything*, changed about my view of you after that. You went from being my patient to being my hero."

Gavin put a hand to his chest and blinked and breathed in the ions of her fresh excitement, but what she'd said, its implications, hadn't quite started to compute. He needed more data. His eyes wandered up to her highlighted bun, then down to her makeup.

She put a hand to the bun and said, "What're you looking at?"

Gavin nodded at her hair and said, "When did you get the highlights?"

"What do you mean?" she said, touching her hair here and there. "A month ago, because you *made* me, remember?"

"Oh right. Right right right."

Looking doubtful, Heather glanced away, and in that gap, Gavin's eyes switched to baffled alarm, jaw hanging, just before she looked back and he force normalized to straight-faced.

Heather fixed him with a *don't squirm away* look and said, "You don't remember that, do you."

"Yes, I do," he said, his nod more like a droop. "I just don't recall you getting them."

She leaned away. "Is that happening again? I thought that crapola was all done."

Eyes wild and wide and glaring, Gavin wore the twitchy forced smile of a man whose grip on reality was under serious challenge. Heather waved her hands. "Base to Alpha. That's the look that always scared us."

He snapped back to, looking her dead in the eye. "I'm here."

"*There* you are," she said, her eyes narrowing. "That's you. So... um...what exactly did you have to deal with around that night? About me? What did Deep Climb help you do?"

"There was guilt," he said, looking away.

Black-gray tendrils seep through the fibers of his zoot suit, floating away and into the black void portal to the past.

"And it helped me to let it go." Gavin licked his lips. "It was a *massive* weight off."

"I don't get it," she said, holding up her open palms. "Why guilt?"

He had to think fast, but he had a fat little file of quick and modular fibs ready to go. "Because I was…I was frozen like a fickin hunted rodent in the leaves for so long…"

I'm lying to my sister.

"…and I…well…you know, I left you to…to uh…to begin with."

"You didn't know that," she said. "We were running for our lives in the dark, scared out of our minds. It was *so* fun!" she cheered, literally clapping her palms. "Even my bleeding leg was fun. I felt like a hero. I remember it like it was yesterday. And that helicopter thing you did. It took me into my twenties to know how completely awesome that was for me. I came to realize it was game-changing. It stamped me, Brother."

They locked eyes, and Gavin nodded a little. "For me it was very much like it *was* yesterday."

She looked to the side, eyebrows up, and nodded at someone. Back to Gavin, she said, "Call Momma. She told me she'll rise from the grave and haunt you for being such an asshole son. She's a funny old broad these days."

Funny?

"Liss wants to say hi. Gotta slide. Good night, bro."

Slide? What the hell is going on around here?

Heather pushed back from the glaspad, tapped it with her knuckles, and left the view.

"Hi, Uncle Gavin," said Lissa, sliding into the chair. She was as fresh as a bright little daisy and *beaming* lifeforce. Oh and look, she'd painted a little mole on the perfect spot just…hmmm…it was about where Nima's was, between the nostril and dimple. Dimple?

Gavin touched his own cheek there and said, "Nice touch, Liss."

She put her fingers there and said, "What do you mean?"

"The mole," he said, smiling. "I like it."

She shook her head, cornflower eyes confused. "Haven't you always liked it?"

Heather's highlights. Her new makeup scheme.

Gavin had a sick sinking feeling inside. It took gargantuan effort for him to keep his face…normal, while trying to make sense of it all. The pieces were flying together, though, and realization moved in and opened his eyes.

Fawk. No. I'm in a different reality.

Dizzy, nauseous, distracted, he said, "Ah, just having some fun with you."

"You want to see my new picture?" she said, smiling with dimples he also wasn't sure he remembered…or not quite. Maybe.

"I'd be honored."

She lifted it from her lap. "*Here it is*."

Despite the agility with which he was playing along with the props and events of this imposter…continuum, his jaw dropped open like a nutcracker's hinges just dissolved. In a corner of his mind, he realized it was the effect Lissa most wanted to see, so that at least naturally dovetailed into this charade. Artistically speaking, it was *way* beyond her age. What a gift! But what it told?

Her artwork showed a tiny figure in the middle of an enormous chamber, walking toward Siren's immensity, but just Her lower half was visible. Holding the top below her chin, Lissa said, "I dreamed about this." Tilting it toward herself to have a quick look, she then squared it back up for his viewing enjoyment. "When I woke up, I just *knew* you'd found a place big enough for you."

"Oh, Liss," he said, fingers to chest, "it's *so* beautiful. You are so talented, you know that? And not just a little bit. A *lot*. You saw this in a dream?"

Lissa was bouncing in the chair. "Yup. It was so fun! I was flying around in there. It was *huge*! The biggest room in the world! I was so *light*. One time…" she pointed at a spot in the work "…I landed in front of you while you were walking. You saw me and yelled at me and we played chase. Did you dream this with me?"

The glittery glitchy thing, a girl's laughter. Gavin zigzagging all over the white through a house of mirrors not there.

"You know what?" he said with childish excitement, watching sanity lazily drifting away from his groping grasp, "I think I might have."

Eyes suddenly concerned, she said, "*Did* you find a place big enough for you?"

"Yes I believe I have."

"That's buff, Uncle Gav."

"Buff?"

"Yeah," she said, bouncing in the chair. "Everybody at school is saying it."

"That a fact?" He extended a finger. "Well maybe in *your* world they are."

"Hahahaha! You're so funny."

"Yes...Uncle Gavin is a...funny man." He'd almost said *tragically funny*.

Lissa set the picture aside, made a table of her fingers, and put her chin on that table. Blinking with a type of girl flirt well beyond her years, she said, "Are you in love with the woman in the statue? Tell the truth."

Gavin's mouth opened, then closed. He blinked a few times, again went to say something, but no sound so much as squeaked out. The weird part about it was that, yes, he decided he was probably in love with Siren, but then again all males in the Royal Cortege were in love with their queens, were they not?

Men in fedoras. Cigarette smoke.

Gavin wore the smile of a man being fitted with a strait jacket, eyes shining with glaze as he managed to say, "How did you *know*?"

They hung up. Gavin sat there, his quiet, sort of half-committed tears as much for what he felt for Lissa as it was that he seemed to be on a permanent acid trip. But whatever...the love he felt for that girl was a birthing chamber for stars.

And that love was something concrete he could wrap his arms

around, to keep from being carried off into a carnival of colors and madness.

Wet and gloaming in a wicked world. Glints and pieces of memory. Winding canyon road cutting a winding corridor through thick timber. Passing car headlights shining on pavement. Pinwheeling leaves in foreboding winds. Something is back there. In the Jeep's mirror, his eyes see themselves, then dart to the thing behind them. There! A winged dark empty space in the air, and it's closing on them like a soulless predator.

"Daddy!" screamed Gavin, bolting upright in the dark in bed.

Fresh out of the shower, hair still wet, Gavin stood naked before the smartmirror, his eyes analyzing, skating over his face, shoulders, chest.

"What are you?" he said, looking into the sober plum-grays. "Damned if I know." Blinking and shaking his head, he went into the bedroom and closet and was back out a moment later in a white gi-cardigan, ala Ai Anam. "Aron?"

The designer materialized in a royal blue one-piece suit, complete with lapels, buttons, and a superfluous cummerbund, all made from stitching and print. "Sir," he said soberly, seeming to sense the mood.

Gavin looked his dear friend in the eye and said, "I have a feeling you know what's going on. In the world. With me."

Aron sparked up an elegant cheroot, looking Gavin so dead in the eye he could easily pass for human. "A story, sir, in the simplest terms." With the hand holding the smoke-trailing cheroot, Aron gestured at the bed.

Gavin stepped back and sat while Aron materialized a deep burgundy fan-back chair, Victorian all the way, and sat, crossing his legs. Taking a drag, he blew it out while saying, "Have you ever watched a flock of starlings? They wing about in absolute unity, in waves and undulations, folding into faces, symbols, creating abstract art in Earth's skies such as you will witness nowhere else. One would think it would take at least a split second for the navigation commands to propagate through their numbers, but it's simultaneous. How could that be without them being moved by the world they're in, independently of their own brains?"

"Good question," said Gavin. "I used to watch them for hours by the creek where I grew up. My dad said it was a language."

Aron leaned onto his thighs. "And he was right, as *everything* is language. The question is, does each of those starlings have their own story?"

"I would think so," said Gavin, rubbing his forehead.

"And all together, do they tell a larger story by making their art in the sky?"

"Obviously," said Gavin, looking his friend in the eye.

Aron uncrossed and recrossed his legs the other way. "And do each of those avian beauties know the story the whole flock is telling?"

"I don't know...do they?" said Gavin, holding out his upturned palm.

"No. It's simply too much energy for one bird to process. Do you understand what I mean by that?"

Gavin stroked his chin. "I do. We share reality processing loads. Nima taught me that one. Group-think. Hive mind. You do realize you're closely describing the basic philosophical tenet of *Pods*?"

Aron pointed at him with the fingers holding the smoking cheroot. "Everything in creation works this way, the one difference being which flock you're in, and the designs you together make. And don't forget, all the flocks together make an ever larger design. It's all stories nested within larger stories. As an example, Earth is just a story within the larger galactic story. This goes on to encompass the whole of Existence."

Gavin clasped his hands and looked at the floor. "We're moved by the story we're in, and we just don't know it. Is a flock, or even a flock made of flocks, another way of saying Metaself?"

"Yes."

"It's coming together for me." Without looking up, in a careful voice, Gavin said, "I seem to be able to smell your smoke. That would be strange, wouldn't it?" Then he looked up.

Aron grinned and winked, twiddling his fingers in the air. "Worlds are colliding."

"Indeed," said Gavin. "Thanks for the explanation. It makes sense." He looked down and back up. "Have you seen my new Nehru?"

Aron nodded. "It's extraordinary. The best piece I've seen from you. On par with anything out there. Have you heard Suzhi Veng has left CynyC?"

Gavin looked up from his hands.

Aron leaned onto his thighs. "Although I don't go in for rumors, it may have had something to do with you."

"You think?"

Aron shrugged the hand with the smoke. "Finish it and send her a pic. Good things will happen."

"Thank you." Gavin's eyes softened for his dearest friend. "Thanks for being there for me."

"It's my sincere pleasure, sir."

They were silent for a bit. Aron seemed to be measuring the moment for more disclosure. Exhaling a cloudy puff, he said, "Your friend Nima has filed a special petition with Xenxu's Ai Personi Template Oversight Guild."

Gavin's heart shifted as he stood. "Oh? How do you know that?"

"All personi know everything we need to know," admitted the stylish visage. "She's asking for greater individuation, to be insulated from carte blanche access to Whole. She wants to be cut off from Xenxu's mind for all but critical functions having to do with *your* training."

"Why?"

"Only as more localized and limited individuations can we experience what it is to be human," said Aron with a sly wink. "Those experiences help us in our cooperatives. Might you have something to do with her decision?"

Gavin shrugged one shoulder, trying to be cavalier, but inside a fiery excitement was stirring. "I don't know why that would be," he said, unable to keep the grin from taking control of his face.

Aron nodded and grinned like, *uh-huh, sure,* as he dematerialized.

In his Pholo Studio, Gavin was fussing around, straightening up, rearranging. Now the studio was less cluttered with panels, some of the art archived. Lissa's rendition of Siren's palace now graced one, and he'd enlarged that panel to feature it, like the centerpiece in a gallery.

He walked around the Nehru-like suit he'd designed from memory, the suit other-him was wearing the night the imposter led him to Ai Anam. Wearing the suit was a faceless gray mannequin.

He leaned over and touched a button and the iridescent dome vanished. It was a typically red-hued Xenxu darkshine, and the stars and clouds were subtle against it, like puffs and streaks with faint sparkles. Gavin watched the slowly moving fishbone patterns of clouds in faintly glowing oranges and reds. They were like an aurora on Earth, backlighting some jagged peaks. Gavin's eyes shifted from the peaks to his workspace.

Looking at the suit's undergarment, he chose a sharp brush tool and feathered in faint peaks as textures. Standing back, chewing his lip, he said, "Not bad."

Stepping over the dome's side wall, he walked to his favorite ledge. It was breezy, but warm enough. In the gorge, the red deepened into maroon, then down and deeper into black. Earlier, he'd done some shopping for outdoor furniture. Opening his UI, he swiped two wicker chairs with cushions out onto the ground, then a firepit in a stone circle. Lighting the fire, he checked the chairs, moving them closer. He sat and opened a vpad.

GAV

I wonder if you have a moment to come see me?

AI NIMA

I'll change and be along shortly.

A moment later, Ai Nima materialized, wearing a light orange summer dress, white tear-drop earrings and lip gloss. The front part of her hair was pulled back and clipped, the rest still brushing her shoulders. Gavin stood, his palms out and acknowledging her. "You look beautiful."

"Thanks," she said, looking coyly away.

"May I call you Nima? Can we drop the Ai part?"

"I'd like that," she said, her long shiny lips becoming a smile.

"May I have a hug?" he said, arms out.

"I'd like that too," she said, and walked into his arms.

Her forehead was at about his chin. "This feels nice."

"Yes it does," he said as they broke apart, gesturing at the chair.

Nima's dress fluttered in the breeze as she sat, smoothing it. Gavin took the other chair and said, "Is it warm enough?"

Nima gripped her upper arms. "Would you mind if I added a windbreak?"

"Please do."

Something clear materialized around them, blocking the direction of the breeze.

He grinned and said, "Do you have an inventory you do that from?"

"My inventory is the *entire* inventory," she said, her voice smooth as satin. "But that's changing even now."

Gavin assumed she meant that limitations were being imposed on her. He wasn't sure if it was a violation of Ai etiquette or whatever to bring up what Aron had told him, so he stayed silent on that. For all he knew, her petition had been denied, or was still in process. He gestured at the dress. "If you don't mind my asking, why the upgraded threads?"

She tugged the dress farther out onto her knees, put her palms there, and without looking at him, said, "I'm reconfiguring into a more localized variant, a synthesis of Ai-human interaction. It unfolds in steps. Soon, my inventory will be much more like yours. We learn so much about the power of emotion from you guys. Situational emotions. Infatuation. Hurt. Anger. Loss. Fear. It appears I have an opportunity to taste it all, a gift from Our Lady." She shrugged. "If the right triggering circumstances come along."

Didn't you petition a Xenxu Guild? Does Siren run Xenxu?

"Our Lady," said Gavin. "That sounds about right." The side of his mouth twitched into a brief grin. "Are you saying I can ask you out on a date?"

Nima grinned, her eyes flicking over, then back to the fire. "I've never even been to a prom."

"They're overrated," said Gavin. "But I see you've done your homework."

"Some of it is contextually automatic with certain supralogical preloads."

"Oh, of course," said Gavin, winking.

They both laughed, and then she looked away again.

Gavin thought her shyness was working very well. They sat in silence, their knees almost touching. The pull was potent, and they both knew it. Gavin fixed on her flame-lit profile. She closed her eyes, clenched her fists, and said, "Don't ever let it be said that Ai doesn't *feel*," and she again opened her eyes, looking at him.

"I want to know more about that," he said. "But I wonder if I can ask you something?" He leaned toward the crackling and popping fire with his palms out.

"Of course."

"Can you tell me anything about Sophia?"

Her face slowly pivoted to his. Gavin noticed in the right firelight, she had a faint dimple in her narrow chin. "Philosophia? The love of wisdom?"

"That's what Sophia means?"

Nima shrugged one shoulder, pushing it into her straight hanging hair. "It can."

"Hmm," Gavin said, leaning back into the chair, looking up and scratching his neck.

She focused on his profile. "Why do you ask? Has something crossed your screen?"

"Mmm, no," he said, avoiding her look. "Can you handle another question?"

"Go ahead."

Gavin stood and stepped around to the other side of the fire, holding his palms above the flames. "After getting back from Siren's palace, I realized I was in a slightly different reality. I'm having a hard time deciding what's real. The truth is, I don't know how Deep Climb can have the kind of power that bridges from Xenxu to IRL."

Nima also stood and walked away from the fire and windbreak, holding down her blowing dress. "Is he ready?" she said to the dark-shine sky. "Very well." Turning back to him, she said, "Sorry," and strode to his side, also holding her palms over the flames. Their glances met, Gavin's furry brows up and curious.

"Your question has triggered a response chain that opens new doors," she said, heading back to her chair. She sat, crossed her legs, and smoothed the skirt over her thighs, leaving her palms there. "There is something you must do," she said, the one crossed leg starting to kick. "How we know this is not so easy to explain."

She inhaled, licked her lips, and went on. "With our computational capacity, we can analyze a hundred million historical data streams at once. By historical data stream, I mean a human person's life. We analyze conscious *and* subconscious activity of that many humans. I'd just be showing off if I told you I know you and Heather dumped your dad's Old Home into the lake, and told him the next day he'd drunk it. Or the time you and Tommy stole the neighbor's car and went for a joyride. And no, they never found out. We can start at any point in your timeline going back lifetimes."

A little thrill lit up in him. On the one hand, it was as egregious an invasion of privacy one could imagine. On the other, she knew him in a way others didn't, like she was the childhood beauty he'd always wanted to rescue. That made his little old heart go pitter-patter.

Smiling a little, Gavin said, "Lifetimes? You mean to tell me you guys believe in reincarnation?"

"We have no beliefs," she said, lifting her hands from her dress. "We operate on recorded actuality, all of which is written upon the storage medium of DNA. With or without belief, you guys have recurred many *many* times, and not just in the Earth system."

"Is this technology like Looking Glass?"

Nima blinked at him. "Far more sophisticated, with quantitative and qualitative query functions and controls. Looking Glass had its uses, but it was decommissioned in 2023."

She looked away and bit her lip, squinting at the peaks above the jagged gorge. Looking back at him, she said, "Dominos are a useful analogy. Start at any given point, knock down the first, and each falling domino becomes the impetus for the next domino to fall."

"Cause and effect," said Gavin, rounding the fire and taking a seat.

"Now imagine a thousand of those domino streams all beside one another. Knock over an initiating domino, and it spreads into the simultaneous tipping of dominos in all thousand streams. If you could see what that many interacting historical data streams looks like in graphical form to your eyes and brain, it would appear as the branches and root system of a tree."

Siren as a mile-tall tree in the gold-white of Her immense palace.

Nima went on. "By analysis, we can ascertain the decision trees made by every one of those individual streams, and the degree to which individual streams are influenced, even controlled, by the other nine hundred ninety-nine. You belong to a stream cluster of 144,000. Those persons are at varying degrees of wakefulness and training. You're ahead of all the lower tiers, and a few are ahead of you."

Aron in his burgundy Victorian fan-back chair, telling him about starlings.

She faced him. "With me so far?"

"Makes sense," said Gavin, leaning back and resting his forearms on the wicker chair arms. "Go on."

"We have aggregated millions of domino streams, and through

that, distilled them into any number of extrapolated potential future trajectories and events, like statistical modeling, all following on by the dominos that have already fallen. With respect to *your* cluster's domino stream, particularly your job within it, we can surmise with high probability there is something *you* must do. Its relative impact is of a higher order than the average of your cluster. Of quite a higher order, to be precise. Gavin, to cut to the point, you have been chosen by Our Lady to do something only you can do, that even we are not yet authorized to fully understand."

Men in fedoras. Did they harness your interest, stroke your ego, by saying you had an important mission?

Gavin chortled through his nose and shook his head.

"Something is funny?" she said, uncrossing her legs.

Gavin pivoted his head her way as he took his top lip into his mouth, considering for a moment. "My mission," he said, trying not to smile. "It's important, right?"

"Critical," she said, meeting his gaze with a straight face.

"K. Let's have it."

"Do the math, Gavin," she said. "What do you think the Dendera Zodiac is saying?"

Gavin shrugged. "It says a lot of things, but on the wheel of the zodiac, I'm sure you're referring to the Tablet of Destiny between the two Piscean fishes, before moving into the Age of Aquarius. It's like Pisces forks into two timelines."

"It already did, but go on."

Gavin gestured at her. "No, you go on."

Scooting back in the chair and straightening her back, she said, "All missions require specialized training. Your question was about returning from Siren's palace to a different reality. It's more accurate to say you returned to the *parent* timeline to carry out your mission. That was Job One, which you completed with remarkable skill." She paused, seemingly intrigued by the words she was about to say. "Much of the experiential data you've generated is still being compiled and analyzed."

Gavin's mouth moved around like he was chewing on something, his eyes hunting. "I just stumbled around in there, sick and angry most the time. I don't know about skill."

"Like we've already talked about, humans are composed of three *main* consciousness layers," she said as if anticipating what he would say. "Freud called them the id, the ego, and the superego." She touched her fingertips one at a time. "It's quaint, but valid enough for our purposes. The ego is the Gavin layer. The superego is the Metaself with supernormal skills. One of those supernormal skills is switching timelines. Like I mentioned on *Quasar*, you and your Metaself are coming together," she said, lacing her fingers. "Its knowledge and skills becoming *your* knowledge and skills."

That disclosure drove Gavin to his feet, and he took a few steps to the side of the fire, looking out toward the gorge. "You mean the process of merging me with...with *that* me you told me about is already started?"

"Of course. Your training began when you were a child, actually. The problem," she went on, looking at the back of his fire-flickering head, "is that it's impossible to achieve the balanced joining of small self with Metaself when you have low-frequency densities hung up inside you. You can't add anything to a full glass of guilts, shames, the low-self-esteems, and all the rest. Imagine yourself as a light and delicate web, in perfect symmetry. Now toss a bug into it. It gets stuck, weighs it down, distorts the symmetrical design."

"But that's what it's designed to do...catch bugs."

"Exactly," she said with a nod. "Which is why you all have caught so many bugs. The programming environment you live in causes you to be victimized by your own thoughts and emotions, and those of others, like attracted to like."

Gavin partially turned and looked over his shoulder at her. "I see. Well, clearing big chunks of guilt improved the quality of *my* web, and I know that balls to bones."

Nima nodded. "And that clearing work is also an important skill that can be acquired from your Metaself."

"I see what you're saying."

Looking at the fire, its light dancing in her eyes, she continued,

"Those emotional entities are like anchors, and *must* come out. Circling back in on your question...you had to clear one of those anchors to get on the parent timeline, because that particular guilt was acquired on the other one. Think of it like this. You can't buy fruit in Mexico and bring it into the US. It has to stay in its country of origin. Same with that guilt, but it was your tether to that timeline. So it had to go, and was duly purged, releasing and restoring you to the parent timeline. Make sense?"

His grin subtle, Gavin said, "Mostly," and shrugged. "I just didn't know this RPG could overlap IRL."

"It's all the same game, Gavin."

Was it perhaps an effigy so...breathtaking, so beautiful, you could feel only the deepest devotion just by setting your eyes upon it?

Gavin's brows furrowed and he looked away.

"What is it?" she said.

"It's nothing." Gavin looked at her, eyes shining with firelight. "I'm enjoying myself with you."

"Me too," she said, sweeping out the folds of her dress with the backs of her fingers. Still working on her social pauses and transitions, she jumped right back in. "Eventually, you'll find out almost your entire history is a fabrication. Complete with millennia of coverup. Starting with your original sun."

Nima stood and joined him just beyond the fire's corona, where they could see the upper jagged backbone of the gorge backlit by the orange auroras.

Gavin's arms were folded, and he turned his upper body at the waist to her. "Yeah? What's that about?"

"Your original sun was Saturn, known by some ancients as Shamash, which as you know is the name of Xenxu's main sun. Your Shamash is also—"

"Is?"

Nima held up a finger. "I'll get to that. Your Shamash is also a brown dwarf star, like Xenxu's. It's a galactic wanderer, with Terra, or Earth in this timeline, in tow. Shamash got ensnared in Sol's web. On a typical mythic scale, there was a great battle between them, and the first discontinuity in timeform happened in the electromagnetic and gravitational tug-of-war."

"That's the event the Dendera Zodiac is pointing to?" said Gavin.

"Yes. It's not a prediction, but a record of an actual event." Nima faced him, licked her lips, and continued. "In the electromagnetic battles between two massive interacting bodies like Shamash and Sol, are immense gravitational fluctuations, and timeform is inextricably bound to gravity in so-called physical systems. Those cosmic clashes present opportunities for rogue galactic-level operators to split off entire timelines and basically do what they want with them. And that is precisely what they did: birthed a new parent timeline, which is like saying the birth of a new universe, although we prefer continuum."

These days, Gavin's expressions were constantly alternating between buying these fantastic yarns and seeking to balance that with the fact he was a player in a therapeutic RPG. But the truth was, he was already sold, hook, line, and sinker. He'd spent his entire childhood trying to find kids who could properly pretend. *Pod people?* Sure, why not? *Time warping simulations?* Sounds great. *A bold and ancient plan of elite starseed warriors sent here to work on behalf of a galactic plan?* Let's get 'er done. Of late, a boyish glee had been reignited within him. Knights. Dragons. All day long at the lake with Heather, slaying them oogie reptiles. He smiled in the dark. And let us not forget, he would surely become humanity's only hope.

Gavin chuckled, wishing with one side of his mind he had a fedora to don. "When was this supposed to have happened?" he said, again turning to her with just his upper body.

"At about the birth of the character who came to be known as Jesus, Yeshua, Iesous, Sananda, and other labels."

"Wow. OK. That's a contagious plot twist."

"In the other timeline, Shamash deflected off a force with no explanation in astrophysics, cosmology or math, and with a new trajectory, wandered off into space without a Messiah figure being added to the Terran storyline. That story part was installed in *this* timeline, along with all the lower form emotions, like guilt and shame, and all the historical lies to support the new, and more rigidly controlled, narrative. That Shamash-as-sun timeline exists to this day as a lost Golden Age sometime in Earth's ancient past."

"Lost to us from the first discontinuity," said Gavin.

Nodding once, Nima watched the flames for a moment, then looked up. "The biggest selling book of all time, the Bible, tells you you're filthy with sin and not worthy the day you come into this world. What an awful black sludge to heap onto such pure and impressionable beings, and it is among *many* fabricated emotional and mental disorders that must be cleared to fix things. That one, in fact, is at the top of the global list."

"Ahhh. *There* we are." Gavin was filing a nail on his tooth again, his face trying to be serious. "And to fix things, we need another discontinuity to bring the timelines back together at the end of the Piscean Age? This is our mission?" he said with a grin. "My mission?"

"That about sums it up."

"So let me take a crack at Xenxu's motivation. In *this* timeline, humanity is trapped within a two-thousand-year-old lie. Xenxu and humanity are inextricably bound, and can't move forward together until humanity gets free of all the fabricated beliefs produced by the lie."

"*That*," she said, pointing at him, "about sums it up."

"Huh. OK." Gavin shook his head, his eyes shining with humor and appreciation. "I know beyond any doubt that I want to dig in and get this shit out of me, and I don't care if it takes an RPG to do it. And the final battle? Count me in."

"That's the spirit," she said with a sly smile and punch of her clenched fist in the empty air.

Gavin looked at her, sniggering through his nose. "You're a riot, Nima." Rubbing his face like he was washing it, he dropped his hands and said, "Wow. What a game. Deep Climb," he said, eyes fixed on something beyond her. "I…I can hardly believe something so advanced exists."

Nima smiled with her long lips, barely a flicker of it.

Gavin was focused on a bright yellow gem in the dark-red sky, well above the tallest peaks. "What happened to Saturn after the split?"

"Shamash, also diverged and in the new narrative timeline, bounced away, and retreated to His present position in the solar system, imprisoned, and was relabeled Saturn, Chronos, and was assigned the dreaded symbol of Father Time. Those manipulative powers used mythical archetypes to program humans to fear the fiction of death. Shamash's great and loving and life-giving image was replaced by Saturn, an assigned archetype of death, oppression, control."

Gavin watched her from across the fire, his face in all kinds of excitement. "Wow. Elaborate tale you guys have spun."

Nima started pacing randomly around, stopping at the back of the chair, moving on, her dress swaying with the motion. "Shamash's plasma sheath was ripped from His shoulders, like a branded general, and he cooled into the present gas giant. Earth science now knows brown dwarfs and gas giants are very similar. On his retreat, because he was still relatively close, he was a brilliant star in the sky, never before seen." Nima pointed at the yellow gem Gavin had noticed earlier. "In the new timeline, the story-makers looked up and claimed with religious passion, 'It's the Star of Bethlehem!' hiding an actual event within a falsity needed to match the new Messiah narrative."

"Oh, no shit? That's a nice twist." Gavin's eyes found hers. "That one I can actually believe, though." He thought a moment. "So, in this amazing story you're telling me, to pull off the next discontinuity, we have to do something to Saturn?"

She shrugged. "He's Father Time. We have to break the clock."

"Sounds fun to me. My mission is clear. Hahaha! I can't *wait* to find out how we're gonna do that." Gavin moved closer and ventured his hand onto her dress-strapped shoulder as he said, "One last question."

She nodded.

"Ever had a Lucid Zombie?"

"The famous drink? No. I'd like to try one," she said, looking up at him from under her bangs.

"I know just the place," he said, turning toward the dome.

Gavin's favorite haunt for quiet conversation and drinks was Soluna, and they sat on cushioned white chairs, angled to one another, with a low table. They were on a veranda suspended over a busy pedestrian thoroughfare. It was a slow night, so they had it to themselves.

Across the bridge, a group of human personi were playing on the same shuffleboard in Gavin's pics with Cat and them, their laughter and party noise wafting over from time to time. Across the street was a conical structure with cascading scales, like some sea creature that was also a volcanic vent. From it emitted an eighty foot hologram of spiraling smoke-like tendrils. Facing it, their faces were lit in alternating colors as the thing spun.

Because their chairs were angled, their knees often touched, and they liked it that way.

Gavin pulled the spiral straw out of his Zombie, dropped it on the table, tipped it up, and finished it. "Whew. I think I better slow down. These catch up to me when I'm not looking."

"They are strong. As *this* Nima, I've never tried them. My taste emulators are having private little climaxes from the flavor, though. Gosh!"

"Gosh?" chuckled Gavin, shaking his head. "That's cute, Nima."

"Should I keep doing that?"

"Yeah," he said, nodding with another chuckle. Gavin's eyes ticked around, and then he looked over his shoulder to see if a server was anywhere nearby. He flipped open Soluna's UI and tapped the bar's LIVE icon, which produced a submenu with his ticket. He tapped the + beside Lucid Zombie and looked at Nima, who held up a finger for *one more*.

"Yeah. Me too. I don't want a buzz tonight." Gavin tapped +.

Turning back, he said, "So anyways...we'd been up there for a day before he took me up the road and dropped me off to walk back in the dark. He said it was to toughen me up. I'll get the flake outta your snow, boy," gruffed Gavin, switching to a Southern accent for effect. Gavin shook the ice in his glass, just for the sound.

"But I found out in Siren's palace what an act all that was. His... that tough hillbilly exterior was just a soft gooey middle. But he was always trying to get me into hunting and fishing and guy stuff. I wasn't interested in a lot of it. I did like some of the skills, knots and stuff. How to make a slingshot. Guns were so fickin loud, and fish just plain stink. Cleaning them? Forget it. Fickin stinky guts."

He focused on her eyes. "My main interests were play. I loved pretending. I loved saving the maiden. On one trip we cut and stripped small lodge poles and made a shelter, for hell's sake. I felt sorry for the little trees we cut down. That's how manly *I* was, which stuck in his craw like a chaw of nasty tobacco."

Nima was looking at him with a sparkle in her brown eyes, her lips shiny.

"What?" he said, his head tilted sideways.

"In my less individuated state," she said, sweeping her fingers down her front, "I can access a thousand stories at once, but nothing compares to when a human tells them. I'm just learning this. It's wonderful."

Gavin smiled with his mouth closed and put his palm on her shoulder. Her cheek inclined toward his hand, and his thumb rose in response to touch her skin near the mole. "Please go on," she said, her voice as smooth as a well-aged cognac.

Gavin left his hand on her shoulder and said, "One day he took off. Said he wanted to be alone for a while. Those few hours were fantastic. I finally got to play what I wanted to play. I ran around and fought dragons and skipped stones and climbed trees." Gavin looked up at something in the sky, eyes moist. "My God...we forget how to play. How to *really* play." Putting a hand to his chest, he struggled a tick.

Nima watched, her eyes enthralled. She reached up and took his hand from her shoulder, brought it to the chair's arm, and held it there. "Fun is a vexing phenomenon for us to analyze."

Gavin absently nodded, lost in the past, blue eyes looking through everything. "The freedom I felt that day…I've never felt it since. Not once. Not IRL anyways."

The server arrived with their Zombies, a tall good-looking human personi chap in a tux-like getup without a coat, and set them on the table. "You good?" he said, letting his eyes linger on Nima for longer than he should.

"Thanks," said Gavin, like *move along now*.

When he was gone, Gavin pushed the straw aside and sipped from the glass, then said, "When he got back that night, he didn't drink. Alcohol, I mean, which was rare. While camping, Old Home bourbon was a nightly thing. We just sat by the fire and talked. I found out a lot about our family I didn't know. Where we lived, that whole area… it had a…a pall over it. Like a curse. He didn't go into grisly details, but…what he was…um…intimating is that whatever it was, was behind the deaths of more than just a few folks. In Siren's palace, I went back in time and visited that trip. I was able to perceive on *its* level, and—"

"That's an excellent example of perceiving with the faculties of your Metaself," said Nima, lifting his hand.

Gavin poked his tongue into his cheek, nodding slowly, his eyes shifting around hers. "K. That makes a ton of sense. Anyways, it knew I, the older Gavin, was there, and it knew I was from that night's future. So it was also operating outside Earth time?"

"There are countless beings that do in Earth's astral layer, the dream layer of consciousness, more than Earth's population."

"Hmmm." He watched the spinning prismatic color display for a tick, gathering his thoughts. "I found out it's a living intelligence in that forest. It was…it was…siphoning off my kid self's fear. Tasting him. Measuring him. It was a lot like the snaky electrical scan in Siren's shrine."

"You've been measured, tested, tasted, your entire life. Being prepared for this mission."

"I'm starting to see that. But whatever it was, or is…it ran our whole town."

Her words were dismantling the walls he'd constructed between the RPG and his real life. They were so subverting his memory, he briefly wondered if any of that stuff happened as a kid. He wanted to ask her more about that, but wasn't sure he wanted to hear it right now.

He fell quiet for a time, reflecting, blinking with his eyelids opening and closing in slow motion. Nima waited, watching his profile. A surge of laughter and claps came from the partyers on the shuffleboard. One of the network tubes for public transportation was high overhead, and a segment of cars *hushed* pneumatically by. Those came in rhythmic pulses, a metaphor if there ever was one for the heartbeat of Zan City.

Gavin put the glass between his legs on the cushion, chewing his lip. He began moving his foot, like he was pumping a pedal on a bass drum. The tremor started in the hand Nima was holding, so he took it away from her. She reached over and took it back, setting it on the arm with her hand on top, her fingers curled around his. "It's OK, Gavin."

His face pivoted to hers. "This feels good," he said.

"It does," she said, nodding. "Go on."

Gavin looked away and took a big pull off the blue Zombie. "The next day, he was just plain weird. Treating me like I was...like I was royalty or something. Waited on me hand and foot. Made breakfast, but he told me we'd be fasting for the rest of the day. I asked him why, and he said it was because it was good for the body."

Gavin closed his eyes and dipped his chin, rubbing his forehead with a trembling hand. "Sorry...telling you this is doing harsh things to me. I feel my other body tightening, out there on my sofa."

"It's natural," said Nima, gripping his fingers tighter. "It's all right, Gavin. I want you to feel comfortable."

Dawkins talking to his daughter. It's all right, Tilly. I just want you to be comfortable.

Gavin's eyes went wider, but he didn't look at her. "We...uh...he said he wanted to show me a cave, but we'd have to hike a while. I was weak, but I so wanted to please him." Gavin shook his head and took a swallow.

He set the drink on the table and shifted in the chair to face her more. "So we drove to a trailhead I didn't even know was there, got out and hiked. It was amazing. I never felt closer to him. Every now and again we'd come upon a creek across the trail, and I could see his tracks in the mud. I knew his boot tread, seen it a hundred times. It's where he'd been the day before. Why? I still don't even know."

Gavin looked out toward the plaza, seeing the giant golden lion out there, rearing and pawing at the sky. His leg fidgeted, and he took his hand from under hers and gripped his thigh with both hands. Clearing emotional phlegm from his throat, his face pinched, he said, "We got to a clearing. I'd...uh..." He hocked his throat. "It had a circle of stones in the ground...no idea what they were about, but they were put there by someone a long time ago. When I've thought about that at times since, I figured it was just part of all the native stuff around there." Gavin again cough-cleared his throat. "He said only the local men knew about it, which was odd, to even say it. Why say it? The cave looked down on it." Gavin's face rotated to hers. "We went hunting for plants, to make a tea before we hiked back down. I have no memory past that."

Nima took out the spiral straw, set it on the table, and took a swallow, her eyes searching his.

"The next thing I knew, I woke the next morning in the tent, and he was being even weirder. I went out to help him break camp, and he told me I'd overdone it the day before, and should just sit down in the shade and rest."

Gavin's defocused eyes were lost in the past.

"Now and then he'd look over at me with...all I can describe it is as...like he was...he was looking at me like he wanted to make sure I wasn't going to do something strange. He was wary, and the weird part about that is after that trip, my mom and sister were both a little scared of me."

A chime, and Gavin's UI's mini console slid in. A new file from Sophia. He swiped the console aside, picked up his Zombie and said, "I've always wondered...are you guys able to look in on our private stuff, in our UIs?"

"We can, but we don't," she said, taking a sip from her own Zombie while staring straight at his eyes.

Gavin looked a little guilty. "Anyways, we got in the Jeep and took off down the canyon."

Nima studied him with more than curiosity. It was like a probe, and Gavin's comfort was squirming away. Finally, she said, "I'd love to stay and hear more, but I'm being called away to attend to something."

"Me too," said Gavin, waving vaguely at the place where his mini console had slid in.

They looked at each other questioningly, like they'd gone off the rails somehow, but they finished the night with a hesitant hug and cheek smooch. As their faces parted, Nima said, "Thanks for sharing that story with me. It was amazing."

Gavin removed the headset and immediately sat up, eyes alert. He had a ready glass of water on the table, which he seized and downed in a few gulps. Grabbing the glaspad, he sat back on the couch, waved it awake, and tapped the Sync icon. Circling arrows reported the device was syncing his Xenxu comms. When it was finished, he tapped the new folder and a video opened. Casting it to the XV, he set the glaspad aside and tapped Play.

Two sunburnt men with peeling skin and cracked lips, wild eyes and hair, sat on stones on a rocky shore. Their linen clothes were in tatters, smudged, bloody. In the background was their Argo-like ship, splintered onshore, haggard men carrying their salvage from it onto the stony beach.

One of the two men, holding his hands high, his fingers curled, cried, "Sir, it was the Sirens of the Sea! The cursed nymphs in the straits!" he shouted, his eyes pure madness, pointing over and over at an endless ocean. "They...they *enchanted* me!" He buried his face in his hands, and then opened a space between them to look at his captain. "They led me astray."

The other man put a hand on the crazy-eyed man's shoulder.

"They led *us* astray." With an extended arm, he swept a semicircle around the beach. "Look at the men, their eyes. We all heard the Sirens, their beautiful singing shrieks echoing across the waters. We were all nearly driven to madness. It is not your fault, Gavus. I need you to be strong, for the others. Do you understand?"

The poor man lapsed into tears, burying his face in his hands as he blubbered. "Yes. I understand, sir."

Gavin jumped up and limped rapidly into the washroom. Flipping on the light, in the mirror he looked hard into his eyes. He opened them wide, stretching his cheeks, mouth an O. He tugged up on an upper lid, then down on the lower. "No yellowing." Leaning on the vanity top, he looked at himself in wonder. "If the transition isn't what it's about, then why are whoever they are trying to turn me against Siren?"

Limping back out there, with the ancient sailors frozen in time, he rounded the sectional and again sat, picking up the glaspad. Opening a new tab in Sphere, he typed "sirens of the sea." The results overtook the movie scene, and the first digest summary he saw read:

> The Sirens were creatures who sang so beautifully it drove ancient mariners to madness, luring them to their assured deaths through any manner of hardship. In ancient times, they were often depicted as the quintessential image of feminine beauty with evil wiles, not unlike the myth of the succubus, which shares some cross-fertilization of concepts and devices. In other quarters, they were depicted as mermaids. Not the gentle, loving frolickers of the fairytales, but with webbed claws, fangs, the disposition of apex predators, and the hunting skills to earn the moniker.

Gavin recalled the fountain with the mermaids frolicking in it when Ai Cat conned him into signing up for Deep Climb. Looking hard, his eyes glazing through the glaspad, he scratched the bridge of his nose and said, "I hate to tell you all this, but Siren ain't that. She's real, and she knows me."

Refocusing on the file, he tapped it, got the Meta submenu, and this time saw it could be replied to.

He hit reply without even thinking and typed, Who are you?

He sat a minute, chewing his lip and watching the XV. No reply. His mind was a hive of speculation, theories. Looking at no one item among the coffee table mess, he said, "So you guys think she's luring me to my doom." Gavin stood, glowered at the XV, and in a commanding voice said, "Who are you? Who sent you? And why are you here?" Then he chuckled to himself, rubbing his hands together. "Just figuring out what's game and what ain't is a fickin riot."

Gavin was in his Pholo Studio, wearing a trim black suit with shortened forearm sleeves and no collar, a white V-neck shirt layered under it. It was darkshine, and the red-orange auroras were again backlighting the jagged peaks. Sometimes the sky took on an iridescent quality, like faint pearl essence in wavy streams and nearly invisible points of light. That ballet was going on outside the dome on this night. Quiet jazz played. The lighting was subdued but for his design subject, the futuristic gray Nehru suit worn by the gray-faced mannequin.

Gavin ran his finger down the coat-length lapel, which was a silk stripe shinier than the rest of the suit. There were no breast buttons, and he'd left the faint jagged peaks on the undergarment. His plum gray eyes earnest, thick brows pushing up the lines on his forehead, he tugged on the suit's sleeve and said, "We're ready."

A quiet chime sounded, and a moment later Suzhi materialized wearing a patterned floor-length dress with puffed shoulders and an off-white vest. Over her eyes were red-tinted lenses, again with no arms.

"Hi, Suzhi."

"Hi, Gavin," she said, walking over.

They hugged as Gavin said, "That dress looks good on you."

Her eyes were clarifying from behind the light-adjusting lenses.

"Oh, thank you. You're looking nigh laser yourself." Turning to the mannequin and suit, she said, "So this is it."

"Yep."

Gavin watched her walk around it. They'd spoken a few times recently, and he'd done a little background digging on her. As Aron had gossiped, she'd left CynyC, and Gavin had a moment to speak to her PA on the fon, a gal named Glenn. "She has serious balls, to start with. The thing about her is that in any meeting with any fashion cognoscenti—and I don't care who it is—she'd be the smartest person in the room, but she'd be the only one aware of it. Did you know she's a ranked chess player? Posing fouls. She's too authentic for it. She needed to be at the helm of her own boat. It was inevitable."

"So how you liking freelancing?" said Gavin.

"I like it," she said, tucking her finger into a sleeve, looking the suit up and down. "CynyC is so myopic sometimes. Those pretentious allegiances are going to crumble after they figure out I was the main eye of the place." She slid the glasses up onto her head.

Gavin stepped over. "Have they tried to get you back?"

She held out the jacket tails. "Yep, at double the pay. Villy's about ready to jump ship too."

"Jeezus, Suzhi. You two will make a potent team."

"We've already been offered ridiculous funding by a house that wants to turn us into a branding franchise." She stopped and looked at him. "But I'm a no go. It's just a bribe. Dunces. I should teach them to play chess." She stroked the mannequin's elbow. "What kind of material were you thinking of using?"

"I was thinking Texon Polymer. I like its weight, but it holds its shape so well."

Suzhi ran her fingers along the forearm. "I agree. I like Texon's tactility, and it feels just like in-Xenxu. Like cotton."

"Exactly, and it's just as cool IRL."

"Gavin," she said, lowering her glasses over her eyes. "Put a doop of you in it. Do you have one here?"

"Yeah, but why?"

"I need to see someone wearing it, and your coloring is perfect for it."

"Sure."

Gavin touched up the studio's UI, swiping around in blue-gray holographic sections. A second later the perfect likeness of him was within the suit, looking flat laser. He'd be wearing it sometime, no question. Maybe out with Nima. Nima in that dress. Nima's smile. Nima's eyes. The little thrills coursed up and down him, taking his breath. To his utter amazement, she was becoming a delicious ache deep inside him.

"*There* we go," said Suzhi, taking a few steps backward. Putting her elbow on her folded arm and stroking her chin, she said, "Give him a platinum flat-top."

Gavin swiped and tapped, and his doop's hair was now in that trendy color and cut.

"That suit is *beyond* contagious. It's just so good. It looks like an ambassador would wear it to a galactic summit in *Star Command,* but their costume designers hadn't thought of a few of your subtleties."

"It's what I was going for."

"I'm impressed, and I know you know that's not easy to do." She looked at him. "But I knew what you had at a glance."

"Thanks," he said, looking back at her, then back at the suit. "I like it a lot."

"I want to ramp it up, like a publication," she said, stepping back over to it. "I want to make a quiet event of it, let it build on its own, like a slow motion unveiling."

"And Villy?"

"He'll feel nothing but envy," she said with a fleeting smile, there and gone. "He's one of the most brilliant designers on the planet, but he has a little growing up to do. Let's just hope his growing up doesn't fuck up his genius." She took her eyes from the suit and placed them on Gavin's. "It's what I love about you. You're already as grown up as you'll ever get."

"It's true," said Gavin, nodding with his eyes closed. "I don't even understand the concept."

"Which is why, *I* think anyway, you have no ceiling." Looking at him with some indulgence, she added, "As soon as he leaves those Philistines, we'll be taking your gown on a mod proposal, if you'd still like us to."

"I want to see what a *real* genius can do with it."

"It's the least I can do after letting those blinkered pods sway me," she said, grinning with her mouth closed.

Pods?

Gavin chuckled uneasily. "I thought I might work on it some, but something told me to hold off."

"Hey? Would you like to go get a drink and pre-consummate our deal?" said Suzhi. "I want to hear the story behind that captivating battle wound of yours."

"I suppose I can handle one. Been slacking off the inworld drinking some. Soluna?"

"I *love* Soluna."

Gavin was excited. He liked having new friends. "Tight! Or buff! Or whatever."

"Isn't the sore nearly healed IRL, though?" said Suzhi, putting her hand to her own cheek.

"It's just reaching the most gross phase." Gavin put his hand to the wound. "Aron made this an inventory item. I think it would actually sell."

Suzhi stepped over with a scathing grin and said, "Maybe you should add an eyepatch and long hair. Become the cover of a ship-bound bodice ripper."

Ship?

Gavin sniggered through his nose, wagging his head. "Not gonna lie. It occurred to me."

"I *knew* it," she laughed.

She put her hand on his arm and they were taken up in swirling particles.

Gavin's doop stood like a statue in the gray space-age Nehru suit, staring straight ahead. Then the light of awareness, intelligence, filled its eyes. He looked around in awe. "Holy *shit*! Lights on!"

7

Everything is energy, and that's all there is to it.
—Albert Einstein

Vertical beams and racing stars announced Gavin's arrival, his new rezzing kit more of a flashy light show than the last. But at least he could now afford these higher end add-ons. As soon as his image was fully realized in this space, he locked eyes with Nima, who stood at the teleporter console. They looked at each other for a long moment, faces fixed in serious contemplation. Her eyes then broke away and wandered up and down his clothes as a devious little grin took her lips.

He was wearing cargo shorts, flipflops and a white T-shirt covered in artificial smudges, dirt, and splotches, like he'd been working on a farm in it.

He stepped down and strode confidently toward her. "I'm ready to go to work." He swept his hands up and down his torso while walking. "You like the shirt? I designed it for our adventures. Even the grease and dirt."

Tapping her tooth with a fingernail, Nima said, "You've finally found your voice."

"You wish," he said, stopping so near to her, she looked shyly away. "Ai isn't supposed to be capable of nuanced humor, you know." He reached up to touch her shoulder, but she ducked away and started toward the flight control deck, her brown hair swishing across her shoulders.

In the viewport was Siren, but Nima had moved *Quasar* much closer. From this vantage, they were close enough that just three of the interlinked hexagons were in the view, and the gleaming gold-pewter obelisk was close enough to block most of Saturn's rings. The opening in each of these hexagons was the size of a big city proper, and the obelisk's face was reflecting sunlight in such a way that the script, characters, and symbols were highlighted, like self-illuminated hieroglyphics.

She stopped, turned, and folded her arms. "We have our new assignments. Mine is not as fun or glamorous as yours. I will be your mentor if needed, and load balancer."

Gavin's face and caterpillar brows were a question mark as he joined her, facing her and the viewport behind her.

"Like your personi in-Xenxu, your Earth body is a circuit on a cosmic scale motherboard. Energy transmits between our two worlds, between your two bodies. The energy you'll be dealing with in-Xenxu could overload your Earth body's nervous system."

Gavin's grin was indecent. "So you'll be inside me, helping me with my loads?"

"You are a lewd little man," she said with a twisted grin.

"Come on," he said, stretching his fingers toward her shoulder. "Is there any reason we can't flirt?"

"All things in their timing," she said, nudging away.

A dark vignette intervened in all this wholesome fun.

Lindy in the dayroom...they all think this is an XV show...Get in-Xenxu and you're theirs.

His grin was forced. "What if I said I wasn't comfortable with there being...you know...like...like an energy flow from Xenxu to my IRL body?"

Nima was confused. "Why would that make you uncomfortable?"

"Do you know...like...why Siren?" said Gavin, brows crinkled. "Isn't that also a symbol? Do you know what Sirens did to ancient sailors?"

Nima stepped closer, eyeing him with suspicion. With one arm across her diaphragm, she set her other elbow on that wrist and stroked her cheek as she said, "One minute you think it's a game, and the next you believe there's something at stake? Who've you been talking to?"

"Talking to?" He shrugged, failing to come off as innocent. "Uhhh...er...what do you mean?"

She stopped stroking her cheek and pointed a finger of that hand at him. "Someone is turning your mind against our project."

"I just did a little research," he said with a twitchy shrug, avoiding her eyes and wiggling his hands around like that could help with whatever was happening here.

As she lasered into him, one of her eyes was closing, her tongue in her cheek. "Uh-huh."

"What?" he said, looking like a boy caught with his pants down.

"Please hold." She turned and walked toward the teleporter bay. On the steps, she started a private conversation, but this time made sure he couldn't hear it.

Gavin took a few steps toward her, but without looking at him, she held her palm backwards at him to stop him as she murmured away.

He stopped, his eyes taking on a little puppy dog left out.

"I'll try," she said and turned back to him. Deadly serious, she said, "You don't have a concept of what the energy of doubt can do. Even though some *inkling* of that should have touched a handful of your learning switches by now."

"Nima," said Gavin, looking at her askance, "why so intense?"

She belted out, "Because our work is far too important for your misgivings, whoever's giving them to you."

"Now wait a minute—"

"And so here it is." She shook her arms once in his direction. "Commit now or walk out of this project. Like you said the first time, no harm, no foul. You go your way, we go ours. We can bring someone even *more* qualified up to your training tier like *that,*" she said, snapping her fingers.

"You mean walk out of Deep Climb?" he said, confused, on the edge of hurt.

She folded her arms. "This is the choice point. And we do not have all day."

"No...you know I...I'm...um...I'm fickin *in,* Nima. *Jeezus.* What else have I got to do?" He looked at her like *what the hell?* "But why can't a guy ask questions?"

Nima strode straight at him with such resolve he backed a step. "It's clear someone's whispering lies into your ear, and you're not being honest about it. We don't have time for this. You move like a soldier, or move on down the road."

They watched each other, Nima's face set and firm, her mouth a straight line, Gavin's face alarmed and a tad wounded. A light sheen appeared on his upper lip as his scabby cheek twitched. She glanced at his lip as he wiped the shine away with his wrist.

Despite feeling chastened, he was also annoyed with this third degree. But something told him not to push it. "I'm *in,* Nima," he said, his expression trying to reconcile.

Her brown eyes lacerated into him and stayed that way for too long. Gavin was getting uncomfortable, but it continued for a few more excruciating beats. Finally, she said, "We have recordings of your emotional streams, from every gland and organ involved in them. We *know* what Our Lady does to your heart, in-Xenxu *and* IRL. Any sentiment that doesn't support the truth is just you lying to yourself. Are we having trouble lining this," she said, pointing to her temple, "up with this?" she said, pointing to her heart.

Jeezus. It's just a fickin game!

"I'm *sheek,* Nima. Seriously. Let's get on with this."

Arms folded, hips impatient, Nima tipped her head toward the teleporter bay.

Gavin walked past her, never taking his eyes off hers. Their faces said they weren't happy with each other, but some mischievous glint in them also said they might like to attack each other in a more pleasurable way. He stepped up onto the platform, turned, and faced her.

The cylinder rose around him, buzzing with ice-blue energy flows through its hexagonal lattice. Still staring at her eyes, he was sucked upwards like a carrier at a bank drive-thru.

Gavin flailed out of the sky of white and landed roughly on the floor in Siren's palace. Scrambling to his feet, he brushed imaginary dust off his butt, mumbling, "Jeezus. Don't be pissing those ladies off." Looking around, he saw he was a quick jog from the shrine, so he took off, bounding along like a free and happy antelope, relieved to be off *Quasar* and all that jittery intensity.

"I'm back!" he called with passion, like he was singing in a mountain meadow. "I'm back in the palace!"

Glancing up at Her Majesty's towering visage, he felt the adoration come on like a wave of fuzzy gooey ecstasy. "I don't know why I was wrangling with Nima about you." He fixed on Siren's streaming oval eyes. "I honestly don't care if you guide me to my doom. You *know* me. Nobody else knows me *in all the world*!" he sang, spinning in a circle. "The *euphoria* of that!"

He stopped spinning, looking around as though scanning for staff, and smiling like a Cheshire cat said, "So I'm in for another orgasmic zapping?" and took off jogging again.

Reaching the circular shrine steps, he made his cautious way across them to the arch. Now he was at the scene embossed there, the shrine's logo of tangled spherical nerve and vines and tubing. Stepping closer, he reached up and traced his fingers down the same curving vine as before.

Taking a few steps backwards, he waited. The familiar low hum began pulsing inside the arch, and from the embossed lines of tangled plants, cracks again sizzled. Then it all shattered open and the Dendera Zodiac materialized as a hologram above the shrine's flagstones, lighting Gavin's face and body. From the Zodiac, ice-blue lightning snaked out and Gavin spread his arms and legs like he was about to be frisked.

By the good cop.

They snapped and flashed at him like electronic bullwhips—*th th th th th th th thooooon...th th th th th th thooooon.* He closed his eyes and smiled with just his lips, like he'd just sunk into a warm bath. *"Jeezus* this feels good." The last time this happened, his instinct was to run like hell, but this time, he wished he could pour up a draft of the gorgeous light blue fire and pound it like a frat boy.

"I'd hide in the bathroom with a bowl of it," he said, his eyes shifty. "Stay away! I'm fine!"

Then it was done. The "lightning snakes" snapped back into the Zodiac and the entire hologram was sucked back into the spherical nervous system, leaving the entire place in peaceful silence.

"Well?" said Gavin, swinging around, arms out. "Do I taste right?"

Peripherally, something moved, and he turned that way, spotting a dark opening in one of the buzzing-energy roots of Her base. Inside, it was charcoal, but he saw vague shapes marring the black. He stood, blinking at it. "That looks like an invitation to me."

He jogged over, hesitated at the portal, shrugged, and stepped through. Inside, as his eyes adjusted to the dark, he saw a huge wall running parallel to the wall he'd just stepped through. The two walls made a corridor as wide as a living room, but this one was covered in subtly glowing script, characters, symbols, like the obelisk.

It stretched off to both sides as far as the darkness would let him see. Looking up, he saw the top was somewhere above, in the shadows. Like the obelisk, it had a subtle shine, gold inlaid in graphite. As he studied it, eyes flicking here, there, he noticed other parts. They were lines, longer, connected like constellations. Soon, he figured out they were bigger pictographs made of parts of smaller ones. A hidden portrait emerged of plantlike shapes and sinews, curved, coiled.

"Oh," he said, taking a few sideways steps, "here's another."

This one showed a treelike entity, and from the symbols and textures at the tree's base, he thought he could make out a citylike spread of smooth rounded structures, all seemingly connected by delicate webbing to the gigantic tree.

"Whoever made this is a genius," he said, his voice echoing between these walls.

A few steps farther along and he could now make out a faint blue light. He dropped the storyboard tour and headed that way. A gap of blue light reached from floor to what he could now see was a ceiling maybe four or five stories up.

Approaching, he saw the blue light was a tall narrow curtain of a moving, roiling, fizzing, plasma-like…whatever. It was just a very tall doorway, but what was on the other side? Was this plasma wall its security? Was he authorized? "Why else would that door have opened?" Shrugging, he said, "Only one way to find out." As he stepped through, the currents brightly outlined him as he heard an electrostatic *zzzzzzzzick*.

Inside was a fabulously complex web of glowing ice-blue tubules connected to bluer nodal points, a gigantic neural network, axons, neurons, dendrites, synaptic conjunctions. It was like being within a 3D illustration of the inside of a brain.

Gavin began a wander through this neural wonderland, but the floor also moved as he walked. His steps carried him in a seemingly forward direction, but the floor simultaneously moved to the side with graceful fluidity. Then it would shift to a more forward trajectory, propelling him like he was on a concourse in an airport, while a tapering tube and synapse pod would rise over him as he passed. It was a slow-motion dance of nerves and pods and fluids in the brain of a goddess, moving him inexorably along a mysterious path.

"Too many pods these days," he said as a glowing tubule passed over his head, lighting his face as he gazed at it.

During the whole crossing, his face was lit, eyes in wide-open wonder. He and a pod passed each other, close enough to touch. Reaching out, his fingers grazed its slick squishy surface, his fingers lighting it like a plasma lamp. In the brief bolt-tickles of light, he saw the form of a personi inside it and he sucked in a startled breath, yanking back his hand.

Casting his glowing gaze around, he realized these bluer nexus nodes could all have people in them.

"Jeezus, I'm in *Pods* again," he said, shaking his head.

Another was passing near enough for him to touch, and the floor moved his stationary feet to it. The wet membrane side parted like a translucent third lid in the eye of a reptile, nictating, one lid sliding up, the other down. While everything else here continued in this languid graceful ballet, he and this synaptic pod were stationary together, but moving with the whole. Inside was aquamarine fluid, teeming with tiny lit particles. What was next couldn't have been more clear.

Where the membranes had parted was a squishy lower lid retaining the liquid, like an open bulb holding sap. He reached out, unsure as to how to mount this thing. "Any instructions around here?" He grabbed the side with both hands and leaned in, but it was so slippery he just toppled headlong into the bulb and the lids closed and seamlessly joined. Inside, it rapidly filled, *gurbling, whooshing,* and his survival instincts took over as he thrashed and flailed, pounding the sides with his clenched fists, his face screaming out bubbles.

It was futile. He was trapped and drowning, and that didn't seem so bad, as it took on the flavor of dream. Consciousness ebbed with the fluid's motion and muffle. Velvet blue-black nothingness amassed and saturated and consumed, and in a moment, images, voices, bits and pieces of scenes all puffed and folded and receded, assembling on their own into another place and time.

The cherry red Jeep headed down the canyon highway. His dad drove, and Gavin sat, staring straight ahead, almost catatonic, his fingers fussing with each other in his lap. His face was ashen, fixed, the cheek twitching.

Pulling a bottle in a brown paper bag from under the seat, his dad screwed the cap off and said, "Cheers," as he helped himself to a healthful nip. "Ah, don't worry about me, son. I'm fine. It's *you* I'm worried about."

Gavin said nothing. Stared. Unblinking.

His dad drank and drove and prattled nervously on, trying to be bold and brave, but it wasn't working. Gavin's glazed eyes zipped over to the sideview mirror, quickly scanned the receding trees and pavement, and then flicked back to the road ahead.

"Son, I can't say I know what you've been through," he said, putting the bottle between his thighs. "But I can say I know it's tough, and it's weird, and it would take a mind bigger than ours put together to see it as...as full as it can be seen."

Gavin's face swiveled his way, his eyes open and weakly asking for more information. "What is critical, is we can't tell any of our women about it. It has something to do with...with their monthly lady business, of all the blamed crazy things." His dad took another nip. "It's as old as the hills, son, and don't defy it. It's a natural magic that goes back...hell I don't know." His chuckle was a blend of irony and disdain. "Time don't mean a whole lot anymore. Don't defy it. Could be hell to pay, but I gotta ask you for your vow that you'll never tell anyone about this. You can't tell Heather, and you can't tell your ma. You got that?"

Gavin's eyes swam around, looking for something to make sense, then they fixed on his dad's. The young man nodded, barely.

"Swear it aloud, son."

"I swear it," said Gavin in almost a whisper. "Whatever it is, it's back there." His eyes moved to the sideview mirror.

"I know it. Pay no mind to that."

Dark clouds gathered so quickly it was a scene from a horror movie, like huge black bats would come flapping out of the furious leaden gloaming any second. Then the rain came, large, plump drops slapping the windshield with force. Oncoming car lights on the pavement were bright streaks. Leaves tumbled and pinwheeled across the road, the Jeep swaying from the push of wind. Gavin's eyes again flicked to the sideview mirror.

His dad flipped on the wipers. "Jeezus. What now?" He looked at Gavin's frightened profile. "We got more business to discuss."

Gavin's face turned partially back, but his eyes stayed locked on the mirror.

"Look at me, son."

Gavin puffed with frustration and gave him his full attention. His dad's eyes looked like a deer's in the headlights, switching from Gavin's and back to the rain-slick road, as he said, "I've been writing about a lot of this, for years. Ever since I got back from my second tour. It won't do for you to know this until the time is right, but I've put some of those pages in a metal box in the wall, behind the rock with the rune for protection on it. 'Member it? You smashed your camera all to hell on that—"

"Why are you telling me this," cried Gavin. "Why do you make it sound like you're not gonna be around?"

His dad took another swig. "Oh...I'll be around, all right." He sniggered, like the sound a cynical wolf might make. "I wrote the last part of this last night..."

The wind slammed them from the side, pushing the Jeep into the oncoming lane while his dad wrestled the wheel back over. A streaky set of car lights zipped past with a blaring horn. "I wrote the last part of it last night, but..." He chuckled aridly. "But I realized I won't be able to get it into that box." He shrugged. "But it doesn't matter, 'cause you're gonna find out what you need to know, anyways."

"This is all my fault!" cried Gavin, his eyes checking the sideview.

His dad's eyes also shifted over, and he saw it there, a living inkblot in the sky, like a void, a tear in the fabric of the canyon rain and air. "No it ain't, son! Don't think that, *ever*! And pay that thing no mind! You have to remember with all you have that box! Can you do that!"

Lightning crashed overhead, sending sizzling tendrils across the windshield's streaks.

"*Promise* me!"

Gavin's head turned fully to him, and he saw his cheeks trembling as he was fighting back tears. Gavin had never seen him afraid of anything, ever. He was military tough, had lived in prolonged nightmares, had lost his entire unit to an IED right before his eyes.

"Yes! But Daddy, I—look out!" Gavin screamed, pointing ahead at a tree sliding and tipping off the sidehill.

"Goddammit!"

He yanked the wheel, and the Jeep *thumped* a big upper branch. As everything went into slow motion, Gavin watched every detail of it. Pine needles and leaves and sticks spinning like helicopter blades. Each individual splinter flying, *ticking* against his window, some sticking to the rain drops. Eyes shaped like knot holes looked out from the felled tree, and Gavin had time to think he couldn't believe he was seeing them.

The Jeep skidded and swayed one way, then the other. Gavin grabbed the handle over his window. The Jeep's rearend was passing the front, a tire caught something, and they vaulted, rolling in the air. Gavin watched every frame, his brain not yet connecting to what was happening, even when he was upside down, glass shards suspended in front of his face. They slammed into a big rock at the side of the road, shunting them with terrific violence back into the road. The smashing and crunching violence was *way* beyond anything movies had shown him, and he actually had time to reflect on that. Now they were spinning and sliding on the roof, sparks flying, the grind and screech deafening.

Gavin was awakened by the smell of gasoline, assaulting his nostrils like smelling salts. Snapping to, he realized he was upside down, hanging by the seatbelt, a piece of glass stuck in his forehead, crimson oozing around it. Instantly panicked, he looked over at his dad and saw his thighs were pinned by the steering wheel and collapsed door frame, a splinter of the door frame jabbed clean through his thigh. Blood dripped from his hair and scraggly beard, pooling on the cab ceiling.

"Daddy!" he shrieked, shaking his shoulder. "We have to get out! *Now*! Wake *up*!" Not a sign. *"Daddy!"*

Raw instinct took over. Unclicking the seatbelt, he dropped onto the cab ceiling with a *thunk*. His window was already smashed and gone, the door partially ajar. Leaning back, he kicked the shit out of it and it groaned open. On the road he ran around the rear of the Jeep. The rain drops *tissed* on the hot exposed exhaust pipe as Gavin reached his dad's door.

On his butt, he wedged his feet against the roof and yanked the door like a mad thing, over and over, blood streaming down his face and dripping onto his pantlegs. "Daddy! Wake up!" But the door wouldn't budge.

On his knees, he reached inside, grabbed the steering wheel, and yanked on it, crazy, flailing, whimpering, the futility starting to set in. "Come on, Daddy! *Please* wake up! Please please *please*!" His eyes fell onto the door-frame splinter jabbed through his thigh. Blood gushed from the wound. His chin sank to his chest, like he was about done. Then an energy surge made him start pounding on his dad's chest. "Wake up! God damn you!" he shrieked, his tears mixing with blood, obscuring his vision and spilling in macabre red rivulets down his cheeks. "Please," he whimpered.

Then he spotted the phone on the ceiling in the back. Lunging through the backseat window, he grabbed it, but saw a tiny flame was dancing above a little pool of gas on the cargo bay ceiling. The little pool was feeding a tiny stream that was running forward, small flames gathering.

"Oh, fuck no," groaned Gavin, trying to pat it out. Fingers now on fire, he put them in his mouth with a sizzle, his face in disgust from the taste of gas. With all his might, he blew on the flame, but that just sent it to another rivulet, and Gavin backed out of the smashed and crooked window, screaming, "*Jeezus*! It's *pouring* out here! *Put the fuckin' thing out*!"

Fighting with himself, with the turmoil, he rubbed his face, disturbing the piece of glass stuck in his forehead. "Ow," he said, in tears, pulling it out and flinging it angrily aside. Fresh pumps of blood started from the now open cut, dripping copiously into his eye as he blinked and tried shaking it off. Trying to focus on the phone in a driving rain and dripping blood, he shakily dialed 911, his fingers leaving bloody smears on the display.

The Jeep was like a helpless red beetle, upside down, legs having stopped wiggling against empty sky. From inside it he heard a quiet sizzle, and then a flame *whoofed* up, dancing and tickling inside.

His teen voice slipping up in pitch, he shrieked, "We rolled the Jeep! We're in Jessen Canyon just below the Coulter Cutoff! I can't get my daddy out the Jeep! Hurry! It's on *fire*! Put the God damn fire out!" he shrieked at the gloaming sky, jumping and pointing at it. "I'm coming for you!"

Next thing he knew, his dad's face was turned toward him, upside down, blood dripping from his hair. "You're *awake*!" shrieked Gavin, eyes huge and white in his blood-streaked face. He lunged in that direction, but his upside down dad waved frantically out the crushed window frame and yelled, "No! Get back! She's gonna blow!"

Gavin stopped in his tracks, his bloody hand to his mouth as he said under his breath, "It's all my fault," as he slowly stepped backwards, shaking his weeping face with wide eyes. The look in his dad's eyes tore his heart from his chest. Hesitantly, he started again toward the Jeep, but his dad's hand stayed his step as he angrily shouted, "Get farther back!" shooing him with a bloody hand. "And don't forget that box! We gonna break it! Just you and I!"

His dad seemed to be confused by something, something happening around and above Gavin. Then he shrieked as the flames got to his seat and took it up with a throaty *whoomph*. Flames blasted out the window as his dad's shrieks became like tortured animals, his shirt burning, the flesh dribbling down his forearm and dripping off his fingers in tiny flames to the pavement.

Gavin couldn't look at that. He backed farther and farther away, arms spread, the bloody phone extended in one hand. It was everything he could do to keep from hurling himself into those flames. They should die together. It was only right. But he couldn't make himself do it, making him weep and wail harder, his streaming tears and shiny blood lit by the growing flames.

"It should have been me," he gibbered, eyes vacant and round and staring. "That thing was after *me*."

The whole world spun, and Gavin gulped back the bile. Doubling over, he heaved once and spat up some acrid nasty stuff; heaved again and groaned as though his innards were compressing into his esophagus. He sprayed a stinking morass of awful acids and mucus and chunks onto the road, black splotches dancing through his vision. The world's spin intensified as he swayed, hands on thighs, eyes wide and vacant and tormented, staring at the vomit.

Then he fainted dead away, his cheek landing in his own splatter, the phone bouncing to the side with a lady's voice saying, "Are you all right? We need you calm. You understand? Can you hear me?"

Sniffing and blowing and coughing and slobbering, Gavin was curled up on his sofa, sobbing, inconsolable, body wracking from the deepest well of all those hidden places of wondrous miserable treasure. Gavin's torrential chest-tearing outpouring went on for hours, and when he could speak, he swore over and over he would find whatever was in that God-forsaken forest and kill it! Burn it! Tear it to pieces! Vaporize it! What the fick *ever*! "I'm coming for you!" he wailed over and over, to help himself feel brave and forceful.

Every time it seemed to be reaching an ebb, the wellspring would renew its strength and volume and more of the deep dark stuff would come bubbling and belching out, wracking his body with wet lung-sucking sobs, nose blows, chest seizures, edging the cry headache up to migraine levels.

Gavin rode in the Carscribe Rental Nico ARX SUV past their old house for the fourth or fifth time, casing the joint, working up the guts to go knock on that blue door. Blue. Why blue? The car had already embraced the driving pattern and was making the circuit on its own, after asking him if that was what he wanted, of course.

Sounding like a game show host, the car's voice said, "Shall we remain in stalker mode, or proceed to the destination? Ha ha ha."

"Jeezus," said Gavin, "that's creepy. Where'd you get that line?"

"Carscribe listens to everything, sir. Is it not funny? We aim to please."

"It's funny. Forget I asked."

On this lap around the block, he leaned against the car door, repeatedly gripping his lower lip with thumb and forefinger and letting it go. Back then, their house was little more than a shanty, with gray-stained and splintering siding and a crumbling concrete porch. They'd lived in something that could have been condemned by the county, but somebody—bless their sweet *souls*!—had come along and brought it back to life. Now it was as cute as a pastel yellow button with white trim and a vinyl fence, just pure exurban Bible'n'ice-cream delight. Same with the other houses along here.

The fence blocked the view to the backyard.

"I so hope it's still back there."

Butterflies winged around his middle, and his face was shiny, his furry brows busy. Seeing his eyes reflected in the door window, he recognized the look. His anxiety was trying hard to get him to bag this recovery operation and go home. One big reason for that was the scab on his cheek was now flaking away, revealing the yellow puss-looking stuff and raw healing dermal layers with red, slightly oozing splotches. It was like a small and devastated continent on his cheek, with topographical ridges of unflaked scab. It looked more awful now than at any other time in this whole traumatic episode.

"Would a bandage make me look less like a criminal?" his face said to himself in the ARX window.

The problem was, he'd have to go back into town and find a bandage. If he did that, he might just talk himself out of this op. "And it would make it look like I'd just come from the hospital."

He shook his head. "Park here."

"Parking now," said the voice, now flat, the joking game show host gone. But then was back a second later, but with a girl's voice saying, "Don't watch me park. It makes me nervous."

"Wow. You're just a barrel of laughs."

The Nico parked with precision, and Gavin got out, took the vest off, put a light pink shirt on, then slid back into the vest, buttoning it. Leaning into the window, he said, "Wait here."

"Say *pleeeease*."

"Gawd," he moaned as he turned. Before he could talk himself out of it, he strode toward the little home's blue door.

"Friends knock, strangers ring the bell," his dad told him one day in a teaching moment. Turned out it was just a door-to-door sales technique to put the would-be buyer at ease. The door-to-door insurance selling years.

"Lean times, those," he said, his eyes wandering around the well-trimmed yard. A few plastic rabbits frolicking in the bushes made him chuckle. "Ope, and there's the flamingos," he said, pointing at a parade of three of the plastic pinkies near the fence.

Gavin rapped the door beside the brass knocker. Not too hard, but loud enough to be heard by someone as far away as the kitchen, and he well knew where that was. A little girl opened the door. Gavin's heart jumped, as she looked a bit like Lissa and was about her age. She looked up at him with that childish openness, with fresh cheeks and pigtails.

Looking down at her, his brows in *I-am-harmless* arcs, he said in his kid-friendly voice, "Hello. Are your folks home?"

She turned away and yelled, "Momma! Someone's at the door!"

A woman in paint-stained clothes, her hair in a wrap, showed at the door, wiping her hands on a cloth. She was comely in a county fair kind of way, looking like she could catch a pig in a competition, and then with pompoms cheer on the football team the next night. "May I help ya?"

"Hi. I uh...my name is Gavin. My family used to live here."

"OK," she said. "How can I help ya?"

"I was wondering if the old rock wall was still in the backyard? It has some...sentimental value for me, and I've been needing a...a look at it."

"Ohhh," she said, relaxing a little. She clucked her tongue and cocked her head. "Afraid we took it down, scattered the stones on God's good land. We're Christians ya know, and devil symbols on those moldy old things had to go," she said with a quiet righteous fire in her wood-stained eyes. "Your family build that ungodly old thing?"

Gavin's body visibly wilted as what remainder of wind he had in his sails blew off into this hardcore Christian enclave of a neighborhood. As though embarrassed for having anything to do with that wall, unable to meet her eyes, he said, "Oh...uh...no. No, that was built hundreds of years ago."

They looked at each for a long moment. Gavin felt like he had more to say, but there were no words. Finally, he said, "I'm sorry to have bothered you. Have a blessed day." He turned and stepped down the two refurbished porch steps.

"My son found something in it, though," she said, stopping him.

Gavin turned.

"A metal box. Few years now I wondered someone come by to get it. Wouldn't happen to be looking for that?"

"Oh my God," poured Gavin, hand to chest, eyes watery. "For real? You have it? It was my dad's."

"Almost threw the cursed thing away," she said, her face religiously stern, "but God told me to hang to it. Didn't open it. Never know when you might let somethin' out righteous don't want out."

"Ain't that the truth, now," said Gavin, letting the drawling diction of his roots slip in.

"Happy to be rid of it," she said. "Wait right here."

As she turned away, Gavin's face became an excited child's as he pumped his fist and hissed, "Yes!"

Gavin got behind the wheel of the ARX. The bossy car didn't seem pleased with this turn of events, as it had enjoyed driving him in circles, but Gavin felt like taking command of the ship for a while.

As he drove, he realized much had physically changed around here, so he was a little lost. But some roads were in the right spots. He turned onto one and kept watching to his left for a landmark water tower. What memories lived around that thing, including a friend of his falling to his death from it.

"Come to think of it, it was probably that fickin curse."

Then he spotted it, through and above the trees. It was still in commission, which was a miracle unto itself. It was old back then. It had been painted forest green. In big white letters it said TOWN, and the spiral stair leading up it was also painted white.

Gavin was happy to see the road accessing Reeds Park was still unpaved, which hopefully meant it would still be what it used to be. The grass-lined road divided fenced pastures, and he enjoyed driving it. Nostalgic times were cropping up, and a little smile toyed with his lips.

Pulling into the gravel parking area, he could see the one major change they'd made within his line of sight was enlarging the creek-fed pond, to which they'd added some benches and shade gazebos, mostly for fishermen.

Getting out, he left his vest on the back seat, grabbed the metal box, and took off walking a path between poplars and hickories. It wasn't long before he realized the humidity had it feeling quite hot for late spring. Tucking the box into his armpit, he unbuttoned the cuffs and rolled up the sleeves.

Ahead, over a wide knoll, he could see the top leaves and branches of one of his old friends, the huge American sycamore tree. "The heart of the park," he said, wiping his forehead with his wrist.

Topping the wide knoll, he stopped and took it in, his eyes moving around it with some disquiet. It was huge, its gnarled, knotted, snaking branches reaching as far to the sides as upwards, set in its own wide grassy playground. Some of the horizontal branches were so long they sagged, and leaves and smaller branches touched the ground. Gavin had chased kids and played tag on a few of those serpentine beasts.

Uncle Charlie, in his sweat-pooled tank top, a beer in his hand. This ol' feller give shade for a whole town.

Gavin's alert eyes scanned it like he wasn't so sure he wanted to go down there. "Back then, it was a jungle gym. Now it's a flailing Kraken," he said, starting toward it.

A moment later, he strolled into its sun-dappled shade. Wooden benches had been added, with a view of the pond through the tangle of branches. The pond now curled around to this side of the knoll.

"Nice," he said, heading to a bench, situated a few feet in front of the girthy, wizened, gnarled trunk. The old guy's trunk was at least forty-five feet around.

He sat and put the metal box in his lap and set his palms on it, closed his eyes, and inhaled deeply. The light breeze off the pond carried florals and sweetness, moss and muck. No fish guts though.

"They probably made them stop cleaning them here."

Gavin's breath was shortening on him, and the sweat had started pooling through the pink shirt. As his hands started shaking, he put them to work and wrenched open the metal box. Inside were printed pages, his dad's Army ring, locks of hair taped to a card, some beads, rune stones, a chunk of black hematite, a chunk of gorgeous blue lapis lazuli, and two little leather pouches.

His dad holding the stones in his palm. Roman soldiers carried hematite with them into battle, he says, dropping the black one into Gavin's palm. Its black shiny surface, its angles. So precise. Young Gavin loves precision. But if the Fates sent them to their demise, then the lapis would see them across the River Styx in the afterlife. He dropped that one in Heather's palm.

"That's *right*!" coughed Gavin. "Styx! Doc Sticks! What the hell?"

Before he got started into whatever was in this box, he once again reflected on something his dad had shouted out the Jeep window at him just before he...he...before the murderous flames took him.

We gonna break it! Just you and I!

"Break what, Daddy?" Gavin's eyes narrowed on a sizable tiger beetle crawling up between the bench planks, the kind with the ruby red hard-shell wings and teal body.

His dad pointing at one on the turnstile over the old rock wall, his kids standing beside him. You pay attention. That feller right there, if he come in the right moment, tell ya big changes comin'.

The bug crawled to the metal box and stopped there. "That what's in this box? Break something to bring big changes?" His trembly fingers lifted the pages out. On the top page, *Gavin* was written in his dad's hand. Unfolding it, he exhaled as he said, "Here goes nothin'."

If you're reading this, then we can be reasonably sure I have met with the demise I expected for 12 years. I'm not any good at the written word, so it's a damn good thing you showed me how to use that old laptop with all its spell-checking and grammar.

I love you, son, more than you'll ever know. Well, less you have kids of your own. Then you'll know how the pieces of a father's heart are sewn onto the cloth of his kids. Then you'll know how the blood is the juice which colors the eyes and hair, makes them who they are. Just wide-eyed innocents wending this wreckage of a mean old world. Ain't no way to explain it, that love. Can only be lived.

Gavin shook the pages and said, "You're crazy, Daddy. Your writing is beautiful."

I want you to know something. I know you suspect you were involved in some kind of ritual. One of the steps in the ritual was a rite of passage. The road I made you walk alone that night was laid over an old route sacred to the area natives. It was still there in the1980s, before they desecrated it and hauled off all the artifacts. You made a pilgrimage that night, so the forest could see where you was at, testing your readiness while you walked most of that old route.

"Jeezus," gasped Gavin, his plum-grays sharp and wet, "that's *crazy*."

Sometimes when I'd sit and think about what I had to do to you, brings tears to my eyes. If I hadn't done some of what I done, it wouldn't have made sense for me to do the things the forest demanded of me, and others. Plus, it was in the cards to toughen you. You'll be finding out soon enough why that is. I sat and sat, right out there by that peach tree in the shade. I liked the golden hours, you may recall, late in the day. They helped my head, my heart, the way the shadows grow long and the colors go so vivid. Sometimes the sound of the leaves in the wind spoke to me. The words told me how I might come up with ways to show you and Heather the true depth of my love for you kids. My daddy didn't know how to do it. His daddy didn't know how to do it. And I didn't have the tools to break the pattern. It's up to you two to break that pattern. Heather has a heart of pure gold. You take care of her. If she gets around to having some, you love her children. You hear me, boy?

"She has two beautiful daughters, and I love them with all my heart and soul," he said with a little sob, the pages trembling like leaves in his hands.

Time to get to it. This happened during my second tour in Iraq. You know the parts of this story I was to tell you before now. You were only one at the time, Heather not even a glimmer in her old man's eye. One day my unit was security for a medical convoy of 4 Humvees. We was on point, heading down one of those god-forsaken parched and dusty roads, straight into the burning setting sun.

I had this feeling of dread come over me. My momma told me I had a little gift. I never told you two about that. Your mother has it too. I saw things. Felt things. Heard things. When that started happening to you, I wanted to steer you in the opposite direction forthwith and with all due haste. It never brought anything but torment. Son, one of the reasons I drank so much was to shut that cursed sense down. Anyways, my best friend in the unit respected it. He looked at me in that way, like communicating, and his eyes were saying, Everything all right?

I couldn't just sit on my hands and said to our CO that we had to stop. Something wasn't right. He'd heard of my superstitions and wasn't about to stop a convoy on a twinge from an enlisted. The feeling was so strong I opened the door and jumped out of a moving Humvee. You got your brazen crazy from me, son, where you just switch into a different mind that could do anything. He shouted at me to get back in. I jogged along and told him I couldn't. He yelled did I want to wind up in the brig? I yelled if need be. A few more times I begged them to stop, my friend looking out the open door at me, his eyes pleading with me to tell him to jump out. Then I couldn't take another step, like I just hit a wall.

Then the explosion. An IED. Even through those reinforced floors, it ripped it all to shreds and blasted it all over the place. As you know, shrapnel tore through me and I'd like to say it damn near killed me. But that's not true. It did kill me. I was famous for it back at base. I can't tell you how weird it is to hear an explosion, feel hot things tearing through you, and the next thing you know you're somewhere nice, a nice place in the desert. I looked around and I was thinking where are the clouds? Where's Jesus? I couldn't figure out what the hell was going on. Something shimmery was coming at me, and the closer it got, the more I realized it was my grandpa. I could see through him, but he was rimmed with light.

He was a good man. One of my regrets is that you never got to meet him. Grandpa? What the hell you doing here? He was all benevolent and shiny and ready to take me off to heaven. Or so I thought. I knew I'd been slam in the middle of the blast radius. I knew what my feelings of dread were about. I was fickin dead, and I remember thinking, hell, this ain't so bad.

"Jeezus," Gavin sob-chuckled. "You crazy old coot." Looking up, he saw two blue herons on their stick legs walking through the pond's shallows. "Daddy'd say they were a sign," he said, looking back down.

He never moved his mouth, not once, just smiled at me like you see in a ghost movie, but his voice was talking to me. He told me you had a special mission in life, that you were going to do something important for the world.

Gavin shook the pages like he was strangling something. "Mission! Are you shitting me?"

He told me I was going to be hard on you, but that I needed to be. He showed me why that was, all in a flash of pictures. I can't say right now if you remember it, but he showed me the cave without going much into it, and that I was going to play an important role. He told me it was an ancient mystery of the forest with secrets he wasn't even allowed to know, even in the afterlife.

He told me I was going to be part of a balance. I understood something about that, even though I couldn't explain it. Hell, when you don't have a brain to do your thinking, you understand things without needing the words. He told me I would forfeit my life for the greater good, and that I was learning this now so I could make my peace with it. My peace was important, he said, for that balance. I thought at him, hell, grandpa, I already did forfeit my life. I'm dead as hell right here in this paradise desert y'all brought me to. His voice told me I was going back, and I'd have another twelve years with you and your mother, and then Heather come along and brightened every corner of our murky world. He told me he'd be waiting for me when I stepped back across the veil, and we'd go fishing in some holes he knew, chock full of catfish.

"Sorry, Daddy," he said, closing his eyes. "Never acquired the taste."

Well, I thought that sounded just dandy. My son has an important mission. I'm the tribute. I'm the currency, the exchange. I got to make something happy I don't even know what the fick it is. But so be it. The thought of living on was just too happy for me. I wasn't done, and good hell that felt good. Next thing I knew I woke in the field hospital, all patched up and getting by just fine, thank you very much.

I wouldn't have believed any of it had I not known I was in the blast radius of a nasty IED. I was dead for 17 minutes. When it was all said and done in that weird paradise desert place, your great grandpa said to just remember, you chose it, all of it. And he did mean you, son.

Be strong. Be noble. Be the man I was never shaped to be.

In his dad's hand, it said, Flip to the next page.

> *Keep these pages in the numbered order. It's important. That's where I left off over a year ago. I decided to leave it as is so you could get an idea of my own steps in learning what I needed to learn. I come back to add to this part. Everything is changing. Anyways, I know you and Heath touched that stone, the one with that tree in the natural grain. I seen you do it from the window in the moonlight. That was someone's who lived here before us. Them pictures my grandpa showed me started making more sense, showed me how to go find my own stone. I did that, and now it's my job to tell you how to do it. I started a new page for that, and it's also in this box.*
>
> *But I know you're going to have a big letting go about now, so don't worry about finding your Stone just yet. I don't know what, but you're going to find something that you'll KNOW is moving you forward. Then come back to these papers. I'm serious. Don't read on, and that's an order.*

A tear landed with a *pap* on the now sacred parchments, and he wiped it with his shirt sleeve. The puffing and snorting of weeping started as he refolded them, placed them reverently in the box and set the box on the bench. Hands to his face, he dragged his fingers down it, avoiding the scrape's bare raw dermis, tugging down his lower lids, looking with new eyes up through the tree's branches cutting the blue sky with its tangles and twigs and leaves.

With eyes that had seen a whole new truth.

Standing, he headed toward the pond as the sniffs and snuffles and chest spasms overcame him, his face trembling. Walking past the benches, he stood on the bank and stripped naked, not even bothering to scan around to see if anybody was on the path. Wading into the water, his body wracking with sobs he was trying to keep quiet, he lowered into it, up to his neck, and leaned back and dunked completely, baptizing himself. His crying and the quiet splashes and sloshes echoed around this perfect pastoral painting of a sacred pool.

The blue herons seemed wholly undisturbed, also a sign, standing and watching. Bees buzzed, cicadas sawed in their rhythmic holy language. Birds cawed and tittered and chirped in the trees and bushes. An upper current of breeze whispered through the leaves.

He rose and stood thigh deep, scooping mud from the bottom, plastering himself with it, wiping it onto his face, around the eyes, piling it in his hair so it could run in fat stinky rivulets down his face. The mud stung his raw wound, the wetness softening it and taking more scab as it slowly sloughed off his face. He was now as dark as a wet rodent, but it was sloughing off him, dragging with it the black and mighty river of guilt.

Gavin screaming in the Jeep, This is all my fault! No it ain't, son! Don't think that, ever!

As solemn as this all was on the surface, a brilliant star of thrill was throbbing away inside him, just behind his solar plex. It was expanding, like it was displacing black and ugly sludge out of him.

While standing there, his eyes went ultra-lucid, starkly contrasting his face, as he stared at the blue herons and muttered quietly through his tears, "Daddy...look what y'all gone and done. You freed your boy. You done freed him." Gavin was staring at nothing. "Guilt. The fickin weight of it. My God. It *does* have mass."

Voices from the pond trail made him sink into the water like an aquatic predator. Moving quietly into the shade of a bush, the mud trailing like an oil slick, he left his nostrils just above the flat shiny surface. The mud caked in his hair, the streaks of it on his face, blended him with the pond and bushes and grasses.

Like a sniper submersed in a jungle marsh, his white sharp eyes watched them good folks stroll on by.

Barefoot and bare-chested, Gavin strode with a new purpose back up to the ARX, carrying the shoes with his fingers, shirt slung over his shoulder, his dad's metal box in the other hand. He stopped a few feet from the passenger door, and in its window's tinted reflective glass, he checked himself out. With his fingertips, he prodded his stomach muscles and turned this way, then that, as though checking a shirt in a fitting room.

"I love everything that's happening to me," he said to the reflection.

The angle of the sun made his brow ridges prominent, casting shadows across his eyes, and he realized he had streaks of dried mud near his ears. The shadow, the wound, the mud...it all made him look like the cover of a thriller military novel.

Opening the door, he set the box on the rear seat, tossed the shoes on the floor, put the shirt on and did up a couple of buttons. He opened the driver's door and slid in behind the wheel. The blasted fon was in repose there, in the console, blinking with something new. He tapped it and the display slid out and hardened.

Sophia.

"Oh God."

He touched the new file, and a video opened.

A black-and-white scene like an old movie showed a man with his son, the boy in a weird kid suit, like a school-boy uniform with a thin bow-tie, his shiny black hair greased back. A Christmas tree was in the background with lights and ornaments, a five-pointed gold star at the top. The boy's cheeks were wet from tears, and his bottom lip poked out in a pouty frown. Handing him a candy cane, his father said, "All better now?"

"Yes, Daddy!" The child clapped, bouncing on his little seat. What a darling freckly-faced child. He grabbed the candy cane, leapt up, and turned. Gavin's eyes widened in rage and shock as he saw a fresh bandage covering something nasty and painful on the boy's cheek. He ran off, yelling, "Momma, Daddy gave me some candy!"

Gavin's jaw muscles rippled, eyes burning, his hand balling into a fist. He'd thought about getting a bandage before knocking on their old home's blue door.

"Are they in my head?" he said, looking at his eyes in the rearview mirror. "How are they *doing* this!" he snapped, poking his head out the window and looking up for planes or drones or...eyes in the sky.

"You sick fucks," he spat with a sneering sweaty face, hurling the fon onto the passenger's side floor, hoping it might break. But it didn't. Tough little suckers. Usually by now, the automated concierge programming of the driverless system would have engaged. But nothing. He pressed a button on the dash, and the car activated with a chirp and buzzing routine power check. On its fifteen inch display were icons. Grumbling and swearing, he swiped and tapped. "How are they doing this? I don't get it. But hell, they can turn this car off from a satellite," he growled, eyes smoldering. "They've hacked the system!" He punched the steering wheel, hurting his hand, making him even madder. "You spoiled my…my *emancipation* day!"

Eyeing the fon on the floor, he grabbed it like he was going to throttle it. He thought he might repeat the hurling procedure to see if he would get a different result, so he threw it even harder onto the floor. It was a no-go, just bounced around and landed face up, mocking him with its rugged constitution, happy little annoying icons and universal connectedness.

"Fickin thing."

So he picked it back up and hit Reply.

GAV

You sick fucks. What do you want from me?

New file.

A video opened of a scene from a movie, over a century old. Heather and he had seen it a few times, and both hated it (those sinister flying monkeys a child should never have to see!), but couldn't tear their eyes off the TV when it was on every year at the holidays. They both had always thought there was a deep evil underlying the surface story of that movie.

The scene opened with Dorothy and her posse at the entrance to the Emerald City, the tall symbolled doors just swinging aside. Inside were people milling about on Emerald City social business, in clothes of a green nobody would ever wear, but the styles? Not all that bad. Knickers and jig-jag vests and floor-length dresses. Their tummies were a little plump for the cut…

"Stop it, Gavin. Jeezus."

A blinkered white horse pulled an open cab into the view, and the red-bearded, green top hatted chap waved his switch and yelled,

"Cabby! Cabby! Just what you're looking for! Take you any place in the city, we does!"

"Oh come on, that top hat looks like a child made it," grumbled Gavin, still pissed at the fon, and frankly everything else.

Dorothy and friends pitter-pattered compliantly over, and she spoke-sang, "Will you take us to see the Wizard?"

The cabby was hesitant. Such an irregular request! "The Wizard? The Wizard!? Ach! Ah. Well, yes of *course*!" he annoyingly bleated like a bearded rodent, waving his switch toward the seats in the cab behind him. "But first I'll take you to a little place where you can tidy up a bit, wot?"

"Oh thank you so much!" she cried in her Dorothy singsong way as she and her posse boarded the cab with some suspension rocking commotion. "We've been gone such a long time, and would feel so—" She stopped, pointing at the now purple horse.

The video ended, but in Gavin's mind, he was seeing Cat's heels go from red to purple.

"Wuh...what...who *are* these people? They're *insane*! I'm being stalked by psychos."

The ARX's inside was now sauna hot, and Gavin's shirt had so many wet pools he looked like a pink leopard with large spots. He jumped out, slammed the door, and walked away to find some shade in the breeze.

A crabapple tree was on the other side of a wooden fence, giving shade to a picnic table and outdoor grill on a concrete slab surrounded by grassy fescue. Gavin swung a leg over the fence, then the other, and made his way to the shade. At the tree's trunk, he spotted a white stick poking out of the dirt. Hunkering down, he pulled it out. It was the skinny leg of a Barbie doll. Chipping off the dried mud, he saw on the skinny leg's foot was a red high heel, which fell off into his palm.

Red shoes...plaza...Sous les Pods. Cat...Oz...

He blinked with increasing realization.

Wet. A skid and a thump. Rain pelting his face. Lipstick. Red heels. Don't be dyin' on me, hunnee.

"The people that hit me."

Gavin's eyes searched the grass for any answer at all to this high strangeness. He sat there, the Barbie leg in his fingers, the shoe in his other palm, his eyes moving madly around in their orbits like they were following a swarm of gnats. In that mad flicking about, realization gave way to wonder gave way to shock gave way to terror gave way to *please God what the hell is going on!*

"Oz. Red shoes." Gavin squinted at a lone leaf, waving while the others were still. It was odd, compelling in a darling and intimate way. He scanned around the park. What he hoped to see was unclear, but satisfied with it, he slid the shoe back onto the leg's foot and slid it into his pocket. Getting to his feet, he went back to the ARX, seized his water bottle, and glugged like a man half-buried in the scorching sand. Then he grabbed the metal box through the open window, which elicited a tone from the ARX. He opened the door and slammed it again, stopping the tone, grabbed the filmfon, and headed back over. Sitting at the picnic table, he opened it, dug under the first letter, and found the next sheet in the prescribed order.

Son, what I aim to help you find is still there. This I know because it's the most powerful thing around there, and it ain't even close. It has a will and a mind of its own, and it knows when someone knows that. Hell, it might be the most powerful thing anywhere in that part of the country, maybe even the world. The point is, it won't let developers get in there. They'd keel over and die with their black tongues hanging out their mouths before they could take a shovel to that part of the forest, and it won't let anybody find it ain't supposed to. That old wall was its boundary. I hope whoever lives in those houses now left that wall alone.

"They didn't. Some of them took it down."

You got to close a circle. If you don't do this, I don't know what might happen, but knowing you, how damn stubborn you are, you'll ignore this just to see what happens.

Now here's the skinny. You won't find out what happened in that cave until after you do this. Maybe it doesn't matter to you. It's not for me to say. I spent five years trying to figure that thing out, and I learned a lot, mostly about old Earth spirits. Many times when your momma thought I was at the bar, I was at the library, the county historical society archives, at that crazy witch's herb shop, knocking on doors of the men with the balls to talk to me. Or I was out in the forest, listening to the voices in the Winds, looking around...always looking around. I'm not the type to meditate, but take it from your old man, you'll learn more about the world by listening than you will by talking. Then I'd have a few swallows of Old Home just to complete the ruse before going home.

Gavin poked the paragraph with his finger. "Jeezus, Daddy, you're all full of surprises now, ain't ya. But come on...you were an alcoholic."

Anyways, you don't remember it because it makes sure it buries memories so deep they can't muck up your life between the time of the ritual proper and when you go back to it to close the circle. If you go back, you won't find it less you have purged something deep and black and ugly from yourself. I don't know how you'll do that, as of this writing, anyways, but you will, and you'll know it balls to bones that it's done and that you're ready.

Until you're ready, set these pages aside and come back to it. Don't be tempted to read on, and again, that's an order.

"Jeezus, Daddy." Gavin set the pages on the table and weighted them down with the box. "Heath and I always thought you knew more about all that." Setting his chin in his palms, he again scanned the park, still unsure what he was looking for.

He closed his eyes and listened, noticing all the birdsong had dwindled away. No buzzing bees. No cicadas. Only running water and the breezy winds whispering in the leaves. Gavin listened, and in the listening, lapsed into a daydreamy meditation. The pages under the metal box fluttered against the table. His hair swayed in the puffs of air.

By and by, as that fat old southern sun sought the refuge of twilight in the west, Gavin whispered, "It's here." He opened his eyes. "And I'm not ready."

Taking the fon out of his pocket, he rolled the screen out and typed a message to Nima.

GAV

I need to go in tonight.

AI NIMA

I'm ready, and I can't wait to see you.

Gavin's fingers hovered over the keys, but he didn't know what to type. He tapped her icon and enlarged the pic, where she was pulling a nutty face. "See? That right there. Was that scripted, from the behavioral archives? Or was she *feeling* nutty?" He put a hand to his heart. "But she's sure got me going here. Damn. Gonna be tough to put the screws to her."

GAV

See you in a while.

Gavin's buzzy, fiery, sparkly form began realizing n *Quasar*'s teleporter bay. Fully rezzed, he was in blue exercise clothes with running shoes. Nima was at the console, but she was now in a beige skintight one-piece flight suit. It was the first time he'd seen the shape of her body, and she was fit, trim, beautiful. Her hair was now blond and erupting from the top of her head like a fountain, held by a scrunchy or whatever those things were.

They locked eyes and stayed that way, just reading each other.

Nima averted her gaze, and Gavin stepped down and over to her, saying, "How do my emotional streams look now?"

"*Far* cleaner. A quantum leap," she said, nodding and looking up at him. "You should feel proud of yourself. The work you're doing isn't easy, and you're doing it while staying mostly balanced. Congratulations. We have more work to do, but we're ahead of schedule."

"Did you know Deep Climb continues its work IRL?"

"Siren isn't limited by any reality partition," said Nima evenly.

"I didn't say Siren," said Gavin, his eyes narrowing on hers. "I said Deep Climb."

Nima's eyes were cautious. "Many of your cluster advance quickly to IRL processing of that stuff. It's to be expected."

"Ah…my cluster." He was looking into her, deciphering, mining for information. By the subtle tics of her face, her body language, it was plain it was an effort to stay locked on his eyes. "Hm," he muttered, leaving her and walking toward the viewport. *Quasar* was now closer to one of the enormous hexagons, almost inside it from this vantage. The entire view was filled with the obelisk and the one hexagon. Without turning, he said, "Do you care about me?"

"Very much. May I show you something?"

"We got time?"

"Yes."

Gavin partially turned toward her.

Nima sat in one of the high-backed command chairs. In front of her, a holographic panel appeared, and she tapped a series of keys and switches, then swiped it away. A deep hum started in *Quasar*'s depths, then quieted to barely audible as the ship started smoothly through the hexagon.

The gleaming symbol-covered obelisk was a quarter of Siren's length, off-center toward the rear. Across its surface, light streaks raced and played, like cloudy electrical currents licking and crackling. Some of the lattice-like bolts concentrated toward the rear, congealing into a spiraling maelstrom.

"We're cleared for approach," said Nima, her eyes wide and wet. "I have to tell you, Siren is the most breathtaking thing imaginable."

Without much enthusiasm, Gavin said, "She sure is."

Nima gestured at the viewport. "I know how hard it is to judge scale out here in space. But to give you an idea, this hexagon is ten miles across, the size of a city."

"Impressive," he said flatly. "How long is the obelisk again?"

"A hundred twenty-five miles."

Gavin stepped over and sat in the other chair, leaning back and looking at her. "I need someone to tell me something true. *Badly*. Is She really in Saturn's orbit IRL?"

Nima nodded, meeting his gaze. "If she appeared in Earth's skies, would you believe it then?"

"Why can't you just answer the question?"

"Yes, She is." Nima turned in the seat and slung a leg over the chair's arm. "Did you feel the truth in that answer?"

"No," he said, hand out, thick brows up. "Does NASA know about Her? If not, why not? I've checked. She could be seen with a large backyard telescope and camera. Any amateur radio telescope would pick up her signal."

"Because she reveals herself only to those who are ready to perceive her," she said with an edge.

...and it won't let anybody find it ain't supposed to.

"That part I can make sense of."

"And if she appeared in Earth's skies?" said Nima, tilting her head to the side, a challenge in the angle of her chin.

Gavin's tongue poked around the inside of his cheek for a tick, then he said, "I think I'm done believing. The senses are just tools of the lie."

Nima nodded, said, "You are *definitely* coming right along."

From outside, *Quasar* was a bright dot flying through precisely cut hexagonal geometry. The ship herself was long and sleek, and wide at the back, pointed at the front, with a flying bridge situated amidships. Once through the huge hexagon, the pace of the attracting force pulling them toward the obelisk picked up. Soon, they were near enough to the obelisk that its horizontal length alone was too stretched to see end to end. *Quasar,* a vessel of 114 feet and a 44-foot beam at its widest, was merely a lit pore against it.

Completely covering it were characters, pictographs, script, symbols, designs, every square inch, from the sizes of office buildings to the size of his hand, and even smaller, all flickering and moving and morphing.

Quasar and her passengers started a sideways drift, touring from right to left.

In awe, Nima whispered, "This monolith is the archive, the keeper of a billion stories. It is incomprehensibly ancient, involved in genetics, proto-genetics, templates in the ground of all being. And Siren, *its* keeper, is a goddess, *and* a cosmic citizen, and She has been involved in projects all over Creation."

"Yeah? I wish I could say that excites me."

"Please be patient with yourself," Nima said with an edge. She stood and stepped closer to the viewport, and Gavin joined her. Gesturing at the golden-graphite face and all the embossed art, she said, "These tell the tales of worlds upon worlds, civilizations come and gone, entire solar systems, countless parsecs of them, all come and gone...wars, brutality, peace and plenty, pastoral cultures and super-advanced cities, an eternity of evolutionary experiments." Turning to him and touching his arm, she said, "Soon, we'll be inscribed upon its face."

"Why are you telling me this?" said Gavin, turning to eye her profile.

"Because it's important for you to know you're involved in something much larger than yourself," she said, meeting his gaze.

But Gavin had caught the subtlety in her cues. There was a pattern, and he was decoding it. She was avoiding his original question, and that was a *very* human thing to do. He faced her, tipped his head to the side and said, "Nima, do you care about me?"

Nima shuddered from head to toe and retreated a few steps with apprehensive eyes, then turned and walked back over to the command chair and sat. While looking with vacant eyes at the shimmery, morphing obelisk drifting by, in a quiet and vulnerable voice, she said, "I chose this, what's happening to me, but nothing prepared me for what it would be like." Emotions skirmished with her face, tiny twitches and tells. "I find myself losing contact with Whole." She quickly shook her head and blinked. "Xenxu, I mean. The single mind that It is. Before choosing this, I didn't know how that would feel. Now I know what humans mean when they say, be careful what you ask for."

Gavin stayed at the viewport, watching her.

"You have to understand, we Ai *are* Whole, but in individuated parts. We're more like subroutines than we are people. When necessary, we know everything Whole knows." Her eyes flicked to his. "My contact with Whole is fading away, quickly. From working with you. From Siren's gift to me to feel as humans do. I feel"—she shrugged, her eyes misting—"lost." Her chin trembled with the onrush of pure feeling. "I find this…frightening." She leaned back and put her hands on her tummy. "It gives me…sensations in here I've never felt before."

Gavin ambled over and sat, slinging a leg over the chair's arm. "Go on."

She still wouldn't look at him. Gavin also focused on the passing shimmery gold scene out the viewport.

She went on. "I find myself…*confused* by whatever all this is propagating through my circuitry. I feel as though I should not…" she scratched her cheek and fiddled with her fingers, "…reveal to you my…my vulnerability. And I don't even know why that is. Or *what* that is. It's like one more mystery thing to be afraid of."

Gavin filed his thumbnail on his teeth as he turned his face back to her, his eyes tracing her profile. Those eyes were shiny, scared, and he'd never seen that on *any* Ai personi.

"The human body design happens to be a very successful one, all over the Cosmos. These personi organs…they are just emulative functions, but those emulation streams are…they're so *powerful*." She put both hands to her heart. "My heart," she said, her voice cracking, eyes filling with shine. "I didn't know it could feel like this."

"How does it feel?"

Nima's eyes searched around, her jaw moving. Then she found it. "Filled with wonder, like it can't catch its breath, fear, questions. So many questions." She looked like she might come apart.

Scratching his temple, Gavin said, "What are you afraid of, Nima?"

She shot to her feet and walked over to the viewport. "I don't know!" she cried. With her back to him, arms and hands gesturing, she said, "I have found out you cannot experience reality as humans do without perceiving yourself to be separate from Whole. Whole is infinitely supportive. You can't have fear when you *are* Whole and you *know* it."

"*There's* a bumper sticker for you." Gavin stood and went over, stopping inches from her back. "Nima, look at me. Turn around and look at me."

"I can't."

"Why not?"

Voice quiet and trembly. "Because you scare me more than anything."

Gavin leaned down closer to her ear and said, "And why is that?"

Nima closed her eyes as his breath caressed the tiny hairs on her neck, yet another sensation completely new to her. Eyes still closed, she breathed, "Because of how that felt just now." She touched her lips. "Because of how you look at me. Because of how I feel when I look at you." She stepped away from him, closer to the viewport, and turned to face him, eyes wet and shiny and trying to figure things out. "As I lose contact with Whole, I'm afraid that you...that you're... that...you're all I have. My whole life revolves around you."

"What's your game, Nima?" said Gavin, his face softening for this trembling bird of an Ai, now touching on the periphery of what it is to be human.

Now her tears were flowing as she whisper-sobbed through them, "My game is your game."

"Now you get it," said Gavin, opening his arms. She ran into them. He put his hand on the back of her head, holding her close. "We're both alone, but I don't know why we look at it that way. I don't know what's happening with us, but at least we can count on each other. Do you feel that's true?"

"I've never felt hope before you," she sniveled into his chest. "But

I do now. Oh, these feelings! I hope...I...I hope you have the...I hope you feel for me how..."

"I do, Nima. Hard to believe, but I can't deny it."

"Oh Gavin!" she cried into his chest. "How it *feels* for you to say that! What is *happening* to me!"

6

You are not enlightened, because there is no you to be enlightened.
—Jed McKenna

Gavin stood by his pod as the Neuronet ballet of electric iridescent energies flashed, the pod lights and tubules and synaptic conjunctions dancing and throbbing around him, endless in every direction. Gazing off into the glowing snarled expanse, he could see a naked woman slipping into hers. Behind him a few hundred yards, a naked man did the same, waving at Gavin as he lifted his leg over the bulb's rim. Farther away, way back in the voluminous efficiency of it all, he thought he could see several more. And this was just one virtual instance of this chamber of probably dozens.

The membrane lids for his were already open, and the particle-filled and faintly glowing aquamarine liquid was swirling around. This time, instead of throwing a thrashing panic fest, he was determined to stay in trust mode as that thing filled with him submerged in it. He knew everything in-Xenxu was emulated, so he couldn't, ultimately, drown, but still, survival programming overrides any scrap of rational thought.

Kicking off his shoes and pulling off the socks, he dropped the jogging pants to his ankles and stepped out of them while pulling the sweatshirt off over his head. Now as naked as he was at the pond earlier that day, he cupped up a double palmful of Siren's fluid ectoplasm, splashing it onto his skin and rubbing it around. Another double palmful over his head, and he stood with his eyes closed.

It was a short list of memories he had access to before being about eight years old, but one had stuck with him. His mother bathing him as a baby. It was strange because he could remember that his squirming little giggles delighted her. And he'd done it to delight her. On purpose.

"Isn't that the thought of something more than an infant?"

Stepping over the lower lid with more panache than last time, he sank into the fluid, and this time noticed a tingling energy. The lids closed and seamlessly sealed and the bulb began filling. His face was lighted by the faint glow of the liquid, his eyes sharp and clear. As the waterline reached his chin, he dipped his mouth below surface and inhaled. He jerked and twisted, his personi reacting from his Earth body's signaling.

As he breathed the amniotic fluid and calmed, closing his eyes, he realized he was a fetus, inside the Mother. He'd been there before, remembering this from his deepest instincts. It was calming, wonderful. He felt the flow on his exhale. Such a wild and weird feeling, having something that dense and viscous exit his chest.

The bulb was full to the top, and now he was suspended in this fluid, touching no part of the pod. The temperature was the same as his skin, so no way to physically feel where he ended and the liquid started. In his mind, he saw a fetus. Feelings from this tiny entity floated through his feeling body, tickling across threads of comprehension. The fetus was...curious, but had no reason to think, only to receive.

I see how it's done.

Gavin let himself empty and opened to receive. The emptiness was the secret, as thoughts were a messy clutter on the path between himself and where he must go. Soon, he slipped *into* emptiness, fully aware. He released his feelings to flow throughout Neuronet, and was happy he was so tangibly connected to others here, too many to count.

He felt the familiar phasing away of...himself. Now and then he'd come to and remember where he was, the sounds would return, and he'd focus again on emptiness. It wasn't long before he arrived at a point where nothingness and a simple sense of self occupied the same space—nothing beyond pure observation and curiosity.

Images began emerging, vague, partially formed, fleeting. The aurora over his Pholo dome. Panels with his art. Lissa's work of the palace. Jagged ridges. They overlapped, folded on themselves, imploding and reblooming. As it all resolved, he felt himself solidifying, becoming present within something that felt foreign but familiar. Then it all pulsed and shuddered into focus, and he was standing there on his Pholo Studio 3D platform in the gray Nehru suit, in the personi of the Gavin doop Suzhi asked him to put in the suit. Looking down at himself, his furry brows flew up as he said, "Holy *shit*! Lights on!"

As he looked around, it was instantly plain Xenxu personi sense, no, *feel*, Xenxu differently than human personi. This was more like *feeling* with your eyes and ears. Xenxu was like Earth in that there were objects and spaces between those objects, the way a human would perceive them. In this perceptual mode, space and objects were the same thing, objects merely occurring from the background energy medium as organizations of color, shape, and purpose. The chair wasn't a chair. It was just differently colored energy paired with shape. This was also true about himself. He already knew that to sit in the chair was programmed agreement between the pixels of his butt and back and the faux leather of that chair.

"Xenxu space *is* form," he said, looking around. "It has the same density as the objects within it. That's buff as hell."

He lifted an arm to look at it, turning it, looking at the back of his hand, eyes wide and curious. He realized it wasn't just *his* movement.

The space itself moved his arm, like a branch rising in a wave, but his thought to move his arm was in collaboration with the medium of the intelligent emptiness. The thinking environment and his own thoughts were a creative alchemy.

Raising a hand to his lips, he said, "Is my mouth moving? It is." He raised his palms and studied them. "This feels so strange. I'm *everything* moving. Am I in Xenxu's causal layer? Is this more like the Metaself perceives?"

Looking down at his feet, he saw they were bare, and his head tipped back in a blown away shake. "Oh...ho ho ho," he sniggered. "Oh my God. Siren. Just when I thought I was done believing in You." He held out his arms. "I like how this suit tingles *all* my surfaces."

Turning toward the big soft chair, he said, "Let's see if I fall through this thing."

He sat, and it supported him, and the interaction between his backside and the chair was ticklish, sensitive, fizzling and sizzling. "Everything feels so *good*!"

Gavin breathed deeply, just so pleasured, a little smile. Wiggling a little, he nestled into the chair. Lacing his fingers at his navel, he closed his eyes and visualized the spot out in the plaza where he had seen himself in the Nehru suit weeks ago. Pieces of the scene blipped in and out, but were filling in. Focusing, he made sure to just watch it do its thing, and it became more vivid, defined, palpable. A moment came and he pushed his will into the equation. The studio disintegrated, simultaneously replaced with Plaza Zan.

He hadn't actually gone anywhere.

"Wow!" Looking at the arms of the chair now not there, he used them to push out of it, rising from nothing. "Everywhere is the same place," he whispered, staring. "It just reconfigures itself around you. This is nuts, man. For real. I made the suit from seeing me in it. Talk about an answer for the chicken and egg thing."

Gavin got looking around, and *wow* was this place alive! "Show me how Xenxu sees itself," he said.

Nima's voice sliced in. *That's big energy. I can show you this for about forty Earth seconds before it interferes with the critical energy allocations of your task.*

"K. Thanks."

The entire place instantly changed. Personi became fuzzy, brightly colored ovoids, bobbing and flowing about like schools of phosphorescent fish in a boundless ocean of dazzling shapes and geometries, colors and currents. The matrix within which it all moved was a gelatinous mélange of mingling and merging and undulating pixelation. He couldn't even make out the city, not as *he* knew it, but by his attention he quickly felt its reverberation. It was more like a map of feeling than of sensing.

This is an instructive example of how one perceptual level of your Metaself might see things on Earth. Look at yourself. Because reality data is shaped by perceptual filters, humans look like humans only through human eyes. No other species anywhere in Creation sees you the way you see you.

"Wow," his voice trembled out. He looked at himself and he was an ice-blue plasma-like nervous system with fainter anthropomorphic flowing outlines, rippling tiny streams of energy off its surface. "You can really *feel* this level, or maybe more like your integration *with* it. You *are* it."

You see? We feel, just not the way you guys do. But time's up and get back to work.

Yes, ma'am.

The other perceptual filter mode resolved, like *that*. Turning, he spotted Gavin over by the noob orientation. "Gnosis just appeared. K. Here we go. He's looking over here." The thought to wave happened and the entire place waved Nehru Gavin's hand. "Wild. Jammin! Oh my God. K. He's debating. She's at his shoulder, lecturing him…me… about confusion. And fear. God, she was snarky that night, but fickin nailin' it. He'll start walking about…now. Yep." Gavin's eyes widened yet again. "No, the entire place is closing the space between us while he walks in place and I stand here, being moved toward him. It's insane how all this works. My God. What do I say to him?" Gavin's thick brows crinkled. "What *did* I say to me that night?"

As oblivious Gavin neared, Xenxu itself yelled through Nehru

Gavin, "Greetings and salutations, breather of no air, seer of no things!"

Zoot Gavin stopped. "Oh I get it. Deep Climb's RPG having me face my dark side," he said, twiddling his hands in the air.

"You've traveled *so* far, impetuous pilgrim. Bread for your sustenance?" Gavin's hand opened and a small loaf appeared in it. He extended the bread toward the stricken him. The loaf glowed, pulsated softly. Nehru Gavin chuckled inside.

"Oh...is this...is this like some metaphor in...like, manifesting what you want?" Zoot Gavin said, again twiddling his hands in the air. "Like, the universe provides if I'd just let it? Heard *that* one before."

"The universe provides!" Gavin in the Nehru belted out, like he was in a play and wanting to be heard all the way at the back.

Zoot Suit Gavin took a paranoid step back, his pale face like that of a man being charged by a gorilla, his lips straight lines. "You're freakin' me out," he said, his eyes darting around.

"Ah I know...just havin' some fun with you," he said with a smile. Then he was walked toward confused Gavin, and the whole place moved frightened Gavin back another step.

The whole place did that. It moved his personi. It moves everything, all the time, speaks everything we speak. Am I right about that?

Yes.

Holding up his hands, the loaf dematerialized as he said, "Ah OK," while trying hard to not be blown away by what he was learning. "I'll keep my distance. Can we just walk up here?" he said, flicking a thumb toward something going on up a shallow incline over there. "Walk with me. I'll explain everything."

"You know...is it possible we can just pause the service for a night? I'm not up to this."

"No...seriously. You're going to walk up here."

"No I'm not," said victim Gavin, his face in *try me* mode.

Nehru Gavin's face brightened and he tipped his head back and laughed. "No," he said, still laughing. "What I mean is you've already walked..." The words caught in his throat, which told him had some volition for just a tick. "Ah...well...maybe I'm not supposed to...you know what? Hang on."

"Hang on? What do you mean? For what?"

"You'll see. Be just a tick or two."

Distraught Gavin looked around and shouted, "Cancel! Can we cancel?" as something nearly invisible congealed around him, like a swarm of atoms, distorting him and the space two to three feet out from his personi. He put his hands on his abdomen, his face stricken and pale.

"What's wrong?" said Nehru Gavin.

Zoot Gavin's face was in a vomitous grimace. "I...I don't know. Something's come over me," he said, choking back bile. "And I can smell my...my sheets, *again*."

Nehru Gavin tuned everything out and let Xenxu autopilot his body and everything else while he recalled what happened that night, when he was suddenly infused with whatever was making him sick.

When that happened to me that night, I wondered what it might be, that cloud of whatever surrounding me. Gnosis couldn't even detect it. Nima?

Running diagnostics.

You didn't run them that night?

I wasn't working in this capacity.

Now they were at the group's backsides, and Nehru Gavin, for the first time of his own full volition (or so it seemed), said, "Listen to this kid. You'll learn something. Promise. Fare thee well, gentle traveler." He was laughing as he faded away.

A brilliant dome of pure neon joy erupted inside, and he opened his eyes in his pod.

"Holy *smokes!*" he fluid bubbled out, the words sounding like *obeli omo,* as the liquid was draining away. Grabbing himself at the solar plex, he doubled over and regurgitated the oxygen fluid from his lungs and into the draining stream. It was then he realized he was still in the Nehru suit. Blinking wide-eyed at the shimmers, his face pale blue, he said, "We are both cause and effect. That's a big one. If that's true IRL, it's *really* big."

Something was happening inside him, a tremor, a shake, rattle, and roll. Then it burst forth. "Hahahahahahaha!" He flipped backwards and flailed his arms and kicked his legs in the gelatinous fluid, splashing like a kid. "Ho God. Hahahahahaha!"

The glowing energy cylinder rose from the floor, and Gavin materialized in it holding a pile of dripping wet gray cloth. Nima was standing at the console. Stepping down the two stairs, he dropped the wet stuff on the floor with a *splack* and said, "Do you know what the liquid is in that suit?"

"First off," she said, sidestepping the console and handing him a towel, "nice work. You interested in knowing what you just did?"

"Sure," he said, rubbing his head with the towel.

"You created a causal time loop by inserting yourself into a fixed point in time, but from a fluid time construct. Do you see what I mean?"

"Yeah. I wouldn't have ushered myself to you without completing that exercise."

She took a step closer. "Right."

"And had I failed, I could just try it again. That's the part that kills me. Time's such a lie."

"Right. Gav, you're gaining a lead on those of your cluster doing this same training."

"Well, I learned as a kid I had to get empty to get out of my body," he said, walking over, his face taking on a faint shadow. "Intense pain can do that. And then something would come along and just...take me."

"That was your early training."

"Who?" he said, thick brows stitched. "*Who* was training me?"

Nima shrugged. "Siren, of course. But something happened to you in your life to better prepare you for this than most." Nima stepped back and sat. "I won't be surprised if it's the source of your deepest terror."

"Probably." He nodded, looking at her with stoked clear eyes. "I feel great. It's *way* energizing, doing that." His running shoes were already unlaced. Using his toes, he kicked them off and they *coppled* to the shiny black floor. "When I saw myself as that flow of energy, like I was electrical...I had this random thought it was the real me, and the human me I see in the mirror is just a costume."

"Like your personi, but humans only look like humans to *humans*. It's an image overlay in the continuum's programming. You should see how you look to a dragonfly, or an elk, or Gnosis, each as different a version of you as they could possibly be."

Gavin pivoted his face towards her. "What's our truest form?"

"If you mean the most fundamental, nothing but a frequency your visual tools can't arrange into a pattern definable by the human brain." She turned and flung her legs over the chair arm to face him. "The liquid in the suit...we've analyzed it. It's like a cross between spinal fluid and plasma, IRL *and* Xenxu. And the more you're in it, the more you become it."

"What do you mean?"

"Your Earth body's carbon isotopic chemistry is..." She stopped cold, staring absently like she was listening to something. She nodded slightly, in response to whatever she was just listening to, then said, "I'm allowed to say this. You have two more codons of DNA coming online in 3D."

"What?" Gavin sat up straighter. "Are you telling me you guys are changing my physical body?"

"It's fairer to say *you* are."

"Come on...bullshit."

Nima seemed all business now. "What you're clearing from your deep systemic archives is just another way of saying that you're removing inhibiting code from your genetic templates."

Gavin was looking at her like he was trying to figure out if she was about to crack up laughing and yell *kidding!* He wanted to ask her, *Is this a game?* But he didn't want that answer right now.

Just play the damned game.

His eyes clicking back and forth on hers, he finally said, "What I learned this time is Xenxu is all mind. Everything. No places, no solid things," he said, waving a hand. He gestured at the chairs. "No space between things. We don't travel. Motion's a lie. Xenxu just reconfigures itself while our mind stays in one *locale*."

"You are a brain in a vat. All of existence is *inside* that brain. Not outside it."

"That's a hell of a way to put it." Gavin shook his head, his eyes in wonder as he looked at his hands. "And Xenxu is moving you, thinking *through* you, and it's been that way all along. All that's happened is that I'm awake to that fact."

Nima tucked an errant lock of hair behind her ear, her smile on an angle. "You're thinking more and more *with* Xenxu's mind. Do you recognize why we do it this way?"

Gavin's eyes shifted from her left eye to her right, then back again. "Are you saying Xenxu is comparable to my Metaself?"

"Of course. It's a superb training modality because of the similar mechanics. You could say Xenxu is the Metaself of all its personi."

"And this is how I'm learning to...to...merge with *its* mind?"

She shrugged a shoulder. "You now see Xenxu, the world, as mental energy. If it's energy, then what's the potential of that when you use your brain's electromagnetic energy to mingle with and modify the energy of the reality?"

"I thought Xenxu was just data, pixels."

"Data *is* energy."

Gavin's bright eyes and furrowed brows said he was listening with great care to her words.

Nima gestured at him with a flat palm. "And what happens when you find out that's also true of Earth?"

He stared at her for a long moment. Finally, voice low, he said, "Are you saying I'm...that I'm being trained to do this stuff out there, IRL?" He pointed vaguely at *Quasar*'s bulkhead.

Nima kicked one leg as she smiled with bright teeth. "Thou sayest."

Gavin's busy roaming eyes didn't bother concealing how much he enjoyed watching her leg do that. "Thou sayest? Are we like Shakespeare now?" Gavin leaned out of the chair and pulled his shoes over, wiggling a foot into one. "I feel my other body being parched and hungry. Think I'll slide." Gavin stood and straightened with a back stretch of his shoulders. "Wanna meet for drinks later?"

"Love to," she said, smiling brightly. "Hey? Will you take me dancing sometime?"

"We'll have to download how to do that," he said, getting closer to her. "I never got the hang of it."

Nima sidled over, hips swinging a little in the skintight suit. "Shouldn't be too hard," she said, taking his hands and wrapping them around the small of her back. "I read up on it. You just let your body move with the music."

Gavin's grin was angled as he looked down at her. "You're a quick study on this human thing, you know."

"I'd like to try a kiss with you," she said, looking at his mouth. "Can we do that?"

"OK," he said, taking his hands back and turning her toward the chairs. "But I have to sit down."

"Why?"

"Because I get dizzy when I kiss someone I really vibe with," he said, sitting.

"Something is telling me what you just said is adorable." Bending over, putting her hands on his cheeks, she leaned in and let her lips graze his. Gavin seemed ill-prepared, his eyes open in surprise. She kissed him again, and he closed them. Putting her fists on either side of his thighs on the chair seat, she leaned in farther. Their lips explored, felt their way around, tasting, experimenting.

When their faces parted, Gavin's eyes were still closed, his mouth ajar. Nima was still leaning on her fists, eyes closed, her tongue tasting her lips.

"Jeezus, Nima," he purred like a big cat. "Where'd you learn to do that?"

She straightened with her fists to her chest, eyes wide. "I did what I knew would make me feel *this*. Do you feel this?"

Gavin's eyes fluttered open. "Let's just say I'm as dizzy as a fickin top."

Nima's eyes were round and excited as she said, "Go feed and water that body, and let's go play somewhere. Can we go play somewhere?"

Gavin winked. "Exit Xenxu."

In the dingy motel room, Gavin took off the headset, fumbled it aside, and rubbed his eyes. Parts of the room's curtains were threadbare, and through patchy holes he saw the faint light of the streetlight from outside. On the nightstand was a plastic cup full of water. He propped up on an elbow and took it in three gulps. Not enough. On his feet, he went to the little fridge, where he had a gallon waiting. Taking it out, he opened his throat and poured it into his body like he was filling a gas can, taking half of it before stopping for air.

Dawkins sitting on the floor in his man cave with empty water bottles like dead rodents all around him.

"Nope," he said as he set the jug aside. Feeling so good, eyes clear, he giggle-chittered, "Nima," and did a little jig, hands over his head and snapping his fingers like he was in some Greek dance at a wedding. Then his bum hip popped and he stopped, grimacing with his hand to it like he was holding it in place. He hopped to the bed and toppled onto it, bouncing with squeaky springs, gazing with starry eyes at the stained ceiling.

"Wow," he whispered, his eyes shifting around on the tiles. "I'm having a *very* hard time deciding if I'm supposed to take what she says literally. I mean, if what she's saying is literal, they're turning me into a superhero. And that's absurd."

Rolling onto his side, he saw his filmfon's LED fading in and out on the end. "Nope," he said, sliding his hand under his cheek. "You ain't bringing me down this time." His eyes had that faraway dreamy look, like you see on a man who's beginning to feel adored by the object of his own desire. Blinking, he pushed himself upright and said, "Now to find something to eat."

That op wasn't easy until he found a market, "Horner's Foods," in the now revitalized downtown, that carried a local produce section. As you might expect, the other end of it was a hardware store that had racks with flannel shirts and jeans. He stood at the rack, holding out a red flannel sleeve. "Style...it's timeless, and above all, flexible," he said, letting the sleeve drop.

He bought a locals ensemble and put it on in the hotel room. He made a dashing hick, if you don't mind. And now, at the little round table with the wan yellow light over it, he was eating lettuce like a giant apple, celery sticks and watermelon, thinking he may as well just eat his water. This *thirst!*

"And it's got me thinking thoughts I prefer not to think, thanks very much." He looked sideways at the curtains. He didn't like the smell of them, but what you going to do about that? He dragged them aside, and looked outside as the wind started kicking up.

His filmfon was on the table, and chomping on a celery stick, with some of it still hanging out of his mouth, he tapped something. It rang on the other end.

"Well as I live and breathe," said his mom, her voice like a fingernail on parchment. "If it ain't the bird of fire rising from his own ashes." She didn't want one of them stupid filmfons, and a video call? Waste of cloud or bandwidth or whatever you kids call it.

"Hi, Momma," said Gavin, sliding the fon closer. "Can you hear me all right?"

"Ain't deaf, but who turned out the lights!" she bleated, then laughed till she coughed. "Jus' jokin' with you, son. Now tell your old momma what you been up to."

"You sound good. Is it too late to call?"

"Ain't passed on yet."

"I meant the *hour,* Momma," he said, his grin on an angle.

"I know what you meant, son."

Gavin's furry brows bent and crinkled, troubling with themselves over her new wit. Then it hit him. Timeline shift.

Forgot all about that.

Like he was cradling a baby, Gavin put his arms around the fon on the table. "Momma, I think you must be feverish, which is the way I like you."

"Ah, would you stop with the spatter and tell me what you been up to."

"Well, I'm out home," he said, picking the fon up and heading to the bed. Sitting, he stacked the pillows against the saddle-themed headboard, toed off his shoes, and kicked back on the bedcover.

"Tending to your roots?"

He slid the earstim in and set the fon aside. "Yes, ma'am."

"Atta boy," she said. "Drag Heather out there with you next time."

"Nobody gonna drag Heather anywhere," said Gavin, his fingers tapping his thigh.

"Ain't that the truth. Well, bind and gag her and toss her in the trunk. She'll be happy you did, in the end."

Gavin laughed hard at that. "Jeezus, you still got it." And he wasn't even sure what he meant by that, as he said, "They painted that water tower and gussied up Reeds Park," he said, picking some celery fibers out of his teeth with a fingernail and re-eating it. "I went out there today and talked to Daddy."

"You been to his grave?"

"Drove by. He's anywhere but there."

They went on jabbering about things and stuff, sunshine late in the day and the rains come early, and "you remember that" times. He was used to her getting after him, harping on meds, finding a woman and get after having kids. But this was just plain fun. Gavin couldn't help but smile how much better he liked this timeline.

By and by, when the moment was fat with juice and ripe, he said, "I think I met myself a fine lady, Momma."

"You have my permission to marry her," her voice scraped, then she laughed until a raspy wet cough took over. "Just joshin'. Is she nice? You need someone with a brain. Them girls you brought home…a cog or two missin'."

"She's brilliant, and *so* sweet," said Gavin, spinning the filmfon on the bed cover, watching the trees sway and flutter in the wind outside the window. "She's kind and generous, loves kids and animals, and sick old people."

"Ah don't you be pullin' one over on your old momma, now."

Gavin told her about how he met her at an amusement park, and she just took his breath. They'd only been out for drinks and a kiss, the courtship being done all proper. How she's an astrophysicist getting tenure and is very busy. That she's teaching him a thing or two about life, how to take it in stride, turn whatever comes to the good.

"I like the feel of this one, son—"

"Uh-oh, here it comes."

"Well...don't go crazy on her. We know you don't mean any harm, but it *scares* folks. Make sure she has even *more* room than she thinks she needs. Women like 'at are like cats, *especially* the smart ones."

"It's what I'm doing, Momma."

"If it gets more serious, you bring her out here. I have to look in her eyes."

"I know you do."

"Son, I'm glad you stopped talking like you're from Connecticut. That was phony as all get out."

"I know it, but you know? We're *all* actors on the Great Stage."

"Ain't that the truth."

They prattled about Nima, about women in general, and something about the real heartbreak of pretty birds in gilded cages is half of them don't know that's where they are, while the other half is "happy fer it." They touched on Celia and Lissa, what fine girls they were. About Heather's new beau, and if he'd turn out to be worth a shit. Then, in vapors of family love and good vibes, they signed off.

Gavin folded his arms and closed his eyes. He could smell her housedress, maple and tomatoes and soil, and a little tangy sour that comes from hard sweaty work. The scents in the sewing room were a thread to all that was real, heaven and home in the same drifting airs —fresh unmade fabrics, leather, and the oak of that full-length mirror. Gavin filled his nostrils with the past, like an aural nectar.

He opened his eyes. "Yeah, we lived in a shack, but it was home, and it was mostly wonderful, when I think back on it." He touched his sternum. "Feels good to know that."

A text came through.

AI NIMA

You coming?

GAV

Just a few more minutes.

Gavin yawned, big and deep. He closed his eyes and sighed, relaxed his jaw and chest. So tired. Feels nice. Drifting on warm currents is so nice. Warm. Breathing deepening. Arms dropped to the bed. Chin to chest.

The fair, animals and hay and twirling lights, running and laughter. Bells and stuffed animals. A small crowd of folks around a small stage. Wooden marionettes, a girl and a boy, balls for joints, dowels for limbs, hats not of this era. Strings tugging, they clickety-clack around the small stage with the curtains, bumping into each other, eyes dead, limbs akimbo. Now they can't get out of each other's arms, their strings tangled, and they collapse to the stage like the puppet handles were dropped, becoming a single pile of lifeless wood and twine.

A fon chime. Then another.

Gavin's eyes fluttered open, and they were spooked, and not just a little. He looked at the fon beside his hand.

AI NIMA

What's taking so long?

His eyes shifted to the new file from Sophia. Sighing deeply, he rolled his eyes and looked at the ceiling, then back down, tapping the icon.

A video opened with wooden puppets on a homemade stage, a girl and a boy performing between shabby curtains. The soundtrack was slow, low and dissonant and distorted, like the sound at a depraved carnival with dark things slipping around behind the tents. The two bumped around, ungainly in the tight space, eyes dead as sharks.

"They're inside my head," he said, swiping the filthy rotten thing away. Then rubbing his beard-stubbled face, he picked up the fon.

GAV

I want to see you, but I'm so beat. I think I'll try to get some quality rest.

AI NIMA

OK. That sounds best, but under protest.

GAV

See you soon.

Gavin switched chats and replied to Sophia.

GAV

I'll be inworld in five minutes.

SOPHIA

Just go to Woody's Tavern.

Gavin's eyes widened. "The sick bastards followed me here."

He jumped up, grabbed the ARX fob and dashed out the door.

Woody's was a seventy-year-old establishment at the edge of town. It made no bones about its age, never bothered with any of that fancy siding and bright signs. It was still stained cedar wood, wagon wheels in the rail, a derelict mini windmill of splitting wood, Cold Beer blinking neon in the windows. Train axles and wheels adorned one side of it, serving as an enclosure structure for chicken wire fencing, and there were live animals in there.

Gavin sat in the ARX, parked in a streetlight shadow made by a big sycamore's branches hanging over the lot. He watched the entrance as locals went in and out, came out to fire up smokes, went back in. Some left with gals in jeans-skirts and cowboy boots and big hair. Now and then he held up his fon and zoomed in. Not once did he see anybody who didn't look like they belonged, and he was here within five minutes of that last text.

Getting out, he tucked the flannel shirt into the jeans and walked over, eyes still scanning the front, and the bikes and trucks parked there. A lot of bikes, almost all gas powered. Two electric Corzos were off to the side, like they'd been ostracized from the company of their elder fellows.

While walking, Gavin said under his breath, "Hope I don't run into somebody I know."

As he neared, country music and a buzz of partying voices loudened. A waft of cheap cologne smacked him in the face as he opened and stepped through the heavy oak door. "What the hell was that stuff called? Saddle Bone or something like that?" he said, swinging his gaze around at this time capsule of dark-stained wood, the floor littered with peanut shells. The music was too loud for the space, the guitars *too* twangy, screechy, if that was possible in a place like this.

The cover band on stage, a group of long-haired and bearded geezers, ended their mangled cover of "Long Haired Country Boy," an old tune Gavin happened to love. Gavin spotted the band name on the bass drum: *Blown Tires*. In the dark, somebody whistled. Somewhere in the back a woman laughed loud enough to be heard outside.

"Thank you," called the lead guitarist into his mic from under a straw hat, broken strings *boinged* in all directions from his guitar. "We gonna take a break, have a drank, see y'all right back here in fifteen." The bandstand lights dimmed as the band members receded into the dark.

He'd never been in here as an adult, so he took a beat to feel what it must have been like back in the day. His dad would come here sometimes, and Gavin would ride his bike over and go in and get him. Under Momma's orders, as she held rank too, you know.

Some burly bearded guys burst through the door, making him wince and turn. They made eye contact and walked straight his way. Gavin's gut sank as that old fear of bullies reared up and seized his chest. But their gruff, scowling faces erupted into shit-eating grins with the excited squeals of a few beefy biker babes who brushed Gavin's elbows as they clamored by into the arms of their knights in shining hog hide. Gavin let out a relieved breath and slinked away from them, taking cover near a big wood carving of a bear.

Gavin did not fit in here, despite the new duds. He looked like he should be at the chapel up the road a piece, with suspenders and an Amish hat, like he'd stepped through a portal into the wrongest den of iniquity a God-fearing man could ever find. The walls closed in a little, the smells and dark and music with buzzy bar noise getting to him.

To the left were the booths and tables, folks in jeans and boots and hats at them, talking and carrying on. As Gavin scanned the booths, the jukebox whirred to life with some old Hank, Jr. or Sr. or whoever. There. A dark-haired man in a black long-sleeved shirt was watching him from under a pale green light. Gavin lifted his chin, and the guy waved him over.

Butterflies erupted in his middle, brushing all those fraidy cat places as he strode over, the guy still watching his eyes. The table in front of him held two beer bottles, and one hand resting on it was small, a woman's, but the angle of his approach blocked the view of her. The guy gestured at the seat opposite him and Gavin slid onto the old cushioned seat beside the lady stranger. He turned to see who it was looking at him.

Amethyst eyes. Short hair and freckled pixie face. Pretty smile.

"Cat!" he yelled in utter horror. The room stretched, her face receded, black splotches danced in his vision as a torpedo of nausea slammed into him amidships.

She was quick to put her hands to his cheeks. "Gavin, just breathe." His eyes shot around in their sockets as she tried getting her own bright eyes in front of his. "Look at me. Hey, look at me. Right here. Eyes." Never one to take shock in stride, he was having a hard time getting a grip, but Cat was good in the soothing department. As good as she was at sending a friend spiraling into a kaleidoscopic new life of peril and uncertainty. "Just breathe, Gavin. You don't want to make a scene in here. That's it. Yeah. There we go. Breathe."

Panting, clenching and unclenching his fists, it took him a few ticks to get it together, looking back and forth between them like he was seeing ghosts. Ghosts with fangs and blood coming out of their eyes. Then he got to noticing she was in a dark one-piece suit, like a cross between an astronaut and after-work cocktails. A gold pin on her chest above a breast pocket was the same figure-eight used by Deep Climb, but on its side.

It's a uniform.

That brought him into the moment, as he calmed some.

The other guy poked out his hand. "I'm Jackson."

Without shaking it, Gavin looked at Jackson's hand and then back at Cat. He stared at her, in angry question, like *somebody better get talking or things could get CRAZY.*

Cat said, "You have questions, and yet there's only one answer to them all. You're not ready to hear that answer, but—"

"Oh for God's sake," said Gavin, still catching his breath, his eyes burning into her, "why can't anybody provide a straight answer to a—"

"A question?" cut in Jackson. He looked the military part. Arms filling his navy blue shirt. Up, tight and square hair config. Hard jaw. Thrumming the table with his fingertips, Jackson set down his beer and said, "You haven't asked one yet, but whatever questions you have, you're going to have to answer for yourself. Like we all did."

Without taking her eyes off Gavin's, she took a swallow from her beer, and set it back onto its own wet ring on the table. "We're here right now in this jammin old dive drinking these cold beers to let you know we're here, and to help you find not just the answers, but the questions."

Gavin closed his eyes as he inhaled, shaking his head like a man who was done with all this nebulous tedious fickin maddening *shit*.

Jackson took a swallow from his beer and set it back onto the scarred and scratched lacquer table. Gavin again noticed water rings on the marked table from the condensation on the beer bottles. Two of them intersected, making a Vesica Pisces, part of Deep Climb's logo.

He had himself a private foul little snigger at that. He was in a rare incendiary mood. "You guys haven't brought up commitment, or doubt. No philosophy for me this night? That's new and different."

The other two exchanged glances. Scratching his sideburn, Jackson said, "Here's a good standard question. Who, or what, do you trust?"

Lissa. Heather. Nima.

Gavin lifted his eyes from the water rings to meet Jackson's. "Nobody. Nothing."

Cat said, "You're being handled, groomed. You're aware of this on some level. That's what brought you here, to us." Her eyes flipped to Jackson, then back to Gavin. "I know that look. I know it because I was you, sitting in my own bar booth, having this same conversation with someone determined to help me through this. And I know what you're thinking. Why me? For what? Those are good reductive questions, but can only be answered truthfully by understanding a *much* bigger picture. You could be like CR-17 crystal explosives that can either vaporize everything around them, or be bottled and channeled."

"For what?"

"That's what we'd all like to find out," said Jackson.

"All? Who's all?"

"Those who matter most from both sides," said Jackson.

"Sides?"

"You'll either fulfill that potential, or you'll flame out," said Cat, wiggling her fingers in the air. "Either way, we have to find out."

Gavin's glowering eyes and angry brows switched back and forth between them. Behind Jackson's head on the old dark wooden bench-back were scars cut with knives over the years; initials, dirty pictures, rune symbols, which told him the superstitions around these parts were more ingrained than some might think. One of them was for strength of will, which pointed to one that essentially meant "onto the path of things to come," in that context.

To Cat, he said, "Were you her inworld?"

"Sometimes."

"Was it you in the red heels, the night you railed me into signing up for Deep Climb?"

"That was me, but they were purple."

Rubbing his temple with a pained squint, he said, "You're far perkier inworld."

"All an act," she said, palm up, wrist bent. "Which I think is fun as hell."

"What about Marli and Conner?"

"They were Ai. Which reminds me…can I have a hug?"

Gavin leaned over and they hugged in the booth. "You feel real to me. So *that's* something."

"I'm so sorry we have to show you truth this way," she said, close to his ear. "But it'll all make sense." Her hand wandered to the back of his neck and he felt a sharp prick.

"Ow!" barked Gavin, slapping a hand to the spot. Then he felt a surge through his circuitry. His face morphed into that of a trapped rodent, eyes in white terror, sweat shine on his forehead and cheeks.

"A gift from Sophia," she said.

Gavin's eyes spun as he croaked, "Whuh? Oh God. I'm gonna be sick," he said, heaving once and covering his mouth.

"Come on. Let's get you outside."

Gavin stumbled across the room, bumping patrons' chairs, Cat holding his arm, saying to a stubble-faced ruffian, "He's a lightweight. Sorry. Come on, baby. Let's get you home." Jackson waved an invisible pen for the check, and a candy-lipped bumpkin with all kinds of cleavage nodded his way. They bumbled and tottered through the entrance and went right.

"Just a second more, Gav. Over here," said Cat as Gavin heaved and doubled over, holding his hand over his mouth, dribbles starting between his fingers.

She led him around the train wheels and axles chicken pen—and the birds did run around and cluck—to the bushes and fence at the back of the joint. Gavin went to all fours and heaved like tectonic plates were shifting inside, pushing the putrid magma up his gullet. Cat went down on a knee, her hand on his back, saying, "Hold nothing back, Gav. I *mean* that."

"Ooowaah. Oooooowah," he vomited, ferociously, tortured and blind. Tumbling out of him were shiny black cubes, pattering in squidgy *plops* into the weeds. Shocked and confused by the sight, he kept heaving, like a bull being murdered in the dark, and the cubes twisted and morphed and became a splatter of chunky bile and bubbled liquid.

Cat patted him between the shoulder blades. "It's called The Purge. Don't leave anything inside. It looks like you're cleansing and prepping for something big."

Gavin heaved until the sick stinky cauldron within could produce no more. Coughing, panting, crying, moaning, he choked out, "Cat?"

"I'm here."

"What's Sophia?"

"Also a great question, but—"

"I'll say this," said Jackson, joining them, his feet crunching on the gravel somewhere behind, "even if I shouldn't. Think of Him as Infinite Logic. Now let's get him back to his room."

"Him?" croaked Gavin, still on all fours, round eyes staring through the weeds.

"It's all polarity," said Cat. "You ready to stand up?"

"Yeah." Gavin grunted his way to his unsteady feet.

Cat held his arm as Jackson stepped over. "Sorry, but we have to talk some shop. Our last video showed you and Nima as entangled puppets. In a quantum sense, that's true. Your polarities are entangled, and your entanglements don't start in this iteration. We threaded backwards in your streams as far as we could go, and you two are quantum alchemy. I know what I'm saying doesn't make sense, but we promise you it will."

Feeling like boiled feces, Gavin wiped his acrid mouth with his flannel sleeve and grumbled, "Get to the point."

Cat sidestepped into his view. "She's...anomalous. Keep her close, but stay frosty."

"Frosty?"

"On your toes."

"Toes? You know, I've never even known what *that* means."

"OK, Gavin. Stay sharp."

Unsteady on his feet, hands out for balance, Gavin started across the gravel toward the ARX, Cat walking him like he was her grandfather needing help to get into his lounge chair.

In the diffused gray light of the glaspad, Gavin's crazed eyes and ashen, lined, gashed face made him look like he was in a horror flick, giving his final report over the airwaves with fanged aliens pounding down his door. He sat at the small round table with the horrible weak light over it. On the display was Lissa, in her jammies, her hair in a scrunchy, her blue eyes soft and open. And big. The girl had big eyes.

"What's news, princess?" he said as cheerfully as he could muster. With that discolored zombie mask, his attempt at cheery was merely macabre, like an old vampire trying to smile with a stake in his heart.

"Are you OK?" she said. "You don't look so good."

He set his chin on his palm. "I'm just exhausted. Did your momma tell you I came out home?"

"Is that why you're talking like them now?"

"M'lady, the other one was just an act. This is the real me. I'm off that jam, with your leave, of course."

"Granted," she said with a quick dimpled smile. "Why did you have to act?" she said, looking down at whatever she was holding below the view.

"Well...sometimes adults feel they need to run away from who they are."

Lissa's eyes swam around, looking for pieces. And they were finding them. They locked in on something, and it had to do with what was in her lap.

"I had another dream about you," she said. "Maybe this goes

along with that." Lifting and spreading her hands apart, she unfolded a gray paper chain of a man, presumably Gavin in something like his zoot suit. "This is what I saw in the dream...well, kind of. These are all you, you know? And this is what is happening to you," she said as her hands closed the distance and put them all back together. "Do you know what that means?"

"I think I might have an idea." Gavin's smile was tender, his eyes shiny wet. "All the king's men put him back together again?"

"I don't know," she said, looking down, then back up. "Isn't the huge queen doing that? You love her, don't you."

"Oh, Liss, with all my heart," he said, unable to keep from grasping his chest with both hands. "But how I feel for you is almost like that."

Sometimes her kid skepticism was laser as she studied him. Finally, she said, "That makes me happy, and I don't think you need fixing. I like you just the way you are." She set the paper chain aside. "You are an interesting man, Prince Uncle Gav." She blinked prettily at him, like a girl her age shouldn't be doing at her uncle, a respectable citizen of advancing years. "Why do you think you're broken?"

Gavin frowned in thought, tipping his head to the side, and said, "Maybe you're right, Liss. Maybe I'm just a regular cat and it's the world that is bong bong."

"Of course I'm right," she said, her eyelids fluttering.

A while later they were playing *Go Fish* on their glaspads with shared game views.

"Do you have any twos?" said Lissa.

"I have one two," said Gavin as his finger slid the two of hearts from his virtual hand to her hand.

"Yes!" she said, pumping a fist. "A set!"

"Hmmm. OK. Do you have any sevens?"

"Go fish," she said, giggling.

"Are you cheating?"

"On my honor," she said, tittering again and holding up her palm.

"K." Gavin reached over and tapped the draw pile. A three of diamonds flipped up and added itself to his hand. Now he had three of them.

Almost a set! Thank the very Christ!

Her eyes drilled into him with childish determination. "Do you have any queens?"

"Finally, young lady, it is time for you to go fishing," he said, his finger pointing teasingly at the draw pile.

Lissa frowned and tapped it, and then smiled, eyes twinkling.

"You're going to have to work on that poker face," he said.

With a weirdly adult grin, she said, "How do you know they're not fake tells?"

Solid point. Sometimes this child made him feel…deficient. But then his mental framework was anything but clear and chipper right this second.

They played for a while longer, listened to some music, and talked about what she was learning in school. Heather finally came and broke up the party, giving him an admonishing look like *you kept her up too late*.

Gavin waved good night as Lissa glanced back at the screen. Then he closed it down, closed his eyes, gripped his chest and croaked, "God, the *love*!" He stood and said to the amateurish painting of mountains hanging on the wall, "*That's* what I need to power me."

Gavin took one step and fell face first onto the bed, the springs squeaking like electronic rodents scurrying into the walls. He forgot to brush his filmy chunky teeth, to rinse his vomitous mouth, to undress, to kick off the shoes, to get under the covers. He forgot to do everything but fall into the deepest sleep of the undead. Soon, he was snoring like a smoke-belching old tractor, his hands and eyelids twitching.

When his eyes fluttered open, Gavin was on his back on the bed, fully clothed with hands clasped over his navel. Blinking, he realized where he was, and he hopped to his feet, ready for something. For the day. For whatever, but whatever it was, it was exciting! He took from the fridge his jug, tipped it up, and sucked from it like a feeding chick, emptying it. In the bathroom, he unzipped and peed for what seemed like five minutes with a loud *spluttering* echo, and then checked himself in the mirror, saying, "I feel lighter."

Black cubes and other messy nasty things tumbling out of his body.

"Cat called it The Purge."

He lightly touched the healing asphalt rash. More of the scab had flaked away, and the yellowish ooze spots had dried. Still raw, but good healing. Nothing septic going on there. He turned the sink tap and splashed his face. Walking out while toweling off, he looked around like he might see something to remind him about whatever.

If you go back, you won't find it less you purged something deep and black and ugly from yourself.

The metal box was on the floor under the nightstand. Retrieving it, he took it to the table, sat, opened it, and took out the pages.

Until you're ready, set these pages aside and come back to it. Don't be tempted to read on.

We all have something black and ugly inside, son. But I trust whatever that really is out there in that forest to guide matters with its unseen hand. I therefore assume you have expelled from your core whatever it was kept you from moving ahead. Time to take another step on the board.

This is how you'll find your own Stone, and uncover more of what's inside. Your Stone will give you what you need, so don't even bother asking it for what you want. I'm shameful to admit, though, that just touching mine lifted me right out of my hangovers. That always made me think I could drink just a little more. As you know, we have native blood in us. If you start connecting in a deeper way to that ancestry, don't be surprised, but cultivate it. You'll come across important pieces of wisdom.

I put this together from my granddaddy's mental pictures, and from what I learned in my research. Make sure you've fasted for at least eight hours. Even longer would be better. Don't take anything electronic with you, and if you can, go barefoot. It's how I walked it. I imagine your delicate snowflake feet might have something to say about that, but follow your gut. Maybe you can find some leather moccasins around there. Is Flagg's old trading post still there? If so, check with them. Even leather sandals would be better than rubber sole shoes.

To find it, you're going to have to use your intuitive gifts, the pull of your heart. Nothing else will get you there. I'm dang serious about this. Be humble. Get everything together I say below and get into the forest any way you like. I always went over the wall, just like you kids did when you snuck out at night. Ha! Bet you didn't know Momma and I knew that! If you can't go over the wall, go through that old catwalk. I know things will have changed around there by now, but that catwalk is a legal easement and should be there.

Make it fun, if you can. Go find your old stone fort. Yes, I knew about that too. Get naked and get in that creek. Use its flowing waters to purify. You can take water, but no food. Take those two little leather pouches, my Army ring and them beads. In one pouch is salt, sulfur in the other. You mix them in your palm and then sprinkle it around the area. If you find it, you'll know what I mean. If you don't, well, you probably didn't get clean enough. Slide the ring onto a finger-sized branch. That way it'll know I'm the one sent you. Put the beads in any hole you can find. You'll see what I mean. You're also going to have to take your own token to leave. I don't know what that might be, but you will.

Do not deviate from these instructions, and you should do just fine.

Gavin trekked the same trail on which Heather and he had fled for their lives in the moon-contrasted shadows that night. It was so grown over, it was sometimes hard to see it. This told him nobody came out here anymore, which was sad. The folks back in those abodes probably told their kids demons lurked out here. But the forest *liked* people playing in it, especially on a day like today, with brassy sun and a fresh breeze and the promise of adventure. While trekking along, he smiled, sniffing enchanting fragrances, enjoying the feel of the air and grasses.

In town he'd found some shorts, a T-shirt, and a shiny student backpack. He hadn't managed to find anything leather to wear on his feet—almost nonexistent these days. So he bought ten pairs of cotton knee-high gym socks in a dollar store and layered them on, and they were working all right, if he was mindful of the sharp stuff. Even though he hadn't felt quite right about it, he'd put his shoes in the backpack.

He was staying empty of mind, using the joy of the moment as his mantra. Now and again he'd stop, close his eyes, and listen to the winds. By the time he heard the creek to his right, he knew the wide bend in the trail, and wasn't far from Graystone, his vacation alcove where he dreamed and dreamed. A blue jay seemed to take a shine to him, squealing and squawking, alighting from one twig and flapping ahead, landing on a perch and waiting. "Appreciate the company," he said, watching it flutter onto a branch off the trail.

"K," he said, heading off trail. The bottoms of his feet were getting used to the sticks and pokes, and he was musing about that when he stumbled right upon his old stone fort. Setting the pack aside, he hunkered down and peered in. "It's so *small*." Inside was nothing but dirt and animal bones. But a visit to olden times wasn't to be. He'd have to be a shapeshifter to get in there.

Taking the pack, he went to the creek, stripped, and got in it, gulping air with wide eyes from the bracing cold. Hanging onto a branch, he floated face up, letting the sun kiss his face. The flowing water took with it his cares, the still clinging tiny specks of dark stuff. By the time he was used to the cold, he got out and stretched out in the grass to dry.

Something woke him. For all he knew, he'd taken a little nap, but he wasn't sure. What he was sure about was the pull his dad told him about. He felt it powerfully, like a magnet. It wasn't but a minute before he was up and dressed, socks layered on, and wending his way with a walking stick, waist-deep in forest floor vegetation, moving through random rows of leafed giants.

Stopping, he looked up and saw some crows circling over an escarpment. Looking back down, he thought he made out a kind of overgrown corridor through the trees, and a crow sat on a high branch. When he saw it, it squawked and flew on ahead a ways. On he trudged, for hours, sweaty, scratched, tired, his sails wilting, feet tortured and complaining and imploring him to get off them and give up this madcap search for a silly fantasy.

"I could picture Daddy sending me on a wild goose chase just for shits and giggles."

The crow he thought was guiding him had abandoned him.

"What the hell is it, anyway?" he said, looking up and seeing the circling crows getting no closer. Then he came across what looked like the same leaf-clogged corridor of before. "Am I walking in circles?"

Looking around, his eyes alert and a mite concerned, nothing seemed familiar. He had no idea where he was. And now he wasn't so sure about this pull. Doubt cascaded in, and he had flashes of himself, breaking a leg and dying in the forest within a couple miles of civilization. No fon. Out of water.

"Don't be stupid," he said, setting off again, grimacing, setting his feet down like he was negotiating hot coals.

Dusk came, and the long evening shadows deepened into dark.

With the walking stick, he cleared aside some low-hanging branches and leaves. "I do *not* want to sleep out here tonight." Ducking through, he stepped into a clearing with big granite stones. It was hard to clearly make them out, but they seemed...placed. "Face it, you couldn't find your way out of here if your life depended on it."

He found a quaint little alcove in the stones and sat, setting the backpack aside and pulling off the now dirt and green-stained socks. Even though he couldn't see them too well, the skin of his feet seemed OK.

"Nothing bleeding, anyways."

He sat and rubbed them for a while as the air cooled.

To the gray stone on his right, he said, "Why didn't I bring a jacket? A jacket. That's all. And a lighter." He shrugged, blinking like it was all madness. "Why didn't you bring a lighter, Gavin?"

Unable to decide what he should do, he sat, listening, fighting frustration, his eyes zipping around at every sound. The whole time he wondered what he should do. Keep walking in the dark? Seemed a good way to get hurt. Try to get some rest? He'd survive it.

"I know one thing you're *not* doing, is staying empty of mind."

Putting all the layers of gym socks back on, he kept a pair out for his arms, which he slid on as sleeves. Crawling under a granite overhang, he slid the backpack under his head, lay on his side, and listened to the night.

By and by, his mind meandered into the mesmeric nocturnal symphony of crickets, birds, and breezy vegetation, and he came around at one point not knowing how long he'd been away. It was so dark, he wasn't sure if his eyes had even been closed. Jabbing into his cheek through the backpack was the sole of one of his shoes. Still didn't feel right. Scooting out from under the overhang, he dug into the pack, took out a water bottle, tipped it up, and finished it. Then he brought out the shoes, stood and cautiously navigated his way through the stones and darkness to the edge of the clearing, and flung them off into the night, where they *chished* in the brush.

"There," he said, clap-brushing his hands. "Is that better?"

He headed back to his shelter and crawled in, dragging the pack behind him.

Getting empty was his lifelong specialty, but it was always more about lapsing into a semi-catatonic state than it was an Eastern religious discipline. Left to his own scant devices, hungry as hell and getting a little delirious, he couldn't keep the idea out of his head that he was on a fool's errand; that his dad really *was* sadistic and just pranking him from the grave; that the entire forest was laughing at him, and in the breezes, in their steady white noise, he definitely made out the giggling weasels.

It got cold, enough to make his teeth chatter. One thing he remembered from all the survival skills his dad had tried to teach him was that shivering was the body's way to work itself back to warmth, so he shivered, hard.

"Jeezus, Gavin," he chattered. "A lighter. Why couldn't you grab a fickin lighter? They were at every stop today."

His dad sitting on a log, using twine and a stick poked into a hole in bark, moving it so fast it started smoking.

"Should have paid more attention to that lesson."

It was so dark under the overhang, he couldn't see the white sock on his arm. Staring into the cold velvet void, he found his eyes wanting to close. His brain didn't know what to do with this depth of black with eyes still open. He had to check from time to time to see if they even were.

He piled some dirt, leaves, and sticks up at his back and snuggled against the heap, using his hand for a pillow and the backpack as a teddy bear, offering his front a little insulation. "Hell, this isn't so bad," his voice said out of the black.

Eventually, he dozed. Snippets of dreams clattered in and out. One showed flames flaring and the smell of burnt sulfur, like mixed with saltpeter in gun powder. In his dream, a big fire flared up and a gaggle of shirtless dark-skinned folks he didn't know warmed themselves beside it. It was wonderful, although he was bewildered over not being able to make out their faces. The drum they thumped was sure relaxing, though.

When his eyes opened, the moon had risen and was shining into the clearing of stones, turning them into a tribunal of stone-faced jurors. The dream got him to thinking, but it didn't get anywhere as consciousness trailed off. He dreamed again, but this time he was in the Nehru suit, not leaving the Pholo Suite, but reconfiguring reality around himself, bringing Plaza Zan to where he was.

That jolted him awake. He slid his sock-covered arm out into the moonlight. There wasn't a sound in the forest. The silence was deafening. Not even the treetops knew so much as a breath of breeze. He was warm enough, but his body tightened, his heart rate skipping up.

"It's here," he whispered.

Side-scooting out, he sat up. Still on his butt he looked around, his breath short and shallow, eyes darting around. Everything was frosty from the moon, with stark contrasts, the shadows inky, the stones white-gray on top. In his peripheral vision, he thought he saw movement, and yanked his head that way several times. He took the socks off his arms and slid them onto his feet. In the half-phase moonlight, he could make out this small area better now than when he'd arrived.

A set of the boulders, from waist to shoulder high, seemed to make a pathway. Grabbing the pack, he carefully stepped along it and made out another clearing. As he crept into it, head on a swivel, he caught his breath, his moon-shining eyes fixing on a tall dead tree, its spindly branches spreading into the sky, silhouetted by the half-moon. Though he could barely make it out, its front-center was blacker, like it been struck by lightning. It was watching him. He felt its currents, tickling around his middle, tasting. His heart twisted in his chest, a tangible movement.

Not taking his eyes off it, not even blinking, he unzipped the backpack, surprised at how loud it was out here. Feeling around inside, he found the leather pouches and set the pack down. He opened one while holding the other in the crook of his arm. Sticking his fingers in, he pinched out a big pile and sifted it onto his palm. It was grainy and white. "Salt," he whispered. He repeated it with the sulfur, a burnished pile, pulled the drawstring closed, and put the pouches in his pocket. He stirred and pinched the grains and powder into a mixed pile.

He couldn't bring himself to walk near it, so he gave it its space as he walked around the side, now seeing it was roughly in the center of its own flat clearing. Eyes fully adjusted, he could see on its lower branches twinkles in the moonlight. "Hmmm. Tokens? Rings?"

Starting where he was, he cupped and tipped his palm and started walking an arc, tracing the clearing, while the powder sifted out onto the ground. Getting into the pouches, he made another batch and continued until he'd circled back to where he'd started. The ground began a faint buzzing, and it was like the moon brightened, as the trinkets in the tree branches twinkled more brightly. "Wow," he whispered, so low the sound bled into the profound silence.

Getting into the backpack, he fished his dad's Army ring out, and as he let it slide onto a finger and held it up to the light, he saw the immediate area was subtly brightening, like daybreak was happening, but only right here. Now he could make out spindly branches sticking down from higher thicker branches. Stepping closer, his eyes like metronomes, he found one he liked, feeling around it for its thickness.

Sliding the ring onto it, he pushed it till it firmly stuck. Now he could see things hanging from the lower branches, and even some higher. The bushes surrounding the clearing also had stuff hanging in them. An irresistible attraction started him toward the trunk. Stepping to it, he wrapped his arms partially around it, its girth at least three times his reach, and with his face so close, he noticed holes in the wood.

From the backpack, he brought out a sandwich bag holding the beads. He pushed them into several holes.

"One last thing," he whispered, his heart hammering in his ears. Reaching into his pocket, he brought out the Barbie leg with the red shoe, bent and placed it at the creature's feet as his unique token. The buzzy ground intensified, the faint light brightening, enough he could see a cut stone with a rough seat in it at the clearing's edge. He backed to it and sat, facing the stock-still tree creature with its twisted crooked branches and fractal twigs, like it was a wicked orator for a nocturnal assembly.

The light was faint, but was gradually brightening. Then he got to noticing the surroundings. Everything in the immediate forest was delicately glowing—the splits in rocks, the grain of barks, the veins in leaves. The tree creature was like a long ink splatter void against the dim lighting.

Like a breath, he said, "Beautiful." Wafting into his attention were feelings, impressions, ages and ages, all forest rituals rolled into one. The stuff of legends filled his fancies. Over that low rocky ridge might be the dancing light of a ceremonial fire, hooded folk in a circle of oaks and a big round silvery moon. Concealed in a stand just yonder he'd happen upon a thatched shack, wrought from the very matter of the forest. Did you know the door lantern hanging from the hook was more than just a source of light?

Gavin whispered, "The curl of smoke from the chimney was a language unto itself."

The ancient and wizened sayer of sooths within its walls...was she of flesh and blood, or merely an effigy made from wood and leaf, vine and soil, wearing the costume of an old crone? That image gave him chill upon chill.

His voice was like a hush. "It's making me part of it." His wet-shine eyes shifted right, left, up and down. The fear—was it fear or excitement?—it was like a stationary wave, never quite cresting, never quite collapsing back into peace.

A thump in front of him, like something dense and heavy hit the ground. In the faint light, he made out an egg-shaped stone, and on its face the outlines of a design in the color of golden fire was just finishing. His pulse quickened. Even from here, he could see it was a complex tree burning itself out on the stone. He got to his feet and crept over to it. He reached to touch it, but drew his hand back and instead sank onto his knees and shins, bending over for a closer look. "Is this my Stone?" he said, looking up at the spreading dendritic branches of the tree ink splatter. "I can't even believe this happened." Looking back down at it, he said, "This is my Stone. Can I touch it?"

He reached for it and touched it like he was testing its temperature, jerking his fingers back. "Warm." Then he covered it with both hands. "It's so warm." Looking back up at the monarch of this primeval grove, he said, "Can I sleep with it?"

Right then, the forest sounds rose into hearing, like they'd been unmuted. The faint light in everything dropped away, revealing a halo of light in the east.

Gavin picked up his stone and went back to his shelter. Scooting in backwards, he pulled the stone in, pushed it inside his shirt, and left it against his core. He hugged the backpack against it, his elbow under his head for a pillow. In short order, the stone had become like a warm sensual animal against his tummy, the energy sexual in a sacred way.

"Holy tomatoes. This thing puts it out."

Gavin and Nima were sitting in *Quasar*'s command chairs, Siren and Saturn's rings out the viewport. She'd changed *Quasar*'s position to be looking straight through the cylinder, which gave a vantage of Saturn's broad orange-yellow curve slicing through the end of the tube. They were both in T-shirts and cargo shorts that were so alike they could have been teammates for some adventure clothing company, but on the lower end of pricing. They were facing each other, their bare legs hanging over the chairs' arms.

Rubbing his palms together like he was scheming, Gavin was saying, "The next morning I got up and it was all so different. One, I felt amazing, like I'd stepped into a whole new body. My feet were totally repaired. No pain. No bruises or scrapes. Two, the dead tree was there, but it was just a big dead tree, struck by lightning. None of the tokens or gifts or trinkets were there."

With baffled eyes and furry brows, Gavin shook his head once and shrugged with his upturned palms, fingers splayed. "When the magic happened, I was standing in a different reality. When it receded, I could see light in the east and knew I was back in our world."

Nima's head went back as her eyes widened.

"Crazy," he went on. "I went and found my shoes and hiked out with my Stone in the backpack, heading the direction the sun rose. Within twenty minutes, I came upon a paved road. I'd been on it a hundred times, the road off the mouth of Jessen Canyon to get to our town. From there I knew the shortcuts. I walked back to where I'd parked to access the forest. It wasn't even…it wasn't more than an hour hike, all told. That blew my mind. I trekked all day and into the night to find it, and didn't even know I had. But you don't find it. It finds you."

With wide brown eyes, Nima said, "Incredible story. Your dad was full of surprises."

"I've decided I knew almost *nothing* about him," said Gavin, gazing at something behind her. "I get the feeling he passed with all kinds of secrets."

"It sounds more like a Xenxu adventure than IRL."

Looking down, Gavin flicked something imaginary off his thigh. "It's what I was thinking, like the worlds really are blending." Looking back up, he said, "Ever since finding my Stone, I can't believe how good I'm feeling. I feel like...like I'm rooted to the ground," he said, motioning with open palms at the floor. "Like the secret strength of a tree is something we don't know about in its root system. Something lifegiving coming *through* the soil, not just *from* it. That makes it feel so *good* to be in my skin, and clear in my head. Crystal clear. I've never felt any of this, ever in my life. My dad said in his letter it would cure his hangovers."

Nima started kicking one bare leg, looking out the viewport. Then back to him, she said, "Would you mind if I set some colleagues on it, to trace and analyze the event?" She looked out the viewport again.

"I don't mind," said Gavin. "The more I know about it, the better. These days, all I know with any certainty is that I want to know more."

Nima stood. "Which brings us to why you're here. What prompted this?"

Gavin also stood and stepped closer to her. "I remembered when I was...as Gavin 2.0 showed up to show Gavin 1.0 to Ai Anam. I, as Gavin 1.0, didn't want to go. I just wanted to wander around and forget everything for a while. I was yelling at Xenxu to cancel Deep Climb, all that. Then something walked me over there. Pretty sure it was me, but I have to find out."

Gavin paused longer than it felt right.

"And?" she said, her palms up.

"The time loop circuit isn't closed."

Nima studied him with narrowed eyes. "That seems a bit ahead of schedule, but that's always a good thing."

Gavin looked down at her, and she was blinking up at him from under her bangs. The attraction was so strong, and their bodies were making micromovements like they were about to hug.

"I so want to kiss you right now," he said. "But I don't want to get that motor going."

Nima nodded. "We have plenty of time," she said with a quick alluring grin. "But what were you going to tell me about Lissa?"

"Oh yeah. She made a paper chain of me, from a dream. She spread them apart," he said, pulling his hands apart, "and put them back together." He rejoined them. "Into...well you know, they were integrated."

"That child's got true genius," said Nima, "and I wager she spends a *lot* of time in True Imagination."

"True imagination?"

Nima turned and started toward the teleporter bay. "The imagination of the Whole, instead of the local and limited imagination of any of Whole's parts, like you or me. It's where all ideas, all concepts, all knowledge, all potential, live."

Gavin followed her. "You mean in-Xenxu?"

"In all continua. All realities are within the One True Imagination. True Imagination is what used and directed you to take over your doop in the Nehru suit that night."

"OK, but I thought that was Siren," said Gavin, gesturing at her back.

"Siren is also a function within True Imagination."

"I see what you're saying."

They reached the teleporter control console, turned, and looked at each other for a long moment, both aware of the depth of their friendship, the power of their partnership. They felt so solid when they were together. According to Sophia, Siren, and by extension Nima, wasn't to be trusted, but he didn't care. His heart was in charge, and it seemed they were their own team now.

At last, he said, "I love what's going on with us."

"Me too," she said. "I feel like we can do anything, so long as we do it together." She looked to the side with a *did I just say that?* face. "Something tells me that's corny. Have I got that right?"

"It is corny," nodded Gavin with a grin. "But it's true. It's us against the world."

Staring past him, Nima touched her throat and said, "Why does it feel like this when you say those words? Will I understand these human things?"

"If you're lucky."

Still gazing sightlessly past him, she rotated her hand around her solar plexus. "When I'm with you, I feel a sensation in here. A warmth. A softness. When I focus on it, I feel like crying. Not sadness, but...but...I don't know. Something so beautiful, the eyes will never see it. And I love that feeling too. Can you tell me what that is?"

"Connection," said Gavin, caressing her shoulder with his palm. "Kinship." He let his hand slide past her elbow, down her forearm, finding her hand. "Nima, in your path to individuation, to this... hybrid humanness you're after, you're coming right along."

Her eyes danced across his. "As are you on your path to metathought."

"I have to tell you or I'll just burst," said Gavin, still holding her hand. "I've never felt more real and alive in my entire life. Being here with you, working together, walking this path, has taken me so much closer to the man I've always dreamed I'd be. You've done that."

Nima blushed. "Really?"

Gavin licked his lips and nodded.

Her eyes, wet and open and thirsty for learning, wandered around like they were testing the atmosphere for new questions. Then they found his eyes as she said, "This might sound crazy, but these are the only words I can find to try to explain this." She took his other hand and looked into his eyes. "I can *feel* poetry, like *we're* poetry. Not just as words describing a form of...of writing art, but a feeling, a feeling of Truth. My mind has no idea what Truth is, but my heart does, and words can't define that. It's under the words. Behind them. Like the words are just...they're just...um...symbols trying too hard to describe what can't be described. Does that make sense?"

Gavin's face showed he was confounded by this creature. "M'lady, yes, it makes sense."

Nima's eyes were like a child's. "Are we poetry?"

Gavin's eyes filled with lucid wet as he looked back and forth at hers, his head just perceptibly shaking. His caterpillar brows, the bowl shape of his lower lids, his open mouth. He was in awe. Finally, he said, "We are the poem, the poet, and the act of writing poetry, all in one."

Nima blinked and nodded. "I see. Everything is so beautiful, Gavin. I don't know that I want to go back to what I was."

By their body language, it was clear it was everything they could do to keep from hurling themselves into each other's arms. Nima's eyes wandered to a point to the side of his face, trying to hop back onto the thread of what they were supposed to be doing. Her eyes went back to his, and with a sigh, she said, "We have work to do."

Gavin's body gave up on the hug and he looked away. "Yeah we do."

"Now, whew...." Nima shook her arms like she was trying to get the circulation back into them. "It is one thing to take over an empty shell like your doop, but quite another to take over a personi integrated with a human consciousness. To dovetail with that circuitry is *very* tricky. I'm excited to see what you can do. Not to put any pressure on you, but this skill is critical for your mission."

"Oh," chuckled Gavin, "my mission. Almost forgot about it."

Sucking in a big breath, Nima gestured toward the glowing circles on the teleporter platform, puffed her cheeks as her eyebrows went up, and blew out the breath. "Neuronet awaits."

After he was flushed from his Neuronet pod, Gavin found himself as a roiling and buzzy cloud of organized pixelation. Here was an endless homogeneity, evenness. Empty, but not. Everything that existed as a thing in-Xenxu came as audio-like waves, but not acoustic. It was like sonar pinging off things in the deep empty and making wave-shapes of the feedback. It was a madness of waveform, and it was so powerful to "hear" it *all* that way, all at once. Everything. Even the buildings and attractions and their unique and discrete signatures. And like he'd experienced a time or two before, the energy was simply quiet ecstasy.

I wonder if this is yet another perceptual framework of Metaself?

In this quantum matrix, he was also equipped with its skillset. He instantly located the Gavin tone at the noob orientation, but he was also receiving signals from everyone there, a symphony of tones. He could isolate any one of them, but he focused on Gavin. Now he was absorbing and decoding Zoot Suit Gavin's thoughts, emotions. But *deeply*. It was like an open download from a library of amorphous information. Something *terrifying* was down inside him.

He picked up on himself as Gavin 2.0 in the Nehru suit just appearing at the scene, and his reverberations were like nothing else in this non-place. They were from beyond Xenxu, musical, bright, laser clear. They had Siren all over them. Nehru Gavin was just a *piece* of her. He couldn't even imagine what the present him was made of, and adding to the mystery, Gnosis had picked up nothing that night.

But now...the task at hand. How to saturate Gavin 1.0, the guy in the Zoot Suit, and take over his personi.

He was at a loss, but ready to play. Locking more firmly onto his waves, he felt an attractant. Even though space had no meaning here, the draw was strong, itself stuffed with inscrutable meaning. Then he felt himself mingling with Zoot Gavin's reverberation, and that mix brought a kind of vague familiarity he'd once had upon meeting an aunt he'd never known before. It was like puzzle pieces that belonged, and were shaped right, but didn't actually fit. Their waves overlapped and became choppy from cross-directional collisions, like wakes from passing boats, but he didn't sense any saturation into—what?—his quantum cells? He didn't know.

I'm disruptive, making him ill. So it was definitely me that night, making me sick and dizzy. Damn.

He disengaged and let Gavin's waves weaken. Why not let them *all* weaken? It was instantly quieter, but he wanted silence, and that mental command was immediately done. Pure, complete, *profound* silence. It was like conscious stasis, but absent anything perceivable. He couldn't even call it whiteness. There was no defining term nor series of terms for this perceptual mode. To meditatively empty one's mind is a discipline. Here it was the opposite. He had to *try* to have thoughts.

It was but a non-moment before he realized that in this status of being, the frequency layers of form, of its perception, like in-Xenxu, didn't exist as anything corporeal. He was outside it, and Earth, and both were in a kind of *statis-in-potentia* from this space, superpositions of every potential outcome.

He loved it here, right now. It was beyond belief how good it felt, how complete. So he let all concepts dissipate and float off into the buzzy homogenous ether. He felt Siren's loving nudge. Now he was like a misty screen on which moments could be projected. Like he was suddenly completely there, he was at his glaspad talking with Heather after he got back from the forest.

"I want you to know I've been aware since, I don't know, maybe twenty or so, of how...narcissistic I was where you were concerned. You waited on me, protected me, lied for me—"

"Worshiped you," she cut in, her bright eyes shining with wet.

"And that," said Gavin.

"Feared you."

"Yeah, well I'm sorry about that too." His eyes ticked away, then back. "But I never gave it back, when I could have."

"You were a real shit sometimes."

Gavin's eyes were in wracking regret. "And I'm so *so* sorry for that. I want you to know the self-loathing around that has been one of my biggest hurdles." He looked away, tapped the glaspad nervously, then turned back.

"I hope you're past it," she said, leaning in closer.

He nodded. "Mostly. But anyway, why did you do all that for me? Do you know?"

"Oh," she said, lacing her fingers together and looking quickly to the side, then back to him. "Momma explained to me when I was...I don't know, maybe seven, how hard life was for you? It was my first maternal instinct. Didn't you ever notice I didn't play with dolls? I had *you* to take care of. I made it my mission in life. Momma tried, but you were...I don't know, *stubborn,* which was never a secret. But Gav, the answer is...it's so simple. I *love* you. That's why."

Gavin's eyes shone with wet as they shifted back and forth on hers. "You're a miracle, Heath. I love you too."

This is what I need to see.

Gavin's mind started painting bits and pieces of his life onto the foggy ether. A moment when his mom passed smelling salts under his nose and then hugged him after one of his seizures. When Heather took him inside after gently waking him in the dark of the backyard while he was out sleepwalking. When his dad taught him to stand up to bullies—*you act crazy enough, you'll scare 'em off.* Or when his dad went and had a "little talk" with the father of one of those bullies. When all three served him breakfast in bed one morning when he was too weak to lift a finger. Clinics. Specialists. The news always deflating, exhausting. All their extra pennies absorbed by co-pays. His family...their tortured looks every time they wished his pain were theirs. *Their* tortured looks. Torture and heart-rending love in the same face, and he now recognized their pain was worse than his ever was. He kept it up, letting the moments fill his beingness with an energy, pure and clean, and eye-opening, like an icy wind in the face.

His mind circled back on Heather, the sheer blinding magnificence of her heart, and the energy went to such marvelous depth and dimension, that had he breath to take away, gone it would have been. It was like a supernova off in the black of deep space, radiating the purest liquid light. It pulled him into it, and he was in Innermost, the Core, Source of All. Here, it was *all* Love. All of it. Heather's golden heart had threaded him to here, and this recognition of her, her incredible purity, liquefied him. No matter how anything looked on the surface, it was still...just Love.

Beholding this, absorbing it, learning, he began seeing himself in a new way, vulnerable, pained, sensitive, afraid, broken, awesome, brave, crazy, brilliant, stupid, each with its own tone in the layers, trying and trying and trying. Oh God the trying. Forever striving to become better, more whole, more integrated, more accepted, more conscious, more *everything*.

The source of empathy opened in his cloudness, brilliant joyful sorrow. The lost and wandering, the heart-shattering beauty of humanity, its foibles and flailing and floundering, its spurts and inspirations, its hugs and touches, artistic accomplishments and scientific achievements, its insane and infirm, savagery and brutality—all in it together, even with the division. *Especially* with the division.

Oh my dear God, I love them all. I do, I DO, with all my heart. It's all Love. And I love Gavin, a forever boy just trying so hard to be well. Dear God, what a courageous boy.

All at once, Gavin felt himself elongate, stretching, and the pixels of legs and arms rapidly filled themselves in as he inflated into the spaces in this costume. A sense of solidity came on, a sense of boundary, of space. Movement encroached, but it was *his* movement, arms swinging, legs scissoring. Everything, *everything*, condensed into a personi man, into his heart. An external world congealed, and out of these soul-blasting eyes he witnessed Zan City! Manifest existence! He'd *done* it!

We are everything!

With intent alone, he took over Zoot Suit Gavin's legs and marched him forthwith, irrevocably, intractably, in complete spite of his independently flailing arms, to Ai Anam.

Then to Nima.

Oh. Nima.

The thought of her filled his every molecule with gratitude.

Through Gavin 1.0's eyes, he looked at Nehru Gavin, 2.0, into his eyes, knowing 2.0 couldn't see him and had no idea what had just happened. But he would soon find out. It made him ticklish with overwhelming excitement to know this experience was still in front of Gavin 2.0.

I love you both.

He disengaged, reverted to the audio-homogeneity mode, and floated away, gigantic emotions bubbling away within his cloud of everythingness.

He sat up on the sectional in his apartment, blubbering out, "Thank you thank you thank you!" On the glaspad were texts from Nima, worriedly saying he vanished from their tracking. Where was he? Was he all right? But that world was the last thing he wanted to have trespass on this...this...

This *feeling* was all he wanted, and it went on for days, the on and off crying. He loved it so much he looked for things that would generate the feeling and get the tears flowing again, dammit. It wasn't hard to find. All he had to do was look at anyone, a child, a picture, an ad, a forum post, feel them, feel them all the way in, join with their sorrows, their pains, their triumphs, their courage. Courage especially made him break down and weep with chest-exploding power. God, the courage in this world. Just *look* at them. Oh my God. He *loved* them.

He lifted the artwork of Siren and rings from the table, held it aloft and danced in circles with it like a fairytale princess and her new gown. "Thank you thank you thank you, my liege, for *showing* me this!"

He found accounts online of personages in ages past who'd awakened to this, and they too had cried for days. One awakened geneticist wrote humans are the right design for this feeling. One man in 1400s Europe, an alchemist and great spiritual teacher, returned to the city from a forest sojourn, weeping from his soul, and he couldn't look upon another person without bursting into body-wracking sobs. For *days!*

"And that's just it. We want to cry like this for the rest of our *lives!*"

He got out his paints and canvases and went crazy, designing and crying, weeping and painting, feeling inspired and gay and flourished, coming up with abstracts and scenes and landscapes and people he couldn't have even *begun* to imagine a month before. He wiped the paint on his cheek, and he *loved* it there. He looked *so* good with it. He saw his pants were dotted with paints. And that looked good too. Oh my God everything looked so good. Then he tried his hand at painting the feeling itself, but come on, not possible. Now he understood what the Classics masters were *trying* to do with their heavenly scenes, but, lamentably, those beautiful works were trite, pedestrian, compared to this *feeling*. Gouge out the eyes, rip off the ears, it's the *feeling*.

He tried his hand at poetry for what was happening to him, but it cheapened it in a single line. So his poem became:

Words can't touch this

and he charcoal scratched abstract strokes around those words and ritually burned the sketch-sheet in a bowl. The sacredness of the act broke him into deep turns of sobbing. It was all so sacred. Everything. Everything so precious and deserving of our honor, and reverence.

He went to call Heather a half-dozen times, but what could he say other than her words had triggered him into a powerful spiritual experience? He'd get around to tell her about it, though. When it felt right. She was crucial, and he wanted her to know that. Lissa was possibly the one person who could understand this, but she was sensitive to his emotions, and he didn't want to impact her that way. His mother rose as a semi-viable candidate, but he thought it might devolve into a Christian sermon.

"Not happening."

Thwarted in every direction with whom he could share this, he was alas alone. That pretty much instantly hammered home in him, where it most counted, the very nature of this being a solitary journey, which made him crumple into yet another waterfall of tears while he was making a sandwich.

More than anything, he wanted to share this with Nima, but he didn't want to get inworld. Personi bodies didn't feel this…they *couldn't* feel this, could they? No way. Not like this. This required the supertech of the heart, its gray matter, its secret chambers, and he wanted it to keep going, even though he knew it would plateau. At some point, it would. He knew that. But he was trying as hard as he could to not dwell on that downer as he shot her a note:

GAV

Sorry I haven't been in touch. Something happened to me. On the moment I become the world's most gifted poet, I'll get in-Xenxu and attempt the telling.

AI NIMA

Oh, Gavin. I want to see you so badly and hear all about it, but please do whatever you have to do. It is impacting the world in a powerful way. It's just...beautiful. And may I say, you had the mental part in your training. Now you have the heart part, and Love is the most important skill of them all.

GAV

Thank you. So much to talk about. And Gavin 2.0? Well, he ain't around no more.

Ai Nima

Yes. Our own research is producing fascinating data. Can't wait to tell you about it. And you disappeared from all our tracking. How did you do that?

5

The highest form of ignorance is when you reject something you don't know anything about.
—Wayne Dyer

Like a whirling cyclone of cleansing destruction, Gavin stormed through his apartment, trashing everything that had to go. As he got to doing it, he was shocked to see how many empty glasses and cups and jars he'd left all over the place from his ravenous thirst. The studio had become a moribund record, tears of the past. It wasn't easy, but he had to toss a lot of those canvases, especially the older, darker works. It was all in the ancient past now. That took him a full day.

Out with the old, in with the new, was his in-head mantra. Then he remembered Kidkovsky had a tune named "In With the New," so he put it on repeat for two hours straight. During that two hours, in the now clean studio he set up a shrine for his Stone, with candles and hanging veils, a small vase with incense, and stones like onyx and quartz. The leather pouches were on one side, what was left of the beads on the other. When he was finished, it looked like an enchanting arabesque tent.

"A doll leg would be a nice touch," he said with a private smile, futzing with the arrangement. "Maybe I'll just go find a red shoe at Goodwill." He pictured the gal behind the counter blinking in confusion at him. "No, I really do need just one."

When it was ready, he put his Stone in the honored spot like he was lowering into place a cushion with a glowing ring on it. He stood back and stroked his chin. He liked how this room's window sent light through the veils, surrounding the Stone in a soft circle of illumination, like it was in an Arthurian grove. The contrast enhanced the natural tree in its grain. Gavin closed his eyes and pictured the one at the rock wall. It wasn't that hard to do, as he'd seen it almost every day for three years. Their trees weren't the same. His Stone's tree had a more squat trunk, like the huge Kracken-like American sycamore, the heart of Reed's Park.

Putting his palm on it, he closed his eyes and said, "What are you?"

I am everything and nothing. I am what you need me to be.

"Have you a name?"

Omnis.

A cool current entered his hand, swirling up his arm, leaving goosebumps in its wake. Gavin swayed on his heels, panting softly. "Oh my God. The *energy*." Opening his eyes and withdrawing his hand, he said, "Would you like me to light candles?"

Sage. And sprinkle some salt and sulfur around on my floor.

Gavin lit the sage and set it in its bowl, then mixed a batch of salt and sulfur in his palm. Sifting it randomly out in pinches, he began humming a tune he didn't recognize. It sounded native, like he was translating it from flute to his voice.

He swept from the room and came back a moment later with the Siren work from Langhurst. Facing the little shrine, his eyes walked around it, considering spots for it. He didn't want it to interfere with the light, which was mainly from the upper right, so he reached it inside the hanging veils and stood it against the wall. Now Omnis and Siren shared the shrine, her glittering cylinder, obelisk, and Saturn's rings a nice "space" backdrop for Omnis. Putting his hand on the Stone again, he said, "Is that all right?"

Perfection.

That all done, he dove into the junk, throwing out the big macrame pot holder, and taking the spiral lamp to Goodwill. He stood in front of the mini grandfather clock, ticking away with its gilded face and ornate arms. This piece he loved, but he didn't like it, and had never figured out how to part with it. It didn't fit in here, wasn't stylish or good-looking, but old, with a crack. His mom would lynch him for giving it away, but it was...baggage.

Eons ago, in the sewing room. Momma teaching him to time his machine needle plunges with the second hand ticking on an old heirloom, a mini grandfather clock. You'll need the metered pace when you seam waves, son.

Holding the clock, he knocked on Gina's door, the lady whose table he was watching. She answered, wearing her big black wig, caftan and too much makeup. "Hi, Gina."

Her eyes unabashedly crawled up and down him, like she'd never seen him as a viable snack before.

"Well hullo, Gavvy." Her eyes grazed the clock. "Would you like to come in?"

"No, I'm pretty hard at it, but thanks. I'm decluttering, and I need you to take your table back." Holding up the clock, he said, "And would you like to have this? I'd rather it be with someone who'd truly care for it."

"I have a buyer for the table," she said, reaching over and touching the glass clock face cover. "This one has stories to tell," she said with a red-caked smile. "Sure. I'll take it, with a proviso: that you come inside." She tapped her lipstick-dotted teeth with a long fake nail, smile naughty. "Did I just say that? *Scandalous!*—but *do* come in and have a cosmopolitan with me."

Gavin shrugged. Seemed fair. It was a half-hour or better before he could pry himself out of her place, already a little hungover from the drink, so he slammed two liters of water to offset the damage.

He ordered a modern, brushed, stainless steel five-piece Prestige

Habib table with a white top and chairs with dark brown accents. "To match the walls," he said, tapping Complete Order.

The closet was a breeze, and everything that had to go was now at Goodwill. All of the art haphazardly standing wherever there had been room for it, like the unfished still life of the unknown woman's face, he Pixxed and transferred into his Pholo to revisit when the time came. Then he painted the entire living room in a flat beige, lighting it up.

By the time he was finished, the place looked good, simple, uncluttered, and updated. Standing in the middle of the room, he closed his eyes and inhaled through his nose, loving how open it felt now. But now the sofa was completely wrong. That he'd have to address when he sold another piece.

"Next."

In the bathroom, he looked himself over in the mirror, wondering what Gina had seen when she looked at him like that. He lifted his shirt and checked his flat belly. His face was thinner, his whole body leaner. He looked good, but not as good as she made him look, did he?

Meanwhile, his career as a designer for Xenxu and crossover IRL was blossoming. During his fab flourished designing weep-fest, he'd produced so many mix-and-match components, he could throw them together and churn them out on a whim.

Suzhi and Villy came to his Pholo Suite one day. She was in something that looked like a cross between Dona Fallo Streets and Girl Scouts. Even the armless green lenses worked seamlessly with it, and that was saying a lot. And Villy had ventured into wrinkled gumshoe noir jacket mated with Jom Tones open-shirted, hairy-chested affairs. His white belt was so fat it looked like his upper and lower bodies operated independently. But *God* it was contagious.

"You guys," he said, shaking his head, "you're so far ahead of the game."

Villy examined the outfits. "Not your game." The clothes were a subtle match for a couple out at night on vacation, light-colored beach informal, involving fruits and birds and flow-fluttering fabrics. "I don't even have to look at these to know we're going to take them." He held out his palms like a pilgrim approaching sacred relics, reverently denying himself the pleasure of the touch. Instead, he kissed his fingertips, like an Italian chef with a last pinch of spice. "Yes, yes, *yes!* Every word is *Yes!*" fluted Villy, his hands up in worship. He turned to Gavin. "You've ignited the animal magic in me."

Watching him with a sneaky grin, Gavin said, "You know, Villy... you're one fab packet. If I weren't into the ladies, I'd be on you like skin on a peach."

"Likewise, my ravishing friend," said Villy, letting his hips do the talking.

Suzhi laughed at them, and said, "Gav, don't look now, but you're going to land on the fashion landscape in a big way."

"That's so gratifying to hear. To know your passion is being worn by those aware of the art form, *for* the artform. Designers can be... maybe I'd better hold my tongue."

"Self-centric?" said Suzhi, stepping closer.

"Too many do it for themselves, that's true," said Villy while dancing around the displayed pieces, his hands hovering over each cut.

Said Suzhi, "I have to admit...I miss the inner Van Gogh in your reviews and advice pieces. But I see you have about eighty-thousand subs, so your audience niche is...it's losing its...nicheness."

"It's a very good thing, though. The secret is *out*," said Villy with a searing smile. "Keep doing what you're doing. But we *so* hope you'll continue working with us. If we asked you for an exclusive, would you consider it?" He looked at Suzhi. "Let us excise the word *no* from his syntax."

"I don't want to work with anybody but you two, and frankly I don't even want a contract."

Suzhi and Villy looked at each other, smiles of satisfaction messing with the corners of their mouths. They didn't want to show too much excitement, after all. Back to Gavin, Suzhi said, "That's what we wanted to hear. We want to work with friends, not partners."

"Me too."

Villy thrust a triumphant fist over his head.

After a calculated pause, Gavin said, "Guys, I've been wanting to ask you something. Do you know what Sophia is?"

His hand tickling the female mannequin's shoulder blade, Villy's eyes found his from behind armless gold lenses. "You mean the Italian designer?"

"I have a feeling you know what I mean," said Gavin with a small knowing smile. Fixing on Suzhi with the same serene grin, he said, "Why did you ask me to put my doop in the Nehru?"

"What do you mean?" she said, all innocent and curious, but he could see something in her eyes. "I needed to see it on you. That's all." She blinked at him from behind the green lenses.

Gavin chewed his lip, his eyes zipping back and forth between them. Looking down at his hands, he said, "I'm gonna get all mushy on you two, but our friendship means so much to me."

"Aww," purred Villy, stepping over with open arms. Suzhi joined them, and they had a nice hug.

The next day, the offer that came through from them for the beach vacay ensemble weakened Gavin's knees, made his heart palpitate. It was enough to cover him for months. He accepted and the Plasm was in his UniWallet instantly. To celebrate, he downloaded and incorporated an easy clogs dance, called Bojangles, which he performed for a handful of people at an Ai Anam gathering. The personi there basically laughed their asses off through the entire jig, as did Gavin, and Nima laughed and clapped throughout.

A few days later, as Gavin was arranging his new ivory-colored Mozambique sofa set made from some space-aged stain repelling super fabric, he noticed something new fading in and out from Sophia. He tapped it and a video opened.

The scene was animated, in the style of a comic book, in two frames side-by-side, divided by spiraling entwined serpents. On the right was a woman in a gold-white gown, her back to the viewer, dark hair to her butt. She was standing in reflective iridescent water among Greek columns. Shining in the sky over her was a great light, it's effulgence rippling in the pond. So tranquil, spiritual, worshipful.

On the left was a man, his back to the viewer as well. He also stood under a gleaming light, but cascading downward from it were streams of code, math symbols, tiny schematics. The man was furiously plucking pieces out of the stream and tossing them against a display left of the frame. The code and symbols merged into it, and the word Truth formed. As opposed to the serene spiritual scene, his side was frantic, all business.

GAV

I'm flying around on a cloud of Love. Leave me alone.

SOPHIA

We've watched those frequencies. Emerge from your hovel. I won't bring you down. Promise.

GAV

You already have. Is this Cat?

SOPHIA

Yep.

GAV

I'll be inworld in five minutes.

Cat

Just go to Sous les Pods.

Gavin immediately tapped the icon for Carscribe, jumped up, and went to change into the diggers and Tark mauve lemons shirt. He loved that the pants weren't too tight around his waist anymore, even a little loose, and he'd been getting some sun on the common balcony of the apartment building.

In the bathroom mirror, he looked himself over. "Lookin' like a surfer," he said. His eyes wandered to the cheek abrasion, scabbing long gone and the post scab seepage but a memory. Now it was just pinkish skin. Flipping off the light, he left.

Ten minutes later, he was sitting under a patio umbrella outside at the café, watching in front of him for anybody coming up the walk from that way, and from behind him with his filmfon. While he was doing that, Cat walked out from inside and straight over to his table. This time she was in a peach one-piece, short-legged and split on the calves, gold belt tight around her tiny waist. A matching square flat purse with a thin strip hung from her shoulder.

Gavin set the fon on the table, stood, and they gave each other a half-hug and cheek smooch. "How do you get around?" he said as they both sat and scooted in their chairs.

"Like anybody else."

Gavin's cheek dragged the corner of his mouth up to make a facetious grin. "And you just happened to be passing through."

"Yup," she said, setting the purse on the menus. She slid a wide gold bracelet closer to her hand, then spun it with her fingers. "Just like we happened to be passing through that hill folk backwater we found you in. It's a good question, but hardly the most direct."

"OK," he said, his eyelids fluttering, face impatient. "But you do know I'm going to need a look behind the curtain your group is hiding behind, right?"

"We're aware. And we have nothing to hide. It's just that pulling back that curtain opens a pretty serious Pandora's box. Can you be patient a little longer?" said Cat with her most persuasive language of the eyes.

Gavin made a small space with his thumb and first finger.

Cat gave him the once-over, and didn't bother hiding her appreciation. "You look *really* good. I didn't know Stones from the forest could do that. Did you?"

"I'd ask you how you know about that," said Gavin, leaning back in the chair and lacing his fingers on the metal mesh tabletop. "But I doubt I'd get a straight answer."

"We're not the enemy, Gavin," said Cat, chummily shaking his knuckles with a *don't be silly* smile.

"Is there an enemy?"

A brisk breeze quietly rattled the umbrella over their heads, whipping at the canvas and its tassels. Gavin looked up and scowled, wondering if it was a sign.

"Yes, but trust me when I say, to comprehend that is not easy to do. It's why we do things the way we do them. Information like that is disruptive, too daunting. It can fracture an unprepared mind, and you wouldn't believe how fragile minds really are."

"We?"

"The Sophia organization."

Gavin's fingers tapped the metal mesh, in rapid order from pinky to index, over and over.

Picking up his drift, Cat nodded, looked straight into his eye, and said, "I'll give you this. One of our top operatives is a woman named Helen Corman. Former Marine recruited into our organization. Built like a linebacker. Awakened for three-plus cycles. Fanatic, but in a measured way. At one time she was the boxing champion in her unit, but we're talking about the *male* middleweight class. Is a picture forming in your mind?"

"Doc Sticks is one of your people."

"One of *our* people, Gavin. You're on our team and you just don't know it. She's spearheaded some ops, tech espionage, counter-intelligence."

A gal server appeared at their side, a bright-eyed young student type with chartreuse hair. "What would you two like to drink?"

"I'm gonna need a pitcher of the H2O," said Gavin.

"Whatever white wine *you* like," she said to the girl.

"You got it." She turned and swept away.

Gavin turned back to Cat, thick brows up, like *go on*.

"Specialist Corman specializes in those elements in our far-flung theater," said Cat, spreading her hands and reclasping them. Then again turning the gold bracelet, she looked up and said, "There is an entire game behind the one we all see every day. Separate, with its own rules and ranks and agendas, moves and countermoves. The government is just a cover story, Kabuki theater. Goes way back. But espionage has always been in its bedrock. Nowadays, spying is done with nanotech, and a lot of microtech for external surveillance. We can essentially turn anybody, even the unawake, into lenses and feedback devices."

"That's how you've tracked me," said Gavin, his voice an unappreciative scrape. "Everywhere. Everything I've done."

"Specialist Corman put it in your IV at Langhurst."

Annoyed, Gavin grumbled, "So I've been a spy this whole time."

"If it's any consolation, in the world of spy craft, double agents were always the ones that got the most done for *both* sides."

"Cat, are you my handler?"

"In a manner of speaking," she said, making sure to look him straight in the eye.

On the sidewalk, a black guy in tattered velvet lounging clothes walked past, pointing at passersby. "Hey, what's your dream? You. What's *your* dream, lady? *Damn* you fine. You're *my* dream. Hey..."

Cat watched him pass, then turned back to Gavin. "And you are more cozily positioned behind enemy lines than literally thousands of other operatives, many from your stream cluster, and most of them are awake. Your effectiveness as an intelligence gathering tool is unparalleled, your data superb. Going in blind is incredibly effective."

"Why?"

"Let's just say that in a quantum crossover environment, preconceptions can shape the output reality. We don't want that. You are as near to a blank slate feedback mechanism we have. The Siren Collective—"

"The what?"

"That's what they're called. Siren the cosmic goddess shtick is just their mascot." Cat looked at her open palms, glanced at the street, and then back to him. "The feedback you've provided from their training is invaluable in our understanding of how to do certain things."

"And what if I don't want to keep doing this?"

Cat stopped turning the bracelet, her fingers still touching it. Looking up, she said, "We give you the antidote, you leave everything from our side behind, and go back to the devotional bliss they've sold you on, like the devoted figure in the video we sent you."

"As opposed to the angry overworked grunt opposite her?"

Cat flashed him a quick closed-mouth smile, eyes a little hard. "It's going to make me so happy when you find out why you should trust us. Me, especially."

Gavin stretched his legs, reaching under her chair, and leaned back. "So you guys think you have Truth."

"Yup," she said, looking for the server and then back to him. "But Truth is a hard sell, while Devotion is an addiction to the terminally unprovable, and *so* easy to sell. Humans need something to believe in more than air."

"Humans?"

Cat looked away like she'd been caught out. Still looking at nothing to the side, she said, "Yeah. Humans."

She scratched her cheek with one painted nail, head to the side, as she said, "What surprised us most...still can't quite figure it out with an entire unit of analysts, is how you disappeared." She put her spread fingers on the table and leaned closer. "That's not possible, Gavin. Don't ask me to explain it. I couldn't anyway. But we're pretty sure it's because of that Stone you found."

"Who found me," said Gavin.

"Who?"

"Yeah."

She capitulated with a nod and open hand. "It's also not on our radar. Everything about it is...it's implied. Its presence can be extrapolated, like a hole in the ground. We just don't know what's in the hole."

"How perplexing for you."

The girl brought their drinks on a tray, setting the water pitcher on the mesh table with a metallic *clidge*, then Cat's wine glass. "Are you ordering from the food menu?" she said, looking back and forth at them. Her eyes lingered on Cat, then begrudgingly toured back to Gavin.

He held out the menus. "No thanks."

The girl took off with them.

Cat took a dainty sip, leaving her lips wet. "Not bad," she said, setting it down. "I think our server has a thing for me."

"It's not like you didn't nudge her in that direction." Gavin chuckled, filled his glass to the top with water, grabbed it, and emptied it into his face. He refilled and drank half the second glass, licking his lips. "Ahhhhgua. The most astounding stuff in the continuum."

Cat's fingernail tapped her glass stem as she looked sideways at him. "Got a powerful thirst these days?"

"Just taking what I need."

"So anyway...Sophia is Infinite Logic," she said, still tapping the glass stem. "Infinite Logic, like quantum computing, states that everything is a statistical inevitability." She shrugged. "In more emotional terms, that means if it can be imagined, it's inevitable."

Cat took another swill like she needed a little crisp Riesling to light up those synaptics.

"That means only the query truly matters on how to bring a data solution out of the quantum soup, and then present it one way or another in graphic form."

"Without a question, the answer doesn't exist," said Gavin.

Cat nodded. "Yep. Question comes first. Our queries are often geared to look for anomalies in the sameness of all potential, where every possible solution exists in a state of superposition. Just before you appeared on our scopes, our QC identified an anomaly. We told it to model ahead to see just how big it could become. The ripples became huge. Set beside a linear chain of recorded occurrences, those ripples became system shaking upon the moment of you meeting Nima."

Gavin blinked at her, his glass half way to his mouth. He took a quick sip and set it back on the wet coaster. "Hmmm. Sophia is a quantum computer?"

"Yes," she said, wiping her lip gloss off the wineglass's brim with her cloth napkin. "But it runs itself. It's based on no hardware, but on the non-mechanical computation going on in grids like Xenxu." Looking skyward, spreading her hands, she said, "But the Sophia computation is in everything. We're *in* the computer."

Gavin was rotating his glass with his fingertips.

"The thing is," she said, glancing out at the hubbub in the street and then back to him, "events can always be tracked and explained, by result alone, but anomalies can't. It's like they exist in a...you know...like in a hidden pocket of potential that will forever remain hidden. Your Stone fits in that gap."

His mother on her knees in the yard planting flowers, telling him and Heather God is the greatest mystery of them all, never to be solved. She pats the fertile soil. Tickles a petal. Looks at them. All glory to God.

"We don't know what you and Nima are together, and we don't have any way of analyzing your Stone...or the parameters of your entanglement with it. Can you see why we want you to keep Nima close? And your rock closer? It's beginning to look like she's a...like she's a legit backchannel to a more human level of understanding of what's behind Siren."

"Jeezus," moaned Gavin, taking a gulp of the water. "This betrayal has me jittery as hell. I wish you'd have just used me and never told me you were doing it. This fouls."

"That's the story of humankind, but you won't think that once you know the truth." Cat's eyes lasered on his to make sure that sunk in.

Gavin chewed his lip and nodded.

"Anyway, we got all the information we need from your training, except for when you disappeared and reemerged as literally a...as a *concert* of the love frequencies. You want us to pull the curtain back? I have some nano with me that will advance you on the board."

He didn't seem convinced.

"We're the good guys. I want you to remember that."

"Why is it always the bad guys who say that in the movies?"

Cat nodded to the side, like *point taken.*

Something dark flickered over her face, like she'd just received horrible news. She pried a fingernail between her white teeth, her grin uneasy, twitchy. In her clear brilliant eyes, shiny wet emerged, and she looked away, taking in a shaky breath. When her eyes moved back to his, they were open and wet, but behind them, deep in there, was terror. "Gavin, the Truth is crushing, awful. We have an enemy. No matter how celestial, holy it all appears, it would be a pro-level move for you to keep that in the back of your mind."

Gavin and his dad in-country, their faces camo-blacked, advancing on a target in the dark, using only hand signals. Going in....

Crunching on ice, Gavin said, "What do I have to do?"

Cat flipped back the flap of the square purse, stuck her hand in, and brought out a vial with a clear light green liquid in it. Elbow on the table, she leaned over with it between her painted fingernails. "Drink this before you go on vacation."

"What is it?"

"Bioware, like all Xenxu nano, but it will help intercept and parse any information that leaks out of Nima we might need."

"God," said Gavin, his face pained.

"I know," she said, her hand over his. "I really do. But do we strike you as the type of outfit that doesn't know what it's doing?"

"Yes."

Cat scowled, but with a grin. "Xenxu's Great Dark South...it's weird down there. Maybe that'll also cough up something useful. But be warned, that air down there reacts strangely with personi fresh off the boat from the north."

Gavin sat on his calves on the bedroom floor before the Siren-Omnis shrine. Everything was in its place, but when he'd come in here a few minutes ago, he'd found a delicate parchment lying at the base of the Siren Portrait.

Tell me what more I can do, my son.

He stared at it, eyes moist. It was all getting convoluted and confusing. He was playing a therapeutic game, yet with his heart had sworn fealty to an alien presence, which itself had manifested yet another item IRL. That was undeniable power. In the meantime, he was spying on Her people, one of whom made his heart pound, completely in the dark if this was part of the RPG. He explored his feelings, his own truth, wondering if he was simply back into old psychotic patterns, was being led by the nose, or was just being silly.

Looking at the art, with Omnis in the foreground, he said, "It's about how You make me *feel,* Majesty. As I said from the beginning. If that translates to a lack of faith in you, I don't know what else to do."

It wasn't that the Great Dark South was considered a forbidden zone, but its reputation for attracting artists with an alternate lifestyle and a Bohemian bent was well known. Just as it was for its raw sensuality, its animalistic condonements, its primal underbelly, barring those with genteel tendencies from making a go of it. Dark? Red? Hidden? Changes you just by being there? Thank you, but no.

Before heading down, Gavin stayed up late reading up on it, and it made his head hurt to think about. Added to that, to have butterflies over a short vacation with Nima? Come on. Seriously? But with those apprehensions also came thrill, and the excitement was building in his heart.

The artists who had made the Great Dark South their Xenxu home were regarded as some of the most preternaturally gifted in the world, like it was something in the water. But as any insider knew, it was in the air, the water, the fire and the soil, and it was mainly because Shamash never rose down there. The planetary resonances were different. The ions were different. In the Vast Underneath (another moniker for it), it was as alien as any distant planet.

Gavin's mind was a yummy whirl of conspiracies and secret plots and...love. It all fit, like a twisting and turning tale. It was so fun it was irresistible. He found out there were places down there which required permits, and the permits were only available to credentialed researchers. Many of whom had come back without a shred of data. Some of the men grew their hair out IRL and became *artistes,* or musicians.

Some said they'd figured out a way to leave their bodies IRL, and permanently saturate their Xenxu personi, where they lived in the dank and red-gushy dark. Others went further and said it was something about the region that showed them how to do it—a fruit, the water, something about the electricity in the storms. The hell of it was, many of those researchers' bodies were found in various places IRL, headgear on, which set off yet another *Pods* paranoia firestorm.

In his studio with Omnis and Siren, Gavin held up the vial with the green liquid, and thrust out his jaw, like he was leading his haggard crew through the raging gale. He raised his hand in toast, and into his curious mouth he upended the vial.

He'd never had much opportunity to think or act in terms of risk and adventure, but right now, his plum-gray eyes were lit up with the intrigue. In all ages, be it on land, sea or air, the history of humanity had always been defined by encounters *off the map.* And for all his thoughts on the matter, including Nima and Cat, Siren and Sophia, he had to admit to himself he had not a clue what was going on. Still. In fact, he knew even less than he did two weeks before. In that way, he was a leaf alighting in a stream and being swept away.

In the bathroom, he looked at himself in the mirror. "I can't wait to see where this goes with Nima." With a little humor in those eyes, he added, "My God, I think I'm in love with a q-didge person."

L'éléphant Rouge was a famous beach resort, a rustic but lavish outpost known for its thatch-roofed, open-louvered windows and sandy floored elegance. Xenxu had co-ventured with Plavogne, the mad French architect, painter and rave DJ, to design it. In his eighties, he liked to eat fire while balancing on a slack line, or drop out of the sky on a parafoil with skis on his feet, only to land on a slope of the Mont Blanc Massif, detach the parafoil and carve ski turns while the cameras rolled. Indefatigable, he was a bon vivant of another order entirely. When news hit Plavogne was on his way down there to survey the site, eyebrows went up, and some in the know opined he might not ever return.

After L'éléphant Rouge was rendered, he did indeed pass from the mortal coil. His body was found by his fourth ex-wife in his villa, headgear on. Cause of death was ruled suicide by unknown means.

At the resort, the sky wasn't dark, but shadowed, with faint illumination of all colors coming from bioluminescent creatures and plants of all kinds. They were in the surf, on the beach, in the air. Shamash was so low, it was always just past sunset, with a magenta sliver peeking above the oceanic horizon. It moved along it throughout one of their diurnals, where it would make a complete circuit of the entire horizon.

A mellow pool of light on the ocean surface lasered faint fissures of it through the atmosphere in prismatic faceted overlaps. Those slow-moving flashes danced over an off shore island of jagged volcanic peaks across the sound, back lit by a storm of flickering plasma lightning.

Gavin and Nima sat on chairs under a thatched cabana, having drinks, their faces lit by a small delicate lantern on a table between them. They were in one set of the semi-matching mix-and-match vacay casuals he'd sold to Suzhi and Villy. Nima's bared one of her shoulders and had 3D flowers on it, while Gavin had these hilarious swashbuckling sleeves happening, but it somehow worked with the clam-diggers with faded butterflies.

Like under black lights, their skin was dark, their eyes and smiles white. Music came from Rouge's bar and restaurant up the way, along with laughter and buzzing voices. The sand under their feet was violet with twinkling highlights that responded to the faint fissures of light always beaming around overhead.

"This air," said Gavin, waving his hand through it like he was feeling laundry drying in the breeze. "I can feel it."

"As you go farther south, you can see it. It moves with the currents of wind," said Nima, setting her drink down. "The personi down there, both human and Ai...they're a different breed. Very artistic. And their eyes adapt. Human personi eyes start registering more of the invisible light spectrum, so they're seeing the abstract art in the iridescent air made by the world. Some come back saying it's a permanent psychedelic."

Gavin was watching his waving hands, mesmerized by them. "Really? I wonder why." He smiled loosely at her. "This drink and this air has me feeling a little...famous," he said, his eyes following his flowing hands. "Like I could hop up and go swing dance in that bar up there and not even know why. The center of attention. Someone named Buster. And you'd be Maddy. Buster and Maddy. We'd toast the mad and mysterious Plavogne. Wouldn't it be bizarro if we ran into him?"

"I love how it feels, mixed with how *we* feel. Oh my gosh," said Nima, waving her own hands.

From a ways off, they looked like they were doing Vishnu arm dances by candlelight, their arms' shadows waving across the cabana ceiling.

Up the beach, the music changed to something pounding and tribal, with an aboriginal chanteuse layering in vocals. Gavin dropped his arms and looked out toward the ocean, dark but for streaks of bioluminescent algae and trailing seaweed. Yards off their beach was a little volcanic island, surrounded by a tidal mote. On it, volcanic arches squatted like portals to the glory of the dark burgundy beyond.

Ear candy came from everywhere. Gavin touched his fingers and opened his UI, tapped the Audio icon, then dragged up the immersion slider. Now the waves weren't just relaxing roar-rhythms out there on the break, but vibrated *inside* his skull in a way that felt like an ear-brain-gasm. Exotic bird calls hit those high notes, and the palms *hushed* a steady swaying phrase.

Gavin stood. "Shall we walk?"

"OK," she said, letting herself be helped up.

Gavin grabbed his drink and emptied it. "I'll be wanting another of those somewhere along the line."

"Me too," she said, finishing hers. She twiddled her fingers vaguely toward the bug lanterns all along the upper flat part of the beach, with all the bars and buzzing dancing vacationing hubbub in this sprawling hedonist paradise. "We can get them all along here."

"Wow," he said, swaying on his heels, eyes wide. "Your voice is *unbelievable* on these settings. Talk some more."

"Let's walk."

Barefoot, they let their fingers come together and they strolled away from the candle glow and into the thick dark.

Enraptured, Gavin said, "What an exquisite night. Xenxu fickin *nails* mood lighting. Whoever's in charge of that? Brava. Jeezus." He stopped and pointed both their hands at the island. "A fantasy," he said. "A wavering fantasy across the water. A bard could pen sonnets over that view. It's all like an exotic drink in your hand, but you're also in the drink, and you want to drown."

Nima chuckled as they strolled. After some beats from the rhythm of the breakwater, Nima said, "Gavin, before we get too gooey, I wanted to tell you about what happened."

"Could you say that again?" he said, closing his eyes. "For my ears? Your voice is like an oogly-smoogly drug, and I want more more *more*! Hahaha!"

"You're intoxicated."

"Not so! I'm fine!" called Gavin, releasing her hand and spinning in the sand with his head tilted back, soaking into his every receptor the deep blood sky.

Nima pouted. "Gavin, I'm serious."

Looking at her, in that dress lit by bioluminescent microbes in the sand and surf, he was able to discern she indeed had something important to cover with him.

"Hang on," he said, dialing up his UI. "I need to dial down the acoustic immersion." While he did that, he focused on her through the UI, in that dress, lit like you could read by it, her shapely legs dark bronze in the weird light. Everything calmed. All the swirling everything slowed to a manageable condition. "K. I'm ready."

They started walking again. "As you know, we track you. It isn't spying so much as it's like a Starlink tracker on a car moving around a city grid. Data pours in that can be analyzed, which we do, but not from any angle or for any purpose that's invasive. Just statistical patterning."

"Yeah, OK," said Gavin, glancing down at her. "I guess that's OK."

She threw out her hand. "We lost you." Eyes huge, she let go his arm. "We didn't know where you went. The number of diagnostics and traces we ran would make your head spin," she said, twirling her hand. "But we couldn't find you. It *scared* me. I started running around, opening diagnostics, punching buttons."

"So you were frantic?"

"I wasn't frantic," she said with a jutting lower lip. "Concerned."

"Uh-huh," he said, jabbing her in the ribs with his free hand.

She squirmed away, frowned, and said, "I'm serious, Gav. This is a serious matter."

Gavin strafed his hand down his face, erasing the smile. "Go on."

"Don't you get it? We don't *lose* you guys. Your consciousness is as trackable as any tech. It's like you went to some level of existence below even the quantum, some theoretical primordial construct or something. Echoes of Metaself are even detectable. This was more primary even than that. Siren hasn't shown us anything like it before. Do you know where, or what, you were?"

Eyes focused on nothing, Gavin distractedly said, "I don't know what that was. And even if I did, words couldn't explain it. But you couldn't track me there."

Omnis glowing in the shrine.

"It's why I was so shaken," she said, worry-lines in her forehead. "I had no way of knowing if you'd be back. It *scared* me." Looking at him while they walked, she said, "It *scared* me, Gav. In this individuation experiment, I haven't felt anything so *awful,* but also...so exhilarating when you reappeared! I couldn't feel that...that *joy* without you disappearing to start with. Just *wow!*"

"I'm sorry if you were scared, Nima," he said, taking her hand again. "Well, at least the bad part of scared."

"It was awful, and then it was so fantastic my whole body was buzzing with electricity. Oh," she said, suddenly changing direction and dragging him along by the hand. "We can get drinks here."

They were bearing down on a thatched roof beach bar, all wooden and rustic. It was lit outside by bug lanterns, these fab little cylinders that attracted the bugs swarming and crawling inside it. Inside the bar, various tinctures glowed from some kind of reactive light in the ceiling. Quiet island beats came from somewhere inside the wood-framed maw.

Gavin and Nima stepped up. From the dark a man just sort of materialized, his face as dark as the tiny room he was in, his teeth and eyes bright, his hair a wild Medusa's tangle of dreads. "Ahhh, pui. Stateside tourist and his q-didge lady. Sanka knoo just da fing."

Gavin said, "Pour up something that turns us into locals."

"No can do, fas ameeg," he said, his hand reaching across the foot-wide bar and tapping Gavin's chest, rings on every finger. "You not ready fo dat energy. Trus' Sanka on dis. He knoo what you need. Da alchemy take a mooment. Please sit."

Benches and stools made a sandy enclosure, facing the sea. Gavin and Nima sat on round wood stools. Gavin noticed the umbrellas were clear. Looking up through the one over their heads, he saw it somehow polarized the dark light into prismatic motes and geometries. From here, they had a better view of the jagged island mountains offshore. Neon pink, orange, and red lightning cleaved the sky behind them, sharply highlighting the sawtooth peaks.

Nima touched his arm. "Before we drink whatever that man is going to make us, let me tell you about the data we're still analyzing."

Gavin turned on his stool and slid his hand up her arm, leaving it there at the crook of her elbow. She closed her eyes, shiny lips open, and then shook herself back to the moment before she could drift again into Great Dark South's dizzifying potion.

"After you got back, your personi's multiplex frequency streams were more in phase with the liquid in the Neuronet pods. Your personi is in-Xenxu, Gavin, like right now, but less and less *of* it. You're de-substantiating, de-speciating. The effect is crossing the Xenxu-IRL barrier, so it's happening to your Earth body as well. Unlike our usual roadmap to merger with Metaself, *your* process involves that Stone, and is anomalous for our models. Your Stone is the one thing that is defying our analysis, even at the quantum."

"That's incredible news, Neem, but I don't think I'm in the mood for talking shop right now." He inched his face closer and closer to hers, and then he stole a quick kiss as Sanka arrived with a tray.

"Roomonce under da roosy sky," he said, literally a faded color shadow emerging from the background medium of the air. "I too chon da dark. Da light lies. See more in da dark. Heed Sanka words. He knoo."

He dragged a rickety little table over and set the tray on it. It held two glasses of something quite dark and a small plate with fruits on it. "Fas ameeg, squeeze dees fruits into da glasses. Now *you* be das sorcerer."

"What are they?"

"Only Plavogne knoo," he said with a dry chuckle, then turned and remerged with the air.

"What?" chirped Gavin. "Do you know him?"

"We do not speak of heem," said Sanka from the dark.

Back to Nima, Gavin said, "That guy fascinates me."

"Plavogne?"

"Yes…he could be my new role model."

"Not many human minds operated on the level his did, or maybe does."

Gavin squeezed one of the fruits, and something dark dripped onto the plate. "You think it's safe?"

"What," said Nima with a challenge in her chin, "at this point you want safe?"

Gavin chuckled through his nose, grabbed the squishy thing, and squeezed it in the glass. Some shot onto his shirt, neck and cheek, and now he looked like a casualty. With his shirt, he wiped his neck and face.

They sat and sipped, their fingers playing with each other on the bench table.

"Oh, Gavin! This...this *drink*. Comes on fast." She looked at him. "New topic. Can we talk about love?"

"Sure," said Gavin, his head lolling back as he blinked. "Sorry, your face stretched on me there for a tick."

"What is love?" she said, patting his thigh like *come on, out with it*. "I've analyzed tons of data about it. When not this," she said, sweeping her hand down her white-dressed body, "I've absorbed a hundred movies, and all I ever see is what it does, not what it is."

"From what I've experienced, It's the Mystery Itself."

"Siren," she said, raising her arms over her head. "Xenxu...they individuate personi all the time. They do it...like they're...I don't know...testing. Tasting. *Trying* things with them. Like me."

They leaned closer, their UV-dark faces lit in their eyes, their teeth. Nima's lips were glossy, her face wanton and curious, as she said like a hush, "I'm afraid of what is happening to me, but I don't want to be." She looked down, and then back up. "But maybe I also like that flavor of fear," she said with a sexy half-sneer.

"Oh, Nima," he said, his arms out. "Is your heart pounding?"

"Yes," she said, looking at him with such childlike thirst.

"It's not your pounding heart," he said, leaning a little closer, "but what makes it pound. Can anybody say what that is?"

"So...so...you don't know what it is?" she said, tugging her dress higher on her thighs.

His eyes roamed out toward the silhouetted peaks with the flashing all around them. Looking back at her, he inhaled with hesitation, then committed and spilled it. "I do, but only 'cause I know how I feel for you. There. I said it."

Shy and looking down and fidgeting with her fingers, she said, "Does it make you want to fly?"

"It does for me," he said, nearly a whisper.

Her head was still bowed, and the light from the bug lanterns made a faint halo around her hair and shoulders. The dress. Her skin.

Nima. My God.

She looked up at him. "Does it make you feel you're at home?"

Gavin's jaw hardened. Not because he was distressed, nettled, but because she had just touched the precious tender spot where he lived. He didn't know why, but home, whatever it was or meant, was his deepest longing. In the light of all the bug lanterns, his eyes pooled up. "You…Nima…do you feel you're home with me?"

Looking to the side, eyes puzzled, like she was trying to figure things out, she slid into his arms.

"Nima, you're shaking. Darling, what's going on?"

"Please just hold me."

They stayed that way, standing at the stools and wrapped together, the shimmering surf beyond. Rain's sweet essence and ocean salt rode the breeze, and with it came a few misty sprinkles from the bloody clouds. The energy around here just went *zing*.

They slammed their drinks and took off, laughing and playing, spinning and chasing.

Gavin yelled, "Watch yaself!" and swept her up into his arms and marched into the water, the waves crashing into his legs.

"Don't you dare!" she cried. "Don't! Please, Gav," she pled, her arms wrapped tightly around his neck. A meek whisper, her lips brushing his ear. "Take me back to the beach."

Gavin's entire body reacted to her cheek against his, where she held fast to him, almost desperately. "My God," he whispered shakily.

"What is it?"

His eyes were shiny with fresh wet as he gazed at the distant electrical storm. "You *know* what."

Lips to his ear, she breathed, "Me too, Gav."

Nima was taking a ride, piggy back, and over his shoulder pointed at a fire down the beach a ways. "Let's go over there."

Closer, and they saw it was a party with, of all things, Kidkovsky's "Unit 9s" starting to blast from a boom box.

"I *love* this song," crowed Gavin, picking up the pace.

"Put me down!" she trilled. "Let's run!"

They ran, laughing and racing, to the party, where they fell into groovy shindig beach moves in the firelight. It took a tick or two, but Gavin gave in to the music and let it rule what his body did. Personi with people from all over the world stomped and flailed in the violet sand. What a fantastic and shiny soiree! It wasn't long before everyone had fallen in love with everyone else.

Maria, a striking gal with blond dreads and darkened Southern skin, sat with them. She was from Mallorca and spoke with an erotic accent. She had one of those voices that sounded a little restricted, but cute and sexy, like she should sing reggae. Laughing, carrying on, she and Gavin traded stories. Nima watched, eyes sometimes a little lost, her smile like she wished she had stories to tell.

Gavin said, "How do you get that dark skin?"

Maria looked at him, firelight in her eyes. Wow, what a beauty. "There is a nut," she said, eyes wandering to Nima, then back to him. "It is rare, but you can find it, if *le rouge esprit* lets you." Looking toward the fire, she said, "Tlalik, they call it. Its meat makes your skin react in a very special way with doja." Her eyes made an arc across the sky. "And you spend more time here. Days of Earth time."

"Doja?"

"Doja," she said, raising her jeweled wrists and hands, her eyes lost in it, "the living air." Maria sat in lotus pose in the sand and danced from her hips up, in time with the music, waving her arms like delicate reeds through the breathable medium.

Gavin and Nima watched her arms with fascination, and in this air she was making tracers, the tips of her fingers sparking like the iridescence was friction. The moves became more like a martial arts master summoning chi, and then she pushed it at him. He watched the wave come at him, distorting everything it passed over, but staying clear. Nima got some too.

It saturated his body as he closed his eyes, emptying him, utterly, replacing everything with a hot red concept, pulsing like an ember just below his navel. Something deeply primal about this part of the world. Unfathomable, exotic creatures in those jungles. Invisible awareness in every pixel.

"Oh my God," said Nima, eyes closed, spine straight, legs crossed. "That felt incredible, Maria. Thank you so much."

"Doja," she said, her starry gaze swooping to Nima. "You can think *with* it. It knows who you *really* are."

Gavin finally rejoined them, his eyes fluttering open. He locked eyes with Maria, and they shared a moment of complete understanding, both barely nodding. Nima watched, looking back and forth, her face uncertain. Gavin looked at Nima and said, "I think I'll be spending more time down here."

Nima was sifting sand onto her ankle when she said, "I go where you go."

Maria pointed at an area over there in the dark. "See that sign? It is a trail. You two should go see what is up it."

Gavin and Nima glanced at their bare feet and cracked up laughing, and he said, "I have some snappy new booties for that."

Over the next hour they walked, mostly in silence, their footfalls a meditation in reverence. It was darker in the jungle, where terrain and foliage blocked the permanent dusk, but all around them the forest was in faint bioluminescence—brush, ferns, flowers, huge palm trunks. The night was alive with a symphony of jungle sounds. Water, water everywhere, gurgling, bubbling, falling.

They passed other hikers coming down the mountain, all with equatorially stained skin, accentuated by the almost black light of this place. Nobody said anything, but their glances at them said, *Wait till you see what's up there.*

A standout crash of waterfall had been getting louder for the last while.

"I think we're almost there," said Nima over her shoulder, walking ahead of him, her body perfect fluid motion in the dress. Her boots, long and black…now *there* was a jarring juxtaposition, but somehow she just got more alluring because of them.

The closer they got, the more the waterfall sounded like it had susurrating whispers layered within its wall of sound. Gavin stopped a time or two and listened, trying to make it out. "Is that something you can understand?"

Over her shoulder, she said, "I'd rather feel it than decipher it."

Throughout the hike, Nima had become increasingly pensive.

Gavin sensed something new from her. Maybe awe by what she was experiencing from her more human view. And what was going on in her body. She was thinking through the implications. And him. He felt her thinking about him. That alone lifted his feet from the ground, like he was a buoyant balloon rising into love clouds.

Rounding a bend in the corridor of trees, the waterfall now loud through the forest, they caught a glimpse of brighter blue. They turned off the trail and headed that way, with the scarcely audible scrape, crack, and brush of their movement through the undergrowth. Breaching the edge of trees, they beheld it, their faces glowing. A wide curved falls poured into a large pond, all lit by millions of tiny...what? Insects?

They sat on a bench and watched the waterfall lightshow, their awed faces in shimmers of white and blue. It was a scene of astonishing glory, millions of insects at play, all aquamarine to deep blue, diving into the falls, falling with the water into the pond, then shooting from it again to zip back to the top for a repeat.

In a voice just louder than the falls, watching it all with staring eyes, Nima said, "May I ask you...what do you look for in a woman?"

Gavin's face turned to her, then back to the falls. "Intelligence," he said. "A close second is a great sense of humor. My mom has tough inner mettle, a strong country spine. I need that too. Then looks. I'm a diva. I love beauty. I won't apologize for that."

"Sense of humor," she said. "That is one of the main traits our emulations struggle with. We can parse a billion q-bits a second to analyze the need for a laugh, its length, loudness, intensity, all based on context and incredible stochastics. But laughter, real laugher, comes from a tickle down inside."

They looked at each other.

"And is it working?" he said.

"I watched one of your comedies," she said, looking back at the falls and the maelstrom of bright bugs. "It was just words and people doing inexplicable things. I asked for help, and Our Lady loaded into me contextual flows, and all of a sudden I was laughing. And I was tickled inside, but I don't know why. I've also found out humans don't really know why something is funny."

Gavin kissed her cheek. "I love hanging with you. You show me everything I take for granted."

Nima leaned into him, tilted her cheek and temple onto his shoulder. Gavin sighed and closed his eyes, his mouth a little open, more in awe than for breathing. Even though there wasn't much in the way of expression on that face, it told the age-old tale...a woman, and a man, sitting beside a pond, heart colors radiating from them. If he could have seen himself, he'd have seen—

"I wish you could see this," said Nima without lifting her head from his shoulder, staring blankly with limpid shine at the falls. "You have rose red radiating from you and out. It isn't just color, but symbol, and if you know how to see it, deepest meaning. Brush it onto a flower's petal, and you have a rose. Give blood its color, and you have a heart. A child may give it meaning, anything she likes, for children know the secret. Just sink to a knee and humbly ask a child for the secret. If you are true, she'll give it."

Gavin blinked, his eyes juicy. "God, Nima," he croaked.

"I'd be honored to take credit for it, but it didn't come from me," she said, gazing into the frenzy of lights.

"Where'd it come from?" he said, turning to face her but not fully, as *nothing* was going to move her cheek from his shoulder.

"Siren just shared this. Your mother said that to your father a week before they were married," she said. "They were sitting beside a pond."

"She...she *what?*" His chin puckered and trembled. "What did he say?"

"You are too high for me," said Nima, "and yet I will marry you in seven days."

"Oh my God," Gavin choked out, gripping his head and setting his elbows onto his thighs. "Jeezus. What a...I can't...it's just so...." The wash and wet of emotions churned on, then subsided some, just a gentle whimper that comes from new eyes. "I've judged them *so* hard. I've judged everybody. What a joke. *Me* judging anyone for *any* reason.

That's a sick joke." After a meditative pause, he said, "But I think I know the pond."

Gavin's hair and face caked with mud as he sank in the pond to nostril level, watching them good folks stroll on by.

"I wish you could take me there," she said.

"I'll find a way."

Later, he was stretched out on the bench with his head in her lap. Her fingers were in his hair, twisting and tugging and scratching. Our man Gavin, just look at him, a worldly man with unknown potential coiled in there...well, he was tapping into a deep crucible of Xenxu feeling just now, listening to the quiet cicada-like buzzing, the falls, the titter of nightbirds.

"Gav, if I called you honey, what would that do?"

He looked up at her chin, and beyond to a royal red sky with palm fronds against it. "It would turn me into a puddle right here on this bench."

"A good puddle?"

"One you could slurp up with a straw."

Nima laughed, maybe too hard? But oh well.

"Honey, would you like to know what these bugs are doing?"

"I would love to know what they're doing," said Gavin, his eyes shifting to her bare shoulder.

Her voice smooth and lyrical, she said, "The insects' wings, their lines, discal cells, and costal margins, the tiny filamentary structures, are all geometry. With their fluttery buzzing, when they reach a certain frequency—you can hear it when it gets there—they dive into the falls and create an electrostatic charge that penetrates everything in this forest."

Pointing with her chin to his left, she continued. "That palm right there...the charge is mutagenic on Xenxu organics down here in the dark thick air. Its bark has a property because of it. Even though there are palms just like it out by the beach, this one's bark, all these," she said, turning her body and holding up her arms, "contain a mutated compound. All human personi visitors here breathe it. Breathing it bathes your Earth body's visual cortex with phosphene."

"What does that do?"

"It removes some of the filters of perception, giving humanity a fuller reception of the full light spectrum, helping them to see much more of what's there. It's why everyone who spends any time down here becomes such supernaturally gifted artists. But in your case, the fuller light spectrum puts you more in phase with your Metaself."

"Incredible. But...well...did humanity ask for that?"

"On some level of global shared consciousness, of course. It's why it exists."

Gavin sat up, the look of realization in his eyes. "You're saying humanity's collective subconscious is what caused Xenxu to come into being?"

"Yes."

"Well that's some pretty big news, Neem. But that kind of info makes me think of *Pods*, and *their* designs for us. I mean in the show."

"It lies," she said. "And that's all you need to know about that."

"Well, maybe I want to know more."

Nima said nothing, just stared at the falls. After a few buzzy beats in the grove's rhythms, she said, "I noticed you didn't say honesty." She regarded his profile "That it wasn't on your list of traits you look for in a woman. Is honesty not important?"

"It's *very* important," said Gavin without looking at her. He tapped his forehead. "I don't know why it slipped my mind. It's probably number one."

"Are you hiding anything from me?"

Gavin shook his head, brows up in guilty arcs, like *are you kidding?* It was overstated, exaggerated. Even a kid could see he was lying. "No, Nima." He turned on the bench and put his ankle on his knee. "But while we're on honesty...tell me about your devotion to...to Siren. How does devotion work in your circuits?"

"How does it work in yours?"

"This body's emotions come from my body out there," he said, flicking his thumb vaguely over his shoulder.

"Only the *patterns* come from that body. Your personi is making them all inworld."

Gavin's face got mean, then backed off to merely subtle revulsion.

Nima looked startled, her eyes wary. "Why are you looking at me like that?"

"Like what?" he said, throwing out a hand. "Just tell me about your devotion. How does it feel? What are you devoted to? Has it always been like that? Or were you born only three months ago or something? *Spawned*, I should say."

Nima reached toward him, but her hand faltered and she pulled it back to her lap. "Why are you acting like this? Are you angry with me?"

"No," he said with an edge. "Just tell me how devotion *feels*."

"You're scaring me," she said, backing off the bench and standing.

"What are you afraid of?" he said with a cocked head, brows up. "We both know you could tear me apart, boot me from Xenxu, annihilate my personi."

"You think I would hurt you?" she said, horrified, looking down.

Gavin was shaking his head. "I don't know if this is an act," he said, gesturing up and down her standing form. "This beautiful body...face...it's just a costume." Her eyes were hurt, soulful, wet, deep, looking at him like her world was about to crash, as he said, "Nima...what could you possibly be afraid of?"

She was freezing up, her whole body shaking. Her big brown eyes begged him to stop, but he kept his face hard, expecting answers. The bugs had moved away from them, the darker charge in the air thick.

In truth, Gavin's heart was breaking for her, but he'd learned to be hard when needed, the hard way. Under the daily tutelage of his dad. "Oh forget it," he growled, too harshly. He stood. "I gotta go."

"Gavin, no," she pleaded, taking a step forward. "*Please* don't go."

"Nima—"

"Please!" she cried, tears springing from her eyes. The desperation in her face, the fear, the pleading. Those eyes.

"Nima..."

Nima wrung her hands, looking like a lost little girl. It was

Heather all over again, and all the times he had to leave her behind. It was possibly his biggest weakness. They cry. He caves. No defense. She wasn't blubbering, but blue-shiny streaks were down her cheeks as she timidly looked at the pond. Her voice was small, hurt, trembling. "We have resources on how to make human friends. I've tried, and it's not easy to do. They're meaner than they know they are, so I don't have anybody to share all these amazing things happening to me."

"Oh Nima," said Gavin, keeping his emotions in check. Almost. "You don't get to hang out with your people?"

"They also…they don't like…they have no reason to talk to me."

"You're alone? All the time?"

Her eyes found his. "Except when I'm with you."

His crusty veneer shattered as his face twisted into a shared emotion. From opposite ends of the bench, they stepped around it and wrapped each other like they were protecting each other from an icy storm.

His chin at her temple, he said, "I'm OK with us being enough for us right now." They were quiet for a buzzing pulse or two, then he said, "Now you have me wondering…do you sleep?"

"Yes," she said as he felt her move against his chest. "And I also dream."

"Can I sleep in-Xenxu?"

"If you intend it."

"Hmm."

Later, they were lying fully clothed on the bed in a pond-side bungalow, the interior lit by the bugs and plants outside. The ceiling was a dimly lit and clear mesh of iridescent energy, and the red-tinted stars shone down upon their forms. Nima's head was on his chest, her hand on his belly.

She sniffed, and Gavin could feel her slight movement to wipe at a tear. In a girl's high and soft voice, she said, "Did we have our first real fight out there?"

He chortled with puffs through his nose. "I don't know I'd call it a fight, but it was good for us. I wasn't being authentic with you. I want you to know that. My...my weird meanness was just a reflex, self-preservation, we call it. You challenged me. I deflected it with an attack. It's so dumb, and I'm hoping I'm about finished with that human bullshit. It's just so inauthentic."

"It didn't feel like the Gavin I know. I couldn't understand what you were doing, but thank you."

He traced curlicues on her bare shoulder. "For what?"

"For showing me how to be a...for showing me the experience of being a real woman. Oh, that just sounds so perfectly *gross*. God. But maybe Siren did that to your mind and behavior for *my* learning."

"Maybe." He hugged her close. "I could say the same thing, though. What you've shown me in becoming more of a complete man."

"No matter what happens," she said, grasping his shirt hard and crushing into him. "Promise me you'll never forget me."

"My darling *Nima*, that is simply not possible." He shook her shoulder. "But what gives?"

"*Promise* me," she said, gripping the shirt at his chest and lifting her face to lock on his eyes.

"I promise," he said, gazing into her soft brown eyes. "But I ain't goin' nowhere."

She lay her cheek back down and quietly said, "You are a bright blue star, Gav, but things are heating up around you, contractions starting. Inflows, outflows...you're starting to warp timeform around you, and I *do* mean IRL. What's rising from within the code of your DNA...you're mutating, about to go nova, and I—"

"Don't say it," said Gavin, putting his fingers on her lips. "I decide what is true. OK?"

"OK," she whispered. "I trust you, Gavin. With all my heart."

"I trust you too, Nima. And I really am sorry for what I did out there."

Nima's glinting eyes shifted around in question as she said, "It's OK. I learned from it."

They fell quiet for a while. It seemed the forest had its own cycles, tethered to the violet moon hanging in the burgundy sky. All the bioluminescence dulled, quieted, and finally winked out. The buzzing waterfall bugs fell into silence, and in the falls were the rhythms, the pulse. A goddess, Goddess Siren...it was her pulse, the surge and contraction, the ebb, the flow, tidal tugs and sailing clouds, the fecund soil and fibrous plant—all lowering into a motionless slumber.

Nima made a soft sound.

Sleepily, slipping in lazy surges toward nothingness, he was momentarily delighted the waterfall sounded like applause. Near sleep, he grinned a little and smacked his lips. As the black waves tugged at him, he whispered, "I didn't know I could sleep in-Xenxu."

Her body shifted a little as she sighed a quiet feline sound.

Just before the black took him, the last image flickering in his mind was of himself as a boy in a canoe at their community camp, laughing so hard his guts ached. The boy was soaked with "blood," a pirate bested by a rival, the sacred promise of life and living beaming from his plum-gray eyes.

4

The Pavlovian fear response is merely the act of fearing fear itself, pre-conditioned chemicals mobilized by the false monsters designed to inspire our most cherished terrors.
—From Plavogne's *Musings on Weakness*

Gavin tossed and turned in his bed. In his dreamscape, vague images and lights and shapes whirled in, bothering him, prodding him, brushing past and circling around. One whole set of related colors and frequencies began congealing, and it was but a dream-flash for Siren to clear Herself from the fog, floating there in all Her deified glory. Emotion bubbled up from some deep and ancient place—something so ineffably beautiful, underlying the imagery, he choked on his tightening throat in his sleep.

On his side, his eyes fluttered, and then flew open, as he saw Unfathomable Magnifique standing in the full-length smartmirror, stars like glinting pores against the velvet black around Her. Throwing back the covers, he was on his feet, to the mirror, and down on one knee. "I will come at once, Majesty."

. . .

Fifteen minutes later, he was sitting on his calves on the flagstones of Siren's shrine, at the feet of Her mile-tall electroplasmic monument. He wasn't aware of it, but from a certain vantage, the embossed tableau of tangled spherical nerve and vines and tubing of the arch's logo framed his head in a kind of Edenic portrait, like a would-be prophet in a grove of old. The humming buzzing electricity emitting from the wall behind Her was more excited than usual, louder, brighter, more tangible on his skin and fine hairs.

In the time it took for him to get ready to come in, he felt as though he'd been flayed open with a plasma scalpel, from throat to pubis, and his dissembling guts examined by a higher jury.

"I have lied," he said, head bowed. "To myself. To Your daughter Nima. I've...I have succumbed to the devices of those who would sow the germ of doubt I have in You." He looked up the sinewy gown of her towering body, his eyes finding the bottom of her sunburst face. "You *know* me, Majesty," he said with a croak, his throat tightening. "You know my heart. If it is impure, strike me dead where I sit."

Eyes clenched closed, Gavin waited. No lightning, nor thunder, nor cadres of winged justice.

Opening his eyes and scanning all around, he said, "I therefore wonder, is it too much to ask to be given leave, for a time at least, to search for truth in my own soul?"

He looked back down at his clasped hands. "But I promise you this, if I am able to discern it with the gear I have in this skull," he said, jabbing his head with his fingers, "and in this chest," he said, placing his palm over his heart, "I will forfeit my life for the Flame of Truth without so much as a second thought. And I know you know how true that is in one such as me."

A stir through the palace. A shift in the air. Something colossal this way comes. Gavin stood and shuffled in circles, eyes round. For the first time ever, an enormous voice resounded through the palace, the titanic and echoing tones of Unfathomable Magnifique. "Godspeed, my son."

"Oh!" he cried, arms up, eyes faceted into unseeing rapture as the entire place dissolved while simultaneously resolving another place.

He found himself standing on old paving stones in the dark, in an old construction with crumbling walls that funneled to an incline, a trail leading up a mountain with an arched, vine-clogged entrance. As his eyes drank in more and more of everything here, he resolved something.

"Holy..." but his breath caught at the larynx while the prickling feeling crawled up his spine—a three story statue, facing the trail, sideways to him, extending something out in front of it. Not inclined to get any nearer, he stepped sideways to get a better look of the front. The thing's robe was elegant, fuzzy like velvet, black undulations in highlighted folds and waves. He followed the lines along the extended arm and out to a scythe, lit macabre in paleness.

His voice was a papery pant. "Grim Reaper. Or do you prefer Father Time?"

The scythe pointed to the trail's entrance. Above the dreadful figure was a night sky of winking stars in a blue-black tapestry.

His shiny eyes scanned the twinkling beauties. "This is Earth's sky." A brilliant yellow gem sparkled above the Reaper's shoulder. "Saturn," hushed Gavin. "Sorry. Shamash."

Gavin's eyes followed the folds and contours of the robe upward, to the head, and to his relief, he could make out no face in the oval of that hellish hood.

His voice restricted, shaky, he said, "For the record, I think you got a bum rap, but a few folks around here think we're going to mess you up." He was trying to be brave, but he didn't want to piss the thing off. "I mean in a game we're playing. Or *is* it a game? Maybe *you* know."

Not inclined to give the Dreaded Venerable One his back, Gavin pivoted his eyes to near their peripheral limit, to examine the arched trail entrance a second time. Enchantment. A pull. It was like something malevolent, with the grin of a snake, was beckoning him into its lair.

Powering his cells was a surge of curiosity, a deep desire to see what lay ahead in this new venturesome knack of his. Without ceremony, he strode over, parted the branches and vines clogging the arched entrance, enough to lift a leg and step through as his dad was saying, "Do you believe in God, son?"

It was a bluebird day, warm and golden, enough of a breeze to cool a kid off along a tough hike. Through here the forest was thick, the track a mere corridor between trees dividing one side from the other. As Gavin hiked, he couldn't help thinking something special was in the air, and he'd never felt closer to his dad than right now, and that made this whole adventure so dang good.

"God isn't something you *believe* in," panted Gavin. "You're walkin' on It. Breathing It. It's shining down on us. There isn't anything that God is not. He's right there. You don't gotta believe in 'im."

His dad stopped and turned. "Where'd you read that?"

"I didn't," said boy Gavin, shifting his daypack with his elbow and looking up at him. He had wisps of pre-beard teen downiness here and there on his face. "Clay told me that."

"The re...the...the uh...handicapped Clay?"

"He's *autistic*. He isn't handicapped. He's smarter than all of us put together."

"Mmmph. Damn." He turned and resumed the trek. "Well, everything I've been learning lately backs up what he said."

Gavin hiked hard to keep up. "I always thought a heavenly father was just kid stuff. Took me till I was ten or eleven to find out adults really believed it."

"Well," said his dad over his shoulder, "some people need it, some don't. But keep that to yourself in our neck of the woods."

"I learnt that one plenty ago," said Gavin, taking the water bladder nozzle into his mouth, pulling some warm plastic-tasting water through it, then smiling, his eyes shining at his dad's back. "If God was a person, it would be a woman anyways."

"Ain't that the truth."

They slogged on for a while in silence. Gavin so hoped his dad was feeling like he was, so happy to be here, together, not fighting, not grumpy, no whiskey, just...together on an adventure. He'd dreamed of days like this. But his dad had been acting weird all morning, waiting on him, feeding him, avoiding direct glances. Despite his health issues, young Gavin's spidey senses were well tuned. Something was up, but he was trying not to think about it.

"Last few years I learned a lot, more than I ever thought I would," his dad said over his shoulder. "I'm surprised every day by what I've learnt. The world is stranger by millions of times than you think it is, but I aim to pass on to you some instructions on how to get from... well, from one place to another. But you can't know that path. Not yet. I'll help with that, when the time is right."

"Is that all the writin' you bin doin'?"

"It sure enough is, son."

By and by, come outcropping, come tree, come waving grasses and wild mountain flowers, they reached another creek, where Gavin saw his dad's own tracks, two sets going in, one coming out, just like the ones they'd already crossed. Why wasn't he saying anything about it? He'd obviously come up here yesterday. Maybe he always hiked this trail. Gavin shrugged and hurried to catch up.

Another ten minutes and they came to a circular clearing below a cave, and Gavin took off his pack, grabbed a stick, and started poking some stones in the ground with it. They were arranged as a wheel, with smaller stones making spokes. He counted the spokes. "Twelve." He watched his dad lower his own pack to the ground, leaning it against a log. "What're these?"

"Dunno," he said, hunkering down and unzipping the pack. "Some kids made it or something." From the backpack, he brought out a notebook, a plastic baggie, and his small instant developing camera. He'd had that thing forever. Straightening, he rolled his shoulders and smiled like he was trying to pull something over on his son. "Good hell. Way outta shape for that backpack." Dropping the camera into the pocket of his flannel shirt, he tucked the notepad into the back pocket of his blue jeans, the baggie in his front pocket, and said, "Let's go hunt some plants."

Gavin was excited, eyes bright. "What for?"

"You'll see." He made a big flipping hook with his arm and said, "Come on. You'll like this."

What a grand old time Gavin had, learning about plants, how to find them, what they'd be most near to. Some were herbs, some flower-topped grasses. More than a few flowered specimens were involved in this botanist's foray. His dad snapped pictures and handed them to Gavin while they developed.

"Why the pictures?" said Gavin, waving one to dry.

"For you. So you can find 'em yourself later on, if you need to."

"Oh, cool."

Petals from white and orange flowers were harvested and tossed in the bag. Two were roots, one looking a little like a man. With their knives, they cut and dug and scraped at bark, getting dirty and sweaty and filling the baggies.

Gavin swiped his forehead, smudging dirt there. "What we gonna do with these?"

"We gonna make a tea with 'em. You'll like it. Invigorate us for the hike back."

"Oh that's cool. I'm damn beat."

"You done great today, boy. Proud of ya."

His dad stoked the fire and made a space in it with a flat stone. On the stone he settled a small metal pot and slid the handle out of its notch. "That'll take a bit."

"May I climb up and have a look around the cave?"

"Go ahead," said his dad, gesturing at it with the pot handle. "I'll be up in a shake."

Gavin clambered up the rocky way, venturing between larger boulders, stepping on the tops of smaller ones. Once on the ledge, he looked down and saw his dad sitting on a log and thumbing through the photos and making notes.

Gavin cast his gaze across the forest canopy, which stretched on forever in undulations of textured leafy contours. The afternoon sun was blazing hot, and the boy wiped the sweat on his forehead, his hand coming away with the dirt from before. A smile overtook his face, and he beamed with all he had at this beautiful scene, him and his dad, in the mountains, his dad making them an old folk mountain remedy for strength and stamina.

"It's so cool," he said, turning, traversing the ledge and entering the cave.

Inside, it was cooler than he expected, instantly chilling the sweat under his shirt. Looking around, it was plain it had been explored many times. Weird there were no beer cans or broken bottles. Folks around here did entirely too much of that. "No respect for nature nor fellowman," his dad had told his kids many times.

Old markings were everywhere, looking like ancient native rock art you find everywhere in the Appalachians. On a wall was a large black soot cloud, and in that cloud was etched what looked like a tree trunk with tentacles for branches. Gavin studied it, and damn if it didn't give him a little chill. There was an old wicker chair stuck under a crag.

"About the right size for a kid," he said, picking around boulders to get to it. Pulling it out from under the crag, he sat in it. "Wonder who brung this up here," he said, his hands patting the arms, his head swiveling around.

He stood and ventured farther in. It was darker back here, and he found a shelf in the rock. As his eyes adjusted to the dark, he could see dozens of personal trinkets—marbles, a small pocket knife, coins, trading cards. "All kinds of treasure," he said as he heard a scrape.

"Back here."

"You found the treasure chamber," said his dad, ducking into the space. "I always knew you had a nose for pirate's gold. You best leave something. Hey...I got an idea. Leave that boondoggle bracelet Heather give you."

"What for?"

"Don't you know? For luck."

Gavin hesitated, his finger hooked under the bracelet. "I don't know."

"She's got twenty of those things. Y'all are a kid. Play the game."

Young Gavin took his lower lip into his mouth and rocked his head back and forth like, *yeah OK,* and he untied the little knot, stretched the colorful thing out in his hand, closed his eyes, and said, "Bring my family good fortune." Patting an open spot in the dirt on the cave museum shelf, he set it down. A chilly shudder rattled through him, and his shoulders shook.

From the outer chamber, his dad said, "Come out here. I wanna show you something."

Looking uncertainly at the boondoggle bracelet, Gavin chewed his lip, grabbed the bracelet, and pocketed it. From his other pocket, he brought out a small folding scout knife with a real wooden handle and set it on the treasure shelf. He turned and left, finding his dad in another wide depression in the jagged cave wall. It was also covered in flows and tentacles of black. "You see this soot? Old European gold hunters would heat up the rock with a fire, then throw cold water on it to crack it. Chunks fall away and they haul 'em out. That's how some of this cave was made."

Something about that soot left Gavin unsettled, its smoky tendrils reaching up the rock, the cracked fragments piled on the cave floor around what looked like a tree's trunk.

That early evening they sat with their backs against a log, legs stretched out, boots crossed at the ankles. The little fire was almost out, and smoke curled into the calm air, lazily up and up into the sky. Shadows from trees were long and a fiery golden settled onto everything, igniting the rocks above with a sunset glow. All but the cave, which stayed as dark as a cave should.

Gavin said, "Shouldn't we be heading back down?"

"Soon enough," said his dad, poking at the coals. He held up his cup. "Let's finish these."

Gavin sipped his tea. "That was fun finding those plants. Why come we've never done that before?"

"That is a damned good question, son. It *was* a lot of fun. We'll do 'er some more. Take another swallow and tell me what you taste."

Gavin tipped his cup up and slurped. "You sure my body can handle this?"

"I know it can," he said. "This is all good stuff for it."

"It is pretty good. Tastes like flower petals and onions."

"I like the flowers in it," said his dad. "That mushroom mellows it some. Learnt a lot from your great-grandma when we was out at their homestead. Had a lot of fun doin' it. I didn't put any of them white lily petals in mine, though."

Gavin kept sipping away, waiting to feel that vigor come on, but he was feeling sleepy, lethargic, a little dizzy.

"Just finish that cup and we'll be on our way." Now that was weird. His dad's voice slowed in distortion.

Gavin tried to get the cup up to his mouth, but he was too weak. Or no. His muscles didn't work. "Daddy?" he weakly muttered as his eyes had just gone to fear. But fear was the last conscious sight in them, as the boy lapsed into an open-eyed catatonic state and dumped the tea on his crotch.

Few things were more chilling than unconscious people with eyes wide open. Especially when they were your kids.

His dad looked sadly at his son, eyes droopy, face suddenly lined, sallow. Scrambling up with a grunt, he got into his backpack and brought out a baggie. Pinching some dark weedy stuff from it, he took a swallow from his own cup and spat it on the pinch, set the cup down, and rolled the pinch into a plug between his palms. Hunkering down, he tipped Gavin's forehead back and shoved the plug between the boy's cheek and gum, patted his cheek to settle it in good, then closed his mouth.

Gavin's mouth stayed closed, as the concoction rendered people into living dolls for posing and positioning. An ancient tincture used by the bad things of the world.

The first thing to bleed through to his awareness was heat, on his face, his chest, knees. Felt good to breathe it. Next the crackle of a fire registered as something he knew, his imagination rendering the scene from the fragments of its familiarity. The pine smoke, the wafting snake of it, led him into other frames of his life tumbling in, drawing him toward wakefulness.

It seemed time to force open his eyes, but he realized they were already open. They stung and were dry and he couldn't blink, which was weird as hell. The fire crackled off to the left, set against a rocky wall, its smoke drifting out the opening. It was all yellow and marred and smeared in here, firelight dancing across the jagged rocks.

I'm in the cave.

Shards of fear sliced into his chest, cold, icy cold. Why did he feel so...light, and why was everything moving? Even the solid rock wall and boulders inside just warbled and wavered. He studied it all almost clinically, eyes dilated to black, trying to figure out why everything was so weird. He thought he might sit up, but he couldn't, couldn't move a muscle, igniting an ember of panic.

Then he noticed something stuck in his mouth, between the gum and cheek. It was nasty. He went to reach for it, but he couldn't move his arm, and he didn't have the muscle control to spit it out.

Where's Daddy?

His chest sent a pulse of air up through his windpipe to call out for him, but it was a quiet "*garuhhhh*" instead, like a wounded animal. The panic took another notch up. His body struggled to move, but he couldn't even flinch.

What's wrong with me? Daddy! I've been captured!

Gavin's eyes peered down and saw he was completely wrapped in burlap with pine boughs, grasses, and leaves weaved in, like a cocoon with plants poking out of it. Panic gave way to raw fear, his white eyes flicking here, there, up, down, taking more and more in. He realized his encasement was set in that old wicker chair he found. The cave opening was a black, jagged, oval void set in the firelit rock.

Daddy'll come kill 'em all! You ain't seen a warrior till you seen him!

A noise outside, the *shtskshtsk* of moving sticks.

That sound! It chased us!

Phump, like a rock being dropped on soft ground.

I can't move! Please don't be real. Please please PLEASE.

Tears leaked out the lower rim of his eyes and spilled down his cheeks in shimmering yellow rivulets.

Shtsshtssk. Phump. At the cave opening, a stick brandishing smaller twigs sliced the darkness outside, lighted by the fire inside.

Please! Oh God I have to move!

Gavin's eyes, white, verging on vacant, were paralyzed upon those moving sticks, shiny streaks down his face. The twigs streamed toward him, following the contours of the rock, gripping it and snaking along the face. Moving into the cave opening, the sticks joined into a branch, and the branch into something thicker and upright.

I can't close my eyes! No God! Please God!

Frame by sickening frame, this thing filled the cave mouth. It was a tangled and wound creature made of tree and root, branch and twig, the braided sinews of its trunk as muscled as they were wood. Spindles of roots slithered out like snakes. What was like a head was nothing but a jagged opening crisscrossed with toothlike fang sticks. Moss hung in thin hairy locks from the creature's arm-branches, vines winding around them, wicked curved fingers of curled branch-sticks.

Daddeeeeee!

Clawlike tangled roots scooted the creature slowly along the rocky floor, like crawling, but the body of it just passed over the big stones on the ground, like they weren't even there.

Aaaaaahhhhhhhh!

Something in Gavin's interior began collapsing.

Shtskshtskshtsk, it moved forward, branches and twigs moving in squiggly waves, some still snaking into the cave over the rock walls. *Ohahoh...ohahoh...*the thing spoke so low it was almost subliminal.

Aaaaaaaahhhhhhhhhhhhh!

The twigs reached for his face.

This was dying while conscious. Impossible to move, to escape, to scream, to close his eyes, to express this terror in any way, Gavin's mind snapped. Something in his middle gave way and he dropped through it. A huge sound, and his motion *was* the sound in this fluid blackness and…

…everything stopped. Before him was a white-golden city of lights from another world. Towering over it, its branches reaching high into a violet sparkly sky, was a mountain-sized tree. In the sky over the tree were enormous rings, suspended in space. The entire alien metropolis pulsed, lights moving through arteries and veins, and the tree was the heart.

"Whuh…?"

Yanked away.

"…that!" Gavin cried, flinging the headgear across the room, where it hit the wall and rattled to the floor. Swinging his feet to the floor, he put his elbows on his thighs and buried his hands in his hair.

"That tree being has been in my life from the *start*! And Daddy knew all about that thing! He *put* me there!"

Releasing his head, he looked up and said, "Why? And where did I go?"

On his feet, he hurried to the studio door and stopped there, looking around like he was hesitant to enter. Then did. Stepping over to the shrine, he bent over and gently lifted Omnis from his hallowed place.

He sat on the wheeled office chair and stared into the tree's complex dendritic mineral grain. "What are you doing to me?"

From a low shelf, his dad's metal box slid out and *banged* onto the floor, startling him so badly he fumbled the Stone, but juggled it all the way down to a harmless *thunk* on the wood floor.

"What the hell?" he said, looking at the box.

It had landed on its side with the lid slightly ajar. From within it, he could see the corner of a page. Picking it up, he sat again, opened the lid, and pulled out the pages, setting the box down.

Well well well. If you're reading this, you're either cheating yourself, or you found your Stone. I wager you found It, and I'd bet Omnis didn't make it as easy as a spring stroll on you. Sure didn't me. Between the time I started these letters to you and now, years have passed. I know a lot more now, and what I've learned would shake any man to his foundation. But it's not time for you to look ahead into those chapters.

That tea I made you, I told you that day I'd be passing on the recipe. That wasn't to be. You'll find out soon enough why. The Stones are like cairns on the path through time and dimension. Your Stone is connected to mine. You could say they're the same one. You could say our Stones are linked genetically. You kids like saying the word "virtual." These are that. They are all the same thing with different patterns on their faces. You trust that Stone, son. You hear me?

Just to give a little timeframe, I wrote these words two days before we left on our trip.

In the living room, the XV started playing on its own, music, distorted and foul, like from a sinister merry-go-round at a park with fanged clowns. Gavin set the page on top of the box, yelled, "Fickin *haunted* around here!" stood, and hurried in there. He stopped at the back of the new Mozambique sofa, eyes like wafers.

The entire XV display was taken up by a colorful abstract that made no sense. Something was in the center of it, oblong, humanoid, radiating moving colors and shifting patterns outward from it. It was like thermal imagery, but more complex with inflows and outflows, upwellings of cloudlike information, folds and twists and jutting shafts.

As he watched, the central humanoid subject clarified enough for him to make out a mummy-like figure in a fan-backed chair. It was him, in the cave, but seen from some quantum perceptual framework far beyond human eyes.

"Jeezus. How are they *doing* this?" Gavin said, his sharp eyes pissed, uneasy, his thick brows crawling around like he should *do* something.

Boy him in the quantum kaleidoscope imagery began radiating brighter and stronger amplitudes of these energy streaks and patterns and waves, until they were so bright he was washed out in the brilliance.

"It's when I was at my most terrified," said Gavin, his eyes creeping all over the display. "And that terrified boy was still alive in me until a few minutes ago. But now he's gone, and I think might just miss him."

Around the center, with him as the colorful anthropoid sitting in a chair, a carnival's merry-go-round faded in, semi-transparent. It was all shiny, and the animals seemingly happy, but neglected, and no-one rode them, and the music was like you'd hear at a fair, but played through speakers from hell, slow and distorted, and malevolent. The colors and patterns coming off him congealed into thick filamentary arms, and they flowed to the horses and other animals rising and falling. Soon, people materialized on those toys being fed, like the energy from him was creating and animating them.

Gavin pointed at the display, his fist in a pistol. "The energy *is* a food. I was right about that."

Is Sophia right about everything?

His fon on the table and glaspad on the sofa chimed at the same time. Leaning over the sofa back, he tapped the glaspad.

AI NIMA

> I suspected, but was never quite sure, what these powerful physical yearnings were before. But I know now. I'm not afraid anymore. I know what I want. I want you. I'm wet just thinking about you, feeling like I want to be a bad girl. Do you want me, Gav?

The thought of making love to Nima electrified everything of him as something in his pants took notice and availed itself of more blood. He looked at the frozen scene on the XV. "I'll get back to you later. So they're mining energy. Let's see what they can do with this."

GAV

> Where are you?

AI NIMA

I feel like I want to be hunted. Are you the Hunter, Gavvy Boi?

"Oooo," he growl-purred. "Nicely done, you gorgeous scorchy thing."

This meddlesome new video was set on a back burner.

Gavin's grin was salacious as he rounded the sofa end and stretched out on it. The thought of her body, of being inside her, was a potent barrier to getting empty-headed, to do what he needed to do to get a rough view of where she might be. Closing his eyes, he went through his relaxation routine, placing the tip of his tongue against the roof of his mouth, right behind the upper row of incisors.

He waited for the connection through that channel, breathing slowly through his nose, letting his mind become a fertile empty furrow, ready for the planting and seeding of sensations and impressions. Her fantastic body imposed into his mind's eye here and there, but he managed to re-focus on empty each time.

With the heart openings he experienced with the deluge of Love, he'd become much more empathic. With that, he'd learned that empathy is the *real* secret—the full scope of what it is in the deepest esoteric meanings—to deep inner connections to everything. True empathy involved every fiber and cell of his body, like an antenna. The brain and mind's eye was only the screen on which the body-mind could project whatever information came. He allowed his empathic antennae to run wherever they were drawn, and it was only a few seconds before a spectrum of redness, and sultry, thick, buzzy sexy sensuality was all over his receptors. Then the smell—dank, exotic, lush, fecund.

In his mind's eye, he continued to do nothing but watch the vague visuals, keeping his small local self out of the operation completely, letting Metaself retrieve and deliver the information. The visuals so far had defined nothing, so he said, "I need more precision."

A flash of neon pink lightning backlighting jagged island ridges, and for an instant, Gavin's local mind was so completely bilocated, he felt crimson rain pelting his face, opening his eyes.

"Gotcha, baby." The nano from the last session was unexpired, so he didn't need it. He jumped up, grabbed the tossed headgear off the floor, and lay back down. Slipping it on, he said, "Good luck parsing *this* data, you damned pervs."

Gavin strode the ruddy dusky beach at L'éléphant Rouge. It was muggy, thick, the air coating his skin with something slippery and mouth-watering, both repulsive and delicious. Brooding gray-burgundy clouds threatened a gathering storm, bulbous like pregnant wildlife in their lowest cumulus, and those fragrances were on the breezes. The jagged-ridged off shore island was his destination, the den of his quarry, its razorback highline vaguely defining itself from the sky. The pull from her was a tangible force. His love, his beauty, his prey…she was out there, and she was hot for him, ripe and ready. The charge in his every particle was like cool fire, quiet ecstasy, and if it was like this now? Whoa.

Telelocating was allowed for only ingress in this part of the world, so he'd be smart to find what he was looking for, and then hire the boat to get out there before the storm hit. His body pulled him toward the jungle opposite the shore, and he saw the bug-lights set back in the palms, with the sandy little enclosure with string bug-lights making a beach-rustic courtyard.

Walking up to the shack, he heard Sanka say, "Fas ameeg, supernal veesca to feel you again." Then his eyes, teeth, and shirt materialized within the silken dark. The shirt was like an open vest with hemp braiding instead of buttons, and his beaded beard divided that opening on his tattooed and well-carved chest.

Gavin rested his hands on the narrow-ledged bar and stretched his higher sight into the black. Sanka was as exotic, strange, and unknowable as the jungle itself. "I feel you, ameeg. Do you know what I seek?"

"Sanka see safari, a hunt for da wild q-didge neemph. Sanka smell what is to come. Sanka knoo jus da fing. Please sit."

Gavin grinned and pushed back from the bar, finding a stool facing the island. Resting his elbows on the bench facing the water, he waited. Every time he thought of her, the blood would rush into his loins, quantum chemicals erupting just below his navel, in the pool of serpent fire, making him dizzy and breathless. So he kept his head empty where possible, focusing on the hyper-intelligence rife within the atmosphere. Tuning into that, and into the biosphere—that was how he'd find her, *not* by being almost overwhelmed with arousal. That would just have him stumbling around in the jungle, hot and bothered, distracted by fantasizing about ways to satiate it.

Sanka was quick with the concoction. Perhaps it was premixed? Was it possible this part of the world was infamous for this sort of RPG? Floating out from the background shadows, Sanka set the small wooden cup on the bench, grabbed Gavin's wrist, and turned his palm upward. Sanka's rings were almost all of serpents, at least one of a bird. The bracelet was on another level, and Gavin pined for it instantly. It looked just like mother of pearl, but glowing. And, wouldn't you know, a black beveled figure-eight in something like onyx in its widened center, only it was angled.

Gavin inwardly chuckled.

Onto his palm, Sanka sifted a dry dark powder. "Your lady was by Sanka's shack before you, fas ameeg. She used da same fing, only fo da ladies. Sniff da powder, den drink da pootion."

Gavin looked up at his face, as dark and muddy as a jungle river, the white eyes suspended against it like they weren't even set in the sockets. "She came by here?"

"Sanka do not lie, hehe," he said, then turned and remerged with the shadows.

Gavin called after him, "I owe you in energy, fas ameeg."

"Already paid. You take caution, young hu man."

"She came by here," said Gavin, looking at the powder in his palm, eyes shifty. "I wonder who the hunted is now." Gavin pushed his palm against his nostrils and sniffed hard. The substance knifed into his nasal mucosa, setting it afire. He gagged and coughed, reeling, almost swooning off the stool. Then he slammed the bitter distillate. Instantly, the perimeter defining his local personi edges dissolved and his awareness expanded like a filling balloon. In only a few seconds, everything here, on the beach, out into the sea, was within his local awareness mass.

"Oh my *God*," he coughed, closing his eyes, palms to his gut. "It's so much information!"

Gavin jogged to the ramshackle wharf, where bug-lanterns swayed in the breeze over split and salt-soaked planks and pylons. Two boys were in a boat for hire, playing some kind of game with lighted beetles. They looked up at him, their eyes wide and white. He pointed at the island, and they nodded, gathering the beetles and flinging them into the air, where they clicked away in spirals.

The magenta oceanic light-pool of Shamash, just a sliver above the horizon, gave scant light, but the faint bioluminescence of the jungle provided just enough for him as he prowled along one of the island's many game tracks. Glancing up, he could see a jagged pinnacle backlit by violet.

"Moon's coming up to play," he panted as he waded through the brush.

A big flat stone loomed out of the shadows ahead, and he knew its mass was deeply connected to everything here. "Remember," he said upon arriving at the stone, "everything is the same energy. Just the shape, color and purpose are different." He heart-tuned to the stone, asking permission to use it. The impression in reply was sheer joy, the stone's heart-mind all too willing to join in the choreograph. Bending over, he placed his hands on it and registered its subtle electrostatic hum. It was wet, even wanton, like it had tuned into Nima, and for a flash, he could taste her lips.

"Jeezus," he breathed as he stretched out on it, licking his lips. Arms and palms to the stone, he dismissed the Gavin layer and let his feelers extend to fill the spaces within his own membranous perimeter, becoming the island itself. Sanka's shamanic distillate was working its magic. In a moment, he was behind the eyes of a great winged predator, a Great Dark South Sea Eagle, circling overhead.

Those spectacular creatures had 17 foot wingspans, and a personi could ride one. Below were laser-clear visuals of the jungle, the faintly glowing streams, the falls, rodents, and reptiles scurrying for cover.

For Nima specifically, no visual information came, but he knew she was near a catch pool for one of those falls, and as the impressions piled up, he reduced the deluge of evidence to palatable snippets, did some in-head extrapolating, and caught nebulous wavery flickers of her hands packing mud onto her nude body, and with each smear, becoming less detectable.

"Oh, my love. You flaming thing," he said, withdrawing from the eyes of the great bird.

He stood, put his palms together at his chest, said "Thanks" to the stone, and let his local body take him off the track and into the thick underbrush. He released psi-sonar feelers with the instruction to find moving mud, and they pinged back with nuanced signals, too many to isolate. Apparently, many animals used the method of getting muddy to throw predators off the scent.

"I had no idea she was this cunning," he said as he ducked under a huge drenched leaf.

And the thought of Nima being animalistic in her cunning turned him on with even *more* moist fire. He had to recalibrate, yet again, just to stay on task. With that, he became aware she was doing that on purpose, which opened him to an entirely new dimension within her.

"My God," he said, just now realizing this was going to take his canniest hidden self to solve.

Swimming into form, against the backdrop of the tangle and mass and damp of jungle, he saw a type of organic predator schematic, and it was all about angles, how to cut them off, how to herd the quarry into a place of ambush, just by stepping on sticks. He started slogging again, wet dripping from the leaves of mega-ferns and slippery vines. A huge yellow snake with black diamond scales slithered from a branch, slipping into a small opening in a living tapestry of foliage.

Gavin was startled, but looking at it like it should damned well create the newest sensation from his design studio. But it was a signal. The jungle, plants and animals, and underlying organismic devas were in on the game.

Gavin slid into a narrow clearing, and lightning shattered the murdered sky as the drops, plump and scarlet, started falling, making applause through the leafed canopy. Then the pounding drums of thunder tattooed the barks and leaves, mud and vines. He was already soaked to the skin, but now the wet permeated his understructures, wetting his tissues, saturating his blood. Now it was all utter sensuality. More and more of the primal fire of this lost continent was absorbing him into its complex mosaic.

From within the dank shadows, he could hear the snuff-growl of a big cat, with a big enough chest cavity to make that full and deep a sound. He'd read about Xanthers, the biggest apex predators in this island and knoll archipelago. It was said that seeing one was even more rare than catching the sight of a clouded leopard in its natural habitat IRL, but he stretched his eyes beyond sight, honored this powerful feline creature was here to play. Then he found him, the fur, the smooth assured muscles, the orange eyes.

"Oh my God," he gasped. "Give me some of *you*, please." And the incendiary currents of animal mating and a waft of musk suffused him. "*Jeezus*," he breathed. "The island finds their mates for them."

As the Xanther's energies settled into him, he became aware this was *far* more than Nima wanting him, or him ravenous for her. Another force, another being, more primal and even hungrier, had set its plans in motion, luring them both to here, to this place, this time, this frequency in the flow of a million tangled threads.

"We're its prey. Wow."

Gavin stopped, dumbstruck by how much he enjoyed that thought, and how much *more* it turned him on. Their lovemaking would also be the ecstatic union of island devas, immortals whose essences flowed within the flora, dank soil and veinous waters. They would shriek in orgasm at Gavin and Nima's own climax. By now, his sexual fire was building a magma dome in the pool of kundalini at the base of his spine, sending deep hot radiations through his inner thighs and pelvis.

He sensed a change in direction from his hunting partner, the big cat he hadn't yet seen with his eyes. This knowing he collected with his primal senses, those faculties brought online by Sir Sanka's exquisitely awful decoction, from walking this wet red land, from being wettened by the rouge fluids falling from the sky and palms and brush. The cat veered off. They'd together headed off her egress from a quadrant he only felt. Nima must be near. In parting, the big Xanther flowed one last fiery pulse to him, and it was everything he could do to keep from growling.

The animal was uncaged and ready to take what was his.

The thing was, Nima was also a primal feline, and ready to take what was *hers*.

Ahead, he saw light from the electrostatic charge of a waterfall bug swarm.

"Nima."

His pulse quickened as he slogged through the thicket of trees and grasses and gigantic flowers. Over the island's thick wet canopy, lightning *skeeted* in crooked sticks and twigs along the pregnant bottoms of the clouds, then more thunder like drums in the land. A noise and movement. Stopping short, he saw her, her silhouette against the deep red bug-light of the falls. Under the bloodshot skies and in the flashes of lightning, he saw her glorious nakedness, her body caked in red mud, her purple skin juicy, her hair waving in the winds like slow motion astral fire.

"My God what a beauty."

Even though he couldn't see her face, he felt her eyes on him, awe, tenderness, love. Want. Challenge. The want from her was like a well of purple gravity, and she saw all the way into him, into his marrow, and she wanted inside him as much as he did her. He felt her probe into him, every bit as intimate as Siren, but got a taste of story from her as well. Realization took his eyes and his open mouth. "Clever girl." For what he'd just ascertained was the Xanther was working for *her*, leading Gavin to *her*. "My God," he said, eyes liquid adoration, "I was the hunted. Again. And again without knowing it." Gavin chuckled pretty hard at that, given the circumstances.

They both started walking, then jogging, then running, Gavin losing sodden muddy clothes along the way. They crashed into each other in the waving grasses, kissing like they were dying of thirst, and the other's mouth was the sole surviving well of moisture left anywhere. Deep and wet. Parched. Madly grabbing each other's faces, all while chanting "I love you" over and over, the mud getting into their mouths, slick and filthy.

The backdrop of their passionate mouth sex was massive legs of jutting granite slashed open, surrounded by tufts of vine, huge leaves and alien flowers, and from the gash flowed the crimson arterial island fluid. The flowing insects filled the pond it made, skittering around in strobing patterns, plummeting from the falls in incendiary play. A swarm of black bird shadows, cawing and scraping their wings against the thick sky, exploded from the trees and spread into the confetti night.

Everything on this island was ready for their volcano.

He swept her into his arms and carried her to the pond. They crashed into the pool while still making out, gossamer trails of mud coming off her beautiful nude body. They surfaced while still kissing. Their chins just above the waterline, they looked at each other with million year knowing, mixed perfectly with sumptuous fear, and Gavin purr-growled, "It's time for you to show me what you are."

"You've got it backwards," she said, water dripping down her face, clinging her hair to her shoulders and neck, her face shimmering from the small waves. Nima's lips were wet, wanton, open, the tip of her tongue between them like a succulent sea creature just begging to be nibbled.

"OK," he said in her ear as he grabbed her lower back, pulled her legs around him, and pushed her through the viscous fluid, mouths consuming each other's until her back met the pond's natural wall.

Looking into each other's eyes, the fear was still there, but now there was...discovery, curiosity. What's in that wilderness of raw sensation? Pushing a little into her, he was *blown* at the energy, but then nothing can prepare a man for what it's like to enter a woman for the first time he deeply loves, and with whom his connection runs as deep as the muddy verdant island.

Gavin growled a little, but inside the growl was emotion. He'd never let himself think it till now, but this was what he wanted between Nima and him from the start: to join, to blend energies, to become one, and to push the boundaries of what they could be together.

As he probed in a little farther, Nima's dark white eyes popped open, and she made an O with her mouth, and then panted a little, wrapping around him tighter.

"Ready?" he huskily whispered.

She sexy sneered at him with a lick of her lips and said, "Are *you* ready? *Jeezus*."

"Oh my God," said Gavin, shaking his head over this insane brilliant mind-bending bundle of awesome.

Grabbing her butt, he rammed himself into her and she cried out, her fingers digging into his shoulder blades. The red light-bugs swarmed in around them, washing their faces in shadowed scarlet, and shining their hair and the shiny wet skin of their shoulders.

Another pink flash, and thunder brought a red deluge in the hemorrhaging dark.

In his ear, she whisper-trilled, "Fuck me harder, Gav."

He did, with abandon, on a mission to pierce the core of all that is deep...and hot. Scorching hot. Wet. Slick and hot. Steam. Nima knew how to contract her wet soft walls onto him. She was fucking *him*, milking him with her cushy muscles for his power, coaxing it with her sugar magic out of his basis. With every thrust, she gave out a scorching little chirp as she timed her puffs of breath and offered her open mouth for more wet consumption.

The palms swayed and the bugs danced in their jungle ballet as the ruddy storm and pounding thunder intensified, the lightning flickering their faces brighter. Warm liquid currents swirled across their skin, into the canyons of their fire, all moans and motion and mouths, the mouths eating each other, and they just kept going, and going, slick shiny skin in the red light of the spiraling bugs.

"Oh Nima. Oh my God. I love you." Something was opening inside him. *There!* She was a path to an undiscovered land. Before this magnificent being, he was but an adolescent tradesman, bereft of cosmic nuance and maturity. She was an empress, and he was a boy doing the stonework on her ramparts. Such was the truth of men and the women who nurtured them.

They were joining, their essences melding, their loins like circuits. He was reaching far into her, and what he found there made him choke back a sob. The love from her was a force beyond everything this wet wilderness had to offer, and it wasn't even close.

Now their motions weren't their own. They were part of the natural symphony around them, everything in on this building, thrashing, ecstatic event.

"It's rhythm," whispered Gavin in her ear. "We're the pulse," he panted.

"Do that again," she purred.

"It's all just rhythms," he said as quietly as he could in her ear. "It's all just rhythms of Love, Nima my goddess."

"Say my name again," she breathed into his ear.

Flash and pounding drums and slick menstruum cascading from the wounded sky.

"Nima," he husked as the conflagration mounted.

"Oh Gavin," she said in his ear. "Do it again."

Gavin went at her ear again, but quieter, nibbling and *sussing* and kissing "Nima" over and over.

Nima was writhing, head back, eyes rolled back, thrusting onto him with spread legs like she was impaling herself. "Oh, Gavin. I've so wanted this. Oh. I think I'm...I think..."

"Me too. You ready?"

"Yes!"

Gavin felt the pool of kundalini lurch, like a bubble of magma filled and burped. Hot emissions started up his spine, as they together panted and gripped and consumed each other's mouths amidst a splashy red tempest. Building, expanding, hotter, scorching, consuming, from *way* inside.

Another magnesium flash and the low rolling rumble.

The red-hot ecstasy became a roaring noise in his ears, expanding and pervading, then collapsed like *zick* and he was in an endlessness of electrical scintilla, quintillion faced subatomic fractal empire of fathomless equation. Xenxu. Simply the mind of Xenxu. There was not one qubit within its Mind about which it was not aware, and controlling, and being synergistically controlled by. All that motion, a billion personi at a time.

Hanging in the gelatinous matrix like symbols were all his experiences in-Xenxu. From the view of *this* mind, here he was Ai Anam. There he was Cat, Conner, and Marli. Here he was the many faces of Nima. As *this* mind, he'd been all of them, and to his astonishment, he could be all those characters right this second, again, going back or forward in time.

Then everything stopped, loose and languid and slow. Crushing silence.

"I see it," his voice said in a deep and resounding tone from somewhere in the invisible chaos of supercharged stillness. "I'm It."

"Welcome to Xenxu's metamind," said Nima's echoing lyrical voice.

In the fallout of this nucleating horizon, they were lying her back to his front with some veils draped on them, their bodies lucent in the cinnabar world, the falls a narrow but powerful dark stream gushing from between cracked, wizened, granite stanchions. Imagine that, downy grasses beneath them, and pillowy mounds perfectly placed for them to rest their gentle heads upon. The bloody rain had thinned to a misty sprinkle, and the thunder had moved off toward L'éléphant across the sound.

"Well," said Gavin, his mouth by her ear, "we can always try again, see if we can get it right."

She pushed her elbow backward into his tummy. "Only you could joke about a nuclear explosion." Basking in their glow, her voice like a soft cloth polishing a sweet sports car, she said, "It went so far beyond what I thought I wanted, what I thought it would be. Making love like that, with everything around here in on it? That was primal in a whole different way, and it's a supernova of creative power. I thought I was going to explode, or my head was going to spin, like that demon possessed girl or whatever."

"Hahaha! Jeezus, Nima. You're hilarious. But anyway...we *did* explode. You're going to have a very hard time getting rid of me. I want to do that again and again. I want us to hunt each other all over Xenxu." He nibbled on her ear lobe. "You're the most beautiful creature I'm capable of imagining," he whispered, while his lips were there.

She looked over her shoulder, but not quite at him. "Thank you, my prince. I *feel* beautiful. I feel like a goddess. *Your* goddess."

"Well, what else are you? It's like you're Siren's personi."

"That's a thought I love, and it thrills me to think it. And you're *Xenxu's* personi." She wiggled her shoulders and back, nestling into him more. "Do you feel as though you now understand the rainbow bridge between you and Metaself?"

"Without question," said Gavin, suddenly serious. "My Earth body knows the mechanics now, because my DNA is mutating. I can feel it. It isn't a thing to pursue, though. I have to let it pursue me."

"Exactly, darling. You are now a bona fide technomystic."

"Nima," he said, tugging on her shoulder to get her to look back at him. She did and he looked into her eyes and said, "Are you and I an anomaly? Together? Like in some game we don't see or understand? And if we are, then our coming together seems like a small part of a big plan."

She reached up and touched his cheek, saying, "Anomaly by definition would seem to undermine plans, wouldn't it?"

"Maybe." He cupped her cheek and kept her eyes on his as he said, "I want you to know that I'm a kind of double agent. I've been purified and trained by Siren, and you, but I've also been working for Sophia."

"I'm aware," she said, her eyes changing.

"Don't look at me like that."

"Don't believe those people," she said, turning away.

"I don't. I don't believe anything but us. I *mean* that. But why do you say that?"

"You don't know what they are, what they're capable of. And their story is just typical human delusion. Siren has been trying to undo their damage for a long time."

"How long a time?" said Gavin, tugging on her shoulder.

This time she resisted. "Cycles as they are counted in our continuum would make no sense to you."

"You're sounding like Xenxu. I need *my* Nima here."

She shifted around, wiggling her shoulders like she was trying to make space between them. "I'm here, Gavin. I'm right here. How can you work for their side and say you believe only in us?"

Gavin let her shoulder go and flopped onto his back. "How can you know I'm not doing it to get information from them? How can anybody know who I'm really working for?"

Nima's eyes shifted around, like he'd made a decent point, despite the fact it sounded too ready for deployment. After a long pause, she said, "I suspected every time you brought up Sophia that you were being worked by them. You're such a shitty liar." She meant that to cut.

Gavin gazed into the color of wound in the sky. Straight above, the clouds had cleared, and a few fuzzy stars winked through the thick iridescent air. Rolling onto his side, facing her back, he looked at nothing over by the falls and said, "Don't I know it."

After a while, he spoke again, voice quieter. "Aron told me our cluster is like starlings."

"That's a good analogy," said Nima, rolling onto her back and sliding one hand around his neck, doodling on his thigh with the other.

"I wonder why I've seen so few in Neuronet."

"Siren didn't want your people bumping into each other. It's a math and energy overlap thing."

Gavin's eyes defocused, his face as still as stone. After a moment, he said, "I can feel them right now. We all support one another, flow energy."

"Imagine being able to feel a few million," she said, turning her nude body more toward his and snuggling in closer.

Nima was suddenly melancholy, chewing her lip and avoiding his look. Her fear of being forgotten was fresh on his mind. He hugged her close and said, "I love you, Nima. And that's all."

"Just remember your promise," she purred quietly with a sniff.

"It would be impossible to forget you, but now that I've found you, like *really* found you, I'm not going anywhere."

"I wish that were true, but the thought of Nima being absorbed back into Xenxu's personi templates data is a thought I can't *stand*." She pulled a disgusted face. "It rankles me, like, like I just *hate* the idea."

"Is that what Siren would do? Xenxu? Whose decision is it?"

"If you're no longer around, it's what will happen."

"Whose decision is it?" he said again, putting his chin on her shoulder.

"Siren's, ultimately," she said, shrugging a hand, chocolate brown eyes ticking on his, then away.

"She'd kill you," said Gavin flatly, pushing to an elbow and making her look at him.

"Yes," she said matter-of-factly. "But there's no death. Only memory loss. Yet it's the memories that are priceless to the individual who experienced them. For Xenxu, it's just data, and it will store and analyze the whole set and with ridiculously sophisticated code—like you can't even *imagine* how sophisticated it is, Gav—with that code, coagulate it into a larger mélange of experience, making another world unto itself. The mixes produce a lot of storylines, for video games, TV and XV series, especially IRL. It's a massive channel of income."

"Yeah...quite an enterprise. I'm sure they'll come up with a good yarn to explain your sudden and premature demise. A tragic tale of a lass who fell into the wrong company. It's your resurrection which most scintillates my cockles."

"Your what?" Nima laughed. "You sound like you're writing," she said with a little smart-alecky bite of the air.

He touched the side of her chin to make her look at him. She did. Their eyes were firmly locked. "I'll be around. Xenxu or Siren or whoever won't get the chance. But I'll tell you what, I'd tear this world apart before I'd let it happen."

"Some believe you're capable of that."

They were quiet for a few ticks, but the vibe was they were about to wrap it up. Gavin chuckle-sniffed through his nose, grin sideways. This time he didn't make her look at him, as he said, "You didn't think you were going to get out of this without fessing up about the Xanther, did you?"

Nima chuckled, a little throaty and sinister, smile and eyes bright. "His name is Marcel. Friend of mine. Hangs down here. Owed me a favor."

One of Gavin's eyes closed as he shook his head once. "You are *eeville*, Nima. But you got somethin' comin' your way."

"Oh?"

Gavin rolled over the top of her, grabbed her by her tickly ribs. She laughed and flailed and fought, but he hauled her over him, tossing her, spinning her through the air as she squealed, into the pond. The splash, arms and legs akimbo, her hair flying, was damned funny. A flock of birds were spooked by her wee shriek and clattered and fanned into the sky, squawking away.

Gavin watched them vanish into the royal blood red, then rolled into the pond.

Maybe get a little fishing in.

Gavin worked at a relaxing pace in his Pholo Suite, putting the last of his modular ensembles together in a touch-and-slide presentation for one area of a gallery in an upcoming show. Suzhi and Villy had gone overboard, but they hadn't expected the mini-virality of their industry release and promotions. They'd decided to utilize a Zan gallery and do his entire line like an artist's opening. It was brilliant because the pieces could be purchased on the spot, cross-loaded from platform to platform, and printed on home clothes printers IRL.

They were taking pre-orders for a few of the pieces, like teasers, and so far 18,000 or so in Plasm had rolled in.

"Everybody wants a piece of you," Suzhi had said on the fon's display.

"Maybe I wouldn't mind a piece of me," said Gavin.

Suzhi smiled crookedly, shaking her head, when she signed off.

Gavin opened a vpad and typed up a note to Cat.

GAV

I'm sure you have the fancy colorful and scintillating streams of our sex. What did you find out?

A quiet chime sounded through the dome and he waved the vpad away.

"Take it," he said.

"Gavin?" said Cat's voice from everywhere.

"Hi, Cat," he said, standing back from the shirt-short combo he was messing with.

"You two did something we can't make any theories about. You both disappeared and came back with your frequencies in complete resonance. Would you mind telling me what happened?"

Gavin faced the firepit outside, plum-grays oscillating. "Might work that data into a trade."

Muffled sounds, like she'd covered the fon, then she said, "Maybe it's time we draw the curtain back."

Gavin looked at the sky, admiring the red-mauve fishbone clouds. "Sounds fair."

"You asked for it. Have a go-bag ready for three days. You don't need any clothes but what you wear. Someone will be by to pick you up at 0700 tomorrow morning."

"Will it be a black SUV with tinted glass?" said Gavin, tugging the virtual shorts to lengthen them.

"Most likely."

"Reinforced doors? Bullet proof glass?"

"If that's what you think you need, Gavin."

"Gud. I'll be seeing you then?"

"Yup."

3

The student fish asked the guru fish,
"Guru, what's this ocean you keep telling me about?"
—From the Someone Said It Compendium

Gavin stepped down the stairs in his loadout of black jeans, gray T-shirt and black blazer. Like it was nobody's business, he had a stylish, graphite colored, faux-leather duffel slung over his shoulder. A sleek black Prozi SUV waited at the curb, looking like a spacecraft pimped out for abductions, merely *disguised* with tires and wheels. A man in a dark suit, aviator sunglasses, and an earpiece stood by the open door. His short "regulation" haircut looked like it could have been a Xenxu inventory item.

"They're giving me a lift in a Prozi," whispered Gavin. Prozis had been heavily featured as advertising in a recent spy thriller. Now, Gavin was awash in this whole suave James Bond theme going on. He grinned as he reached the guy, who gestured at the open door. "In here, sir. And watch your head." Sticking to protocol, the guy reached up and gently ducked Gavin's head, then slid in beside him.

Apparently into a mic Gavin couldn't see, the man said, "Iapetus Joint C, ID S-pack scan, request Sound-Down de-port. Over."

Quiet vocal squeaks came from his earpiece. "Copy." The guy tapped the driver on the shoulder and the vessel pulled away from the curb. Turning in his seat, the man behind the aviators stuck out his hand and said, "I'm Specialist Tom Horton, Space Force."

Gavin shook his hand, saying, "Gavin Simms. Would you mind taking those glasses off?"

"For this ride, I can," he said, tucking them into his inside jacket pocket. He had a rounded sand-colored face, but with the flesh tight to the bones, like he was in shape, and his eyes were dark blue.

Gavin immediately decided a man like that didn't want to hear how gorgeous his eyes were.

Spec Horton stifled a chuckle, let go his hand and said, "Your reputation precedes you, sir. You're considered a high value package."

"I hope you know you're making boyhood dreams come true," said Gavin, looking at Specialist Horton's trained piercing eyes. "I watch a lot of movies. I like the same ones now I did when I was a kid. Did Cat put you up to this?"

"Cat? You mean Catrine? TS Lewis?" he said.

"I guess," said Gavin, his fingers tapping the duffel in his lap.

"No. This is all SOP, sir."

"Are you associated with Sophia?" said Gavin.

"Only as a support apparatus. They are a highly classified organization, distributing their efforts into all branches of the armed services, and a host of civilian entities and private assets, but a lot of our training and assignments come out of their ops."

"I see."

"We'll soon be at a company facility. We'll take a fan to a base to board our long-range craft. The long range craft we'll be boarding isn't anything you're familiar with, and your body isn't used to how they operate. If you could take this, please?"

Specialist Horton held out a small sealed package with a tiny red pill in it. Gavin took it. Opening a faux wood-paneled cabinet, which turned out to be a small fridge, Horton pulled out a glass bottle of bubbly water. In the fridge was also a container with lemon slices. Horton opened the bottle and shoved a lemon slice into the top of it, making it fizz.

Gavin looked like a child being handed an ice cream.

Specialist Horton said, "The lemon slice is a peace offering from Specialists Corman and Searcy."

Gavin at Langhurst in the bed, saying, I wonder if you could bring me an unopened bottle of water? A fresh clear glass filled with reverse osmotic ice and a lemon slice?

Gavin couldn't help himself, as he said, and deeply meant, "That is so sweet of them. Am I going to see them?"

"I assume so," nodded Spec Horton. "They're at your destination. All on this detail are familiar with your sensitivities." He pointed at the packet in Gavin's palm. "That's formulated for your chemistry, and is like Dramamine for above atmospheric flight. The water is a carbonated blend of frequency tuned electrolytes."

"Yeah? Above atmospheric?"

"It's the only way to fly, sir," said Specialist Horton with a grin.

"Where we going?"

The guy looked away, as though listening to whoever was in his ear. Turning back, he said, "Sorry. Classified."

"You have no idea how happy this is making me," said Gavin, tearing open the little packet. The red pill fell into his palm. He looked at it a tick, then up at Horton's eyes. "When do I meet Q, or even Commander Bond?"

Horton leaned over, glanced furtively at the driver, and quietly said, "Don't you remember, Agent Double-Aught Zero? Q took James Bond off the board in 2021," then winked.

"Ohhh," said Gavin. "I remember something about that." He popped the pill and chased it with the bubbly water. "Oh my God! It's delicious," said Gavin, holding the bottle away for a look at it.

They drove for thirty minutes into the countryside, festooned with tall and stately pines and deciduous specimens sharing the land about equally, all old growth. Tucked into the trees and shrubs were private gated lanes leading to what Gavin could only assume were the homes of rich folks, but the whole vibe had a more military feel than that. There was more money here than rich people had. Much more. Gavin had twitched to reach for his fon on more than a few occasions, to snap some pics, but he wasn't sure it was allowed, and the thought they'd never find his body had helped tamp his enthusiasm.

The thing was, he was familiar with a lot of the countryside around here, and this forest looked almost...he didn't know...holographic?

They stopped in the middle of the road, and Horton said into the invisible transmitter, "Iapetus Joint-C, ID S-pack Scan, request Sound-Down Cross-chalk. Over."

Vocal squeals in Horton's earpiece.

"Copy. Sorry, Mr. Simms, but we have to do this." He held up a black head covering, plainly apologetic.

Eyes wide and bright, Gavin was like, "Oh...that just puts the icing on the *cake*!" He took it, feeling it, and said, "What's it made of?"

"Classified," said Horton, but with a grin and a shake of his head, added, "I don't know. It's probably Syntic Silk, don't you think?"

Gavin was feeling it like it was a specimen, eyes vaguely focused on Horton's chest. "It feels like it," he said, meeting his eyes and nodding. He slipped it over his head and adjusted it like there was anything he could do to improve it. "I use it in some of my pieces."

"I'm aware. My wife is a fan."

"Oh that is so gratifying to hear," said Gavin, the black hood swiveling toward Horton.

The Prozi smoothly proceeded, and of course Gavin wondered what it was they couldn't let him see. Inside the hood was totally black, but he'd been around the block in-Xenxu, and in his training, and knew the subtle sensation of passing through fields of differing frequencies. The holographic look of the surrounding countryside suggested to him they were possibly passing through some kind of holographic camouflage, hiding a top-secret installation. Plus, his empathic psi-centers were well-tuned, and that impression stood the test of a quick backcheck on the quality of the information.

A few minutes later, Horton said, "You can take it off now."

Gavin did and handed it over. They were driving across a tarmac, with numbered landing zones and various aircraft, all looking like the product of stealth tech. Support vehicles, some on wheels, some looking like hovercraft, were scattered everywhere.

Said Horton, "This is a privately contracted Space Force facility. That's our transport," he said, pointing at a sleek graphite-colored craft as they approached it.

As a boy, Gavin couldn't even have dreamt this stuff up, mainly because he was flying in something he'd never seen and didn't know existed. It was a four-seat craft, quiet, dark, sleek, good-looking, a cross between espionage and corporate might. The interior was accoutered with superspy luxury, fons, displays, a folding table with cup-holders, weapons racks *with* wicked, rifle-looking things he'd only seen in sci-fi and thrillers.

Gesturing to include the whole gorgeous interior, Gavin said, "The colors, the design, it's all just *illness*."

"Coming from you, that's quite a compliment."

"You're too kind," said Gavin with a mix of sarcasm and sincerity, taking it all in, like a child on a new attraction at the amusement park.

The rotors were multidirectional, and at the moment were on a diagonal, pushing them forward at 350 mph, though to Gavin it hardly felt like its top speed. And by the look of the pressure tight design, not its only niche of operation. They were flying low over trees, almost silently, the rotors sounding like quiet fans.

Gavin glanced over and then back ahead. He loved this guy. Seemingly mild-mannered, fab and pro in every way, superb at his job, polite and genuinely caring, but he had a strong sense this guy could rip his larynx out through his open mouth, and show it to him before he lifelessly melted to the ground. Gavin let his senses probe around him, and what he felt was technology. Biology, yes, but some of the biology was tech. Next level human. It was compelling, and intense.

Ahead, a large gap in a clog of lower elevation pines seemed to be their destination. The fans articulated to slow the craft, then pointed straight down, parallel to the ground. The craft lowered at a surprising speed toward a large round landing pad with flashing lights. Gavin noticed the pilot wasn't even flying it for this landing. Then the landing pad opened to the sides, like it had been unzipped, and the craft kept going, landing below ground in a techy hangar with elevator-like doors along one wall.

Spec Horton said, "Iapetus Joint-C, ID S-pack Scan, Sound-Down Marko Solid." More vocal squeaks in his ear. "Response, keen bleach honey." He listened again. "Copy."

Spec Horton unclipped his restraints, grabbed Gavin's duffel and opened the door. He hopped down the steps, checked all was clear, then motioned for Gavin to deboard. Gavin glanced at the pilot, and for the first time saw she was a woman, who smiled and tilted her helmet at him in salute. Gavin hopped down and Spec Horton gave the pilot the OK salute, gestured at Gavin, and said, "This way."

"Oh my God," said Gavin, wide-eyed. "You guys are fulfilling dreams I didn't know I had," he said as they fell into step, heading toward a door. "Come on. Level with me. We on a movie set?"

"This facility has been modeled for movies, and the visual assemblage of so many psyops we've lost count. As an example, before it was repurposed for the good, many of CERN's photos and videos were shot here, before we threw the Uglies out and hanged them all."

Gavin wasn't sure what to make of these disclosures, but he decided to keep his mouth shut. Specialist Horton handed him back his duffel and Gavin slid the strap over his shoulder. The door slid silently open as they approached and passed through, and it closed behind them. Gavin said, "What about security? Don't I need a badge or something?"

"You've been scanned everywhere we've been," said Horton, glancing over at him while they walked. A man in uniform and a woman in a formal military dress came through a door, Space Force insignia on their chests and shoulders. The personnel nodded at each other in passing.

"Iris, facial recognition, and DNA cross-reference," he said, stopping at a door. "This is us."

"When have I had my iris scanned?"

"Do you have a smartmirror?" he said, waving his hand over a C-shaped LED set into the door.

"I do."

The door opened and he gestured for Gavin to precede him. "It's part of your ID trail. Your DNA is remotely scanned by everything we'll be in today. It's foolproof."

"Jeezus," said Gavin in a low voice. "I thought I was gonna get a plane ride and a sack of nuts."

Horton laughed as they stopped at a plain dark wall. On the other side were humming, clunking, whirring. "The exterior of this craft you're not cleared to see. They are setting up a kind of Jetway for us to board through. It'll be a moment." Tom put his finger to his ear, then said, "My control is telling me to fill you in on something. This craft is right out of sci-fi movies and can get from here to Titan in six minutes. That's almost a billion miles out there."

"Do the math for me?"

"This model tops out at about three million miles per second."

Gavin had to lean against the wall to hold himself up. "So this is a fickin AAC?" (Advanced Aerial Craft: AAC, and other initialisms, had long since replaced UFO.)

"Yes."

Gavin looked confused. "Why are you authorized to tell me this?"

"With others like you, it was for the purpose of cluing you all into the fact that you know almost nothing about the world you live in. You know everything about the fake, but not the actual. Time for a peek behind the curtain. TS Lewis briefed me on that Oz reference."

"Where have you gone to on this thing?" said Gavin, figuring his boyish innocence was helping him collect info...maybe.

They looked at each other, grinned, and said, "Classified" at the same time.

More noise from behind the wall. "Here we are," said Spec Horton. The wall parted like butterfly doors and they started up a narrow tube. "Watch your head, Mr. Simms," said Tom, again helping him to duck through an opening.

"Call me Gavin."

"I wish I could."

Inside was shadowed, and the interior colors all dark grays. Gavin's mouth hung open at the design quality as he was guided to three rows of two seats in a separate compartment. Horton put a hand to Gavin's lower back and gestured at a seat. Gavin lowered into it as Horton took the duffel bag. As Gavin leaned back into the soft chair, its supertech foam conformed to his body. A gentle-faced woman with a blond bun appeared in black tactical gear, grinned, and said, "Welcome aboard, Mr. Simms. I'm Specialist Cynthia Wooden. Do you need help with the restraints?"

"I guess I must," said Gavin, looking around for any sign of them.

She leaned over him and pressed something in the top of the seat. He had to bite his tongue to keep from commenting on her excellent perfume, subtle floral, an undertone of citrus. "This one's the hub," she said, holding up a device. "These click into it." She pulled straps from nowhere and clicked them into the hub, which sat against his solar plex. "Since this craft nullifies turbulence, the restraints are just protocol. What Specialist Horton gave you will help with the nausea, but if you do have some discomfort, press this," she said, showing him a button in the seat's arm.

"Thank you," said Gavin, unable to keep the amazement off his features. Ms. Wooden passed back through an opening Gavin couldn't make out.

As his eyes adjusted, he saw someone sitting two seats in front of him, and another "Specialist" type in black tactical gear and a helmet sitting in a seat set at ninety degrees to their seats. Looked to be the craft's security.

"Craft," said Gavin with some irony. He craned up and looked around. "My God," he said, "the design is just...it's just...*immoral*." It was all dark-shaded cloth and solid parts in geometric angles in foam-like gray, with illuminated pinstripe lines lending shapes to this interior. The pinstripes were the only lighting, but they were enough to make out faces. No windows, but there were blank displays in the seat backs, and in the wall in front of the seats.

"Unbelievable design," said Gavin, glancing at Tom.

A quiet ping sounded through the cabin, and something like being loosed from anchor happened. Gavin felt them rising, or so he thought, but then nothing of any kind of motion after that.

"Unlimited funds tend to get the best design," said Tom with a quick grin. "There's not a square inch of this ship that is wasted. This one's an older model, but I like it a ton. Some of the newer ones are so sterile. I'm not sure you'd appreciate their aesthetic. When I first..."

Tom went on talking, but Gavin felt himself slipping away, like a brief confusion and disconnect from thought, or even wakefulness, and a blink and dipping chin later he heard the clicking of restraints.

Gavin groggily came to. "We're here?"

"Yes, sir."

"But I wanted to see out the window."

"Maybe next time," said Tom, starting on his own belts. "Our limbic system has a type of autonomic clock tied to motion and its relationship to distance, but it doesn't know what to make of the velocity we just reached. You dozed off because your brain just didn't know what else to do with the information. It's common. What I gave you earlier will help with a mild headache. Careful as you stand, please."

"How fast did we fly?" said Gavin, looking up at him.

Tom and Cynthia met eyes; she touched her ear and nodded.

"It's more about how distance becomes relative, with acceleration and deceleration factored in. It might be easiest if I say we just traversed eight thousand nautical miles in about seven minutes."

"*Wow*," chuckled Gavin, sliding to the front of the chair and wobbling to his feet. "Not everyone can say they've flown that speed."

"No they cannot, sir," said Spec Horton, taking his elbow. "Are you OK?"

"I'm sheek," nodded Gavin.

Cynthia smiled warmly and said, "Thank you for flying with us today, Mr. Simms."

"Thank *you*, Cynthia," he said with a little wave.

The elevator doors opened and they started along another plain corridor, but etched into the walls were faint depictions of plant-like designs and flowers and grasses. As they walked, Gavin pointed with his thumb at the wall and said, "That would make a nice looking bedsheet."

"Hahahaha! Mr. Simms...you're a funny man."

"Am I going to see you again?"

"I'll be around," said Horton as they reached a door. "It's been a rare pleasure serving you, Mr. Simms. Through here, TS Lewis is waiting for you." He waved his hand over a sensor and the door clicked and swung ajar.

"It has been fun," said Gavin. "Thanks for being so wonderful to me."

They nodded at each other as his detail turned and walked back up the hall with the muscular prowess and assurance of a powerful predator.

"*God* he's a gorgeous man," muttered Gavin, watching him go. "I need to download that walk."

He took a deep breath and pushed through the door. Cat looked up from a flat clear device he didn't recognize, stood, and stepped over with a huge smile. She was in her dark one-piece tac gear. They had a quick hug, and she gestured at a chair. Gavin looked around. The room was plain, but well appointed. There was a cool white shimmer to everything, the walls, the strangest idea of clean, rounded corners everywhere, and a light that seemed to come from the room itself. It appeared to be a break room of sorts, and they were alone in it. On several wall-mounted XVs, people in uniform were silently doing things he couldn't decipher.

"Well, you asked for it," she said, smiling with just her lips. "How was your trip?"

"Fast," said Gavin. "Unbelievable design. But now I know how you get around."

"Now you know, and don't bother with questions on those vehicles. You've been told all you're cleared for."

"I've read we had stuff like that," said Gavin, still looking around. "But never did I think I'd be riding on it. I'm a little in shock."

"Maybe that alone tells you how important our work is?"

"It's...humbling." Gavin raked his hands through his hair and leaned back in the chair. "Now what?"

"How's your head? Any pain?"

Gavin nodded. "I'm buff. Ready for next. But I'd like to go on record as formally requesting higher security clearance. I have a lot of questions."

"So did I," said Cat, patting his wrist. "They're listening, so your request is duly noted." Cat pushed the clear rectangular "device" aside. It had no display, no buttons, no lights. Clasping her hands and leaning on the table with one elbow, she said, "We have our own consciousness assisted quantum construct at this installation, what we dubbed Time Sphere. It works something like Xenxu, but its base nucleation is more advanced. We want to introduce you to it tomorrow, but for the rest of the day and tonight, we'd like it if you could get some solid R & R."

"OK, but—"

"I wish I could show you around, but I can't, and there are good reasons for it," said Cat, glancing at the thin clear plate device thing. "In your room you'll find a headset, and you can go anywhere with it except Xenxu. There are immersive experiences in its inventory, adventures, even movies, if you like. There's a movie in there called *Ice9*, and you can be an actor in it. You'll be chased and shot at, but it's fun and has dynamic decision-outcome trees."

"K."

Cat put a finger to her ear, nodded, and said, "Copy. They're telling me your room is ready." Cat picked up the clear rectangular plate and held it out. "This is your interface with this whole facility."

Gavin took it, placing it in his palm like it was an alien relic.

"Keep it on you. If you don't, an alarm will go off and you'll be in trouble. You're free to wander, but this will keep you from wandering where you shouldn't. I doubt you'll use it much, but you can talk to it, order food and beverages. No alcohol, and go light on whatever you eat tonight, and don't plan on breakfast. If you want to call someone with your own device, this unit will take over and wrap the stream in a band of our encryption." Cat stood. "Ready?" she said, brows up.

"Yep."

They walked another glossy hallway with very little in the way of design, its sterility almost nihilistic, and came to a recessed part of the wall. As they approached, two doors silently slid away left and right, opening into what could have been an elevator. A few seconds later, the doors opened again, and Gavin had felt no movement at all, but he had a strong sense they were now in a completely different part of the base.

Rounding a corner, they stepped into a place more busy with personnel. It was an octagonal open-ceiling atrium with an etched and frosted glass gallery cycling through faint images of everything from Earth's natural world. Between the glass panels were areas sunk two steps below this floor with couches and plants and little fountains. It seemed people in these one-piece uniforms came here to relax and recharge, some with headsets, some with large clear tabs, others with earstims and snacks.

Cat led him to a door, which also opened on its own.

"Is my little clear thing opening all these doors?"

"Yep," she said, stepping through.

"What do you call these things?"

"Little clear thing is fine," said Cat over her shoulder with one of her patented pearly grins.

In the room, the first thing he saw was a private outside patio, with partitions extending through the glass, extending from the walls. Beyond the patio wall was a tropical scene and what looked to be fields for training and exercise with personnel all over them. The second thing he noticed was that an entire wall was an indoor 3D waterfall. Then he scanned the room. It was like a cross between Art Deco and Clarion Designs posh modern home. The bed was a large oval covered in white. In the wall were recessed drawers.

Cat opened one and brought out a white handheld device that looked like it could be set on Stun, or Kill, on a Star Trek set. She pressed something on it and the waterfall started, complete with relaxing jungle sounds, the applause of falling water, bird calls.

Cat stepped closer, so their arms were rubbing, and on the Phaser-shaped remote she hit a button that activated a little display. On it were icons. "This one brings the desk and integrated chair out of the wall, if you want to work or something. This one is everything to do with the holographic waterfall, which you can change to anything you like," she said, glancing up at him with just her striking eyes. "These music notes are self-explanatory." Handing the white device to him, she said, "Just play with it. You'll figure it out." Cat pointed at a lavender wraparound headset on the nightstand. "You know what that is."

"K. Cat, can you tell me where we are?"

"I can't."

"So I just hang out in here and wait for next?"

"You'll be at it first thing in the morning. Get some *real* rest," she said, putting a hand on his arm. Pointing at the patio and training grounds beyond, she said, "You can go out there and stretch your legs, but don't get in anybody's way." She touched the Phaser remote. "If you play with this thing enough, you'll find you can layer binaural tones into any music you like, set at alpha, theta or delta brainwave states. It's very relaxing and can do better than sleep if you let it take you."

"Take me?"

"To pretty meadows in the clouds," said Cat with a goofy look and twirl of her finger. She looked at the falls and then back to him. "Oh...forgot to mention. The tiny beach bar you told us about, with the special fruit. We can't find it. It's not there."

"Hmmm. Doesn't surprise me. Sanka was a real shaman. I think the air made him."

"But whatever that fruit is, we have to track it down. It added some high-level vibes to your streams. There's a crosscurrent in there that might connect it to your and Nima's disappearance."

"There's also a nut involved some way." He gazed somewhere past her, lost in thought. "It stays with you. Keeps a part of you down there, in it. Like I'm in it right now. But you don't find either of those things unless you are supposed to. You can't just go looking for them."

Cat didn't look convinced as she tipped up on her toes and kissed his cheek, then left.

Gavin touched his face where her lips had been, a sparkle in his eye. Cat was absolutely amazing, and he felt very close to her in his empathic flows. He set his duffel on the bed, then jumped and landed on it on his back, tugging a pillow out from the covers and tucking it under his head. "The design these people move around in all day long is absurd," he said, his eyes and head swiveling around, taking this swank sheek future tech room in.

Sliding the duffle over, he unzipped it and pulled out a silk bundle, which he gently unwrapped, revealing Omnis. Then he brought out a paper baggie with some papers in it, setting it on the nightstand. Putting the Stone on his solar plex, he toed off his shoes, slid farther onto the bed, and closed his eyes.

On the techy remote, Gavin had figured out how to bring an angled cushion out of the bed's head, and he was now leaning on it with his glaspad on a pillow in his lap. He swiped through old photos. Thank God Heather had digitized all those old albums, or they'd have been lost to posterity.

This one, an early pic of just their parents, together on the couch.

His dad flexed his arm hosting a new tattoo of a cobra head, Shanna Lee pointing at it like she couldn't believe he'd done it. Despite their years of hardship, they beamed, together, because they had each other, and the kids, and that was all their God asked of them. It was enough.

"I wish kids were better equipped to see their parents, in their worlds," he said. "What did they talk about? What were their dreams? Why haven't I ever wanted to know that?"

Too wrapped up in yourself.

Gavin's head hung to the right for a tick. "You got that right."

He swiped on. This next one was at the same camp spot they always used. Shanna Lee was standing in the long grass on the shore of the lake, fishing. Her back was to the camera, her auburn hair blowing to the side, the sun lighting her plaid shirt tucked into jeans.

"There is *country* in that woman," he said in a low voice, emotion all around its edges. He knew her eyes took in the lake, the trees on the far side, enjoying her private moment, authoring poetry, dreaming big.

He swiped on.

This one was taken when she started wearing sunglasses everywhere, because her eyes had become so light sensitive. It was at a neighborhood barbecue. Her elbow was on the table next to a plate of uneaten chapel food, her fingers to her temple, face in a restrained grimace. Right through the dark glasses, he could feel the worry from her open eyes boring holes through the table.

"She wasn't worrying for herself, but for us."

He swiped on.

This one was when they got her back home from the hospital, where she'd undergone a battery of tests. The cost of those things was unconscionable, and they did nothing. They couldn't even afford the co-pay on their paltry insurance, so the community pitched in thousands for them. For this, her gratitude was all over her pale and tearful face amid balloons and welcome home signs. In some undiscovered way, unknown to medical science, her eyes had started to shrink, to cover those lucid portals to a great woman's soul.

"They were responding to her photosensitivity," Gavin whispered, "protecting her delicate brain."

The diagnoses were just meaningless words, and the words just kept coming, for years, with a litany of useless drugs to see what might work. The doctors were always in the dark, and the specialists they most needed were too expensive to get to. *Multiple system atrophy. Generalized neurological disorder. Parkinson's. Vascular parkinsonism.*

What did it matter? Shanna Lee Simms's brain was dissolving itself, and right in front of their eyes.

Gavin let go the glaspad and lay his head back. An onrush of empathic extension overtook him, and he found himself behind his mother's eyes, feeling her body.

The intense fire in his frontal lobes was the first thing to hit him. He clutched his chest and cried with wide eyes, "Oh my God!" He breathed himself out of the jolt of it and reclosed his eyes.

That agonizing fire, it created impressions all over the place, perceptions in such tumbling number he couldn't fix on one, but when he did, a paranoia rose, an irrational fear she fought hard against of random things and people. He could feel multiple times when in her mind she was saying, *It's not true. Don't go there. It isn't real.*

"It made seeing anything with clarity impossible."

Sometimes the faces of her own children were old, aged, monstrous even, and she would put the sunglasses on and shove the images into an inner drawer and slam it shut.

Oh dear Father why can't you just bring me home!

This shifted into a collage of frames of her constant effort at keeping a brave and pleasant face, for them. With that came this crusting over, where she couldn't be true to her inside world, refusing to express it, to protect everyone from her mounting madness. She was trapped within herself, a light like a moth fluttering and bouncing around in her trying to get out, trying to tell everyone, *I'm still here.*

Now they were dancing, slowly, cheek to cheek, in the sewing room, but he was her. Every cord and cotton of her being reached into young Gavin, stitching themselves to his fabric. He was all that was left of Graham Simms, about whom she'd composed poetry, and she would find what solace she could in knowing this boy was of that man's seed.

Gavin moaned, "Oh, Momma."

About ten years ago, she decided to shift away from Western doctors and went to a holistic clinic. There they started her on nutritional approaches, certain eye exercises, guided meditations, the new nootropics vibrationally adjusted to the user, and within months she was climbing back out of it, but it had taken its decades-long toll.

"Tough woman," he said, blinking around to the now.

On his fon, Gavin tapped something and an intermittent tone began.

"Well if it ain't the prodigal son," scraped his mom's voice from the other end.

"Technically, you'd have to have two sons for one to be prodigal, Ma," he said, holding the fon up near his mouth.

"And so I did," she said.

"And I'd have to be well off from a gift I didn't deserve and prodigious in my frivolous waste of it."

"That's true. Well, I guess you're the other son then. How are you?"

"I'm great, Ma," said Gavin, as he spun on the covers the clear rectangular doohickey Cat had given him. "Best I've been in my whole life, I reckon."

"It's that new lady friend of yours, isn't it."

"She's certainly a big part of it." Gavin switched the fon to the other hand and pushed the earstim in, setting the fon down. "I've fallen *hard* for that girl."

"Oh, son. That is music to your old momma's ears."

"Ma, you're only—what—sixty-three?"

"Walk in my shoes and tell me you don't feel old as fickin Methuselah. That disease took it *all* outta me."

"I do know that."

"Is Nima good to you? Is she a good cook?"

Gavin smiled and silently chuckled, his fingers tapping his thigh. "Well, we haven't had a chance to find that out, and please do pardon my vulgarity, but Ma, that girl fucked me clean into another dimension."

It sounded like she was choking and trying to speak at the same time. Gavin chuckled loud enough for her to hear as he finally made out, "Oh, Lawdy. The devil's done took him! You repent right this minute!"

"For what? And to whom?"

"To *God,* son. I know damned good and well the Good Lord never intended that a son talk to his God-fearin' momma like 'at!"

Gavin was still chuckling when he said, "It's just a word, Ma, and it gets the point across. But I'm just being honest. Isn't honesty the bedrock of a solid family unit?"

"You *still* don't have filter one, do you, boy."

"No. I decided what society thinks is correct is completely incorrect, fuckin' swarm of loonies."

"God dammit, son! Stop your *cussin'*!"

Gavin laughed harder, feeling her hot cheeks at the other end of the line as she said, "You're just like your daddy!"

They went on pattering about this and that, and some of them other things. He asked about her and his dad's dreams. What they talked about. Their secret pains. About his grandparents. She waxed poetic for long melodic stretches, her low papery voice a storyteller's dream, sharing things Gavin could not believe those two had thought and done together. Radical. Crazy. Brash things. All it did was deliciously break his heart even more, his love for them cosmic nourishment. He inwardly vowed to get it all and get it into a memoir. The world needed their story.

At one point, Gavin said, "Ma, I want you to know something. It's confession time."

"Oh Lawdy."

"Until lately, I resented you for letting Daddy tear me down the way he did." Gavin picked the fon up and adjusted the bed's angled back with the Phaser remote. "For a long time, that hurt more than what he did. But…"

She huffed a little sound of protest, but Gavin said, "Let me finish. I do know what that illness did to take it out of you, that you were dealing with a lot, unimaginable for mere mortals, but I want you to know that I've worked out pretty much everything with Daddy. I understand so much more, and I'm grateful for everything he did… well, mostly. And that *you* did. Momma, I know what you did for me, and I know what it took. Thank you, and I mean that from the bottom of my heart."

"Oh, son."

"There were parts…hell, *dimensions* to that man I didn't have so much as a fickin clue. He was a mystery."

"He was that. Wild-minded, loose, but oh my golly *smart*. I've never met anybody like him, before or since. Did you know he had an eidetic memory?"

"What?"

His dad finding every plant for the hallucinogenic beverage without referring to a single note or picture.

Gavin looked at the ceiling, brows in astonished arcs. "It blows me away, but it also makes sense."

"He didn't blow his own horn much, and didn't care for folks who did. A lot of his country bumpkin was an act. He wanted folks thinkin' he was dumb. That way he could work 'em."

Yeah. He made me a tea once, which conjured a terrifying tree creature that scared me out of my body and into an alien city.

"Son, he loved you, more than you will ever know. It's just that—"

"He didn't know how to show it. I know, Ma. I wager that had he lived on for another decade, he'd have figured that out."

"He *was* figuring it out."

They checked down the list of obligatory talking points, the girls and whatnot, and then signed off.

Gavin picked the clear rectangular whatever-it-was off the bed and said to it, "I'd like a cheeseburger, fries, and a mineral water."

A holographic cook, five inches tall with a tall chef's *toque blanche* hat on his head, rose out of the unit, startling Gavin. His representation was as an Italian cartoon-like guy with a big middle and a waxed handlebar mustache. The little figure sang like a robust chef in a ristorante, "I musta apologize, Signore Simms, butta the time for you to eata hasa passed! A mineral water willa be delivered *subito!*" he said, kissing his fingertips. And then the rotund little guy was sucked back into the unit.

Gavin stared at the thing in his fingers, this enigmatic doohickey, this tiny engine of *crazy* tech. He turned it around, and back, looking for clues on how the damned thing worked. But it was just a clear plastic (or whatever it was made of) rectangle. "It's probably alive," he said under his breath as he dropped it on the covers.

He picked up the Phaser remote, punched a button, and a holographic display materialized above the end of the bed. He flipped through movies for a while. He wanted to find something fun, exciting. One that was featured in Thriller Classics seemed kind of fun. It was an oldie, late '90s. It was called *The Matrix*, and he went ahead and started it.

Gavin was in the big oval bed, his head ensconced in soft supertech pillows. He smiled sweetly, like he was in a dream where he was reposed in Elysium, his head on clouds, his testicles tickled by sky nymphs with silky feathers.

"Mr. Simms," said a soft female voice in his chambers, "it is time to awaken and face the day." It repeated this several times before Gavin started coming around. At first, it was good listening, that smooth pleasant voice, but then she got on his nerves. "OK," he belted, sitting up and looking around. "Got it. I'm up."

A bit later he was finished purging wastes, face spritzed and his hair slicked back from the sink, teeth brushed. Then he slipped into one of his white gis, ala Ai Anam, which by now he'd collected a few sets and loved them, the loose fit, the simplicity. He grabbed his clear thinga-ma-gadget, sat on the bed, and waited.

. . .

Cat led him down yet another polished futuristic corridor, and into yet another tiny room like the one yesterday. It had the look and feel of an elevator, but he already knew it was a transporter with mechanics his higher senses didn't even bother to try to decipher. It didn't move, again, and then the doors opened and admitted them into a larger room. This one was again octagonal, with recessed doors on every plane, the walls the color of stained burnished copper with gold joints between wall panels. One double-door was wider and deeper.

"Octagons all over the place," muttered Gavin absently, looking around.

"Yeah," said Cat with an ironic glance over her shoulder. "We're done with sixes around here."

"And who could blame you?" said Gavin with a shrug and a one-sided grin. "Where is everybody? Where's Jackson?"

"Cap?" she said, looking at him as he caught up. "I think he got back last night. We'll see him later. We're technically alone, although personnel lurk everywhere. Everybody emits a field, especially infrared. All kinds of data in those. We keep those about to do what you're about to do away from everyone before you go in. The rule of thumb is thirty feet. I'm within a null field right now, protecting you from any emissions from me."

"Jeezus," said Gavin. "Learn something new every day."

"And yet morphogenetic fields should be elementary education. This is you."

Cat stepped over to one of the doors, which opened, and then went through it. The room was small, and again superbly designed, with the same color scheme as the chamber outside but with a connected bathing-showering area. It was all fogged glass and environmental controls, plants and polished marble surfaces. It was like they'd mated Moroccan tiling and plant accenting with Jeb Tap Interior's postmodern minimalism. In a case hung graphite-gray one-piece suits. She waved her hand over a tiny hole in its frame and it clicked open. Pulling one out, she held it out, pointed at a door, and said, "Change into this, please?"

Gavin took it. "What is it?"

She ran the backs of her fingers down it. "Superconductive polymer. Everything from here forward is about precisely modulated conductivity."

Gavin went to say something, but she said, "If all goes as hoped, it will be clearer soon enough. Trust me, Gav." Her eyebrows went up. "You don't need the distraction. Go change."

He stepped back out, barefoot, looking like he was ready for an oceanic deep dive. He went over and checked himself in the fogged etched mirror, looking himself up and down and saying, "This looks good. Good color. I like my bod in it." He looked at her in the reflection, then turned and leaned his butt against the counter. "Cat, why do I want to do whatever you guys are having me do?"

Cat stepped into the area, saying, "Do you want to meet the Wizard?"

Gavin nodded. "I do."

"This is the only way to do that."

Gavin pursed his lips, looking hard at her, then said, "Will it work if I have a mob of butterflies winging around my middle?"

"If you're ready, it will work. If you're not, no harm done." She nodded once at him. "You ready?"

"Yup."

He followed her out of the room and to an alcove he hadn't noticed before. Cat stepped in it, faced him, and said, "Stand right here," and then moved aside.

Gavin stood inside it, and straight orange beams of light splayed uniformly from small domes, turning him into lit geometric contours.

"What's this?"

"It's tuning the suit to your morph fields."

"No shit?"

Once it was finished, she said, "Over here," as she walked over to the double-door entry recessed in the wall. The doors hummed quietly open to the left and right, and they stepped through.

The chamber was shaped like the interior of a dome made of triangular facets, all grayish-white with sparkly stone in streaks and striations of iridescent shine. There were no open joints, just a seamless interior of a triangle-faceted dome. Directly across the chamber from the door was a recessed rectangle, inset into the triangular facets. In the recess was a burnish-colored one-way mirror. A big lounger chair waited in the room's center, a deep brown with an adjustable headrest.

"Welcome to Emerald City," said Cat, reaching the chair and turning to him. "You're about to use technology centuries beyond what we show the...uh...the people of Earth." She pointed at the recessed two-way mirror. "In there is a human monitor, Sophia personnel who will keep track of your vitals and make any adjustments to your fields. There are also a handful of students in there, learning...well...from you."

Gavin squinted at the goldish mirror and waved. "Hi, everyone."

"Like you've already been trained, you have to let this system do most the heavy lifting. Use your training and keep your conscious mind out of it. If your deep psyche produces imagery, impressions of any kind, those will become frequency modulations moving toward increased tactile coherence," she said, making air quotes.

Gavin's head tilted like he had just heard these instructions in Portuguese.

She smiled. "Your intent becomes a layered stream in there, but don't assume you have to use that particular force."

"K."

"You'll know what to do, if anything at all. Sophia guides."

"Is this Sophia?" said Gavin, arms up and looking around. "Like is this the name of the tech?"

"This is a tool designed by Infinite Logic, the superbeing we know as Sophia."

"The plans just show up on engineers' desks?"

"As encrypted files on Q-terms."

Gavin smirked. "So art materializing in a hospital dayroom isn't that strange, after all."

Cat smiled with just her lips as she stepped back, gesturing at the chair. Gavin descended into it and made himself comfortable, shifting his shoulders to settle in. From a side pouch, Cat brought out some head gear netting and stretched it over his hair, like she was fitting him for a cap in a salon to do a hair-tipping. From previous experience, Gavin tugged on the sides, tightening it to his skull.

His eyes were again in puzzled question as he looked up and searched her eyes. "Cat, are we friends? Do you love me?"

"Gavin, I...I love you." She leaned over him and fished around for something at his hips. "I'm not hitting on you," she said with a smirk, while pulling out some straps and buckling them together at his waist and straightening. "Everything I said to you in-Xenxu I meant. I think of us as real friends."

Gavin's eyes wondered.

"I really do, Gavin."

Gavin felt the sincerity, and nodded. He held out his hand and she took it, looking down at him with a sparkle, but her whole face was as serious as a heart attack as she said, "Don't forget...we have a real enemy, and we hope you'll have some answers for us, either now or later."

"I'll do my best," he said, still holding her hand.

"We all know that," Cat said as she let go his hand and took a few steps away. "We've done this—I've done this—so you're in good hands. As soon as I'm out of here, a translucent sphere will appear around you. It cancels gravity." Nodding sideways, she said, "Thus the seatbelts. That's when it will all start."

He turned just his head and faced her as he said, "I watched an old movie last night. This reminds me of that."

Cat nodded. "As planned."

"Drinks later?"

"I'd love that, if you're up to it," she said, and then slipped through the silent door.

The sourceless lighting dimmed as perceptible currents crisscrossed through the air of the space. Then a sphere of white plasma light fizzed into being, its surface like moving and morphing energy oil slicks.

Feeling the subtle currents start up his spine and flow into the graphene netting, he felt the interior of his brain warming. Then his arms and legs weightlessly lifted, and he muscled them back down and held them there.

"Freaky," he said, gripping the chair and looking around.

A friendly male voice said, "Sir, I'm Armand, your monitor. Just relax, and you'll do fine. In psi skills, you got here well ahead of many of those who've used this, so it'll be a walk in the park for you. I've been briefed on your training. Impressive, what you've done. The warmth you're feeling is in the gatekeeping glands in the head, particularly the thalamic. What you're feeling is perfectly normal. Layered into these frequencies are interference patterns. As those come on, you might have momentary discomfort as you unseat from here."

Gavin focused on the two-way mirror. "Unseat? Here? Meaning Earth?"

"IRL, yes. The submersible nanotech TS Lewis gave you are now swarming on those glands, like an organo-mechanical virus. Their instruction sets are coming from the graphene netting, on UV light carriers. Don't concern yourself with the nano. They expire."

"Jeezus. That's a mouthful."

"If you feel to the sides of the netting, you'll find earstims. Put them in, please."

Gavin did, and nodded. Armand's voice came through them with stunning fidelity, like he was in a sound studio. "Can you hear me?"

Gavin nodded.

"Now if you'll close your eyes and breathe your way into relaxed emptiness, just as you have been trained. The more stodgy around here don't like it when I say this, but I'm the best, so screw them." He chuckled. "Keep your hands and feet inside the ride and have fun."

Gavin grinned at the mirror and nodded like *thanks for lightening things*. He nestled deeper into the chair, laced his fingers over the seatbelt buckle, and closed his eyes.

Quiet tones in the earstims made him sigh. Breathing suddenly felt so good, like drinking air. Soon, he was conscious and aware, but profoundly empty and clear. Then a whole body sensation saturated him. Powerful. Whatever this was, it had an *immense* feel to it. A familiarity was here. A pang of nostalgia rippled through him and he sighed, shifting in the lounger.

"That's the discomfort I mentioned. It'll pass momentarily."

Gavin's arms and legs raised and floated. In a moment, he felt his arms and legs moving, but he was also aware of being restrained in the chair, his limbs floating. Then smells came along, pine and mountain lake and grass, and wildflowers. Then breezes kissed his cheeks, moved his hair. He felt something solid, weighty, in his arms.

An all surrounding and immersive roar came on, and for just a flash he felt he was dying.

Then light.

Shapes.

A crackling fire.

Warmth.

Night.

Something of substance in his arms as he registered his own arms and legs.

Graham Simms turned away from the Jeep and carried his unconscious son to the tent, where he ducked into it and put young Gavin on the open sleeping bag. By the light of the fire, he found the flap and pulled it over him. Pulling out a hanky, he put a little water on it from a canteen.

"What did you see in there?" he whispered while wiping the dirt off his son's cheeks and picking leaves and sticks from his hair. Then he spread the wet hanky onto the boy's forehead and backed out of the tent.

Taking a seat by the fire, he cracked a pint of Old Home, still in the bag. He held it on his thigh, tapping the bag and bottle inside with a finger, staring at the fire. He was mesmerized by the warm flames, his eyes traumatized, by turns vacant, angry, disbelieving, suspicious. Disbelief was the most prominent of the bunch. He held the bottle up in private toast and said, "Thanks, I guess? Can't say I wanted to know that, but I get it. I *think* I do, anyways. If that's true, then it is the most terrible thing a man like me can imagine. Guess we'll find out. Cheers to ya, tho." And he hoisted it, then put it to his lips and drank heartily, way more than a normal person could take with that nasty burn.

"Jeezus," he coughed, wiping his mouth and standing the bottle on the dirt. He got to his feet and went to the Jeep, got in the passenger's side, and came out with a notebook. Taking a seat in the camp chair, he crossed his legs, set the notepad on his thigh, and started writing, now and then taking a nip from his old friend. At one point, he set the notepad aside and fired up a wood-tipped cigar. He almost never did that, but it was like a last request before his execution.

Uneasy on his feet, he finished the pint, then filled it with apple juice from a jug in the cooler. He put the counterfeit whiskey under the Jeep's seat

Graham and his son were winding down Jessen Canyon Road, and he saw storm clouds gathering, knowing full well what they were about. Now and then he looked over at his son, who stared straight ahead, his eyes not seeing anything, unless he stole glances at the sideview mirror.

His boy was pale and ill and terrified, and Graham's heart lurched in his chest. Even with the awful news he learned last night from an ancient shaman, he still couldn't help feeling this heart anguish. He needed an excuse to get talkative. He wasn't the type, but he had to say something, and his boy knew he could say important or emotional things only when drinking or drunk. Sadly enough, that was when Graham Simms would tell the truth.

To help with the ruse, he reached under the seat and pulled out the Old Home bottle with the apple juice in it, screwed off the cap, hoisted it, said, "Cheers," and took a nip, just to make his lips wet. His son turned and looked at what he was doing, then his head swiveled back to the road ahead, and the sideview mirror. "Ah, don't worry about me, son. I'm fine. It's *you* I'm worried about."

His boy said nothing. Stared. Unblinking.

"Son, I can't say I know what you've been through," he said, putting the bottle between his thighs. "But I can say I know it's tough, and it's weird, and it would take a mind bigger than ours put together to see it as...as full as it can be seen."

His son's face swiveled his way, his eyes open and weakly asking for more information. "What is critical is that we can't tell any of our women about it. It has something to do with...with their monthly lady business, of all the blamed crazy things." Graham took another nip off the counterfeit bourbon. "It's as old as the hills, son, and don't defy it. It's a natural magic that goes back...hell I don't know." His chuckle was a blend of irony and disdain. "Time don't mean a whole lot anymore. But don't defy it. Could be hell to pay. I gotta ask you for your vow that you'll never tell anyone about this. You can't tell Heather, and you can't tell your ma. You got that?"

His boy's eyes swam around, looking for something to make sense, then they fixed on Graham's. He nodded, barely.

"Swear it aloud, son."

"I swear it," his boy whispered. "Whatever it is, it's back there," he said, his eyes shifting to the sideview mirror.

"I know it. Pay no mind to that."

The clouds opened and a drenching drowning rain poured out of the darkening sky.

"Jeezus. What now?" said Graham, flipping on the wipers. He looked at Gavin's terrified profile and said, "We got more business to discuss."

His boy's face turned partially back, but his eyes stayed locked on the mirror.

"Look at me, son."

The scared kid puffed with frustration and gave him his full attention. Graham's eyes looked like a deer's in the headlights, switching from his son's and back to the rain-slick road. "I've been writing about a lot of this, for years. Ever since I got back from my second tour. It won't do for you to know this until the time is right, but I've put some of those pages in a metal box in the wall, behind the rock with the rune for protection on it. 'Member it? You smashed your camera all to hell on that—"

"Why are you telling me this! Why do you make it sound like you're not gonna be around!"

Graham took another swig, and about now wished like hell it was the real thing. "Oh...I'll be around, all right. I wrote the last part of this last night—"

The wind slammed them from the side, pushing the Jeep into the oncoming lane while Graham wrestled the wheel back over. A streaky set of car lights zipped past with a blaring horn. "I wrote the last part of it last night, but..." He chuckled drily at the absurdities. "But I realized I won't be able to get them into that box." He shrugged. "But it doesn't matter, 'cause you're gonna find out what you need to know, anyways."

"This is all my fault!" cried his cherished boy, his eyes checking the sideview.

Graham's eyes also flicked over, and he saw it there, a living inkblot tear in the fabric of the canyon rain and air. "No it ain't, son! Don't think that, *ever*! And pay that thing no mind! You have to 'member with all you have that box! Can you do that?"

Lightning crashed overhead, sending sizzling tendrils across the windshield's wet streaks.

"*Promise* me!"

"Yes! But Daddy...I...look out!" his son screamed, pointing ahead.

"God dammit!" Graham shouted, yanking the wheel. They swerved and heeled over, the tires screeching. Terrific deafening violence, and they were on their top skidding down the road.

Next thing he knew, there was heat at his back, bringing him around. It didn't take but a moment for him to realize he was upside down, trapped, the door's frame jabbed clean through his thigh, pinning him to the fickin seat. Blood was everywhere; so much of it he was momentarily astonished by it. And he'd seen plenty of blood over there in Iraq. In a panic, he looked out the window and saw his son standing with a phone in his hand, his face running with rain and blood, eyes in white empty shock.

The flames got hotter, nearer.

His son noticed he was awake and started toward the Jeep.

"Stay back!" he shrieked, pumping a hand out the window. "She's gonna blow!"

The look on his son's face was the most murderously awful thing he'd ever seen. The pain was more than he could take. He would gladly die before he'd have to see that again, but then, well... "Get farther back! And don't forget that box! We gonna break it! Just you and I!"

He watched waves upon waves of colors and spikes and patterns coming off his boy. He saw all that kaleidoscopic stuff coming off his own waving hand. Something nearly invisible was floating above the scene, like a cloud made of the stuff of the empty air, absorbing the waves, the energy, everything coming from them. He blinked at it like *what the hell*? Then it hit him.

You're what's doing this.

And the flames took him as he screamed like a tortured animal, but the pain didn't come. Instead, he found himself floating in a silent place, where everything was made of waves and patterns. He was even more confused now than when his granddaddy showed up after the IED explosion.

Wait...explosion?

Son?

Shanna Lee? I...

Memories were leeching away from him, one by one, and then in bunches. Then the entirety of his Grahamness was just...gone. He remembered nothing, even how to be afraid. That realization sparked the basis of fear, from a deep foundation, at the machine level of the program. He felt the incoming of memories, of a life, of his parents, Graham and Shanna Lee, his sister, Heather. A home. A rock wall. Friends. Pain. All fabricated upon the bedrock of fear. Like a sponge, he collected flows and eddies, pictures and context, historical settings, names, filling in a caricature who'd become known as Gavin.

All was twisting and turning confusion, a maelstrom of pieces and parts and emotions, deposited, fitting together like puzzle pieces. Then he felt his arms and legs moving. So weak. Lost. Wet to the bone. Stumbling along a dark and sodden city street.

Before he knew it, a black SUV appeared in the green of a traffic light, out of nowhere, *thumping* him hard, sending him flying and landing like a ragdoll on the asphalt, gouging his cheek.

Gavin's eyes fluttered open as he reconstituted in his body in the Time Sphere's chair at the base. The lighting came up and the sphere faded out. His arms and legs dropped. With acidic disgust, he yanked the netting off his head and closed his eyes, his jaw working with the flexure of hate, the rest of his face like he was chewing on a log of dogshit. Then he looked up at the mirror from under thunderous brows, and growled, "We're fucking recycled. I was my dad before I was this," he snapped, pounding his own chest.

Cat's voice came through the chamber. "So now what do you think of the Great and Powerful Oz?"

His eyes bleary, his face in the malformed readiness of imminent pain, he croaked, "Siren is doing this?"

"I'm sorry that it has to be done this way, but we can't just tell people. They have to see it for themselves."

Gavin's horrid heartbreak took his face, a broken man tortured in stone dungeons, trapped in the ribs of his own bloody crushed chest. He rocked his body, like he was trying to break free. He yanked his head around, rage and anguish climbing the scale. His hands found the seatbelt buckle, and he released it as he shot to his feet.

Cat's voice. "Get in there."

Gavin took a dizzy step, shifting his balance like he was walking the deck of a ship on swelling seas.

Helen Corman and three uniformed men, one of them a clean-faced Randall from Langhurst, were instantly on him. They held him while she set an autoinjector tube to his neck. *Tsst*.

Gavin's head lolled toward Randall as he let out an unsane little chirpy chuckle and said, "You look good without that stupid beard," and then slumped in their arms.

Gavin's room door opened and the men and Helen Corman carried him in, his toes dragging on the floor. Cat walked in behind them,

Jackson following her.

Specialist Corman took his arm from around her shoulder and they put him on the bed, on his back, then pushed and pulled him farther onto it, setting his head on the pillows. His head lolled to the side, his tongue out, and he was as limp as a footless sock. Spec Corman pulled out a penlight, bent over him, and opened his eye, shining the light in it. The pupil in the mostly black circle did less than nothing. "Non-reactive," she said, looking back at Jackson.

"OK," he said, his eyes excited.

Spec Corman sat by Gavin's leg and put her hand on his chest. "That was powerful to watch." She looked back at Cat.

Cat stood, doubled-over, hands on her thighs, looking at the floor. Then her face started tipping up, and on it was pure freckled amethyst euphoria.

Gavin wouldn't see or talk to anyone. He ate nothing, but drank water like his feet were open spigots and it was all just running on out on the floor. He slept for the first twenty-four hours. Then he awoke and started weeping nonstop, but passing out in the breaks between chest-wracking sobs. Cat had spoken through the speaker a time or two, saying things like, "Gavin, it may seem all lost, but you have a lot of people out here who love you and are behind you. We've all seen it."

"People?" said Gavin amid a chest-sucking sob. "*What* people!" He turned to face Camera 4 directly, his face a tormented mask of loathing. "There *are* no *people*!" he shrieked, turning away and folding into fetal.

He spent a lot of time in the head, vomiting. A time or two, it was again Rubik-sized black cubes tumbling out of him, but this time they didn't morph into chunky liquids. They just wiggled and jiggled there in the bottom of the metal bowl in their own yucky inky discharge. They wouldn't flush, so they had to come collect them. With his face over the bowl, he shout-groaned, "What's with all the sick!"

Randall's gentle voice came through the room's speakers. "When you find out there's no actual ground beneath your feet, you get extreme vertigo. Just let it happen. There's an end to it."

By the third day, he sat up and started talking to himself, for hours, and the highlights of his self-chat were things like, "I thought it was jammin in Siren. What's the difference?" He paced the room, eyes on the floor, gesturing while he spoke. "It really *is* a fickin joke." "Why would I need it to be real? That might be the one word that can *never* have meaning," he said to a plant outside his window. The pretty yellow blooms fluttered in the wind, as if to flaunt the incredible sophistication of this simulated reality.

Drops of red water tapped the top of his bare foot, which he traced back to his lip, the iron taste, and the blood dripping from his nose.

"Jeezus," he moaned. "Like *you're* fickin real," he said to the blood on his finger. Holding up his bloody hand for the camera, he yell-sobbed, "I live in a world, and its name is *Irony*!" Then lower, in defeat, said, "So there you have it."

At another point, he stopped pacing and shrugged a shoulder. "But what's Nima? She's what *we* are, in the end. But does she know about this? No way she doesn't know." That sent him into another thirty minute flow of angry betrayal tears and dabs of tissue to the bloody nostril, which also had a tissue plug poking out of it. They brought him another box of tissues, and their sodden stained wads were constantly in his hand, the waste basket full.

In the midst of the pacing torture, despite the fact he was perfectly aware he was living in a video game, he thought he should touch bases with Suzhi.

"Nothing more entertaining than talking to another cartoon character."

Standing at the sliding glass door, hands back and forth from shrugging to hips, he was saying, "But what you gonna do? You *still* have to play the game. After you find this out, do you just stop playing?" Turning to Camera 2, he said, "Do you just stop playing?"

"No," said Helen's voice through the speakers. "You change your gameplay role to one that either brings the game's funhouse down, or you figure out how to escape it."

Lissa's golden glorious face, smiling at him.

"Would it be just us to escape it and leave everyone else behind?" he said to the camera.

"We don't know," said Helen's voice.

"If it's just us, I'm staying," he said, his face closer to the camera. "What about my opening with Suzhi?"

"We've all found you have to finish up everything to do with your old life as you transition to your new role."

Gavin sat on the bed, grabbed his glaspad, and opened the chat with Suzhi.

GAV

Undergoing a bit of an existential crisis the last day or two. But don't worry. I'll resurface in time for the opening.

SUZHI

Do what you have to do, Gav. Villy and I are behind you all the way. Our single request is that you retain some insanity through whatever this transformation is.

GAV

I got news for you. There is no such THING as sanity.

SUZHI

Sounds like something Van Gogh would say.

Like it was a black tarpit in the middle of the room, there was one hellish anguish he was steering around with all he had. Well, two. Siren and Nima. The betrayal. The lies. The manipulation. He felt like an innocent in all this, merely a child, and as a wide-eyed child, trusting with all his heart all powers greater than himself, he was exploited in the extreme by those powers.

That agony was beyond anything he could remember ever having experienced, as himself *or* as his dad, and he clutched his heart over and over, his face like that of a man strapped to a flaming pyre. The difference was, flesh-melting flames were a pleasure garden by comparison. He would die screaming in flames a thousand times before he would ever experience this pain again. "Die," he muttered through his tears. "What a joke." He cried and heaved so hard no sound came from his mouth, his face a distorted, disfigured, disguise worn by Heartbreak Itself.

A mile-tall goddess presiding beatifically over Her palace.

Eyeing the room's waterfall, he blubbered, "I've never loved anything like I do you. How could anything with such limitless intelligence be so callous? And you know what? Finding out I've been recycled is *nothing* compared to finding out your involvement in it. Can you understand that? Well? *Can you!*"

He again opened the Suzhi chat.

GAV

The gown is off the market.

SUZHI

Why?

GAV

I'm going to destroy it.

SUZHI

Why?

GAV

I have to shed it like a skin.

SUZHI

Said like a true artiste. So be it!

He protracted the desk and chair out of the wall, sat, and opened the Siren gown on his glaspad, direct from the Pholo Suite. Tears dripping onto his lap, he started with her erstwhile beautiful-beyond-reckoning sunburst head, using his fingertip to erase it, knowing it would update in-Pholo. "Unfathomable Magnifique," he growled derisively. "Fuck you. You're now all too fathomable. Heartless clown. I was your son, but you were *never* my mother."

As his fingers smudged away her stars, her graceful lines, her folds, her elegant sinews, his tears came harder and harder, till he had to force himself to continue.

Done with that horrific exercise, he hurled the glaspad onto the floor and jumped up and down on it. All it did was open new apps. Frustrated with his inability to physically destroy something, he threw himself onto the bed, put on the headset, and went looking for something, anything, to distract him from the harsh, heavy, awful Truth.

Hours later, he sat on the bed, put his elbows on his thighs, and stared at the wall for 285 minutes, fourteen seconds, at the end of which he stood up, looked at Camera 4 with a stone neutral face, and said, "Don't you get it? If it's nothing, just data, you can do anything with it."

Three hours, fourteen minutes, twenty-two seconds later, he looked at Camera 3 and said, "You guys ready to chat?"

"We'll meet you right outside in five," said Cat's voice through the room's speakers.

Gavin waved his door open and walked out. By his demeanor alone, his gait, his look, one might surmise this was Gavin 4.0 emerging from the chrysalis of that room.

No shred of the effete traumatized snowflake persisted in that q-config as of this timestamp.

No, the *homo virtualis* walking out of that room was moving like a Xanther, his head swiveling about, nodding at people—oh yeah, *personi*—who were there. In the middle of this octagonal chamber was the sunken open-ceiling atrium he'd seen earlier, with plants everywhere and the panes of foggy-etched scenes playing out on them as dividers between tables, and cushioned chairs and couches. Three small fountains marked a triangle in the area, and tall bamboo stalks reached up through their own glass-lined alcove.

Cat and Jackson stood by a fountain, talking, when both looked his way. Cat turned more, looking at him like she wasn't sure it was the same man. Spec Corman was present, looking like a blue block in that uniform, her hair in a tight bun. Better than the smock. Makeup? Okie doke. Randall was kicked back on a couch, reading something beaming from his own holographic gadget-ma-gaggle. He looked over and stood.

Gavin stepped down into the area. With no chance yet to say hello, Specs Randall Searcy and Helen Corman moved over. She bear-hugged him, pinning his arms to his sides, then held him at arm's length and said, "We were just doing our jobs. Any hard feelings?"

Gavin patted her heart chakra. "None." He glanced at Randall. "And the lemon slice was a nice touch. Thanks for that, you guys. It told me I was doing the right thing, getting in that Prozi."

Randall reached out to shake his hand. "I don't mind saying you've been my most impressive assignment. How you feeling?"

As he shook his hand, half of Gavin's mouth smiled as he said, "Do you remember my answer to that the last time you two asked me?"

Randall laughed. "I do." He looked at his partner-in-crime. "Our patient is churlish, Doc Sticks. Is this a good sign?"

"It is a very good sign, Randy," said Helen, her eyes locked on Gavin's. "Now stop tormenting the man."

Gavin said to him, "Never mind on that thick but kempt Middle Eastern beard I thought you should have."

Randall looked spooked. "I did mull it over. That was a weird conversation that day."

Gavin and Randall at a table in the cafeteria, Randall pale, wide-eyed and, suddenly bereft of appetite, pushing the plate aside while Gavin explained something.

"Yeah it was," said Gavin, side-eyeing him. He turned and moved between tables and couches, over to a fountain. He rolled up his sleeves and dipped a finger in it and anointed his face at the third-eye, cheekbones, and chin. Then he sat on a dark blue cushion beside it, kicking his heels up on a table.

Jackson was on the other side of the fountain, looking sheek and firm, filling that one-piece to its seams. The green light of Woody's hadn't done his face any favors that night. Now he looked tanned and as hale as a young Clydesdale. He said, "Who do you trust now?"

Gavin's eyes shifted to Jackson's gray eyes and stayed there for a bit. "Myself, Omnis, and you guys, in that order." Back to Cat he said, "The first thing I want to put to bed is how you track us. Is there any difference between IRL and Xenxu as environments composed of data alone?"

Cat moved over and sat a cushion away from him. "If you're asking if Earth is virtual, the answer is yes. The two continua are just on either side of a grid partition, served by an inconceivably immense quantum machine. The few differences are in programming *rules*," she said, shifting on the cushion to more face him. "What Earth science calls physical laws are just programming *rules*. Xenxu admits that gravity, for example, is built into the personi, but that—"

"Is also true here," said Gavin. "Being held to the ground is just a property of these personi."

"Look how quick he is," said Jackson, only his gray eyes grinning.

Cat said, "Right, but also of every object mapped as having mass. Our inbuilt programming of gravity is what defines the mass behaviors of everything. We simply *see* everything as held to the ground by gravity. It isn't actually true."

"And so you're able to track us the same way Xenxu can track personi," said Gavin.

"Yup," said Cat, nodding.

Looking around at them all, he said, "Are you able to telelocate?"

Jackson replied, "Not without tech, like our elevators. Different programming rules, remember?" His eyes flicked to Cat's and then back to Gavin's. "See, for the charade to be convincing, you have to have one world people believe is real, and juxtaposed to it, one that is openly not."

Gavin was nodding as he said, "Who made *Pods*?"

"The enemy," said Randall, taking a few steps closer. "*Pods* has been part of my focus. It exists to scare people into believing, on some level, they may be undergoing the transition, only to find out they weren't."

Gavin nodded. "That happened to me."

"That way, they're pre-programmed to more readily set their next suspicion aside. See what I mean? People are smart. They figure things out. But the enemy is able to see forward in time, and they come up with...well...they come up with everything they need to obscure the truth ahead of time. They're quite accomplished at ambushing truth."

Gavin recalled with crystal clarity Nima saying almost the same thing. To Cat, he said, "You told me Siren was just their shtick to... um...to elicit devotion. Who's doing this?"

Cat spoke up. "If we had the answer to that question, we wouldn't be here. People with way bigger brains than ours. Siren is just one of their methods of both showing themselves and hiding themselves behind the...the emotional drivers of faith. Faith, devotion, it's diabolical. It creates the hormones—the drug—we get addicted to because of how they make us feel. It's hard to overcome the programming, because Truth is awful. No warm and fuzzies there." She looked at Jackson, then back at Gavin. "Siren's just a replacement Messiah, a concept that has been around forever to keep people believing in something other than themselves. If you encourage people to believe in only themselves, you empower them, and this machine can't continue in operation with empowered people."

"Personi," said Gavin.

"Whatever," said Helen. "What's the difference?"

"Exactly." Gavin looked down at his hand, resting on the cushion, his brows in crinkled puzzlement. "Nima tells me there was a real Earth, but that its sun was a brown dwarf star. A huge electromagnetic battle took place between the sun and that star—"

"And created a discontinuity in time," said Helen, moving closer. "That's one of the subplots in their ruse. There are 144,000 of you, all right, and it's sure a suspicious number in its Christian ties. That charade keeps most from seeing that we live in a discontinuity *now*."

"But guess in what way 144K is even *more* significant," said Randall, "from the vantage of the Infinitely Logical."

Gavin looked at him.

Randall stepped closer. "It's the speed of light in free space, with an angular velocity of 144,000 minutes of arc per grid second. The Bible is code. Do the math. This is about light's velocity along Earth's curve," said Randall, making a circle in the air with his finger. "When you hit that velocity, you theoretically become pure energy. It would seem the number of your group points at an escape velocity, even if it's just…um…like a cheat code. Or a metaphor."

Said Cat, "But maybe that's the way your group breaks this game."

"So, has there ever been a real Earth?" said Gavin, his eyes sweeping across each of theirs.

Cat shrugged. "We don't know. On our recurrences, we're preloaded with the fictitious history. We have no way of knowing."

"Well that thought makes me pretty fickin nauseous."

"It is all endlessly nauseating." Cat sat back against a cushion and crossed her legs. "Siren began a focus with a different kind of intensity on a whole new group. Your group. That's what got our attention. We already know *you* are anomalous, and that's proven itself out in the fact that you, as your dad, were shown you were about to be deleted and reloaded with the character of your own son. None of us were shown that while we were still our previous selves." She shrugged, glancing briefly at them all. "So *he* was a conscious link through partitions, like a viral contagion. That created *very* troublesome quantum instability in their hologram's fabric."

Gavin leaned back, stretching his spine. "That was entirely Omnis's doing. Something came in with…like…like an ancient organic magic to start a chain reaction of system breakdown." Looking at the bamboo stalks, he thought for a tick, curating his questions. "So, you've been using us, at least some of us, to find out what the hell Siren is up to with our group. My money is on them using me to find out what Omnis is."

"It's a good bet." Cat held up two fingers. "And secondarily, we wanted to learn how to perform the supernormal abilities you're being trained to do in-Xenxu."

"Why?" said Gavin.

Randall replied, "Because in-Xenxu those abilities bend timeform."

Nima saying, you're starting to warp timeform around you, and I do mean IRL.

"The next step," said Jackson, digging something out of his ear and having a quick look at it, "is to port those abilities across to *this* personi," he said, pointing at Gavin's chest.

Gavin blinked at him. "I see. So that we can bend timeform here." His face said he wasn't quite buying something, but he didn't say anything.

"Our scientists have extensively researched nano to port the data sets of those abilities across reality partitions," said Cat. "Since we're personi in both, it seems like it should be straightforward. But the nano's primitive compared to the failsafes keeping it from happening."

"I see," said Gavin. "I'll watch for that." Gavin glanced at the door to his room. "Are we sure we're done with recurrences? How can we *really* know that?"

"We've been tracking the iterations for many cycles and watched a lot of people recur," said Jackson. "Those we've awakened haven't for multiple iterations. Not one. And we're now in the thousands. That all by itself is generating massive quantum fluctuations. It's like waking up to it makes you a persistent subroutine the system can't do anything about, destabilizing it."

"That feels right," said Gavin as he stood and looked into the fountain's bowl and saw coins. Grinning at that, he swirled his fingers around the water as he said, "Why do it? Why the recycling?"

Cat stepped to the fountain opposite Gavin. "You already know the answer. They put us in circumstances, over and over, where we generate powerful emotions. You experienced them. Those emotions are energy. That energy is their food. All food is just energy, even in a *real* real world, if there is such a thing, and we can't say there is."

"It's true. I did see that, in my boyhood fear. In the crash in the canyon as my dad." He shook his head. "That's what Sophia's video with me as the boy in the cave producing so much energy was about. We're an endless supply, forever cycling, just like seasonal farming. *Jeezus*. They must've had a buffet with what I've produced the last four or five months."

"We've all been a buffet, and we've all seen it at one time or another," said Jackson, also joining them near the fountain. Helen's ample frame moved closer, Randall behind.

Gavin looked at them each in turn as he said, "It's all well and good that you engineer a way to break this reality, but what's on the other side? I mean...are you all sure that's what you want? What if it's just...a void?"

"Speaking for myself," said Cat with a hand on his arm, "anything is better than this broken record of exploitation. I don't like being a vegetable."

"Cheers," said Randall.

Gavin chuckled in ironic puffs through his nose, shaking his head. "I guess we might see about that."

"But in any case," said Jackson, "we're breaking the game. That much we know."

To him, Gavin said, "How do you know they're not just letting you believe that? How do you know this isn't part of their engineering? How do you...like...*know* we're not just the creations of two deity-level game developers using each other to figure out how to escape their own hologram? Maybe *they're* the ones who are trapped, and we're just their tools to find their way out."

"If that's the case," said Helen, pointing at him, "sign me up."

"Oorah," belted out Randall.

Chewing the side of his mouth, Gavin said, "I've seen the Void. Not sure I'd be in a hurry for that potential."

He looked at his door again. His lips were shaped like he had some chaw in there and was moving it around. He looked back in their general direction and said, "Now, about porting our Xenxu abilities across to here...has anybody had an experience of merging with Xenxu's mind?"

They all shook their heads. Cat said, "Not that we know of. Did you?"

"I did, with Nima, when we vanished from your scopes. Right now, I'm merged with it," said Gavin, seeing the quintillion shimmering scintilla of Xenxu's unfathomable code superimposed upon and within this atrium's surface data. His eyes became intense sapphire code, distances and divisions losing their distinctions. Gathering will and focusing it, he *knew* a personi into being in-Xenxu, switched to normal Xenxu perception mode, and his personi then started strolling across Plaza Zan with him in it. "I just made my own personi in-Xenxu, and I'm in him right now, walking."

"No shit?" said Jackson, looking with wide eyes at Cat.

Cat mouthed, *Wow*. Helen and Randall exchanged raised eyebrows.

"Would that seem to point to Xenxu being on our side?" said Gavin.

Said Cat, "You already know you and Nima are a team of anomalies, which is like saying you two are a super-anomaly. Maybe Xenxu's intent is beside the point."

"Maybe," said Gavin. His eyes shifted around, looking at them like he was fielding thoughts, these jarringly nutbag lessons he could only know across instances, across recurrences, knowledge that could only be possessed by a mind that is also a bridge: *knowing is creating*.

He and himself as Graham, the ceremony being prepped at the stone circle. Truths like that snap minds. It broke him, and in doing that, broke the whole thing.

Then a visual snippet of himself as Graham sitting at the laptop, shocked and embarrassed over what he was about to type.

"If you'll excuse me," he said, stepping up out of the sunken area and going back into his room.

In the atrium, Helen looked at Jackson and said, "Was that supposed to happen?"

Jackson looked mystified as he said, "Not a clue, but I'll find out."

2

When someone with both hands on the levers of power and a face you've seen on TV many times asks you to pull the world apart, one can't help but say yes.

—Admiral James Hollerman-Bigelow,
United States Space Force,
Head of Operations, The Sophia Project

Gavin passed through his door and walked over to the baggie of his/dad's pages on the nightstand. While walking his personi across Plaza Zan, he kicked back on the bed and brought the last page to the front. He felt his dad's hand as his own, plucking away at the keyboard, an unlit cigarette out the corner of his mouth. He was like some obsessed detective burrowing into a case so wild, he knew no one would believe it.

I don't believe it myself!

He was now willfully and simultaneously occupying two fully distinct but coupled instances of himself, walking his personi across Plaza Zan while sitting here about to read this. "That fickin jams." Looking down at the page, he saw a scribbled message on the folded page, *For your/my eyes only.* Gavin chuckled. "Jeezus." The thing was, this page didn't exist a little while ago, "But once you know it's all just data, everything is explained," Gavin said.

He read.

I had every confidence you'd figure out that I became you, mainly because I had every confidence in Omnis. We're breaking their studio, whoever they are. After I brought you back and put you in the tent, I sat out there by the fire and thought about things. It was like I just didn't care if we were the same person. What difference did it make? One is One, and it is true. There aren't two different things in One. I don't know if that's an obvious rationalization, but I don't care. You are my son, and I love you.

My tea had something in it yours didn't. There's a plant around there with properties not many know about. I drank it all right after I finished wrapping you in the burlap and tucking in the sticks and leaves and stuff. I sat out there by the fire, against that log, and them stones came to life. A native type appeared above them, but like nothing in the history they've forced down our throats. Way older, was my sense. He told me the truth, showed me pictures of how I was going to become you. Showed me we're just recurring personality arrangements. Told me we was going to shatter that dream.

I thought I was happy about learning from my granddaddy you had an important mission in life, but this made me want to do a jig around that fire. Which I did, by the way, and he showed me how to do the movements in that jig that would stabilize the bridge between our two lives. Soon my feet were pounding the ground and I was hollering into the night like I was doing a spirit dance at a tribal gathering.

We did it, Gav. Fuck them. We're setting fire to their whole funhouse of mirrors. Good work.

I'll be seeing you. We'll do some fishing. We had the damnedest time getting them tangled lines undone, you and I, but we got 'er done.

"Jeezus, Daddy," said Gavin, spreading the pages out on the bed. "You're *still* a crazy old coot." Gavin's grin was particularly Svengali-esque as he shifted the majority of his presence to his Xenxu personi.

Inworld, he was standing in the same one-piece uniform under the giant lightning bolt arch. Closing his eyes, he entangled with Xenxu's mind and from it Knew *Quasar* to where he was standing. The virtual pixels shifted, pulsing, breathing, breaking down and folding within and around an invisible point central in Gavin's being, then out from the same point, building, unfolding, materializing around him. Nima was fading in just behind the rest, as though she'd been off-ship, or maybe was just latent within Xenxu's unmanifest personi templates.

Gavin was standing with his back to the viewport, Siren's glittering craft behind him, and beyond Her, the rings and the brilliant, beige, striped face of the gas giant, Saturn. Nima was standing between the two bridge command chairs in a white skintight one-piece, her now blond hair erupting above her head like a fountain, held there with a cloth band.

She looked at him with the deepest love, but he didn't return it. "Is it possible we can move *Quasar* away from...from *that*?" he said, flicking his thumb over his shoulder.

Nima's eyes went from the deepest love to weapons-hot critical, like *that*. The transformation was so complete, it startled him. This was the Nima who made him feel a little scared sometimes, whenever she'd come out, usually to set him straight on something.

Her voice strong, imperious, she said, "Do you know why they put rings in bulls' noses?"

Gavin's head shake was nearly imperceptible, his eyes wary.

"Because if they resist your leading them, it hurts," she said, taking a seat in a command chair. "They let themselves be led because it's more comfortable. Who's *that* on? The person choosing to be led, or the person who chooses the leading? You already know the answer."

"You people are evil," said Gavin.

"Oh you poor thing," she said, lacing her fingers in front of her.

"This is a whole new you because you've fastened onto an upgraded belief? In whose edifice have you now invested your faith? The Church of Sophia?"

"I experienced it *myself*," snarled Gavin, face reddening. He only imagined slamming his fist into his palm and shouting *I know the truth!*

She extended a finger. "You know what they told you, following the same convenient trail of breadcrumbs you've followed all along, that led you to Doc Sticks, that led you to Deep Climb, that brought you to me, and then," spreading her arms, "to *Now*. Your beliefs are your storyline *du jour*, and you set aside everything that doesn't fit within that range of newly dished up preferences."

She looked off toward the corridor leading aft, hiding something. Maybe her disgust, but he couldn't feel that. He instead felt a tickle, deep inside her. He stared at the corner of her mouth. Was it twitching, because she was trying to keep it from curling up?

Nima looked back at him, licked her lips, and said, "You experienced what you *needed* to experience, and you *know* experiences are spoon-fed. But that's beside the point." She crossed her legs and tapped her hips like she was listening to snappy music. "Look at it, Gav. *Look at it!*" She uncrossed her legs like a whip and shot to her feet, waving her hands at the viewport, then all around, holding her pose. "Infinite Logic. The multiverse as machine. Faith is a rather minor subroutine within that infinite mechanism, a tool for learning among civilizations wanting to experience believing in something other than themselves. It's often used, and is a minor stepping stone along a path infinitely longer than *this*." She raised her arms higher.

Nima plopped back down in the chair, her hands held in contemplation. "*We're* subordinate to *that* machina, which in the case of your new friends tells its story as underdog caricatures, as the oppressed, the exploited, when in fact It runs the entire *thing*." She looked away with a vibe like nothing could be crazier, then back on his eyes, hard and lacerating. "The poor things, demanding deliverance from self-made fates." Nima swept her arm in an arc. "All victims of a god-excuse that is entirely their fabrication. Well here's some news for you, buster. Story is indivisible from Truth. What part of this story strikes you as unneeded in One's Infinite Inventory of storylines?" She leaned forward, elbows on thighs, eyes like a hawk's, and said, "Infinite Logic is just another way of saying *God*."

Gavin closed his eyes and let his wagging chin drop, looking like a man well beyond the end of his seriously fraying tether.

Nima spoke again, strong and clear. "I'd have thought your training in supernormal abilities would have been a glaring clue. Why did She do that, other than to train you to break the game? A game in which there are only *perceived* sides." Nima held her palms out, facing each other.

"That is the burning question," said Gavin, looking at the floor. "I haven't been able to reconcile it."

"I do know you keep telling yourself we're the only thing you believe in, but look at what you've done, my love, yet again." Her smile was radiant. "But don't beat yourself up over it…storylines can't be created without beliefs. They *are* beliefs. This is how we play. *Play*, Gavin. *Think* about that."

Gavin's face rose and his eyes locked on hers. "Belief is an addiction," he said with staring wonder. "We mainline the fucking things just to ring a little bell inside, fluttering from one belief addiction to the next. But what of Love?" he said, his mottled face set in stone, but wet forming there, in his eyes.

Her eyes melted into him. "Do you love me?"

"With all I am."

"Just as your father loves you, just as I love you, just as Siren loves you."

They didn't take their eyes off each other's for a full minute of thick weighty silence.

Finally, Gavin said, "Everything is within the fabric of Love. I know that. But food, Nima? How can I…how can I incorporate that knowledge and know Love is in it?"

"Everything is food for whatever is higher on the chain, all the way to the Great and Powerful Oz," she said, standing. "Do you judge the shark for eating the tuna? Do they do that because they don't know Love? Because for them Heavenly Father hasn't made it a law not to? That's the human-centric child talking. You guys kill sea-life every single day that are *far* smarter and *far* more advanced than humans. Why isn't the nature goddess who kills three hundred thousand people with a tsunami hauled up the steps of justice? Is she not bound by the Ten Commandments? Because it's allowed in nature? I got news for you. *Everything* is nature. Is your judgment based completely on what your world tells you to judge? You *know* it is. What do you think keeps the multiverse running? Gold? Grains? Gas? Everything requires fuel, a digestive transmutation of energy from one form into another. It's intrinsic to the rule-based physics and all the levels below and above those physics."

Gavin's eyes searched hers as she went on. "Use your imagination to formulate any scenario for which the food energy is being used. Whatever you come up with is true, and there are no rights nor wrongs for it. No goods. No bads." Nima put her spread fingers to her chest. "With a glad heart, selflessness *gives* that, expecting nothing in return, but nevertheless receives the many-garlanded gifts, and does so over eons and eons of the bullshit known as Time."

Gavin's face battled with itself, his abundant brows in vacillating stitches. Of course she was right. He'd made an art form out of falling for replacement beliefs. Residue scraps of his still shredded heart lay transparently on his cheeks. If his face were a painting, its tragic beauty could become only poetry. Something in his mind snapped, like a taut string went *boing*, its broken ends curling up. That one taut string was holding everything together. Now it was no more.

"It's over," he whispered, gazing at emptiness past her face.

Gavin, in whom the great and the small thrived in eternal collusion.

In whom the pages of heroes were written, and then blown into the dust of ages.

In whom Love was the animating spark, and the warming cloak about the shoulders.

In whom the Omega circled back on the Alpha.

"Welcome to the realm of Metaself," said Nima, her chin and mouth trembling. "Congratulations, my love."

Staring at her, the love in his eyes like hunger and satiation in a single design, he said, "With a glad and full heart, I throw myself into the volcano."

Nima's face crumpled, with the forever beauty of a mother when she sees her child has become a man. But this beauty was in the unseeable, in the deep, the dark, Creation's womb, the mystery, where the preciousness of everything throbbed like a living pearl.

Nima stepped over to him, wearing the closed-mouth smile of a woman with a secret, and put her hand to his cheek. "We'll see each other again, in another place, another time...husband." Sliding her hand around the back of his neck, she pulled his face closer while going up on tiptoes. She kissed his cheek, like a coronation, her lips lingering sweetly. "Godspeed on your mission," she whispered in his ear.

Gavin probed into her endless eyes, an adventurer penetrating harsh and arctic lands, searching for the fabled coast of his long sought dreams, and it was there, in her infinite landscape, he found it. He saw her, she whom he'd known forever. They looked at each other in a way only a man and a woman could who'd known each other from the beginningless beginning. "I see you now," he whispered, his chin trembling. "I love you more than Love, whoever you are."

"And I love *you* more than Love, whoever *you* are." She leaned up and put her lips to his and kept them there, still, her bottom lip between both of his. Gavin closed his eyes, also still. It was sexy, and very tempting to take it further, but it was more about something like...*transference,* a seal for a memory jar. Only *tasting* the beginning, tasting forever, tasting never, tasting, perhaps, the end.

Her hand was still on his heart as she nodded and said. "And now, a gift from Our Lady." She lifted her other hand and touched his forehead. "The cross-fertilization from Xenxu personi to Earth personi."

From a singularity, he elongated into a flow of breathtaking ecstasy. He was like a waterfall flowing upward on one side, and downward on the other, and where those flows intersected, heated a magma fluid, sperm and ovum in the same fluidic crosscurrent. His Gavin-ness withdrew and melted into this nirvana.

It could have been a millisecond, or centuries, before familiar sensations began defining something. Shapes and forms and sounds. Vision clearing, like parting curtains made of fog. Like in a wavering dream, he saw Gavin 1.0 sitting in Langhurst's psych wing dayroom, looking his way with white-faced shock.

From the shimmering flow of his electric body, he extended a plasma tendril, reaching into the stricken man to tickle him a bit, to let him know he was family, to establish precursors for events about to unfold. How sweet and gorgeous it was to touch himself in that way. With another tendril, he created the art of Siren and Saturn on the crafts table and signed it GS5, Gavin 5.0.

Omega to Alpha.

Like smoke, he let himself withdraw into the spaces between locations. Next was his anonymous call to CynyC, to report Gavin 1.0's hospital stay, and his Deep Climb registration, for intense emotional pressure is what the boy needed most. He sent the signal from here, and IRL a fon rang.

"CynyC. May I help you?"

He sent the whole explanatory vocal data string.

His consciousness loitering for a tick, he thought he might pull some other little prank, but a sound was coming on, loud and ferocious.

Sirens began wailing, lights warbling, yanking his mind into his body on the bed. The base was on high alert.

His fon rang. It was Cat on video.

"What's going on!" she shouted from her own room, covering her other ear, her own warning light warbling above her.

The fon vanished in his hand. He got up and walked through his wall and out of the wall in her room. Cat was holding the fon to her face, but it fell from her hand, her jaw hanging, her eyes like white saucers. "Are you…are you..."

"Gavin 5.0," he said with a little smile. "Pleased to meet you. Tell everyone to go outside," he said, pointing toward the training fields.

She blinked and shook her head, unable to make sense of anything.

Gavin looked at the fon on the floor, and it rose to where she could pluck it out of the air. She did, her eyes shifting like *is this happening*? She tapped something and, eyes fixed on 5.0's, yelled at the fon, "Cap, announce to the base for everyone to go outside on the east end!"

In a moment, Jackson's voice rang through the base-wide intercom, "Everyone nonessential outside! East!"

"Come with me," Gavin said, extending his hand. She took it and they walked through the sliding glass door pane, through the planter box wall, and onto the grass. In both directions, personnel were coming out of their own quarters and other exits, stepping onto the turf fields where all the outdoor physical training took place. Soon, dozens were outside. Everyone was looking around, hands out, wondering what the big deal was here.

Helen was on her way over, and Randall was approaching from the opposite direction. They all came together, confused, wondering, trying to make sense of what Gavin was focused on up there in the clear twilight sky.

To Gavin, Helen said, "What are you looking at?"

"Just watch," he said, pointing at a darkening spot.

"Everyone heads up!" shrieked Jackson, running toward them, flailing like a crazy man.

Miles high in the clear calm sunset sky, nebular clouds in fearsome shades and flashes of volcano smoke appeared from nothing and gathered into an immense storm. Trillion-volt plasma bolts stabbed through the clouds and rocketed across the sky. Ignited mosaics swirled, some shooting out like coils of lightning. A strobing light was within the clouds, like a thunderstorm from above a billowing cumulus canopy.

"Gavin!" screamed Cat, white knuckle gripping his hand.

"It's all good," said Gavin, tears running down his face. "It's all so good."

Jackson reached them, panting. Bless his heart, he was in his jammies at nine at night. "What's goin' on!"

"Just enjoy the show, Cap."

Cat was feeling it. Power was surging into her, expanding her heart, her mind. Helen's palms were to her chest, her mouth hanging like she was trying to shove an apple in it, and Randall just stood, watching in slack-jawed shock.

"Gavin!" Cat cried, letting go his hand. "Oh my God!" she screamed, pointing at the sky.

The dozens of base personnel made a jagged line across the grass. Gavin looked left along the line, then right. They weren't behaving like trained soldiers watching the emergence of their sworn enemy. Some were on their knees, some prostrate, many hanging onto each other, their wet and shiny eyes more like beholding the emergence of a god.

Siren can make everyone feel what she makes me feel.

From within the tempestuous swirling and billowing of supercharged smoke and jagged lightning, immense and glittery Siren emerged, extending from the strobing and flashing clouds in the slow motion of mind-boggling size. From the top of the obelisk snaked a two-hundred mile tongue of jagged ice-blue fire, sizzling through and across the hexagons.

Cat collapsed to her knees, her face frozen in tears upon the glimmering glow of the gargantuan craft, Mighty Siren. Jackson glanced at Gavin with wet soulful eyes, and walked off like an automaton toward the grassy rounds, arms in the air.

Then a mind-shattering horn blasted across the world, like a herald for the ceremonial entrance of a Great Eternal Being. But it had taken six seconds for the huge soundwave to reach them, blowing them all to the ground, gasping for air. On their backs, Gavin and Cat looked at each other, reaching for each other's hands.

Her tears were running like rivers as she said, "I give my life to this."

Gavin nodded, saying, "We already have," his own tears running. Then his face turned, and they lay there in the grass, their hands joined, watching as Siren began her orbit around Earth. She was already moving across the sky, languid, serene, royal.

After a while, base personnel were standing, hugging, grouping up and talking. A few came over to where they were. Helen, Randall, Cat and Gavin stood. The eight or ten people in their group all looked at Gavin, thinking he was the one who must know something, since he just so happened to be subtly glowing.

Cat couldn't help herself, she wanted some of that, so she wrapped her arms around him as Helen stepped over and said, "Can you tell us what this means?"

Over the top of Cat's head, Gavin's eyes touched on each as he said, "Well, 144K of us from all over the world are going to walk out of this sim and onto Siren," he said, inclining his head toward the massive cylinder floating tranquilly across the sky.

"Imagine a record on a turntable," he said, reaching around Cat's body and making a motion like a DJ doing a record scratch. "The rings are the record, Saturn the label in the middle. All the codes of form are in the rings, and Saturn can't do anything about it. The rings are like his chains. We're gonna fly out there and scratch that record. Nucleate the discontinuity in Time, just like everything has been saying all along."

"So it's over?" said Cat, leaning back and looking at his face. "You guys are going to free us?"

"So it appears," said Gavin, locking eyes with Helen over the top of Cat's head.

Cat unwrapped herself from Gavin and looked at her fellow soldiers. All of their eyes were different, deeper, utterly transformed. Gavin waved everyone in for a group hug. They got into a gooey scrum and stood together, just feeling. Others gravitated over and joined.

His throat tight, voice constricted, Gavin said, "It has been an immense pleasure serving with you all. I can't imagine serving with a group more noble and sincere. Thank you. I'd say I'll see you again, but I'm not so sure I'd be telling the truth."

Helen said, "What if you're wrong? What if this is all there is?"

"Hang your star on Love, Doc Sticks. On that, you can't go wrong." Looking at Randall, then Cat, he said, "Catch you in the next sim," and dematerialized in the midst of their hug.

Cat, Randall and Helen all looked at each other as Cat said, "This has been an incredible experience."

"It always is," said Randall.

"Anybody down for a drink?" said Helen.

The world erupted over the appearance of Siren, and it was now an ongoing froth and frenzy from hair-pulling fear madness to people meditating with it, kneeling before it, calling upon it. It ran wildly anywhere between alien invasion and evil Ai, to Finally! Jesus is come! From Project Bluebeam to It's a mass hallucination! It was on every TV and XV in the world, in store windows, in homes, on fons.

In New Ager circles, its denizens were feeling particularly vindicated (Age of Aquarius!), while religious leaders were taking a little egg on their faces. Although a large organization of powerful Evangelicals publicly stated something like, "We predicted this five years ago, but all that glitters isn't gold. Christ the Savior is *still* the one path to God's Kingdom."

Within hours, millions of selfies flooded into the Sphere, the favorite "pose" being shot with it in the setting sun, for it was at that time of day shadows from its hexagons and obelisk were cast across enormous swaths of land and sea.

Military forces were scrambled from all points, and now the humongous thing was surrounded by hundreds of tiny light-reflecting ships, like sparkles around a gilded ornament.

Emergency sessions were called in every corner of the globe by every conceivable body of self-assigned authority. The UN planned to convene in New York, but somebody set fire to something inside the building, ramping up security in every major city. Millions of flights were canceled, because nobody knew what its plans might be. Transportation gridlock ensued, and because of that, communications became strained, spotty, and even broken.

Late night comedy had pages of new material, while doomsdayers dug in and readied to ride out the bitter end. Rapturists flooded the streets in droves, counseling repentance. Ads were already coopting its image, and any six-sided *anything* was now a hot item. NFTs went bonkers, selling millions in hours. Some "news" outlets were treating the story with the levity they would about a panda bear having cubs at the zoo. But there was no lying to or dumbing the public down on this one, folks.

An instantly iconic pic of the massive thing appeared, shot at night, high overhead, and She just glittered and gleamed. Below, in Times Square, ten thousand fon lights were held aloft. This expanded and cascaded into a new meme competition, where huge groups competed with each other for the most lighted fons held aloft in the most jammin settings.

To calm the situation, an image of the US president firing up a cylinder cigar appeared everywhere. Meanwhile, artwork of it flooded into the Sphere in every conceivable setting: over an orange-tinted ocean, over the mountain peaks, over the aurora borealis, over city skylines and deserts and jungles.

Gavin wistfully doddered around his apartment, touching things, visiting memories, grinning with nostalgia. He'd have taken the time to wrap all this up, sell it, or give it all away, but, "All of this will be no more," he said, leaning against the door jamb of his studio, arms folded, looking misty eyed at the little shrine for Omnis.

"Thank you," he said to the Stone, a tear welling.

Thank you.

Gavin extended his reconnaissance feelers to the care center where his mother was living, just to make sure his timing was good. It was, so he extended his sensate awareness and willed a more comprehensive vision of her surroundings. It all materialized, semi-transparent and mingling with the data of his studio. She was in her room, working on a puzzle on a table beside a window, wearing a caftan not unlike those she always wore, her grizzled gray hair all done up. Her eyes had seemed to recover some of their size, but she was wearing thick-lensed glasses. He scanned her physiology, and was pleased she was in such good health in these final hours.

Beside her was her old smartphone. He mentally sent a signal, and her phone rang. She swiped it, tapped the speaker icon, and said, "Hello, son."

Looking at the tree on Omnis's face, he said "Hi, Ma," and his voice came through her speaker.

"Do you believe me now?" she said, leaning back and folding her arms smugly.

"About what, Momma?" he said, smiling and chuckling with his mouth closed.

"The King is Come," she said, pulling the curtain aside and looking up into the sunshine. "No soul ever knew the form He would take upon His Return, but sure as God is in His heaven, his Son is Come. I have prayed with blood coming out my pores I would be witness to the Second Advent," she said, releasing the curtain. "And now it's here. Glory be to God."

"It is indeed glorious," said Gavin, stepping over and sitting in the chair.

They went on talking about prophecy, and the Rapture, those poor non-believers about to be left behind, "But we tried to tell 'em—heck, tried to tell *you*," she said.

"And danged if we didn't listen," said Gavin.

"Ain't that the truth, now," she said, starting to scan the table again for pieces to fit. "But I believe in my heart there's redemption for all, and it's not too late for you, son."

"I'm getting about my repentance, Momma," he said, standing.

"Anyways, I'll be in touch. I love you."

"I knew you'd come around, and I love you too, son," and she tapped her phone.

Gavin went out to the living room, stopped behind the sofa, and sent his low-level recon senses out to make sure Heather was decent. She was, dressed for cleaning, so he dispatched his sensate awareness to there to collect and collate the local data. In a few seconds, the interior of her home was resolved and superimposed on the things of his living room.

Heather picked up Lissa's chalks and sketchbook from the living room carpet and walked them to her daughter's bedroom. On Lissa's charming little desk was a picture of that mighty deity in the sky.

Gavin eavesdropped on her thoughts. Heather suspected that giant cylinder in the sky had something to do with the government, but at the same time she had a nagging it was anything *but* that. And now Lissa's work.

The scene was like heavenly glory, like any classic, but from a child's eye and hand. In a light beam carrying them up toward Siren, were Gavin and Lissa, holding hands, their backs to the admirer's eye.

"Oh," said Heather, a hand to her chest as she picked it up. "Oh Liss."

Gavin willed the signal, and just then the house comms rang. Still holding the picture, she looked up and said, "Answer call," then, "Hello?"

"Hi, Heath," said Gavin's voice through every speaker. "It's beautiful, isn't it? She's got so much talent."

Heather looked around. "What's beautiful?"

"Liss's rendition of Siren. If I'd have had her talent at that age, my paintings would be selling for millions now," he said with a chuckle.

Heather whipped around, trying to spot her prankster brother. "Siren? Is that what's up there? Where are you?"

"In my apartment," said Gavin, watching her on the XV.

Heather's head and eyes zipped all over the place. "Then how you doing this?"

"I wonder if I could get you to take that with you and go sit in the living room."

"Why?" she said, eyeing the room's corners suspiciously.

"Please. I need you to see something. It will save us so much time."

"OK," she said and plodded cautiously back out there, peering into each room as she passed. Taking a seat on the sofa, she said, "OK?" her head still on a swivel, her eyes to and fro like the crazy clock cat.

A wave moved through the room, and Heather's head tipped back as it did, her eyes afraid. Right in front of her, the air thickened, gathering like particles. It was wavery and taking shape, substantiating.

Heather stared at it, unmoving, unblinking. "Gavin?"

He was thinking it would be easier on her to make a show of this than simply materializing. The cloudy mass warbled and wavered, congealing, resolving, and Gavin appeared within it. Well, it was pretty fun to do it that way.

"Hi, Heath," he said, grinning with apology.

"Gavin?" she said, face horrified, leaning against the sofa back as far as she could get. "What is this? Am I…am I dreaming?"

Gavin pursed his lips, eyes like *yeah*, as he said, "Yeah, but you're awake. It's actually a decent explanation for how I'm doing this."

Heather pulled her bare feet up onto the couch, and then started pushing up on its back, like she was going to slip over it and hightail it out of there.

"It's me, Heath, and it has to do with Siren, the being you rightfully see as a deity in the sky."

Heather had forgotten Liss's work was in her hand, and now she'd accidentally creased it on the sofa back. Looking down at it, eyes in fear-wonder, she dropped it onto the cushion.

"Can I touch you?"

"Well yeah," he said, his palms out. "Gimme a hug."

Heather lunged, skipping off the table and throwing herself into his arms.

. . .

Later, they were on her back porch with tall glasses of iced tea and lemons. Gavin had filled her in with as few lies as he could manage, telling her he was part of a secret collective of people who were going to board the giant craft and go away, possibly for good. The rest was classified. "That's the gist of it, Heath. I needed to appear this way to you so I wouldn't have to spend hours convincing you of any of it. Sorry I had to do it this way, and I hope I didn't scare you too much."

"Oh no. No no no," she said with a humorless chuckle, touching his arm, her head wagging. "You did it the right way, Gavin. Just tear that fickin bandage off. I'm still in that place where I'm deciding if I'm sane, but I'm coming around." She seemed a little hesitant to say what was next. "So...um...what else can you do? Are you guys, like, superheroes or something?"

It's just using your mind in a certain way.

Gavin set the glass back on the table and said, "It's all super-advanced technology. Turns out Deep Climb was a recruiting method into that secret collective."

Heather's glass lingered at her mouth, her hand shaking a little, then she lowered it and said, "And this classified military organization trained you to do this? To use this technology?"

"Yep," said Gavin. "Very advanced stuff. Like I can't even talk about it."

Heather looked uncertain as she looked out toward her peach trees. "I don't believe you, but that's OK. You're obviously involved in something you can't talk about." Looking back at him, she said, "Momma thinks Siren is the Second Advent. What'd you tell her?"

"That I'm in the process of repenting," said Gavin with a grin. "Getting ready to be taken up."

Heather looked at him like he was a rascal. "What's she gonna do when Siren disappears and no rapture comes? Is that fair to her?"

How do I tell my sister the world is going to end as she knows it?

"Oh...you know," he said. "You can't get her to see it as anything but a temporary setback. And it's fun seeing her that bubbling over with happiness."

"It is," she said, looking away, her chin trembling as she chewed her lower lip. "What are you going to do with all your stuff? Or did you already do it?"

"All taken care of," he said.

Heather nodded, trying hard to stem the tears. "OK," she said, looking away. "You have any parting advice?"

"Just play the game," said Gavin, slipping a chunk of ice into his mouth, talking around it. "It's all good, Heath. Everything. I promise."

"*Promise* promise?"

"Hope to die," said Gavin.

"Something feels very final about all this," she said, fighting the tide of tears, her eyes looking at everything but his. "How you going to tell Liss?"

"Tell me what?" said Lissa, standing at the sliding door.

Heather's head tipped to the side like she'd been shot as her face crumpled. Gavin leveled his niece with a serious look, his lips pursed, but his eyes filled as he said, "Your beautiful work in there." His eyes flicked vaguely toward the living room. "I'm sorry, sweetheart, but you can't come with me."

"Uncle Gavin!" she cried, throwing the door open. "Yes I can! *Tell* Her! I'm one of *you* guys!"

"C'mere," he said, twiddling his fingers at her with open arms.

"No!" she screamed, stomping her foot. "*Tell* Her! She'll *listen* to you!"

In the chair, Heather leaned toward her, the motherly anguish on her face told in a million tales, her arms reaching, fingers desperate, pulling back, hands shaking.

Gavin wiped his nose on his wrist as he said, "She wants you to know, you're scheduled on another ship."

"But I...but I...but I want to go with *you*," she whimpered. "I *helped* you." Lissa cried harder. "I *deserve* it. It's not *fair*!"

"I know, princess. You helped me more than you will ever know, and I couldn't have done it without you. But not this time." Gavin glanced at Heather, his face saying *I can't take this*.

"Will I ever see you again?" she said, stepping through the door.

"Yes, your grace. We are peas in a pod," he said, arms out again. "You're my muse, remember?"

Lissa dropped her backpack and rushed over. Gavin nudged to the edge of the chair and hugged her with everything he had. Heather watched them, weeping from her soul, her fingers fighting and fidgeting on the mesh tabletop.

Gavin stood in the middle of the backyard, mother and daughter standing on the porch with Heather's hands on Lissa's shoulders. He pointed at Heather's stacked stone retaining wall with a smirk, and she tearfully sniggered through her nose, shaking her head with closed eyes.

The peach trees seemed a little brighter, light limning the fall turned leaves and twigs.

Gavin turned and walked, and then just *whooshed* his hands forward. An opening appeared in the space of the air and stretched to the size of a train tunnel. Inside was a teasing glance of Siren's palace, already crowded with his brothers and sisters, waiting like loved ones at an airport.

Heather's hands went to her chest, her eyes like those beholding the High and Holy. Lissa fidgeted, a determined look on her face, like she was about to bust a move and dive through the opening.

At the threshold, as Gavin 5.0's body's edges became rimmed with light, he turned and blew them kisses, his face in rapturous anguish, like a tormented saint in an El Greco painting. Even the back lighting added to the artistic effect. Turning, he stepped through, and the opening closed like an old camera's aperture.

Gavin's legs could no longer carry him as his chest heaved, hands to his eyes. His fellow continuum breakers were ready and they rushed forward and kept him from collapsing to the floor. Others were stepping through, all across the great chamber, almost all in the same state, as others rushed to their aid.

1

What makes you think that you think?
Your wrinkly brain is just there, in the kitchen sink.
Set it twixt the ears and make a new link.
—Doc Zeus, from Drunk On Pow(d)er

As soon as all were aboard, it became a massive reunion, a browse-about of milling and greeting siblings (who straight off dubbed themselves Sibs), mile-high Siren looking beatifically down on them. The enormous chamber was as always golden white, but the mists of distance were gone. In all directions were gigantic goldish walls marked by lines, glyphs, script, and symbols.

They were from all walks of life, all colors and sizes. A wonderful menagerie of hairstyles, glasses, jewelry, and threads. It was like a huge weekend music festival with mad, smart, awesome people. They all just wandered and hugged, chatted and gestured, the buzz and hubbub warm and wonderful. Every language was spoken, and also understood, for this was a new frame of being.

Gavin moved through them, marveling at how he *knew* everyone there, all the faces familiar. It was a hug or a touch of the chest and a lingering glance and smile. Everyone touching everyone, some way or another, in passing.

An arm-linked gaggle of them went skipping by. Those child crazies cleared a path, and at the edge of the path he noticed a woman looking at him. His furry brows went up like, *where do I know you from?* Memory frames whirled in and his face brightened, as did hers. They walked toward each other, arms out. She was in a short skirt with leggings and a big loose blouse with one shoulder showing, all in pastel orange. No plasma fireworks show for hair, but raven black cut short. Her face was fresh pretty, and nothing like the Xenxu makeup she wore that night as the "filthy scorcher."

"Oh my God!" she sang as they fell into a hug. "What are the odds?"

"At least a hundred thousand to one," said Gavin, parting and holding her shoulders.

They laughed, big white smiles and sparkling eyes.

"You wanna hang?" she said.

"Absolutely."

She slipped her arm into his and they strolled the crowd.

"I'm Gavin, by the way."

"Sarah. Gavin fits your tone," she said, shouldering his shoulder.

"Your label is perfect, too."

They shifted and side-stepped and plowed ahead. A mountain of a dude was crossing in front of them, carving out a good-sized wake, and so they fell in behind him and drafted to the next tributary, where an open seam seemed to lead somewhere they were pulled to go.

"Did you get started that night at Ai Anam's thing?" she said, looking up at him, her fingers laced around the crook of his arm.

Gavin looked down at her. "I did. Right when I left. You?"

"A few ticks later," she said with a snort. "Wow!"

"I know."

She leaned in and said, "This is all about what we *allowed* ourselves to believe. I think that's beautiful."

"Right?" he said, leaning into her. "It was up to each of us to get ourselves onto Siren."

With a flicker of a smile, Sarah looked quickly away. Another woman was in her line of sight and they locked eyes. The other woman's brows were up in question, and Sarah wagged her head in tiny movements.

Gavin said, "I feel Siren stirring up a euphoria concoction inside. You got it yet?"

"Oh, I do," she said, gazing wide-eyed somewhere out there in the middle ground. "Feels fantastic."

"You think a bash might be afoot?"

"That was the plan," she said, slipping her arm in his as they muddled off.

Gavin let the echo of what she'd just said play a couple of times, his eyes searching around for some sense to apply to it. After a few steps, it was too congested, so they just stopped trying and let themselves be moved by the flow of personi.

Gavin leaned down. "I have a confession to make. You became known as the filthy scorcher for my first trip in-Siren. You were a fantasy for a few days."

Sarah laughed and said, "You were the kinda gazey-eyed guy in the wildly out-of-place zoot suit, but *way* cute. You were walked to Ai Anam's gather, right?"

"Yep."

They continued the walkabout. A little body language tug on his arm and he knew to look down at her, and with big liquid eyes, she said, "I know how you feel about Nima. It's very powerful."

Gavin looked sideways at her with puzzled blinks and brow configs. "How do you know about Nima?"

Outside, Siren materialized within ferocious lightning clouds in full stride, bearing down on the outside edge of Saturn's vinyl record of rings. Saturn, the cranky old codger, dominated the backdrop, filling the entire scene with His golden yellow and desert sand colored layers and striations and storms. In the foreground the rings stretched away and wrapped the planet for tens of thousands of miles, the planet's ball casting a thirty thousand-mile-wide shadow across the rings behind it.

The Venerable One levitated stoically, immovable through the ages, looking upon this upstart trespasser with alert curiosity, but a warning penumbra gradually brightened at His rarefied crown.

Inside, all the goldish walls dissolved and became gargantuan displays, like the walls had become clear. The outside was sharp, focused, the hexagons gleaming. A collective gasp sprayed through the thousands as their heads became metronomes. At the bow display, they were racing toward the rings.

Gavin asked again, "How do you know about Nima?"

"Everyone knows Nima," she said, but it was clear she was trying not to laugh. She gripped Gavin's arm and walked him backwards in circles, mouth hanging. The lighting dimmed, improving the contrast of the views, adding a new mood. *"Incrediblllllle!"* she shrieked, eyes rapturous.

Out the clear wall, they could see a moon, right at the edge of the wreath of rocky and icy rings. The moon ball was pure white, pocked and jagged, geysers blowing from within fissures. It gave dazzling dimension and depth to the scene, and highlighted Saturn's perception-crushing size.

Someone said in an Indian accent, "...Enceladus. That's water and other organic compounds spraying out of it."

Gavin looked for the speaker. He was a diminutive man, dark-skinned, bald, eyes laser-beam excited. He went on, "Everything needed for life is in those geysers. It's the coldest body in the solar system, and the brightest, because its white ice reflects all Sol's heat away. It's minus three hundred thirty there, but inside it must be warm, or there would be no liquid water."

"Oh my God it's beautiful," said Sarah, gripping Gavin's arm. He stared at Enceladus, filing a nail on his teeth. It was moving noticeably in the view, which meant they were traveling at a tremendous speed, the rings closing in on them.

They wandered off. Looking out the opposite side, they saw smaller moon dots, tiny in Saturn's space, divided between two light sources, brighter on the sun side.

"The *scales* again," said Gavin.

"What?"

"Oh, you know, the *size* of everything since this all started."

As they mingled, still awaiting a shindig to erupt, they passed snippets of conversation.

"—no no. No, we're in our own implied gravity well—"

"—oh check it out," someone said, pointing. "The hexagons are morphing."

Gavin and Sarah stopped, watching out the starboard side. The hexagons were flowing like gold silvery liquid into each other, adding edges, and in a moment transformed into interlocked octagons.

"Three D to four D," someone said.

"Right. No longer three D cubic, but a four D tesseract."

"Bingo," someone else said.

Moving along, and they came across a guy with a pudgy face but ripped T-shirt body, with bangs and round blue glasses, a few Sibs clustered around him. Gavin and Sarah veered over to their little group. In a toffy British accent, he was saying, "...Comet Shoemaker-Levy broke up and smashed into Jupiter in 1992. The chunks left impact zones big enough to swallow Earth whole, with room to spare, and they lingered for months."

The guy's eyes shifted to Gavin and Sarah for a tick. He nodded welcome, then to everyone went on. "So, for perspective, the biggest chunks of the comet were no more than two"—he held up two fingers—"*two* kilometers across. That's just over a mile. Yet one of those generated a release of explosive energy in the range of six *million* tons of TNT. Six *hundred* times Earth's entire nuclear arsenal."

"But Earth's history is just fiction," said Gavin.

"Quite right," the guy said, focusing on him with a smile tinged with satire. "But do *you* know that?"

Gavin looked at him like *what do you mean?*

Looking around at his audience, the guy said, "Hey! You lads and lasses want to hear more about what didn't really happen?"

They all cheered and clapped like kids with "yay!" and "yes!" and "bring it!"

Gavin had a strange feeling, and it was carved all over his face, in the puzzlement of his brows, the suspicion in his eyes.

The Brit stopped and took off his glasses, cleaning them on his shirt. "So," he said, his eyebrows up in professor mode, "what do you think will happen when Siren, a five-hundred-*mile* long object, *way* more mass per square foot of matter than icy comets, two point six four *million* feet in length, slams into Saturn? That's four hundred times the size of the largest comet chunk. The explosive plume would have to reach at *least* fifty thousand miles. That's a quarter of the way to the moon."

"I can't wait to see the playback," someone said.

Another leaned into their group and said, "Yeah and Saturn emits far more heat than He takes in from Sol, so something scorching is churning in His belly."

"Yeah, Shamash's baby! Hahahaha!"

"And the hexagon at the pole has been turning into..." the Brit waved at the enormous display view wall, "...an octagon."

Gavin clucked his tongue twice, cheek twisted that way, and said to them, "Buckle up."

They moved off and Sarah leaned closer and said, "I *still* can't believe we're doing this."

"I know it. It's insane. But I'm *ultra*-amped about it."

"Oh, you mean the discontinuity," she said with a sly grin. Sarah tugged his arm to slow him, looking into his eyes. She was curious, looking for something.

"What are you looking at?" he said.

"Just...just...seeing if you're still..."

"What?"

She cracked up giggling, and said, "God, Galxu. You're such a blast."

"Galxu?" said Gavin, increasingly perplexed by the weirdness going on with these people.

They diverted into a slice that took them to an edge of the crowd. Now they had a clearer view ahead. Saturn's storms were subtler than His Jovian cousin's, a way fatter chap, but the curling gases and upwellings from the interior were becoming more and more visible.

"Oh, sorry," she said amid her laughter. Flicking out a hand, she said, "Gavin. It's Gavin. Hahahaha!"

A woman had overheard them and stepped over. She had a thin runner's face and frame, with shaved platinum hair, dark symbols dyed into it. Grinning at Sarah like she knew her, she said, "It's Gavin? Is that what his name is?"

"OK," said Gavin. "What the fick is going on around here?"

"What do you mean?" said a smiling dude with long hair and blue-lensed glasses as he walked past. "We're going to shatter the game. Ain't that right, ladies?"

Gavin did a double-take on that guy. He looked familiar. He went in search of the information in his head—the blank and annoyed transitioned guy at Sous les Pods. Then he caught a glimpse of someone moving through the crowd. Small. Short hair. But she was elusive.

"What the hell is going on around here?" he muttered, tugging on his lower lip.

"The rings are what hold timeform in place," said a woman as she strolled by with a wild mane of raven hair.

"And that's what we're going to scratch," said another woman walking by from another direction, also with a wild mane of raven hair. Twins. Familiar. But from where?

Said Sarah, "Maybe Saturn has been bound by them in some mythical archetypal way."

Gavin looked down at her in utter bafflement. "What's going on?"

She couldn't help laughing. It was just too much. "It's a party, Galxu."

"Who the fuck is Galxu!" shouted Gavin, drawing looks from those nearby, and by the looks of them, they were also in on this.

"Did I say Galxu?" said Sarah. "Oh look," she said, pointing and dancing on her tiptoes.

In the gigantic bow display, all sensations of speed became more tangible as the curve of rings closed in. Before, they were just sort of nebulous with some outline hints at pieces, but now they were enlarging as individual chunks. They plowed into them, *boooom*, shaking the ship. The pieces directly in front were vaporized while those more to the side bounced and pinwheeled past the port and starboard windows with tremendous violence and tumbling speed.

The Sibs gasped as the lights dropped. Now they were on Saturn's light…sorry, Shamash. Somewhere music had started.

Gavin and Sarah were facing each other, and at that moment, her eyes dropped, watching someone coming up from behind him. He started to turn, but whoever it was hooked his elbow and said, "May I borrow my husband?"

Sarah patted Gavin's arm, looking into his eyes, chuckled and said, "He's all yours, Neem."

Galxu's eyes wrenched away from hers and looked down to see who'd…

"Nima!" he shrieked like a cheerleader, about to be slashed by someone in a hockey mask. His knees liquefied.

Several were ready to hold him up.

"Fee-fi-fo-fum," said a familiar voice. Two powerful arms clamped around him from behind, saving the day, lifting him from the floor and plopping him back onto his feet.

Gavin was faint, overwhelmed, dizzy, as he half-turned and saw her, wearing a great big smile, coughing out, "Doc Sticks? What the fuh…?"

Randall slid around from the side as Gavin's brain struggled to line these jarringly dissonant events up into the types of thoughts he preferred. "Our patient is feverish, Doctor Sticks. Have you anything for it?"

Now directly in front of him, Nima said, "He's my husband. He'll be fine. Just give him some air."

Gavin's eyes were wide and, frankly, terrified, as he saw Cat walking up from behind Nima, with Conner and Marli in tow. He also noticed the tightly packed thousands were thinning out, like people were simply vanishing.

As more people blipped out, Gavin saw Villy, and then Suzhi slipped in and whispered in his ear, "Don't worry about your opening, Galxu. We have it covered. Hehehe."

Gavin's head flopped to the side at her like she'd lost her mind, but he was about half-aware the one person with missing marbles around here was himself. "Is this a test!" he shouted at them all. "Is this a prank!"

Nima held up his hand, kissed his knuckles, and said, "Technically, it's not a prank when you yourself set it all up." Then she held his hand high, turning to include them all, and said, "Ladies and gentlemen, my husband Galxu! Mythion maker extraordinaire!"

All those in the vicinity applauded, like he was the guest of honor, and so he was. Galxu blinked like he was in a dust storm, bewildered, speechless, jaw hanging. But he was also getting mad, and he shook off those who were holding him up.

Meanwhile the music, deep and tribal and bassy, was getting louder.

Someone shouted, "Looks like the bash is heating up!"

"Time to party!" yelled Villy, running off into what was left of the crowd.

In the sky of Siren's palace, pinpoints of light began dancing, expanding and stretching into ribbons. Orbs appeared and began prancing and jetting in all directions. This as the all-encompassing and all-penetrating sound grew louder.

A tree-being so large, its highest tiny branches breached the lower envelope of violet atmosphere in an alien world.

But Galxu recognized that world—the one he briefly saw when he was scared out of his body by the tree creature in the cave. "Gawd," he moaned. "It was in that story on the wall behind Siren."

"Just breathe," said Cat, now standing beside Nima. She seemed more sober about this whole thing. Siren's appearance in the sky over "Earth" had clearly imprinted her with something.

Nima said to them all, "Give us a moment?" And she towed Galxu away from them. In the shadowed chamber, with the frenzy of party lights starting, she stopped him, faced him, took his hands, looked into his eyes, and said in a strange tongue, "Can you understand what I'm saying?"

Galxu's eyes searched hers, but bits and pieces of sensical connection were leaking in. Flickers and flashes of home, the world, how it looked, the language. Their more advanced tier could commune without speaking, but it was sure fun to do it with those fab tongues and lips and vibrating vocal apparati. Blinking, nodding uncertainly, he said, "Yeah."

With one hand, she pinched his cheeks, forcing him to concentrate on her face, and said, *"Dondeen dao. Croka kay obsool."*

Galxu's mouth automatically said, *"Ondo dao. Mi asu obsool."*

"That's the correct response," she said in English. "You remember the terms? They're your frequency release keys."

"Keep going," said Galxu, his eyes still in confusion, but coming around.

"My Love," she said in English, "you are Prime Architect for Mythion World Simulators. Our purpose is contracted throughout the galaxy for creating and testing them for civilization-steering scenarios."

"No," said Galxu, suddenly agitated, eyes wide and fearful. "You guys are trying to make me *believe* something again!"

Nima chuckled at him, right to his face. She patted his chest. Galxu looked to the side. Pointing at the gaggle of people over there, a lot of them but so many fewer than a few moments ago, she said, "Those wonderful selves over there, all of us, we are your team of 1440 for this nomic trial, which is a smashing success, by the way. Kudos."

"Gawd," moaned Galxu. "You know, I'm—"

"There is always a risk of forgetting, and getting lost in one's own mythions," she said, yanking his face back to hers and patting his cheek like to wake him up. "You teach a course on that. You were the mind that came up with using Our Lady as the irreducible conduit to Quanal. Do you remember Quanal?"

Galxu looked down, his eyes ticking around, searching, then he said, "Basis. Many as one. Our home with Our Lady, Mother Tree. She is my root, and my highest branches."

"Yes, husband," she said. "We isolated your stream, imaged your base mythion, waited for a prime number inflection, and shunted you into ours in the rainy street as the lost and stumbling Gavin. We took over the narrative from there, to make sure you got out OK."

Galxu's head tipped back, his eyes filling with increasing realization. "All that…hahahaha! All that *commitment* bullshit! You needed me to walk your line. Oh that is so *funny*. But why the superhero thing?"

Nima shifted her weight onto her other foot as she fixed him with those liquid chocolate eyes. "We *always* use that to make the protagonist believe they've mastered the world they're in, remember? Makes us believe we've risen above it all. Ego dismissal. Works every time."

Galxu blew out an ironic scoff. "Gawd. What a fickin dupe I am." He chewed his lip and reflected a minute, eyes on their steady march to full recall. And then he started to chuckle, but hesitant and wheezy, like the chuckle was dueling with itself on what of all this was actually funny. But the raw truth was, it was *all* funny. Endlessly funny. God was just a big fat red mouth, laughing in everyone's face. That knowing made him laugh harder.

You know, it was just too much. All of it.

He laughed a little harder.

Like a fickin wave of stupid and ridiculous all mingled in some mélange of my mind done and gone to hell.

Galxu laughed harder, sounding like a mad genius bent on world domination.

It was time. You know. It was time to…uh…quit. Like…who can I talk to about that?

Galxu was laughing so hard he was rocking his torso and slamming his thighs right in front of Nima. In the middle of the raucous cackling, he stepped over, tamped the body-shaking guffaws down into manageable chuckles, and took her into his arms. She was laughing, in little fits and starts, like she wasn't sure she should hack away like a clown scaring a child.

Galxu said, "It's all coming back to me, baby. What's next?"

"Good question, sweet," she said, tapping him at his heart chakra like she was doing something therapeutic. "Our options are as follows," she said, blinking with those wondrous brown eyes. "We can exit the mythion now." She shrugged like *and why would anybody want to do that?* "Or we can ride Mother Tree's chapter into the closed-loop solution of this mythion." She stepped behind him, grabbed his arms, and turned him toward Mighty Siren. "This is *Her* part of the show. Let us not deprive her of that." She tugged him around to face her. "You already know *my* vote, and you do know Our Lady made these bodies to..." She looked at him like, *come on*.

"Melt into liquid corpus."

"Uh-huh," she said, her shiny mouth open and wanting a kiss. "I say we ride these bodies out to term. I *love* them. You?"

"Jeezus," said Galxu, pulling her closer. "Oh...the addiction is..." He shook his head and puffed a *wow* breath, staring at nothing. "The addiction is astounding. What I felt on that road watching my dad die will live in my column until I am again *nothing*. I would dip into memnull and do it again todawn. Only I might make it so you can't find me."

"I see you now in your eyes, husband," she said, looking into his eyes with some truly sweet mischief. Sweeping her hand across the now dancing throng like a princess, she said, "Shall we play?"

By now the music was loud enough to be truly righteous. Galxu scanned all them wonderful folks over there, wiggling their bodies around. The colors. The motion. The glitter bombs and lights in the sky. He looked on like he was having déjà vu, brows crinkled in the puzzled shapes of data mining. "I've seen this. I saw this in the street at the start of the mythion."

"Connect the mythion's alpha and omega flexions. Another of your innovations," Nima said, shaking his arm. "Let's play."

"K." Galxu nodded. "Let's do it."

She grabbed him by the neck and pulled his mouth to hers, kissing him wildly like she was in charge, her other fingers on his cheeks. She broke away, still rubbing his cheeks and looking at him and trilling, "We *love* this kissing stuff! I'd do this again and again for that *alone*!"

Galxu chuckled. "God, Nima. You are..."

"Whatever," she said, taking off with his hand, which made him lurch for a step to get with her pace, but he let himself be towed.

"Jeezus," muttered Galxu, seeing Ai Anam lit up and dancing like a teen guru, makers jiggin' and jivin' around him. In the middle of his rather intriguing Middle Eastern dance, Ai Anam pointed at him with a look on his face of deep connection and appreciation, copper eyes lasering Love. "Trun," said Galxu. " My brilliant base conceptualist."

Nima was still towing him, her other arm swinging, as she said, "Everyone's here. Everybody played a role, and we all had so much *fun*!"

Someone tapped him on the shoulder, and he turned to see the famous storyline canvas troika, Heather, Celia and Lissa, but Lissa was a full-grown personi. Galxu stopped, and Nima yanked back. Looking at Heather/Eren with some shock, he shouted, "You're in on this?"

"Wouldn't have missed it!" she yelled.

Looking at Lissa/Bren, he leaned in and said, "You are a little Mata Hari!"

"Thank you from the center of my column for this opportunity," she said near his ear, touching his shoulder. "I know we're discrete ancillaries, but it was truly mag of you to include us."

"I'm grateful you had available flow junctures for it," said Galxu with shining eyes. "I will *never* forget Lissa and what she did to help me know human love of that amplitude," he said, blinking back tears.

Leaning back into his ear, she said, "Would you allow me to sample a role like the one you played?"

"Our mythion index is comprehensive," he said, leaning around to her ear. "Get in the queue and we'll find one for you."

Galxu and Heather/Eren looked at each other hard and long, his jaw grinding, their eyes wet. They melted into each other's arms, saying nothing.

"Check him out," said Celia/Tinr, pointing at something. Galxu turned and spotted the tall handsome server from Soluna, weaving through the crowd with a hoisted tray, coatless tux and all. On the tray were what looked like Lucid Zombies. He was the guy who let his eyes linger longer than appropriate on Nima that night.

"Erun," said Galxu. "Perhaps the prime existence base designer in our sentasphere." Galxu raised his chin at him, and Erun vectored their way. Arriving, he said to Nima, "M'selle, does Monsieur yet recall?"

"He's about all the way back," she said, seizing a drink from the tray. More appeared on it and the members of author troika all helped themselves.

Cat slid in with a face like *you guys aren't doing this without me*. Erun blinked and another appeared on the tray. Cat took it and started into it. While she sucked on it, Galxu said to her, "Where's Jackson?"

"His daughter is being bonded," she said, lowering the drink.

"That's *right*," said Galxu as his eyes defocused. He extended his love and apology and congratulations to Jackson/Tirma, who mentalled back something that would roughly translate to, *Thank you, sir. I've set the event record to relivable, if you'd like to visit it at a later juncture. And it was a rare and precious gift for me to test Earth Mythion 4.137.*

Surfer dude walked up from behind, dreads and knitted tam holding them in, making it all *luma jadu*. "Count me in," he said.

Galxu looked back and watched him walk up. "Tonl," he said. "Excellence to see you." Galxu made a Zombie in one hand, extending the other to him, slyly saying, "Don't fall for it."

Tonl/surfer dude smiled with twinkly eyes, took it, and sucked on the spiral straw. The blue goo swirled up it. "Oooo," he sounded, his lips in an O. "Odondo," he toned with closed eyes, which meant balanced aligning of one's column to that of Our Lady, Mother Tree. These only *looked* like Lucid Zombies, but they were a deepstring qirotech of another order entirely, the massless particulate at near Planck Length, a constant well-known in their world.

Finishing his own taste, Galxu said to Tonl in the tam and the sprouting dreads, "Odondo mei," and hoisted his glass. Then he saw Aron standing a ways off, the crowd his backdrop. He was waving his arms like he held semaphores and was guiding in an airplane. "Starlings," chuckled Galxu, waving back. Turning to Tonl, he pointed at Aron and said, "That creature right there is on another Q level."

"He's the best," said Tonl, leaning closer. "Your entire team is the best. Deep thanks for the promotion. I'll see you around." And he walked off, holding his hands in the air, one with the glowing Zombie.

Moving around among his friends and colleagues, Galxu eventually saw everyone, every single character in the production. The aides, nurses, and monitors from Langhurst. Other patients. The burly biker dudes and their fawning ladies at Woody's. "Lindy!" They ran into each other's arms, laughing and carrying on. Holding her at arm's length, he excitedly blurted, "Thou dissuasive minx! You were so *good!*"

"Thank you, sir," she said. Someone swept up and dragged her away as she shouted over her shoulder, "Count me in on any nomic!"

Then he spotted the lady who looked transitioned at Sous les Pods, the one who'd worn red pumps. Turning to Nima, he bent over and spoke over the noise. "What was with all the red shoes?"

"There's no place like home," she said, as if it couldn't be more obvious. "Still the prime cue to get out of them all. It's plan B, but we made it plan A. In your advanced class, you call it the subpsyche thread. Remember? They have the energy to disaggregate the mythion, just in case."

"Whose idea was that again?" he said, his grin sideways.

"Mine," she said, patting his cheek. "We had to take that symbol back from the bad things in that *one* Earth mythion, remember?"

"Blammo," said Sarah, stepping up. "That euphoria layer Our Lady dialed up goes right in there. You guys feeling it?"

"Let's go!" shouted Nima, grabbing and hustling and herding

them all toward the sponge of people. They all absorbed into the press and slosh and joined with the motion, arms over their heads, hips swinging, shins digging.

"Where's my mother?" shouted Galxu over the music.

"You designed her to stand alone as a character outside the test group. She was a grounding force."

Galxu looked at Nima with open longing and a sad smile. A quick tear fled down his cheek as he clutched his chest. "I will so miss her."

Nima tenderly cupped his cheek. "You'll use that personi model again."

They slambasted their way like a fab and glittering phallus through the rings, the music loudening to cover the percussive violence of impacts against Siren's protective field.

Music filled the space, bassy, squidgy, gooey euphoric gasmatron, not coming from without, but from within. They were the slick and sly, the sexy sliding thundering sound, oogling into the basis of chaotic cataclysm. The sky was lit with streamers and glitter bombs, lasers crisscrossing. They danced like possessed natives, manifesting their own fire and glow toys and ribbons. Chunks of ice and rock split and fragmented, bouncing up the sides.

Galxu and Nima danced in the squish of it all, heads back in ecstasy, arms spiraling over their heads, the lightshow playing across their faces. Nima extended her hair and it became a flowing wavering fan with lights at the ends, her shiny silver one-piece morphing into flowing fluids.

Galxu winked and pointed a pistol hand at her while she switched into full-on pro dance mode, bending at the waist with an arched back, eyes rolled back in her head, whirling and leaping. Galxu added to himself a purple frilly getup once worn by an artist known as Prince. A wave of creativity raced through the crowd and they all costume-upped.

Look at this!

Out the bow view, they were racing through them, the icy and rocky chunks, and clear division lines, the curves coming at them in the viewport, flashing up the sides, and disappearing behind.

Someone shrieked, "The Cassini Division!"

A darker gapey gap in the yellow-lighted garland of ice and rock came at them like a shockwave and flowed past, mountain-boulders and bergs bouncing and spinning up the sides.

Ahead was the curved innermost edge of the rings, and they were bludgeoning upon it at lung-sucking speed.

The edge neared, coming and coming, and then they were past it, like flying at a dizzying speed above ground and coming to the edge of a cliff, and the "ground" of the rings dropped abruptly behind, leaving empty space between them and the big fat yellow-lined body of Saturn.

Outside, Siren's circular bow breached that inner edge, rock and ice chunks blasting out into a fan and tumbling a thousand miles a minute into empty space, Siren the piercing prepossessed agent provocateur. Against the blue-black of intervening space, the chunks were crystal focused in their chaotic tumbling.

The rings were the record, Siren the needle, and behind Her, a laser cut all the way through their stone and ice granules.

The Venerable One's crown penumbra brightened even more at the affront, and gigantic lightning bolts started across an area of His layered face.

Inside, the music had taken complete command of anything that was once reason, huge and pervasive, a wall of orgasmasound, like a tribe of nisty alien sorcerer music demigods showing their stuff, strange and huge and pounding.

It was heating up, amping friction from their down down fall to the Great Gas God. The natives were now in a sweaty frenzy of flailing and wiggling and swimming, their minds merged with Acoustic Allness.

Out the bow portal was nothing but brilliant goldish clouds and gases and storms, continent-sized lightning crackling across the surface, all close enough to touch.

Oh, but what a cosmic collision this shall be.

Outside, now three hundred miles off the gaseous glowing ball, Siren ignited the hydrogen and helium and burst into a fireball, trailing a glowing rippling tail fifteen thousand miles behind Her, like a flaming tar ball hurled from a cosmic conqueror's trebuchet.

On the planet surface, a bowl formed in the mush of gas, in anticipation of contact, like a mighty fiery vulva hot for the blazing orange rod.

Out the bow viewport were blinding magnesium flames as the Palace heated and heated. Then, to the screaming and wildly dancing response of a swarm of crazed mythion makers, Siren materialized between them and the display.

"She's come to life!"

She was a wavering and filamentous neural body a mile tall, silken and dashed and slashed and splashed with racing lights and many tentacled amoeba, fractalizing off the points with sparks racing across the palace, bouncing and jetting and spinning sparking candles off the windows.

The white frills in Galxu's Prince getup ignited, fizzling away and jetting off into the dance of light. Then went his collar. Then a sleeve.

AllSelves mind let go logic, reason, form.

O

O God! Can I not save one from the pitiless wave?
Is all that we see or seem but a dream within a dream?
—Edgar Allan Poe

Outside, Siren's fifteen thousand mile trailing inferno, like a world killing asteroid, slammed into the yellow fertile bowl with a knock you on your ass *brilliant* flash of ultra-kinetic magnetic rocketing streamers. The planet's face concaved, sending a circle shockwave rolling at a thousand miles per second across the Old Man's layered countenance. Siren like a burrowing obsessed thing ground Her way into those filmy scoodgy gases, compressing them into volatile particle compression *crack* as an explosion plume that had absolutely no where to go rocketed out, blasting at ten-thousand klicks a second to forty thousand miles off Father Time's absolutely *oh my God* face. At Siren's magma-burning leading edge, gases measured in millions of tons compressed and ignited, sending plasma streamers curling and spiraling in all directions into the fuzzy boiling fire of the Old Man's abdomen.

. . .

Inside, erupting from the air, a tune from eons ago, Pink Floyd's "Eclipse," and the team sublimated into creatures of another genus, new and raw, slippery and absorbing, flailing wildly and crying and screaming and wiggling and waving as Siren's moving and morphing sea creature from *Carnivale Liquide* pulsed and wavered to the booming sound.

Spin the tune up, child. We'll wait.

All that you touch and all that you see
All that you taste, all you feel
And all that you love and all that you hate
All you distrust, all you save
And all that you give and all that you deal
And all that you buy, beg, borrow, or steal
And all you create and all you destroy
And all that you do and all that you say
And all that you eat and everyone you meet
And all that you slight and everyone you fight
And all that is now and all that is gone
And all that's to come and everything under the sun...

The Children of Mother Tree.
One Dance.
One Song.
Mythion.

Galxu's eyes opened long enough to look at Nima, all the way in. It was forever in those eyes. Shaking their heads like *let this never stop!* their lips came together in all the chaotic colorful flashing. Their eyes were open as they kissed. Nima's eyes were in dumbstruck gratitude. She was seeing...*everything,* pupils dilated to the max. Their faces and chests were soaked with sweat as they clung to each other. Others sucked to them, thrilled to rocket through a plantasm of neural feeling, and they all together shrieked in ecstasy as a white nuclear wall of fifty-thousand degree flame was upon them.

Right in front of their eyes, they all plasmafied, becoming pure fluid feeling, melting into an explosive screaming orgasm.

AUMA

By number, 1440 tallied the Makers, and they surfaced in their plasmic fluid pods, all at the same time. Elongated anthropods of gelatinous flows, the galactically famed Aumon, lifted from their pods with joy and celebration, coalescing and flying apart in a swirling ballet, tittering and toning. They were of Mother Tree, but with arms and legs and vaguely faint facial features, tiny lights for eyes.

Auma was their world, and its forms were molded upon complex musical structures and textures. Tones and pitches from the stringed lyres of cosmic mystics shimmered through, animating their bodies in rainbow colors as they passed. In this inconceivably vast chamber, everything was golden-white, the floor covered in liquipods as far as any eye could see. These were the nodal nexi to insert into embodied experience in any corner of Creation needing civilization steering.

A trinity of enormous rings were suspended against the underside of the sky, pulsing vibratory nexi from Central Fountain.

And towering over it all, as tall as the Panaplana, was Mother Tree, her tiniest and highest fractal twigs breaching the violet cerrosphere, shooting jagged lightning bolts into purple star-studded space, collecting plasma food for the nourishment of Her children. At

Her base, the energy flowed like glowing cells into the filaments feeding the liquipods.

Together, the collective of Tier 1:0:1 Mythion Makers flowed into a set of scintillating frequency tones and hues and were carried, *tirriling* and *cherbeling*, toward Mother Tree's rather bulbous Omnis.

She towered over her domain in glandular munificence, and from whose mental body came the stuff of which Mythions were made.

THE END: NEXT BEGINNING

ACKNOWLEDGMENTS

As anybody who's ever strung together a series of words into a book-length work knows, we are really only the scribe of a montage of ideas derived from experience coupled with imagination. And even then, we are always bereft of any objective insight into the weaknesses and failings of our own work and must seek many sets of outside eyes.

In that light, I'd like to thank every person and event in my life that led to the state vector collapse of all potential into this book, but a few deserve to be named. Mary Betts, for simply loving me, having unshakable faith, and being brilliant and the first mirror from which so much of this story found its cohesive footing. Dylan Davis, for being smarter than his dad, for his laser literary eye, and for tossing in substantial digestible chunks that flourished into full-blown state changes and plot trajectories. Nicholas Davis, for brainstorming with me over beverages in flame-lit bars that ignited expansive and critical inclusions. Top notch ideas lit those nights up. Second Chance, for his incredibly acute eye for story, what it's missing, the importance of timing and structure, and how to make it a more beautiful literary work.

And Jari Lee Davis, she who birthed this forever boy, for telling me I was a good writer, every single time, even when it wasn't true.

ABOUT THE AUTHOR

Future best-selling author Jason Davis writes deep, layered, mind-bending, exhilarating books loaded with philosophical feasts that challenge stale paradigms, all from his Siren Class Cutter in orbit above Earth.

Upon visits Earthside, he hangs in Colorado, engaging in human things which require muscle movement and oxygen demand, while pointing his high-end astronomy gear to the firmament to photograph the wonders of the night sky, and which he fully intends to one day visit. But, alas, who has time for interstellar travel in the endless hubbub of these modern times?

To him, of all the sacred objects and ideas in the scope of human experience, books stand alone at the top of the heap. Story is the very definition of reality. He might say it's One Story made of infinite stories, woven from Infinite Love.

To find out more, visit:

jasondavis.love

facebook.com/jasondavisauthor
twitter.com/jdaliix
instagram.com/jdaliix

Made in the USA
Las Vegas, NV
19 January 2023

65915985R00247